BLIND MAN'S
ALLEY

Also by Justin Peacock

A Cure for Night

·BLIND MAN'S·
ALLEY

JUSTIN PEACOCK

DOUBLEDAY ■ NEW YORK LONDON TORONTO SYDNEY AUCKLAND

DOUBLEDAY

This is a work of fiction. Names, characters, places, and incidents either are the product of the author's imagination or are used fictitiously. Although numerous actual locations in New York City are referenced in this novel, their depictions are entirely fictional. Any resemblance to actual persons, living or dead, events, or locales is entirely coincidental.

Library of Congress Cataloging-in-Publication Data
Peacock, Justin.
Blind man's alley / Justin Peacock.—1st ed.
p. cm.
1. Real estate developers—Fiction.   2. Family-owned business enterprises—Fiction.
3. New York (N.Y.)—Fiction.   I. Title.
PS3616.E225B58 2010
813'.6—dc22   2010002640

ISBN 978-0-385-53106-1

PRINTED IN THE UNITED STATES OF AMERICA

1 3 5 7 9 10 8 6 4 2

First Edition

To Melissa – still and again

"Blind Man's Alley bears its name for a reason. Until little more than a year ago its dark burrows harbored a colony of blind beggars, tenants of a blind landlord, old Daniel Murphy, whom every child in the ward knows, if he never heard of the President of the United States. 'Old Dan' made a big fortune—he told me once four hundred thousand dollars—out of his alley and the surrounding tenements, only to grow blind himself in extreme old age, sharing in the end the chief hardship of the wretched beings whose lot he had stubbornly refused to better that he might increase his wealth."

—Jacob Riis, *How the Other Half Lives*

PROLOGUE

THEY WERE three hundred feet in the air when the floor gave out beneath them. The floor crumbled into pieces; it stopped being floor. Instead it was a mass of disintegrating concrete, collapsing in a groaning roar.

How do you run when there's nothing beneath your feet? The mind screams flight, but the body cannot follow. There was no more than an instant of this, a failed scramble against collapse.

There were three of them working out near the building's edge, their legs kicking uselessly in sudden free fall. There was a safety net below, but they were past its reach, unlike a dozen of their fellow construction workers who would emerge from the accident injured but alive. For these three, there was nothing for twenty-five stories to stop their fall, no possible sanctuary from gravity's remorseless pull.

Kieran Doyle, Dmitri Szerbiak, and Esteban Martinez: they weren't men New York City had ever noticed. The first time their names would ever appear in a newspaper was in the wake of their deaths. Doyle was the only one of them born in the States, growing up in Hell's Kitchen back in the neighborhood's last days as a rough Irish neighborhood, before gentrification turned it into an extension of Midtown. Szerbiak had immigrated as a child from Poland; Martinez, an illegal, had come from Honduras in his early twenties, made his way into the union with a forged social security card.

They were all three experienced at construction. The work they did was hard and dangerous under the best of circumstances, and it'd long been clear to all of them—to everyone on site—that the building of the Aurora Tower was not the best of circumstances. Not with the dizzying speed with which one floor climbed above another, the cracks in the settling concrete, the various shortcuts taken in the upward dash. There'd been plenty of talk among the crews: talk of bringing a grievance to the union, talk of going to the bosses with a list of demands, even talk of walking off the job.

But the time for talking was over, at least for talking that might have kept what happened from happening. Of course, there'd be plenty more talking in the accident's wake: there'd be investigations, lawsuits, head-lines, but for these three men it would all be so much useless aftermath.

How quickly an entire mass of concrete could turn itself into rubble and fling itself to the ground. The deep rumbling roar grabbed the attention of everyone in earshot, filled their minds with panicked thoughts of what such a sound could mean. New Yorkers kept the echo of the Trade Center clenched within them, always ready to bloom when a steam pipe exploded or a crane fell, the urban cacophony now shaded with a darker menace. Nearby pedestrians fled the noise before they even understood what was happening. But for Doyle, Szerbiak, and Martinez, there was no place left to go, just a mad jumble of whooshing air and rattling debris, spilling them out into the falling sky.

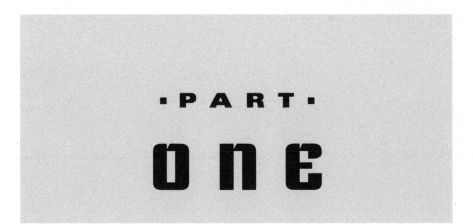

·PART·
ONE

▌ **REMEMBER** when I used to get things done." Simon Roth was already speaking as he entered the conference room. "I went to a meeting, things got *built* out of it. Now I sit in conference rooms with lawyers and accountants all day. Number crunching this, produce documents—you fucking lawyers, you've made what you do so complicated and endless it's all anybody has time to do. The sideshow's taken over the stage."

"Good to see you too, Simon," Steven Blake replied, standing to shake Roth's hand. Duncan Riley, who'd been sitting next to Blake as they'd awaited their clients' arrival, quickly rose beside him.

Duncan was a senior associate at Blake and Wolcott, where Steven Blake was both a name partner and the leading rainmaker. They were in a conference room at Roth Properties, there to update Simon Roth and his people on the various legal tendrils extending out from the previous year's fatal construction accident at the Aurora Tower.

Roth Properties was a private, family-owned company. Simon Roth, the company's founder and still its CEO, was in his late sixties, although as his deliberately over-the-top entrance demonstrated, he made a point of carrying himself with the angry energy of a much younger man. Simon had a full head of gray hair, every strand carefully lacquered into place, a perfectly tailored suit, a striped blue shirt with a white collar, and heavy gold cuff links. The only place his age clearly showed was in his craggy reddish face, like that of a sailor too long at sea.

A small contingent of Roth Properties executives had followed Simon Roth into the room: Roth's two children, Jeremy and Leah, both of whom were vice presidents, followed by the general counsel, Roger Carrington, and the CFO, Preston Thomas.

Leah and her brother were very young for their positions, not far north of thirty, although that was hardly unusual in a family-controlled private company. Jeremy was heavyset and jaundiced-looking, while Leah was thin and ascetic, both appearing older than their years, although in entirely different ways.

Carrington and Thomas were each well into their fifties. Carrington looked like an old-school WASP; Thomas was African-American. They were dressed virtually identically: both in dark pinstripe suits with pocket squares in their jackets and cuff links in their crisp white shirts.

Duncan took his turn shaking hands after Blake, offering his best bright-boy smile and hoping he didn't look ill at ease. Simon Roth was a notoriously demanding and prickly client, prided himself on it, and Duncan would have been perfectly content to leave the client interactions to Blake, though he'd dutifully feigned enthusiasm when tapped to come along. Duncan was on hand to be the details guy; as a senior partner, Blake had scant involvement with the nitty-gritty of a case.

Roth Properties was the developer of the Aurora Tower, thirty-six stories of luxury condominiums going up in the heart of SoHo. The cheapest apartment, a five-hundred-square-foot pied-à-terre, was listed at just under a million, while a top-floor penthouse was on the market at twenty-five. However, advance sales for the building had been only a trickle, not good news for a half-billion-dollar construction project. The luxury aura had been tarnished by the accident and the resulting flurry of investigations and lawsuits.

First up had been the Department of Buildings. Construction had been completely shut down for a month while city inspectors nosed around the building site. The lawyers had coordinated the turning over of documents and been present at interviews, but had generally stayed in the background while the agency did its work. Unsurprisingly, the DOB issued multiple violations relating to the accident (the site had collected over a dozen violations from the city before the fatalities, which wasn't an unusual number for a large-scale Manhattan construction project), levying relatively small fines against both the subcontractor, Pellettieri Concrete, and the general contractor, Omni Construction.

Even before the DOB had issued its findings, a wrongful-death suit had been filed on behalf of the families of the three construction workers. The suit named Roth Properties among the defendants, although generally it was only the contractors who were on the hook for a construction accident. But Roth was the deepest pocket and the highest-profile company involved in the Aurora, so there were strategic reasons to include them as a defendant, even if there was virtually no chance of the plaintiffs actually seeing a dime of Roth's money.

The accident's aftermath had been proceeding predictably, with nothing but minor headaches as far as Roth Properties was concerned, when the article had appeared in the *New York Journal*. The story claimed that the concrete company had failed to provide the standard secondary supports for settling concrete. Even after workers had warned that cracks were appearing, Pellettieri Concrete did nothing to shore it up, ignoring the obvious risk. The article went on to mention that the company's cofounder was currently in jail on racketeering charges out of a prosecution aimed at weeding out organized crime from the construction industry.

But the main focus of the article had not been on the accident itself, but rather on the city's response to it. The story claimed that the DOB inspector in charge of investigating the collapse, William Stanton, had originally recommended referring the case to the district attorney for a criminal investigation. That recommendation had supposedly been rejected by the head of the department, Ronald Durant, who'd then watered down the investigator's findings before issuing a public report. Shortly thereafter Durant had resigned from the DOB and joined a prominent architectural firm that had been hired by Roth Properties to design a wholesale transformation of a city housing project. Although the article didn't come right out and say so, the suggestion was that the city agency charged with policing construction accidents had gone out of its way to issue a toothless report in exchange for a plum job for Durant.

The *Journal*'s story had sparked immediate outrage and was quickly picked up by the rest of the New York press. The district attorney's office promptly announced that it was opening a criminal investigation into the accident. Although Roth Properties was not a target of the probe, the developer had been hit with a subpoena seeking virtually every document in the company's files relating to the construction of the Aurora.

If that wasn't enough to get the billable hours flowing, Simon Roth had also directed Blake to file a libel suit against the *New York Journal*. They'd just survived the paper's motion to dismiss and were proceeding with discovery, which Duncan was heading up. He was scheduled to depose the reporter who'd written the article, Candace Snow, later in the week.

While there were a dozen or so Blake and Wolcott associates working on the various Roth matters, Duncan was the only person besides Blake who was connected to all of them. For the past six months virtually all of Duncan's working hours had been occupied with the affairs of Roth Properties. This wasn't ideal from Duncan's perspective, but it wasn't the kind of thing he could complain about either.

Aside from providing a general update on the state of play of the various cases, the purpose of the present meeting was to discuss a particular piece of bad news: the firm's motion to dismiss Roth Properties from the wrongful-death suit had just been rejected by the court, meaning the company would have to proceed with turning over documents and submitting its executives to depositions.

"What did I just say?" Roth burst out, interrupting Blake's summary of what the company would have to produce. "They want to depose me?"

Blake shook his head. "For starters, they want your son, and Preston. If they do drop a depo subpoena on you, we can always try to quash, since it's a matter of public record that Jeremy was taking the lead on the project and you weren't directly involved. The good news on the documents, anyway, is that we've already collected everything relevant for the DA's subpoena."

"You know how much time I've spent being deposed the past year? Three full days. That's more time than I spent on vacation."

"As I recall, you were down at our place in the Caymans for most of February," Jeremy Roth said to his father.

Simon glared at his son, who didn't meet his eyes. "Just because I'm in the Caymans doesn't mean I'm not working," he growled. "I can get more accomplished down there than the rest of you get done without me up here."

"I'm sure you actually believe that," Jeremy said. Duncan was surprised by the adolescent nature of Jeremy's sullenness with his father, and that he was willing to indulge it in a business meeting.

"I believe a lot of things that are true," Simon shot back.

"In any event," Blake said, ignoring the sniping, "discovery's going to happen. We need to prep everybody, go over stuff. You know the drill."

"I'll be coordinating things from our end," Leah Roth said softly, her cool demeanor a world apart from her father and brother.

"Duncan here will be our point guy on the day-to-day," Blake said, draping a paternalistic hand on Duncan's shoulder. Duncan smiled at Leah, who looked back at him, her own expression unchanging.

"So, you need to take up any more of my day with this crap?" Simon said, pushing his chair back from the table.

"We still on for lunch?" Blake asked him.

Simon checked his watch. "As long as you promise you're not going to try to bill me for it."

Leah looked at her father, then back to Duncan. "You have time to set up a to-do list now?"

Duncan readily agreed and the meeting broke up. Leah picked up a phone on a side table and asked her assistant to have lunch brought in for them. Duncan was annoyed with Blake for not bothering with a heads-up about his own lunch with Simon Roth, although he should be used to such offhand slights by now. Blake wasn't a yeller or an all-around prick like a lot of partners, but he was brusque and elusive, as well as expecting something like mind reading from those who worked for him. But the law was not a profession for those who wanted their hands held.

And besides, part of the idea of coming to a meeting like this was for Duncan to get to know the next generation of Roths. Duncan was at the point in his career that was less about acquiring new legal skills and more about developing relationships and connections to start growing his own book of business, assuming that his approaching partnership vote went as he hoped. Ideally he would establish the same sort of relationship with Simon Roth's children, who were roughly his age, that his boss had long ago built with their father. Blake had been Simon Roth's primary litigation lawyer for over twenty years, one of many blue-chip clients he'd maintained. Blake, who billed just under a thousand dollars an hour, was widely acknowledged as one of the country's leading trial lawyers.

Leah looked over at Duncan while on the phone with her assistant.

She didn't smile or otherwise blunt her gaze, just openly evaluated him. Leah was attractive in a stringent sort of way, with dark straight hair and deep brown eyes, her coloring complemented by her dark pantsuit. She had the particular sort of confidence that Duncan had first encountered a decade previously upon entering Harvard Law: that of the born to it.

Duncan wondered what she in turn saw while looking at him. He was medium height, with honey-colored skin and green eyes that stood out against his complexion, his dark brown hair cropped so short a comb could barely pass through the back and sides. Despite the July heat, he was dressed in a gray Brooks Brothers suit, with a blue oxford shirt and a striped navy blue tie. Duncan had picked out the most conservative outfit in his wardrobe for this meeting—even his business attire usually had at least a little more flair—and such clothing still sometimes felt like a disguise. But he was a background presence at a meeting like today's, meant to be a quiet backstop for Blake, speaking if spoken to, and he therefore did his best to blend into the environment.

"So," Leah said, once she'd rejoined him across the conference room table. "You're Steven Blake's protégé?"

"One of them," Duncan said. "Blake brings in too much work to have just one."

"But you're the one we get," Leah said. "Hope we're not keeping you from more important things."

Duncan wasn't actually a fan of the work he was doing for Roth Properties: there were certainly sexier cases at the firm, including some of Blake's. But there wasn't an instant where he contemplated giving an honest answer, and he had no doubt Leah wasn't expecting one. "You're one of our firm's most important clients, obviously," he said instead. "It's an honor to be trusted to work on your matters."

Leah smiled dismissively, signaling *nice try*. "The bills from your firm go across my desk," she said. "I saw that you billed over two hundred hours to us the other month. That can't leave you much time to work on anything else."

Duncan shrugged, a tad uneasy, not sure what Leah was looking for him to say. "It doesn't really," he said. "I've got a pro bono case, but that doesn't take much time. As far as paying clients, right now you're pretty much it. But it ebbs and flows."

"What's your pro bono case about?"

Duncan was surprised by the question, not expecting any actual curiosity about his professional life from Leah. "It's just defending a family in an eviction proceeding."

"Is that all?" Leah said archly.

Duncan felt a mix of annoyance and embarrassment, but tried not to let either show. His dismissiveness had not been directed at the case itself, which he took seriously, but just at the prospect of talking about it with Leah Roth. This was especially true because the case had a connection, albeit a tenuous one, with Roth Properties.

His clients, a grandmother and grandson named Dolores and Rafael Nazario, were residents of the Jacob Riis housing project on the far eastern edge of Alphabet City. That project was receiving a radical makeover into mixed-income housing, a hugely ambitious transformation in which Roth Properties was partnering with the city. The eviction was based on the grandson getting arrested for smoking a joint outside his project. He'd been busted not by the cops, but rather by private security guards who'd been patrolling around the ongoing construction work.

Rafael had pled guilty to a disorderly conduct charge stemming from the weed, not realizing that doing so would open the door to eviction proceedings. Rafael insisted that the whole thing was a lie, that he hadn't actually been caught smoking pot, although Duncan didn't necessarily put a lot of stock in the denials, especially since they were being made in front of his client's grandmother.

Duncan managed a smile at Leah. "I didn't mean in the sense . . . Obviously, it's very important to my clients to stay in their home, especially since they live in public housing—at Jacob Riis, actually—so it's not like moving is an option. I just meant that it's not some big save-the-world-type case."

Leah cocked her head, her curiosity roused. "We're not involved, are we? Because of Riis, I mean."

"Only through the security guard who busted my guy, if that counts."

"It must be one of Darryl Loomis's crew," Leah said. "It's an outside security firm we use."

"All things being equal, I'd prefer not to have to cross somebody who's working for you."

"I didn't know Blake and Wolcott even did pro bono."

"Neither did I," Duncan replied with a grin, immediately second-guessing himself for being flip, even if Leah had started it. She was a client, after all: just because she wanted to poke at the firm's hard-nosed reputation didn't mean he should. "We're trying to be better about giving back."

"Is that what it's about?" Leah asked skeptically.

The firm's recent hits to its public image had been well chronicled in the press, and were obviously not news to Leah, but Duncan wasn't about to meet her halfway on the topic. "As compared to?" he said, playing dumb.

Leah shrugged. "Self-interest?" she offered.

"You'd have to ask Blake as to the underlying motives," Duncan said. "I'm just more in the, you know, doing-what-I'm-told stage of my career."

"A loyal foot soldier?" Leah said as their lunch was brought in.

Duncan smiled. "That's me," he said.

·2·

DUNCAN WALKED into his favorite conference room, which was on the thirty-third floor of his firm's Midtown office building. Two walls were entirely windows: the longer one looking out onto other skyscrapers, the shorter one facing west, offering a narrow slice of the Hudson River. A Cindy Sherman photograph—one of the Untitled Film Stills—was on the wall behind Candace Snow, although it was partially blocked by the blue background screen that had been set up by the videographer. Duncan, who was on the firm's art committee, was responsible for their owning the Sherman print. He was proud of this, but had never once found a way to mention it to anybody, for fear of sounding like a pompous ass. He certainly wasn't about to bring it up now.

Duncan extended a hand to Candace, introducing himself. Candace looked down at his outstretched hand, her mouth curling. She was clearly not contemplating shaking it. "How long is this going to take?" she asked.

"It's going to take how long it takes," Duncan said, leaving his arm extended, wanting to highlight her rudeness. "It really depends on how quickly you confess."

That at least got Candace to look up, though it didn't otherwise break the tension. Duncan shrugged off her hostility and went to pour himself a cup of coffee from the breakfast array that had been laid out by the window. He had better things to do than this deposition too. Although the libel suit had gotten some attention—Simon Roth's seeking $150 million in damages had helped see to that—in reality it was small-time, at least by Blake and Wolcott standards. It lacked the factual complexity, the vast array of moving parts, that was a mainstay of the sort of litigation the firm usually did. It was also perfectly obvious to Duncan that the case was a loser; he thought it had virtually no chance of surviving the paper's inevitable motion for summary judgment. Duncan didn't like being given a lawsuit he couldn't find a way to win.

Libel claims were always hard, especially when the plaintiff was a public figure like Simon Roth. That task was made considerably more difficult because Candace's article had not contained any explicit allegation of wrongdoing on the part of Roth or his company. It had therefore required a certain amount of ingenuity for Duncan to draft a libel complaint. He'd gotten around the lack of any actual libelous statements by instead alleging libel-by-implication, which allowed the case to focus not on what the story actually said, but rather on what a reasonable reader would take the article as implying. The suit alleged that the article implied that Roth's half-billion-dollar condo project had mob connections; that Roth had knowingly or negligently allowed his contractors to create unsafe working conditions; and that Roth had engaged in a backroom quid pro quo deal with Durant in exchange for his whitewashing the DOB investigation.

It had at least been enough to survive a motion to dismiss. Duncan was reasonably sure that Simon Roth was fully aware he wasn't going to win, that the case was more about sending a message: Fuck with me and I'll tie you up in court for a couple of years, make you rack up a small fortune in legal fees.

Coffee in hand, Duncan sat down across the table from Candace and her lawyer. She was an attractive woman, this Candace. Although he'd taken a couple dozen depositions in his eight years of practicing law, virtually everyone Duncan had ever deposed had been men: fleshy senior executives who viewed being raked over the coals by some smart-mouthed young lawyer in a Hugo Boss suit as a cost of doing business.

Not Candace. She looked to be in her mid-thirties, with a curvy body whose outlines were visible even in her formal attire. She was wearing a white ruffled shirt with a black skirt and a tight jacket, the arc and swell of her breasts visible against the fabric. Her hair was a vibrant red, curly and untamed. Duncan guessed it was dyed, then blinked the thought away: he had more important things to worry about than whether the witness was a real redhead.

Duncan started the depo off with basic background questions. Although he could be aggressive when necessary, Duncan generally found that a deposition was far more productive when he was friendly and low-key, tried to establish a conversational rhythm, rather than thundering and posturing. He was hoping to get Candace to relax a little, let down her guard.

That didn't happen. As Duncan took her through her résumé—college at Brown, followed by j-school at Columbia, then three years at the Albany *Times Union* before joining the *New York Journal*—Candace's hostility only seemed to increase. The mere fact that she was being asked questions at all seemed to offend her, Candace looking at him with murder in her eyes even though what he was asking so far wasn't any more intrusive than a typical job interview.

"How did you come to report on the Aurora Tower accident?" Duncan asked, abruptly shifting gears, deciding there was no point in holding off getting into the real issues.

"I had a confidential source who came forward with information," Candace replied, her arms folded across her chest. Duncan wondered if her posture was just a manifestation of her general hostility, or because she'd noticed him checking out her breasts before.

"And who was that?"

"Is there something about the word 'confidential' you don't understand?" Candace said tartly.

Duncan didn't react, just calmly met her glare. "Are you refusing to name your source for the story?" he asked. He'd fully expected her to do so; this was theater more than anything else, although if the paper's source was going to remain anonymous, that meant it couldn't rely on that person to establish the truth of the article.

"Objection," Candace's lawyer, Daniel Rosenstein, spoke on the record for the first time. Rosenstein was twenty years older than Duncan, a name partner in a boutique firm specializing in media law. He was not an imposing man: short, with a smile like a wince and a perpetual squint even though he wore glasses. But Rosenstein was a lawyer Duncan had heard of: a man who'd won First Amendment cases before the Supreme Court. He'd always been perfectly cordial to Duncan, while also constantly reminding him that his case was hopeless. "The identity of a confidential source is protected by New York's shield law, as you no doubt know, counsel," Rosenstein continued. "I instruct the witness not to answer the question."

"Do you intend to follow your lawyer's instruction?" Duncan asked Candace, following the script.

"As compared to what?" Candace shot back sharply, seemingly oblivious to the rote nature of the whole exchange. "Following yours?"

"Why did this source come to you?"

"That's still fishing around for the source's identity," Rosenstein protested. "Don't answer the question."

"Like my lawyer said."

"But this source prompted you to investigate the accident at the Aurora Tower?"

"I'm not sure I agree with your use of the word 'accident,'" Candace countered. "But yes, it's what made me work the story."

"In your opinion, Ms. Snow, the city initially failed to properly investigate the accident at the Aurora Tower, correct?"

"Mrs."

Duncan paused, momentarily unsure he'd heard correctly. "Excuse me?"

"It's Mrs. Snow."

"Okay," Duncan said, unable to resist a smile as he marveled at the depths of this woman's petty hostility. "Does Mrs. Snow need the pending question read back?"

"I don't know whether they failed to properly *investigate* it," Candace replied. "They failed to prosecute it."

Duncan took a moment with that one, trying to figure out whether he could make it into something useful. "Are you saying the investigation revealed criminal conduct, but then that conduct wasn't prosecuted?"

"Objection," Rosenstein said. "Misstates prior testimony."

Candace ignored the hint. "That's certainly what my sources were indicating," she said.

"You just referred to your sources, plural," Duncan said. "How many unnamed sources did you have for this article?"

"Any such fishing around relating to the identity of Ms. Snow's source or sources is inappropriate," Rosenstein said, more sharply this time. "I again instruct her not to answer. Please stop asking her questions that impinge on the reporter's privilege."

"I believe that's *Mrs.* Snow," Duncan replied.

"Indeed," Rosenstein said with a mock bow. "But my larger point stands."

Duncan was ready to change tacks anyway. "Mrs. Snow, your article stated that a relative of Jack Pellettieri's was connected to organized crime, correct?"

"Yes, his brother, Dominic Pellettieri."

"Had this brother been convicted of a crime?"

"He had, yes. Racketeering."

"And does this brother presently have a position with Pellettieri Concrete?"

Candace shrugged, taking a sip of water. "Kind of hard to hold down a job when you're in jail," she said.

"So was this brother involved in any way with the Aurora Tower?"

Candace looked a little uncomfortable for once; Duncan thought he might be pressing on a weak spot. "Not that I know of."

"Do you have any actual knowledge that organized crime was in any way involved with the construction of the Aurora Tower?"

"There's still a lot of mob involvement with the construction business."

Duncan didn't know why she bothered to offer up such a nonanswer. "Do you have any actual and specific knowledge that organized crime was involved in the construction of the Aurora?" he asked, adding a little edge to his voice.

Candace tapped a finger on the table, then caught herself. "No," she said.

"So the only reason to mention Pellettieri's brother in your article was to imply such a connection, something you couldn't come out and say because you didn't have any factual support for it?"

Candace looked like she was counting to ten in her head before responding, her eyes cast down. When she spoke her words came slowly. "Pellettieri's brother is, or was, connected to the mob, to illegal acts. What the article said about him was true—obviously, seeing as he went to prison. What a reader chooses to make of that information, that's up to them."

"According to your article, the Department of Buildings' field investigators initially recommended that a criminal referral be made regarding the Aurora accident, correct?"

"That's right."

"But they were overruled by the head of the department, Ronald Durant?"

"Correct."

"Did you speak to Mr. Durant himself when researching your story?" Duncan asked, knowing the answer from the article itself.

"Mr. Durant was no longer with the DOB. I called him several times and left messages, but he never called me back."

"What if any basis did you have for claiming that Roth Properties had any sort of quid pro quo arrangement with Ronald Durant regarding his decision not to refer the Aurora accident for a criminal investigation?"

"Objection," Rosenstein said. "Assumes facts."

"My article doesn't say that," Candace responded, after first glancing over at her lawyer. She's learning, Duncan thought.

"Putting aside for the moment what your article said, would you have any basis for making that allegation?"

Candace sighed heavily, again offering a display of her pique. Given that she was the one being videotaped, Duncan was happy to have her visibly annoyed. "I'm not sure how I'm supposed to have a basis for saying something that I never said. No, I don't have evidence of an explicit deal like that; if I had I presumably would have reported on it. It's not exactly the kind of thing that Durant and Roth would have put in writing, or looped a lot of other people into, if they had made such an agreement. There're certainly questions raised by the chronology of events. But this isn't what my article focused on."

"In your article, you imply that Roth Properties bore at least partial responsibility for the accident, correct?"

"Objection. The article speaks for itself."

Duncan's eyes never wavered toward Rosenstein, his focus entirely on Candace. She met his gaze coolly, then turned questioningly to her lawyer.

"You can go ahead and answer," Rosenstein said.

"The article's focus was on the problems with the city's investigation into the accident. It wasn't focused on the accident itself, and it certainly wasn't focused on Roth Properties. Which is why I still don't really understand why we're even here."

"The pending question, Ms. Snow—excuse me, Mrs.—is whether your article implied that the developer was at least partially responsible for the accident."

"Asked and answered," Rosenstein objected.

"It's been asked," Duncan retorted. "Maybe this time it'll be answered."

"My article said what it said," Candace said. "It's not a poem. It's not meant to carry a hidden meaning or convey some message between the lines. A news article is supposed to deliver the facts, let the reader draw whatever conclusion they want out of them. That's what my article did."

Duncan wasn't going to get some kind of grand-slam admission out of her, but at least now he could say he'd tried. Time to shift directions once again. "You work as an investigative reporter, correct, Ms. Snow?"

"Yes."

"How many pieces of investigative reporting had you done prior to your reporting on the Aurora Tower?"

"All reporting is investigative in nature."

Refusing to give an inch wasn't a very effective way to get through a deposition, although it was a common one. Being unwilling to admit basic points always ended up looking bad. "But you are now part of the investigative reporting team at your newspaper, correct?" Duncan said with a show of patience.

"Yes."

"And how long before this article appeared did you join that team?"

"Two months or so, maybe a little less."

"So this was your first story as an investigative reporter?"

"It was my first published story with the I-team. That doesn't mean very much, though. I've been a reporter for about a decade. I've published hundreds of articles."

"You wanted your first investigative story, just after joining the investigative unit, to have an impact, didn't you?"

Candace rolled her eyes. Duncan thought she wasn't going to be very happy with herself if she ever saw the videotape. "Any reporter wants their story to have an impact."

"But you particularly wanted this specific story to have an impact, didn't you?"

What little was left of Candace's patience was visibly fraying. "If you're implying I wrote something untrue to be sensationalistic," she said, a slight quaver in her voice, "that's completely false."

"It is true, isn't it, that you were looking for a big story to help make your name as an investigative reporter?"

"I wanted an accurate story too," Candace said. "I resent the implication that I would bend the truth to further my own career."

"Would this be a good time for a break?" Rosenstein said.

"Sure," Duncan said, knowing it was a waste of time to fight it.

The videographer took them off the record and shut off the videotape. Candace stood quickly, stretching her back in a catlike arch that thrust out her breasts. She turned toward her lawyer. "So what we say now isn't part of the official transcript, right?" she asked.

"That's right," Rosenstein said.

Candace turned toward Duncan, her look so angry that he wondered if she was about to throw something across the table at him. "Nothing personal, you know, Mrs. Snow," Duncan said quickly. "I'm just doing my job."

"Lucky you," Candace said. "Finding a line of work that lets you be an asshole for a living."

DUNCAN MET a junior associate from his firm, Neil Levine, for a drink after work. They walked over to the lobby bar of the Royalton Hotel, less than a block from their office. Duncan had a thing for hotel bars, and the Royalton was one of his favorites in the city: dark and low-key, its ambience both swanky and decadent. There was something vaguely illicit about the place; it felt like a good rendezvous spot for an affair.

Duncan had recruited Neil as a Harvard 2L. Neil had summered at the firm two years ago, and then started as a full-time associate last fall. The two of them had become friends, although it was complicated by the fact that Duncan was essentially Neil's boss by virtue of seniority. He also sometimes found it difficult to put up with Neil's adjustment process to life as a big-firm associate.

"So I got called an asshole today," Duncan said, once they'd ordered drinks from the waitress, a beautiful woman in a black cocktail dress. It was a New York cliché that bartenders and waitresses were drop-dead gorgeous, but it was often true.

"I'm surprised that even warrants a mention for you," Neil replied. He was short and tousled, his hair perpetually uncombed, his clothes often on the far side of business casual.

"I've never been called an asshole doing my job before. Lawyers are much more refined in their name-calling. And besides, I'm not an asshole lawyer except when I have to be."

"So who called you an asshole?"

"I was deposing the reporter in the Roth libel suit, and on the break she said it. Her own lawyer actually dragged her out of the room, made her come back and apologize."

Neil didn't look impressed with the story. "You're honestly comfortable suing a reporter just because she dared criticize Simon Roth?"

"If you think something like that is going to be the toughest thing you're going to have to do at our firm, you're in for a long career," Duncan said as the waitress placed their drinks before them. "Or a short one. Besides, it's not like the reporter's own money is at stake. Her paper's owned by some other billionaire; we're picking on somebody our own size."

Neil shook his head in mock disappointment. "I can understand how lawyers defend rapists and child molesters," he said. "But how you can live with representing a New York City real estate developer is really beyond me."

Duncan understood that Neil's banter was standing in for real discomfort. He'd felt it too, back when he'd first started at the firm. Duncan remembered his own alienation as a junior associate, the sometimes painful acculturation process. Law school did virtually nothing to prepare people for the often dreary nature of practicing law, let alone the amorality of big-firm practice. The reality of representing the interests of some of the most powerful people on the planet was quite different from the abstract idea of doing so.

But it wasn't exactly exploitation: first-year associates at the big New York firms now received starting salaries of $160,000 a year. Duncan had a limited amount of patience for anyone's struggles with the job. If you didn't like the deal, there was a long line of people who would happily take it. He didn't feel the need to nurse Neil through the growing pains of becoming an actual lawyer.

"I actually met the great man himself the other day," Duncan said.

Neil took a sip of his brimming Manhattan, hoisting it with two hands so as not to spill. "Simon Roth? Total prick?"

"Actually, yeah, pretty much. But it seemed a little going-through-the-motions, like it was what was expected of him. How's the review going on the Roth documents for the DA's subpoena?"

Neil shrugged. "Slogging through."

"Find anything interesting?"

"God, no. It's mostly back-and-forth negotiating the contracts, which are endless. Boring as hell."

"I get the feeling you're not enjoying your time at our law firm," Duncan said.

Neil looked away. "It's just the whole cog-in-the-wheel thing," he said. "And most of our cases—it's not that we're repping the bad guy; it's just that the whole thing seems sort of pointless. We're just a small part of some huge business strategy. We have no idea what's really going on."

"You remind me of myself," Duncan said. "Back when I didn't know what the fuck I was talking about."

·3·

GOOD NEWS in the mail: a court order granting the motion to dismiss that Duncan had filed on behalf of his pro bono clients. In reality the motion was little more than a stall: the summons and complaint hadn't been personally served on his clients, but just left wedged in their apartment door. The dismissal based on this technicality was without prejudice, so that all the city had to do was refile with proper service.

In addition to buying his clients some time, the motion had been intended as a warning shot, a way of letting the Housing Authority know that he'd be fighting the eviction every step of the way. The hope was that the city would decide that kicking the Nazarios out of their home was more trouble than it was worth. Sometimes simply showing a willingness to outwork the other side was the difference maker in a case. It was hardly an ideal strategy, but Duncan didn't have a way to win on the merits.

Duncan was still a little surprised to find himself defending the Nazarios at all. Blake and Wolcott generally had more work than its lawyers could handle, meaning not only that associates routinely billed between twenty-five hundred and three thousand hours a year, but also that it lagged far behind more established firms when it came to areas like pro bono. But in the last six months the firm had created a pro bono committee and put a partner in charge of reaching out to various legal service organizations, the goal being that every lawyer would do at least a little free legal work for the disadvantaged.

It wasn't exactly a secret that this sudden interest in pro bono arose not out of the goodness of the partners' hearts, but rather as a concession to a series of blows to Blake and Wolcott's once sterling reputation. In its first years of existence, in the late nineties, the firm had received a cascade of good press as it piled up high-profile victories, much of it focused on Steven Blake. For a couple of years it'd seemed like every big corporate case in the country had Blake on the winning side. He'd been profiled not just in trade magazines, but in *Time* and *Newsweek* as well.

But all that attention, and the firm's exponential growth, had unsurprisingly brought about a backlash. As was inevitable, Blake had lost a couple of cases, tarnishing the myth of his invincibility, and the press that had been so eager to deify him now reported instead on a gender-discrimination suit brought by a female former associate who'd been passed over for partner. The firm had then landed near the very bottom of *The American Lawyer*'s associate satisfaction survey, which in turn had led to a series of increasingly snarky articles on *The Wall Street Journal*'s blog covering the legal profession. All of it inevitable schadenfreude bullshit, sure, but there was no denying that such things hurt recruitment, taking the firm down a peg or two from its former perch as the place all the Harvard and Yale hotshots wanted to spend their 2L summers.

While Duncan had been a little surprised to thus find himself taking on a run-of-the-mill eviction case, let alone doing it for free rather than the $450 an hour the firm normally charged for his time, he made a point of bringing the same perfectionism to his work on it as he did any other case. Despite his cynicism about the practice of law (a cynicism shared by all of his colleagues), Duncan still believed in being a lawyer as a profession, and to him providing his best effort to every client was part of being a professional. Besides, he liked the Nazarios, who, based on his couple of meetings with them, seemed like good people.

Duncan called to tell them about winning the motion, Rafael answering. Duncan gave him the update, trying to play it down, not wanting Rafael to get the idea that they'd really won.

"I knew you'd be able to beat them, Mr. R," Rafael exclaimed, sounding distinctly more excited than Duncan would've liked. "I told my *abuela* you were going to hook us up."

"I really doubt the city will give up this easily, Rafael," Duncan said. "So don't assume the case is over. We've still got quite an uphill battle if they do refile."

As soon as Duncan had hung up with Rafael someone appeared in the open doorway of his office. "Am I interrupting?" Leah Roth asked.

Duncan made no attempt to hide his surprise. Unexpected guests from the outside world were generally nonexistent at the firm: they'd never make it past the lobby security.

"Of course not; come in," Duncan said, instinctively standing up, then gesturing Leah to a seat.

"Sounds like you had a satisfied customer there," Leah said as she sat down.

"What, you're surprised?" Duncan said, sitting himself, looking around his office and wishing it wasn't such a disaster: there were stacks of paper on the floor; his desk was so crowded with papers that no more than an inch of its surface was visible. He didn't think such chaos was likely to inspire confidence in a client.

"Blake assures my father that our cases are staffed with the best lawyers this firm has to offer," Leah said. "He wouldn't lie to my dad, would he?"

"Lawyers never lie," Duncan said. "We just deceive, inveigle, and obfuscate. So what brings you to our humble law firm?"

"Your real estate group's navigating a long-term lease with Ogilvy for us. I've been here all morning. You just deposed the reporter in the libel case, right?"

"Yesterday, yeah."

"Want to give me a report?"

Duncan did his best not to show surprise. "Sure."

"How about we do it over lunch?"

Duncan didn't say yes quite as quickly as he would've liked, at a loss to understand why Leah Roth, the daughter of a man who was worth something like a billion dollars, the VP of a company for whom Duncan was at twenty-four/seven beck and call, wanted to break bread with him.

They went to Blue Fin, a seafood place on Broadway a short walk from the firm's office on the Avenue of the Americas. The restaurant was large and open, with a dramatic staircase and a billowing white wall evoking flowing water. They were seated upstairs, the room crowded and loud with a mix of businesspeople and tourists.

Although it was a restaurant where Duncan routinely brought summer associates and interviewees for lunch, he worried that it wasn't exclusive enough to bring Leah Roth. He told himself that was silly: she couldn't walk into his office unannounced, invite him to lunch, and expect him to have a table waiting at Le Bernardin. Or could she?

Duncan was rattled by her wealth. It was one of the ironies of his job that while he made far more money than anyone in his family ever had, more than he could have readily conceived of while growing up, it also surrounded him with people who were so obscenely loaded that they made him feel like a peasant. Last year Duncan had cleared a half million, thanks to a year-end bonus that'd matched his annual salary, but in Manhattan in the summer of 2008 that barely felt upper middle class. Even someone like Blake, who made about ten times what Duncan did, hardly qualified as rich when you put him next to people like the Roths.

"So, Duncan," Leah said after they'd ordered. "What's your story?"

Duncan was not sure what she was asking for. "You mean my life story or my résumé?"

"Surely you have a life story?"

Duncan wasn't in the habit of reciting biographical information to clients, and wasn't particularly comfortable with the prospect, but then again he was trying to build a long-term professional relationship here, which certainly had a personal component. "I grew up outside of Detroit, went to college in Ann Arbor. I got lucky enough to get into Harvard for law school, so off I went. After clerking I wanted to go to a firm where I'd have more responsibility and less hierarchy than the white-shoe places, so I joined Blake. And here I am."

Leah narrowed her eyes at him, although Duncan couldn't say if her disappointment was real or just for show. "I have to say, even for a lawyer that's a pretty boring life story."

Duncan hadn't been trying to tell her anything, but he still felt a stab of resentment at Leah's response. What was she expecting him to offer up? He wondered how she would react if he actually told her a fuller version of who he was, but he wasn't tempted to find out. Although Duncan didn't consider his background to be a secret, at least not among his friends, it wasn't something he routinely disclosed in professional situations. Telling people complicated things, and his interaction with Leah Roth was already complicated enough. "You didn't expect me to give up my secret identity right off the bat?" he said instead.

"Are your parents lawyers? I've noticed it often runs in the family."

Duncan was the second person in his family to graduate from college, the first to get an advanced degree of any kind, but he wasn't tempted to admit that to a woman who stood to inherit a family fortune.

Instead he just shook his head. "My father does a lot of negotiating for his job, but he's not a lawyer. He chairs a local for the UAW in Detroit."

Leah cocked her head slightly, Duncan guessing she was recalculating her initial impression of him. If you only knew, he thought. You think you know who I am, where I come from, the road I took to get here. But you're wrong about it all. "So what are you doing representing the corporate overlords?" she asked.

Duncan grinned. "My dad asks me the same question every Christmas," he said, not truthfully.

The waiter brought Duncan's tuna and Leah's lobster salad. "So," Duncan said, once they'd started eating. "Why are you interested in the libel case?"

"I'm not, especially. I tried to talk Dad out of it, but he wouldn't listen. He hates reporters. He thinks they exist to take people like us down, look for anything they can find to smear us with. He knows that we'll probably end up losing, but he'd still really love to teach the newspaper a lesson."

"Win or lose, their legal bills will help see to that."

"Why, that never occurred to me," Leah deadpanned. "Of course, Dad's known Sam Friedman forever, so that's part of it too."

Friedman, another wealthy and well-known developer, was the owner of the *New York Journal*. Duncan felt an uncomfortable awareness of being a pawn in a much larger game: two real estate moguls pissing in each other's flower beds. If the lawsuit actually went back to some personal beef between Simon Roth and Sam Friedman he didn't want to know about it.

"Wheels within wheels, I'm sure," Duncan said. "Anyway, as for the deposition, it went okay. The reporter was defensive and testy, didn't come across very well. So in terms of atmospherics it was a win. But the case is an uphill battle, and she didn't give us anything that changed that in terms of substance."

Leah nodded. "I remember from Con Law 101, actual malice and all that. It's part of why I told Dad not to waste his time."

"That's right," Duncan said. "You're a lawyer."

Leah smiled thinly, not bothering to feign surprise that Duncan knew this about her. "Only technically; I never practiced. I was dual degree at Columbia with the business school."

"I don't imagine you ever planned on joining a law firm."

"It was more about the skill set. When I was growing up Dad wasn't exactly enthusiastic about the prospect of my joining the family biz, so a law degree seemed like a way of keeping options open."

"Why didn't he want you joining the company?" Duncan asked, wondering as he did so if it was too personal a question.

Leah didn't look bothered by it. "Commercial real estate is still a very male world," she said. "Even more than law, if you can believe that. Not that my dad was any more fond of the idea of my going to law school. I'm not sure how a man who's as litigious as he is can complain about lawyers so much."

"He and Blake are friends, though, right?"

"I don't know that my father has *friends*, as such. But Steven is definitely a family ally."

"Allies are important."

"They certainly are, Duncan," Leah said. "In a few years my father will retire, and I'll take over the business. Blake has to be what, sixty?"

Duncan noted that Leah had said that it was she alone who would be taking over the business, with no mention of her brother. "He's around sixty," he replied. "But spry."

"So he'll presumably be out of the trenches in five years or so, certainly in ten. Hopefully we can be allies one day too, Duncan."

"We're allies now," Duncan said, smiling.

Leah shook her head, her expression serious. Whatever it was she was getting at, it was clearly not just banter. "We're not yet. Being my lawyer is something, but a true ally is more than that."

Duncan hoped he was keeping uneasiness out of his expression. "We go to the wall for our clients," he said, unsure whether this qualified as a reply.

Leah just studied him in response, Duncan having no idea what she was looking for. "We're having a party for my father's seventieth birthday next Saturday," she finally said, pushing her half-eaten salad forward a little and dropping her napkin on top of it before leaning back in her chair. "I believe Steven is coming."

Duncan raised his brows, trying to look interested. Leah was clearly waiting for a response from him, but he wasn't sure what. "Blake doesn't exactly keep me apprised of his social life," he finally said.

Leah still with her evaluating look. "It would probably be useful for you to come," she said.

This was certainly the most passive-aggressive party invitation Duncan had ever received; he wasn't entirely sure it *was* an invitation. "For my future as a rainmaker, you mean."

"Precisely."

"Does that mean you're inviting me?"

Leah looked at him quizzically. "Wasn't that clear?"

"Not completely," Duncan said. "But sure, I'd love to come." In truth he could hardly imagine a party he'd less like to go to.

"I'll e-mail you the details," Leah said as the waiter brought him their check. "So tell me, Duncan, does family background still matter at the elite law firms?"

Duncan had been doing his best not to be provoked all lunch, but he couldn't fully contain his irritation. He got the feeling Leah was going to keep poking at him until she got some kind of reaction. "Certainly not at our firm, though it probably doesn't hurt if you're talking about a place like Sullivan and Cromwell. But I've never felt that being a working-class kid from the provinces was particularly hampering my legal career, if that's what you're asking."

Duncan had said it with a smile, but it came out harsher than he intended, and there was a moment of silence between them. "I apologize if I offended you," Leah said, her expression unchanged. "You'll find that I'm somewhat blunt on occasion. I didn't mean to sound snobbish. I am quite snobbish, admittedly, but not in the classic Upper East Side sense. I don't actually have much patience for people like myself, if you want to know the truth. I admire people who've worked hard to get where they are. My snobbishness is entirely a tyranny of the interesting."

"That's true of this whole town," Duncan said.

"I was brought up suspicious of inherited wealth, odd as that might sound. The family money's all tied up in trusts—I actually live on my salary, believe it or not. Which is certainly not that hard to do, but still."

"I wasn't offended, anyway," Duncan said. "And I do think having to work for everything from scratch has its advantages."

"I've no doubt it does," Leah said, with a smile that Duncan tried not to take as condescending. "So who were you talking to before? Back in your office?"

"My pro bono client. We won a motion to dismiss, though it's without prejudice."

"Meaning the case is still going to go forward."

Duncan shrugged as the waiter returned with his credit card. "I hope not," he said. "My only defense on the merits is likely to be going after your security guard who busted my guy in the first place."

"Who's the security guard?"

"His name's Sean Fowler. You know him?"

Leah shook her head, though Duncan thought she'd reacted to the name. "Loomis's crew are mostly ex-cops. They can probably take it. So do you enjoy doing pro bono work?"

"I take it as seriously as anything else," Duncan said. "But honestly, I prefer working on the big-ticket stuff. What's the point of being the smartest person in the room unless you're doing something that no one else in the room can do?"

"I guess it's no surprise that you're ambitious," Leah said. "What is it you want your ambition to get you?"

It wasn't a question Duncan knew the answer to, and he wasn't inclined to try and come up with one for Leah. "My ambition is just to win," he said instead. "I win for a living."

.4.

CLEAN AND sober at eleven at night: this was not Jeremy Roth's customary state. Especially not when coming out of a three-hour dinner in the private dining room of Per Se. The restaurant was arguably the most exclusive in the city—not that Jeremy even so much as glimpsed his fellow diners from the private room, which was just past the entrance.

Dinner had been with the Al-Falasi family from Dubai: Ubayd and his sons, Ahmed and Mattar. As a concession to the Al-Falasis' religion, Jeremy's father had instructed that dinner was to be entirely sans alcohol. The Roth family was courting the Al-Falasi family as potential silent partners on the Aurora. As was common, Roth Properties was directly covering only about ten percent of the Aurora's construction costs. About three hundred million dollars' worth of short-term, high-interest loans—the mezzanine loans—were coming due on the building. The plan had been to pay off the mezzanine loans as apartment units sold during construction, but suddenly the market had been asphyxiated. Even that wouldn't normally have been a problem, as banks traditionally extended mezzanine loans as a matter of course. But credit for commercial real estate was drying up fast, everybody was getting nervous, and their skittish financiers were looking for an excuse to bail on the project. The largest source of their short-term financing was a Greenwich hedge fund that wouldn't hesitate to play hardball if there was a problem with repayment.

Although Roth Properties had a few billion dollars of commercial real estate in its portfolio, it had little liquidity, and coming up with a few hundred million dollars on their own was going to be a problem. They'd probably have to sell a building, and with the market rattled they'd inevitably sell for a loss, which would in turn raise alarm bells about the health of their company.

Unlike their biggest project of the moment, the transformation of a tract of public housing, which was being done in partnership with the city and thus heavily incentivized with tax breaks and conservatively financed by major banks with long-term loans, on the Aurora they were out on a limb. So they were looking for major money: $250 million would make the Aurora a real partnership. They'd settle for a $100 million loan, which would at least cover what they owed the hedge fund. With the dollar in the toilet and oil prices in the stratosphere, it was becoming increasingly common for financing for New York City development deals to come from the Middle East. It wasn't a secret, but it wasn't something people were vocal about either.

Not that they talked business over the endless dinner. At least not explicitly. As his father had said on the way to the restaurant, doing business with Middle Eastern families was like trying to get into a prim virgin's pants. You were going to have to spend a lot of quality time together before you made your move.

Family was part of it. Family and business were much more intertwined there than here. The ruling families controlled the money; there was a very limited circle of people to talk to about business and they all shared the same blood. Being a private family-run company was an advantage in dealing with Middle Eastern investors, but it also necessitated evenings like this.

It was the fathers who did most of the talking at dinner. Jeremy and his sister, as well as Ahmed and Mattar, spoke only when spoken to, which was mainly to answer rote background questions about their education and interests. Jeremy drank three bottles' worth of sparkling water without clearing out the itchy dryness at the back of his throat. His knees kept jamming up against the bottom of the table as his legs bounced.

After dinner he called Alena from the back of the waiting Town Car. "I'm on my way over," he said.

"Is that your way of asking?" Alena replied.

"I'm not asking."

ALENA PORTER was living off the books at a Roth Properties building on the far western end of Manhattan, on the outskirts of the

Meatpacking District. It had been the model unit used to sell the build-ing: the furniture and decor from the interior designer had all been left in place. Alena was traveling light, had barely left a mark, so the apart-ment still felt more like a model unit than a lived-in apartment.

Jeremy let himself in. Despite having keys, he'd never once shown up unannounced. He saw no reason to run the risk of an awkward sur-prise.

They'd met at a nightclub a few months ago, Alena not quite work-ing there, but not quite a customer either, arm candy for the VIPs. She'd come to the city to model at seventeen, recruited by Elite, had a per-fectly good run but never really broke out of the pack. Okay, so it wasn't love, but Jeremy was wild for her waifish body, her perfect lips, the purring sound she made when she came.

Alena was in the shower when he entered the apartment. Despite himself, Jeremy felt a jab of something he was pretty sure was jealousy. He couldn't stop himself from wondering if she was washing away another man, one who'd been in this apartment when he'd called. He walked into the kitchen, helped himself to a generous glass of the twenty-one-year-old Lagavulin he'd brought over the previous week-end. He noticed the bottle was nearly half-empty. Then again, he'd def-initely had a fair amount of it the night he'd brought it over.

He took a gulp, then another, too quickly, so that it burned going down. This was no way to drink an aged single-malt, Jeremy told him-self. Part of why he bought the good stuff was so that he would drink it like a grown-up, not guzzle it down like some frat boy, but it didn't always work. Especially not lately.

He realized the shower had turned off; a moment later he heard the bathroom door open. "Are you here?" Alena called out.

"Somebody is," Jeremy said, taking another sip of the whiskey, then eyeballing the amount left in the glass. He opened the bottle again, the cork top making a little popping sound that he suspected Alena could hear, and splashed in another finger.

Alena, dressed only in a thin bathrobe that clung to her still-damp frame, was sitting on the couch combing her hair. Jeremy kissed her hello, settling in beside her, taking another sip of the scotch before put-ting it down on the Noguchi coffee table.

Jeremy picked up an antique silver cigarette case off the coffee table, pulled out a joint and a lighter. He inhaled deeply before offering it to Alena, who leaned forward to take a drag without reaching for it. The humming in Jeremy's brain was fast fading, the propulsive beat in his body finally lulled. Jeremy took another hit off the joint, ashed it before it spilled onto the white couch, then washed it down with a proper, civilized sip of scotch.

Alena put down her comb, looking at him. She was tall, thin, and tan, her complexion practically matching the brown of her slightly highlighted hair. "Why so tense?" she asked.

"Dinner with my family's bad enough without throwing in these fucking Muslim royals. They come over to New York now the same way you go to the Barneys warehouse sale."

"I've never been to Barneys."

"They're bargain hunting, scooping up the city because the dollar's too weak to defend it," Jeremy continued, feeling on a roll, the pressure of the evening coming out in his contempt. "And we've got to go hat in hand to these motherfuckers. Play by *their* rules, even though we're in the middle of Manhattan."

"Their rules? Oh, meaning you had to stay sober?"

Cleverness wasn't an asset in a kept woman, something Jeremy had mentioned to Alena on more than one occasion. It inevitably led to more of a fight than he had the energy to deal with at the moment, so he hit the joint instead. Alena took it from him, had another drag.

"What about the other thing?" Alena asked. Jeremy looked over at her, hoping he'd misunderstood what she was getting at, but seeing that he hadn't. He didn't remember telling her about his recent problems, had no recollection of any such conversation. He could only hope he hadn't gone into too much detail.

"That's being taken care of," he said flatly, making clear that the subject was a dead end.

"Why do you need the Arabs anyway?" Alena asked. "Why don't you just borrow the money from one of the big banks? Isn't that what you usually do?"

Jeremy hadn't made up his mind how he felt about Alena's occasional displays of the rudiments of business acumen. He needed to vent about work sometimes, so it was occasionally useful, but at the same time he wasn't sure how much he really wanted Alena privy to that side of his life. "The credit market's gone dry," Jeremy said. "The banks don't have a spare three hundred million to lend, especially not for real estate. Plus this project is already so leveraged—we've only got fifty million of our own money in, which makes them more nervous."

Alena had clearly grown bored with the topic; she crossed her legs, the robe opening to midthigh as she did so. Jeremy burned his thumb a little hitting the dregs of the joint. He stubbed out the roach in the ashtray, then finished off the scotch in his glass, his gaze lingering on Alena's exposed inner thigh.

"You find peace over there?" she asked him, her smile more taunting than welcoming.

"I'm actually going to freshen this up," Jeremy said, reaching for his glass. "But why don't you meet me in the bedroom?"

"I can do that," Alena said evenly, her voice lacking either anticipation or hesitation. She stretched as she stood, the nipples of her small breasts visible against the thin fabric. Jeremy reached out and ran his index finger down the middle of her robe, parting it. Alena stood as though posed, looking back at him, her expression unchanged. "You know where to find me," she said after a moment, moving past him toward the bedroom.

Jeremy watched her go, his dick alive in his pants, the familiar heat in his blood. He walked to the kitchen, opened the bottle, took a long hard swig straight from it before pouring himself a generous double. He winced down a long sip, getting the amount in the glass to a respectable level. He was foggy now, numbed, but also relaxed.

He was ready. He made his way to the bedroom, unbuttoning his shirt. Alena lay propped up on the bed, the robe off now, nothing on but a pair of strawberry-colored panties. "Why, hello," she said.

"Time to pay the rent," Jeremy said, grinning. Alena's whole body stiffened, her face breaking like a dropped glass. Before Jeremy fully understood what was happening she had her robe on again, her back to him.

"It was just a joke," Jeremy said, his words sounding a little thick to his own ears.

"I'm not a fucking whore," Alena said with cold fury.

"Of course not," Jeremy said, reaching out to her shoulder, Alena sensing it and slapping his hand away before he'd even made contact. "I was just kidding around."

"Calling me your hooker is not kidding around."

"That's not what I— I didn't mean anything."

"You can stay if you want, but I'm going to sleep," Alena said, sliding under the covers, still with her back to him.

"Alena—"

"Good night."

"Don't go to bed angry."

"I already have."

"It was just—"

"You said that already."

Jeremy sat there helplessly, looking at her stiff body under the blankets, the body he would be about to fuck if he hadn't been so stupid. He picked up his glass, finished the dregs of the whiskey—how was it all gone already? Not knowing what else to do, Jeremy stood, glass in hand, and made his way to the kitchen to pour himself another drink.

·5·

GRAVEYARD FOOT patrol in the NYPD's Housing Bureau: no cop's idea of a plum assignment. Officers Dooling and Garrity had done consecutive verticals in two buildings, walking up and down the stairwells, fourteen floors. Garrity, a smoker, started huffing after a couple of flights, his beefy face going red, sweat rolling along his jaw-line.

After the back-to-back verticals Garrity insisted they skip a round, so the two of them stood behind the building they were supposed to be patrolling, Garrity lighting up a cigarette. Nightfall hadn't broken the thick July heat: the air was muggy and still. Garrity, still sweating, logged it in his book that they were doing another up-and-down. Everybody skimmed on verticals, and in Garrity's view two out of three was a reasonable compromise.

The last straw for Garrity had been halfway up in Tower Two, when he'd turned in a stairwell, skidded in something wet, only a quick arm brace on the wall keeping him from falling on his ass. A cursory sniff confirmed his suspicion that it'd been somebody's piss that had almost tripped him. He'd muttered to himself through his ragged breath for the rest of the climb, Dooling knowing to let his partner work through his anger before riding him about it.

"You drop of a heart attack while the two of us are out here, you best believe I'm not doing CPR," Dooling said. He could hear the faint rumble of traffic from the FDR Drive, which marked the eastern end of the project.

"Like your black ass knows CPR," Garrity replied. They'd been partnered for almost a year, rookie cops stuck in a dead-end beat. Like most partners with nothing in common, they interacted with a rude banter meant to cover over the fact that they didn't actually like each other.

"I know a man who needs to be put out of his misery when I see him."

Garrity took a deep drag off his smoke, blew it out at Dooling, though it dissipated in the air before reaching its target. Dooling took a step back anyway, going into a boxer's crouch, feet dancing in the scuffed dirt, a show of energy.

"I can bench four hundred pounds," Garrity said. "So don't get any ideas just because I don't like going up and down twenty flights of stairs."

"So we going to do Tower Four?"

"Half an hour," Garrity said, after checking his watch and then pulling out his activity log, calculating how much time their phantom patrol of Tower Three was taking.

Dooling scanned the empty surroundings. There'd been a couple of people on a bench twenty feet away when the two cops had crossed over from Tower Two, but they'd ghosted away as soon as the uniforms had planted their flag along the building's back wall.

"Standing out here isn't much better than walking a vertical, you ask me," Dooling said, mostly just to say something.

"I didn't," Garrity said, lighting a fresh cigarette off the nub of the one he'd been smoking.

"I'm sure usually when you smell like piss this time of night, at least it's your own."

"Hey, I get that you feel right at home trolling the projects, but I had a father growing up, was raised in a house."

Dooling's retort was lost to the snapping sound, three quick bursts, the noise echoing a little in the valley created by the high-rises. Garrity looked a question at Dooling, who replied with a curt nod, taking out his gun before launching into a sprint down the walkway between two buildings in the direction of the shots. Garrity dropped his cigarette before getting his own gun out, taking off behind his faster partner.

Dooling rounded onto Tenth Street at a small traffic circle, eyes scrambling for danger, spotting a crumpled body across the street, a man in a uniform crouching nearby. Dooling skidded to a stop, looking for movement, anything wrong in the scene beside the guy on the ground. Although the streets would still be buzzing with people a few blocks over in the heart of the East Village, on the far side of Avenue D it was quiet, nobody else nearby. He heard Garrity catching up, Dooling on his walkie-talkie now, calling in shots fired, person hit, asking for backup and an ambulance.

Garrity jogged past Dooling toward the fallen body. The crouched man put his hands up by his shoulders, fingers spread wide, showing them he wasn't a threat. Dooling recognized the uniform: the private security company that was patrolling the construction under way throughout the northern part of Jacob Riis. Dooling had interacted with the private guards a little: there'd been at least some effort to coordinate with them; plus the security people, mostly ex-cops, had fed some low-level busts to the Housing Bureau rank and file. This had made them friends among the beat cops.

"Chris Driscoll," the security guy called to them as the cops approached. "I was on the job at the Three-two."

"He conscious?" Garrity asked.

"I wasn't catching a pulse," Driscoll said, shaking his head, looking down but not quite at the fallen man, who was also dressed as a security guard. "I think it's already too late."

"What happened?" Garrity said.

"I was coming over to sub Sean out for his break, saw him arguing with someone. No sooner had I turned the corner on D than the shots went off, Sean going down. I got a decent look at the shooter: male Hispanic, young, close to six feet, thin."

"Where'd he go?"

"He ran into the project, must've been running along the front side of that building right there while you two were coming along the back."

"He ran in there?" Dooling said, pointing to a walkway about half a block from the one he and his partner had just come down.

Driscoll nodded. "By the time I got over here and checked on Sean, I figured there was no way I was catching him."

Dooling sprinted off in the direction Driscoll had pointed. Garrity asked Driscoll if he was okay staying with the victim till backups and the EMTs arrived, then went chasing after his partner.

When he caught up, Dooling had buttonholed a couple of sullen young men from off a bench, Garrity pegging them as dealers, or at least lookouts, teenagers he recognized on sight but whose names he didn't know. They'd rousted these kids from their perch before, threatening loitering collars, but never actually busted them. "I'm making it simple for you," Dooling was saying. "You tell me where he went, we're on our way, leave you alone. You don't tell me, we're going to take you to our house, hold you there as witnesses for the rest of the night."

"I ain't no snitch," the taller of the two dealers said.

"This ain't no snitching," Dooling replied. "This is saving yourself a night at the station, which is more likely to get you a snitch jacket than just telling me here and now who you saw and where he went."

"We didn't see nobody," the other kid said. He was maybe younger, a good twenty pounds overweight.

"Last call to tell me, or I'm bringing you in," Dooling said.

"Didn't nobody go past us," the shorter one said again.

Dooling looked at Garrity, who shrugged. "You mind them; I'll do a last sprint?" Dooling asked.

Garrity nodded, and Dooling took off. He ran straight for a block or so, then cut east, deeper into the project, looking for anybody who wasn't moving right, any kind of reaction that he could use for a stop and frisk. There were few people around, nobody alone, just some loose clusters of young men, everybody giving Dooling reflexive hard stares as he went by. He ran in a rough zigzag for five minutes, but nothing snagged his attention, and he gave up and headed back to the crime scene as he heard the sound of approaching sirens.

There were already a couple of patrol cars and an ambulance on site, not surprising, since the Housing Bureau's local HQ was just a few blocks away. Dooling didn't see his partner, so he made his way over to Driscoll, who was sitting on a curb by himself. "I didn't spot anybody who looked wrong," Dooling said. "But we've got pictures of everybody who lives in the project. You think you could make him from a photo?"

"I think I sure as fuck would like to try," Driscoll said.

"WE'RE UP," Detective Alexander Jaworski said, blinking the lights in the interview room on and off. His partner, Jorge Gomez, was lying sprawled across three metal chairs arranged into a makeshift cot in the far corner of the room.

Gomez groaned in response. "You can't have a hangover at one in the morning," Jaworski said. "It's not natural."

"Working graveyards isn't natural," Gomez said, nearly falling to the floor as he sat up, the chair his legs had been resting on skidding away.

"We've got shots fired, possible DOA at Riis," Jaworski said. "We gotta be out the door now."

Gomez stood, rubbed at his face, following Jaworski out of the interview room. Jaworski handed Gomez his sports jacket as they descended the stairs to the back parking lot.

It was a short drive from the Ninth Precinct on Fifth Street to the Jacob Riis projects. While Jaworski drove, Gomez pulled himself together, tightening his tie and combing back his disheveled hair. Gomez was a good detective, but his wife had kicked him out three months ago and now he was going on daytime benders, coming in for his graveyards looking like he'd just rolled out of bed, still needed a few more hours to sleep it off. Jaworski had told himself that he'd hold his tongue so long as his partner was only showing up hungover and not drunk.

The carnival was well under way by the time he pulled up at Tenth and D: a quick scan showed at least a half dozen uniforms, EMS, two ambos even though there was only one vic—private companies monitoring cop frequencies, looking to pick up a fare. The only small mercy was that Jaworski didn't scope any press: one advantage of an after-hours shooting in the projects.

Jaworski recognized the night watch commander from the Housing Bureau, Sergeant Fitzgerald, shouted out to him as he approached, "What we got?"

"One of Loomis's guys, working construction security," Fitzgerald said. "Ex-cop, I hear, Sean Fowler."

"Fowler," Gomez said. "I remember him from the job. What's the status?"

"They took him to Beth Israel, but from what I hear they're just running due diligence on a miracle. He didn't have any vitals when they put him in the ambo."

"Ex-cop, huh?" Jaworski said, shaking his head. He didn't like hearing it was a brother officer, but he also didn't like that his run-of-the-mill projects shooting had just turned into a red ball. The bosses would be all over him once they knew the vic had worn blue.

"Good news is, we've got an eyeball witness. A sharp one too: another ex-cop."

"Where is he?" Jaworski said.

"Our house," Fitzgerald said.

Jaworski wasn't happy with that. "Why isn't he at the scene?" he asked brusquely.

"We've got him looking at photos."

"Shit," Jaworski said.

"What?" Fitzgerald said defensively.

"Who's showing him photos?"

"The patrol guys who were first on the scene."

"They fuck up the procedures, a defense attorney will get the ID tossed."

"My men know the rules," Fitzgerald said, a little pissed now too.

"Are your men homicide detectives? Then they should leave the homicide detecting to me." Jaworski turned to his partner. "You run things here; I'm going to go down with Fitz and see where the eyeball's at."

JAWORSKI WAS trying to remember whether he'd ever been this lucky. By the time he and Fitzgerald had arrived at the Housing Bureau station and found the patrol officers who were taking the witness through photographs, the guy'd just made an ID. Rafael Nazario, nineteen years old, lived with his grandmother in Tower Six. The patrol cops had run a solid ID procedure: pulling out forty or so photos that matched the witness's general description, handing him a stack to sift through all together.

Things were moving, and Jaworski wanted to keep them that way. He borrowed a bulletproof vest, even more uncomfortable than usual in the summer heat, then took the two patrol cops, Dooling and Garrity, and headed into Riis while Fitzgerald radioed over for additional backup to meet them.

"You guys were first on the scene?" Jaworski asked.

"Yeah," Garrity said. "We were maybe a block away when we heard the shots."

"Just a block? But you didn't catch a look at the shooter?"

Garrity shook his head. "We lost a little bit of time on the scene, getting the four-one-one from the witness, Driscoll. We took off in the direction this kid had run to, but he must've made the project already by then."

"You were on foot patrol?"

"We were doing verticals of the buildings, stairways, roofs, that sort of thing," Dooling said.

"You were doing verticals when you heard the shots?" Jaworski asked.

"We'd just come down," Garrity said. "I was taking a quick smoke before we did the next one. So we were on the ground when the shots went off."

Jaworski decided not to follow up. Anyone looking at Garrity would make him for somebody not built for going up and down stairs all night. Experience told him that the patrol schedule and their actual whereabouts wouldn't sync up.

Jaworski called his partner on the walk over, caught Gomez up on what was happening, asked him to coordinate getting a warrant on the apartment rather than helping out with the arrest.

A cluster of uniforms were waiting for them outside the building, so Jaworski led a small army up to Nazario's apartment. Jaworski considered taking down the door, claiming exigent circumstances for a limited search, but decided there was too much risk that it would come back to bite the case down the road. Besides, it wasn't like the kid could flush a pistol down the toilet.

Jaworski reached out to knock, identified himself as police, then stood away from the door, his heart bouncing around in his chest like a pinball. The last place you wanted to be standing when knocking on the door of a cornered suspect was in the doorway; if a blind shot was fired that was where it would go. After a minute he knocked again, louder, again identifying himself as police. Finally the door opened, still latched on the chain, and a small, plump, elderly woman stared out at him. "*Dios mío*," she said. "You see what time it is?"

"IT'S LIKE this, Rafael," Detective Jaworski said to the young man across the table. "We've got guys searching through your apartment right now. They're turning the place upside down. Your grandmother's room too."

Over an hour had passed since they'd brought Rafael in. The uniforms had driven him back to the Housing Bureau, where they had Fowler make a confirmation in-person ID. Once they'd brought him to the Ninth they'd left him to cool his heels for a while, running his sheet, waiting till the warrant was granted and the search of the Nazario apartment was under way. They'd also run Rafael's hands and clothes for gunshot residue.

"You got no reason to be dogging me," Rafael said. He was loose-limbed and lanky, maybe still growing.

Gomez shook his head. "Oh, but we do, Rafael. You going to deny you had a beef with Sean Fowler?"

"I got no love for the man, sure, after what he done. The only reason they got those fake police there is to throw us out of where we live."

"I know it's hard to believe when you live in the projects, Rafael," Jaworski said, "but smoking weed is still illegal in these United States."

"He didn't catch me smoking no weed."

"We have the police report and the court file, Rafael," Jaworski said. "We know you pled out."

"I pled to disorderly conduct is all. That's not even a *crime*. Besides, I only pled to that to get out of jail. It don't mean I did nothing."

"Actually it does," Gomez said. "Or don't you remember the part where you told a judge that you were guilty?"

"I was just doing like my free lawyer told me to do. She didn't believe me neither, but I wasn't doing shit when Fowler came up on me that night."

"I understand why that's your story now, Rafael," Jaworski said. "I guess your Legal Aid lawyer neglected to fill you in on what could happen if you pled guilty to a drug charge."

"This is all just bullshit," Rafael protested.

"You didn't realize that pleading guilty on smoking a blunt would lead to your losing the roof over your head, did you?"

Rafael winced in frustration. "How am I supposed to know that?" he said. "If my stupid-ass lawyer don't bother to tell me, then how'm I gonna know?"

"Let alone that it would mean your grandmother's looking at being out on the street too," Jaworski said. "Can't feel too good, doing that to the woman who raised you."

"We got a new lawyer now, a real lawyer, taking care of all that."

"A real lawyer, huh?" Gomez snorted.

"Let me make sure I have this, Rafael," Jaworski said. "You're saying that Sean Fowler framed you on a drug charge, that now because of that charge you and your grandmother are getting evicted from your apartment, meaning that the woman who raised you up is looking to be out on the street in the *twilight* of her years, and you're saying that with all that you've got no motive to kill Fowler?"

"Anybody do that shit to me and mine I'd have something to say about it," Gomez added.

"I got plenty to say about it. But I'm saying it through the lawyer. He's straightening all this out."

"Maybe, maybe not," Gomez said. "But it's all because of Sean Fowler."

"Look, Rafael," Jaworski said. "We're all reasonable people here. Now, we obviously know that you and Fowler had a history. We've got an eyewitness that puts you at the scene. The lab will be back to us within the hour, let us know whether you've got gunshot residue or blood spatter on your hands or the clothes you were wearing. If you're going to help yourself by talking to us, now's the time."

"I got nothing to do with a murder, and nobody going to say I did."

"You're a lying-ass piece of shit," Gomez said. "You think I don't know a lying-ass piece of shit when I sit across the table from one?"

Rafael leaned back in his chair, away from Gomez. "You got no reason to talk to me like that," he said, his voice low.

"I got no reason to talk to you with respect, you murdering son of a bitch."

There was a knock on the door. "That's going to be forensics," Jaworski said. "You want to help yourself, now's the time."

"I never shot a gun my whole life."

Gomez stood up and walked out of the room, slamming the door behind him. Rafael flinched at the sound, then shook his head, disappointed with himself for showing weakness. He knew Jaworski was studying him for just such signs.

"This is really it," Jaworski said quietly. "You make a statement right now, we write it up that you cooperated, that you came forward and admitted what you did. You might even be able to plead down to man one. Once we get a residue hit, you can still help yourself, but it won't mean the same thing. You'll be looking at murder two at best. That white security guard was hassling you, throwing your grandmother out of her home, all that fuss over you smoking a blunt. I understand, son. I do."

"You don't got the right to call me son," Rafael said, glaring back at Jaworski, the two men locked into a staring contest broken only by Gomez's return.

"What're you gonna have to say for yourself now?" Gomez said. "Your hand tested positive for gunshot residue."

"You lying to me," Rafael said. "I know you all are allowed to lie. I haven't shot a gun, not tonight, not never."

"I guess we'll just have to see who a jury believes, your lying ass or forensic science."

"I'm done talking to you. Get me my lawyer."

"You agreed to speak with us, Rafael," Jaworski said quickly.

"You hear me? What I say? Lawyer. I want my lawyer."

·6·

"THIS IS all fucked up," Duncan said.

"Don't shoot the messenger," Lily Vaughan, the other senior associate on the Aurora case, replied.

It was around ten in the morning, the two of them surveying a conference room in their office. It was their team war room for both the wrongful-death suit and the DA's subpoena, the entire room filled with boxes and binders of documents.

"How did this get so fucked up?"

"We left it in the hands of first-years. First-years don't know what the fuck they're doing."

"And so they fucked it up," Duncan said. "And now we're supposed to fix it?"

"If not us, who?" Lily said, looking over at Duncan with a slight smile. "If not now, when?"

"Somebody else and later?"

"That would be nice, yes. But no."

Duncan wondered if he and Lily were flirting, something they still occasionally fell into doing, though their relationship had ended some time back. Lily had lateraled over from Paul Weiss a little more than two years ago. She'd been personally recruited by Blake after he'd defended a deposition she'd taken. Duncan had tried not to feel threatened, though at the time he'd been Blake's sole lieutenant, the two before him having both made partner the year before.

He had found Lily attractive but hadn't acted on it, wary of a workplace involvement. But then a few months after Lily had started, the two of them had spent a long week in Denver interviewing the sales force of a pharmaceutical company as part of an internal investigation into allegations of off-brand marketing of a prescription drug. Their third night they'd ended up emptying the minibar in Lily's room, trading stories of the various lies they were being told, and one thing had led to another.

Their relationship had officially lasted less than nine months, although they'd continued to occasionally sleep together for nearly a full year after breaking up. They'd finally put a stop to that a few months ago—Lily's idea—and were still negotiating where exactly that left them.

Things between them had been complicated from the start, and not just because they were coworkers. There was also that they were both biracial: Duncan the son of a white mother and a black father, Lily the daughter of a Japanese mother and a white father. The roll of the genetic dice had played out very differently for them, however: Duncan appeared Caucasian, while Lily looked conventionally Japanese, at least to American eyes. While their racial backgrounds had been part of what had brought them together, the differences in how it had played out for them—the way appearance had formed their respective identities—had a major role in breaking them apart.

Navigating their breakup was made considerably more complicated by the intricacies of their professional relationship. They were both Blake protégés, so they worked closely together, but they were also competitors. They'd each be up for partnership in about six months, and there was always the chance the firm's partners would decide they had room for only one of them. Or, for that matter, neither.

There'd be a few other associates up for partner at the same time, but Duncan and Lily were widely acknowledged as leading the pack, and not just because they had the firm's most powerful partner in their corner. They were both gifted strategists, able to predict what the other side of a case was going to do and counter moves before they'd even been made. Lily was small—barely over five feet—and quiet—the rare lawyer who listened more than she talked. As a result she was regularly underestimated by people who let her physical presence and demeanor blind them to the fierceness of her will and the depths of her intelligence, which processed information at a speed even Duncan couldn't match.

As a smaller, newer, and less stuffy firm, Blake and Wolcott tended to attract associates who were less rigidly conventional than those who flocked to the more established white-shoe firms, although it was every bit as selective. Perhaps that was why Duncan and Lily had ended up there. They were members of the new multicultural meritocracy that was increasingly replacing the mainline WASP establishment that had traditionally dominated the city's elite law firms.

Duncan and Lily were supervising both the discovery in the wrongful-death civil case and the response to the DA's subpoena. The overlapping document productions were a massive undertaking: there were hundreds of thousands of pages to sift through, an attorney having to look over each page before they'd turn it over. Such document review was, if not the absolute worst part of big-firm practice, a pretty serious contender for the title.

In addition to checking for relevance and privilege, the other purpose of the review was to try to uncover whatever documents would actually tell any kind of useful story from their client's perspective. The goal was to assemble a collection that would fully exonerate Roth Properties from any knowledge of, or complicity with, safety shortcuts at the Aurora; failing that, to establish that the company's files were simply a dead end in terms of understanding the accident's cause.

This task, along with the rest of the document scut work, had been left to a couple of first-year associates, along with a handful of contract attorneys—temps who made their living floating around the big firms, assisting with the most mundane aspects of discovery. But instead of an organized collection of helpful documents, what they had was a sprawling mess of disorganized papers, veering between the irrelevant and the unhelpful. Neither Duncan nor Lily had been paying much attention to the document review, so it wasn't until this morning that Lily had popped over to check in. She'd called Duncan five minutes later.

"I thought Neil was your golden boy, Dunk," Lily said. Duncan had every confidence in Neil's intelligence, but clearly something had gone wrong here.

"Don't call me Dunk. I'll talk to Neil."

"Do we need to tell the Blake?"

"Let's fix it first, then worry about the Blake," Duncan replied as the phone in the conference room rang. "Expecting anyone?" Duncan asked.

"I'm sure it's good news," Lily said dryly. Duncan nodded as he made his way over to the phone: nobody would have tracked them down here unless there was a problem.

Duncan saw on the caller ID that it was Joan, his secretary. "Your pro bono client is calling for you," she said after he'd picked up. "I told him you weren't available, but he claimed to be under arrest."

Duncan snapped to full attention. "Under arrest?" he said. "What for?"

"I wasn't particularly able to understand him," Joan said. "But he seemed to be saying it had something to do with a murder."

Duncan was at a loss as to what could possibly be happening. "Okay," he said after a moment. "When you say it had something to do with a murder, do you mean that he's under arrest for murder?"

"I really don't know," Joan said. "Shall I transfer him?"

ALTHOUGH HE'D worked on a number of white-collar cases, Duncan by no means considered himself a criminal defense lawyer. The criminal defendants the firm represented were either corporations or their senior executives: Ivy League–educated blue bloods who were worth millions of dollars. The cases were often regulatory in nature, brought by an agency such as the SEC, rather than the district attorney's office, which handled more blue-collar crime. Defending such cases had as much to do with defending a murder as brain surgery did with oral surgery. Duncan had never even been to the city's criminal courthouse on Centre Street before, which was far dirtier and more run-down than the federal courthouses where most of his cases were housed.

Duncan's main exposure to conventional criminal law had come almost five years ago, when his half brother, Antoine, had been arrested for armed robbery in Detroit. Duncan hadn't been directly involved in the defense, but he'd ended up as his family's unofficial liaison with the criminal lawyer they'd hired. Duncan had gotten a copy of the file, done his best to keep as close an eye on the case as he could from New York, but in the end he'd agreed with the lawyer's recommendation that Antoine take a plea.

Antoine had gotten out of jail just a few months ago. Duncan hadn't seen his half brother since his release, had visited him only once in prison, and that over two years ago. They'd never been close, never lived together, but Duncan still felt guilty that he hadn't been able to do more to help Antoine.

It took Duncan a while to navigate his way to Rafael. Finally he was shown to a small row of stalls in back of one of the arraignment courtrooms. Duncan entered the tiny room, which barely had enough space for its lone chair, closing the door behind him. In front of him was a metal grille separating him from where his client would be.

Rafael was brought in through the opposite door a few minutes later, looking both frail and angry. All of this was as foreign to him as it was to Duncan: other than the disorderly conduct charge coming out of the pot bust, Rafael hadn't had any run-ins with the law. Yet here he was, suddenly in the major leagues.

"Let's start at the beginning, Rafael," Duncan said, doing his best to ignore their surroundings. "They've really got you here on a murder charge?"

"That's what they say," Rafael said.

"Who are they claiming you killed?"

"Sean Fowler."

"Fowler," Duncan said, surprised. "The security guard who busted you?"

"He didn't bust me doing nothing," Rafael said angrily. "I told you that's just some bullshit."

That the victim was Sean Fowler was not good news, Duncan thought. Rafael had an obvious motive for killing the man who was directly responsible for the fact that he and his grandmother were facing eviction.

"You got to get me out of here," Rafael continued. "They've had me here since last night. I haven't been to sleep."

While Duncan wasn't sure what all might happen next, he was confident that Rafael's just getting to go home was not among the possibilities. "We'll see if the judge agrees to set bail at the arraignment. But even if he does, it's likely to be a lot of money—I don't think you should assume you'll be going home today."

"They're just making all this shit up," Rafael protested. "How they gonna have somebody say they saw me do something I didn't do? How they gonna say they found gunpowder on my hand when I didn't shoot a gun?"

Duncan was not keeping up, but was getting a sinking feeling nevertheless: any hope that the police had picked up Rafael only because he had a motive for shooting Fowler was out the window. This looked like a real case, with solid evidence. "You've got to back up for me here," he said. "Tell me everything that happened."

Rafael nodded and took a deep breath, his eyes wet, trying to collect himself. He ran Duncan through the police coming to his apartment and arresting him, telling him they had an eyewitness, their finding gunshot residue on his hand.

"This doesn't sound good," Duncan said when his client was finished. He saw no reason to sugarcoat the obvious: Rafael was sunk deep into serious trouble, and it wasn't going to just go away.

"You really think I popped Fowler? I got you working on keeping my *abuela* in her home. You just won in court. We're fighting it the right way."

"I know you are, Rafael."

"So what do we do now?"

By training and personality, lawyers rarely admit when they don't know what to do. Duncan didn't feel particularly tempted to tell Rafael how little he understood about how a murder case would play out. He was also virtually certain he wouldn't be around to find out: his firm had signed up for a straightforward eviction case, something that would presumably take up less than one hundred hours of Duncan's time. Defending a murder was a different level of commitment by an order of magnitude. Plus it wasn't exactly what the firm had in mind when launching a pro bono initiative. And even putting firm politics aside, defending a murder fell outside of Duncan's skill set. "I can represent you at arraignment, see about bail. But I think it's unlikely I'm going to be able to keep your case past today."

Rafael looked like he couldn't believe what he was hearing. "What do you mean? You're my lawyer."

"I'm your lawyer on the eviction. But this now is a murder charge. I'd be way over my head, Rafael."

"I'm not taking no public defender. That's how come all this got so fucked up in the first place."

Perhaps because he needed to believe that his grandmother wouldn't be evicted, Rafael had clearly put his full confidence in Duncan's abilities from the first time they'd met. Duncan suspected that Rafael assumed that having a rich person's lawyer would get him a rich person's justice. There was some kernel of truth to that, Duncan supposed, but it didn't mean he'd really be able to stop the eviction, let alone the murder charge. People often viewed a legal case in the same way they viewed a football game: there could be the occasional bad call or stroke of luck, but generally speaking the best team won. But Duncan knew the analogy didn't really hold: the underlying facts and the relevant law were determined before the lawyers ever took the field, and often a case was virtually unwinnable or unloseable from the start. While a bad lawyer could always find a way to screw up, and a good lawyer could make it more difficult for his opponent to win, experience had taught Duncan that in most cases the outcome was not determined by anything the lawyers did, but was rather a largely inevitable application of the law to the facts. There was no magic bullet in Duncan's arsenal.

"I understand why you don't want a public defender, but this isn't what I do, Rafael. I wouldn't have the first idea what I was doing in a murder case."

Rafael looked at him with a mix of pleading and anger. "But you got that hardcore firm you work for. You got connections. I get some lame-ass free lawyer, I know where that shit's going to end—me in jail for the rest of my life."

Duncan was uncomfortable with letting Rafael down, but he didn't think it was helpful to be unrealistic. "I hear you, man, I do," he said. "But it's not really going to be up to me. My firm would have to sign off on it, and I gotta tell you, I don't really see that happening."

"You won't even ask?"

"I'll ask," Duncan said. "But you have to promise me you won't be surprised when the answer I get back is no."

There was a knock on the door behind Rafael, which then opened before he had time to respond, two uniformed court officers in the doorway. "We're ready to take your guy before the judge," one said to Duncan.

Duncan had never done an arraignment before. He'd faked his way through plenty of things practicing law, but never an actual court proceeding. He didn't get to stand up in court very often, so when he did he was always meticulously prepared. Here he was winging it, but he couldn't back out: Rafael was his client, at least for now, and besides, Duncan had already identified himself as Rafael's lawyer in order to get to see him. He made his way to the crowded courtroom, sitting in the front row, which was reserved for lawyers. The room was loud, people constantly shuffling in and out, a bored-looking judge spending no more than a couple of minutes on each case.

Duncan waited a half hour for Rafael's name to be called, spending the time studying the parade of other arraignments. They were all pretty straightforward, but then again, none of them were murders.

Finally it was Rafael's turn before the judge. The ADA, Andrew Bream, was young and blond, with a jock's body and a frat boy's smirk. He made his appearance, Duncan then doing the same, stating his name and that of his firm. The judge then turned back to the ADA. "People?"

"The defendant is accused of killing a former New York City police officer," Bream said. "An officer who was a witness against him in a prior criminal case. We have an eyewitness, another former police officer who ID'd the defendant the same night as the murder. The People seek remand."

"The victim was working as a private security guard, not as a policeman," Duncan rejoined. "And the prior case was resolved with a disorderly conduct plea. My client lives in public housing. He has no resources to speak of. I'd ask that bail be set at one thousand dollars."

The judge appeared to find this funny. "On a first-degree murder charge? The defendant is remanded until trial."

And with that they were finished, the court officers set to take Rafael away. "My *abuela*," Rafael said urgently.

"I'll go see her," Duncan said, a little disoriented at the speed with which things were moving.

He'd just stepped out of the courtroom and into the hallway when he heard someone call his name. Duncan stopped and turned around, found himself facing a man he'd never seen before. He looked to be in his thirties, was wearing a tie with khakis, and was showily chewing gum. He wasn't a lawyer; of that Duncan was sure. Against his better judgment, Duncan shook the man's outstretched hand.

"Alex Costello, *New York Journal*."

Duncan barely restrained the impulse to yank his hand away. It was one thing to quietly handle this arraignment before checking in with the firm about the sudden change in Rafael's case; it was quite another to be talking to the press about the case. "Look, I don't have any comment, okay?"

Costello tilted his head quizzically at Duncan's reaction. "But I haven't even asked you anything yet," he said.

"I've got to go," Duncan said, turning his back on the reporter and walking quickly down the hall.

"Can I get your card?" the reporter called out behind him.

"Left them in my other suit," Duncan said.

THE FEELING of being in over his head at the arraignment was nothing compared to how Duncan felt at the prospect of discussing Rafael's arrest with his grandmother. Duncan took a cab to Tenth and D, the project buildings occupying the entire east side of the street for blocks. Nobody paid him any attention until he had to check in with building security. Once up to Dolores's floor, Duncan found her standing in her opened doorway, a shredded Kleenex clutched in her hand.

Duncan followed her inside, sitting down across from her in the living room. The apartment was a mess; Dolores explained that the police had executed a search warrant, looking for the gun, and they'd made no effort to put things back. Trying to look past the chaos caused by the police, Duncan could see that the apartment was relatively spacious and bright, but Dolores's attentive decorating couldn't fully disguise its dilapidated condition. There were numerous cracks running along the walls; the ceiling was blotched and sagging with water damage; the outside of the windows smudged with layered grime.

"Rafael didn't kill nobody," Dolores insisted. She was a small, portly woman, her English thickly accented and pocked with Spanish words.

"We just went before the judge. I'm afraid Rafael's going to be held in jail until this is resolved."

Dolores shook her head, tears wet on her cheeks. "But if they understand he did not do it," she said.

Duncan knew it wasn't going to be that easy. "I'm sorry, but whatever this is, I don't think it's just some misunderstanding we're going to be able to clear up."

"But you can do something, no?"

Expecting the question didn't make answering it any easier. "I'm not sure that I can," Duncan said softly, forcing himself to make eye contact as he said it.

"But please, Mr. Riley," Dolores said, looking at him with her brimming eyes. "If you do not help my *nieto*, who will?"

· 7 ·

CANDACE SNOW arrived late to the five p.m. news meeting, ignoring the looks as she made her way to an empty chair in the corner, all the chairs around the table already occupied. She was the only reporter there among the editors—the I-team sent a reporter to the meetings to see if there was a story that looked like it might be worth going deeper on, something with more meat on the bone. The I-team's editor, Bill Nugent, believed that what separated investigative reporters was an ability to see the big picture, to make the connections those in the daily trenches might miss. He wanted them looking into the daily slash and burn in order to see past it.

As with any city newspaper, the bulk of the *Journal*'s stories were ephemeral, the endless loop of there-but-for-the-grace-of-God tales of city life that nobody much remembered a week later. However terrible for the people involved, their outcome did not affect the larger patterns in the city's grid of power and influence. The I-team stories were different, or at least they aspired to be. At their best, their stories altered the city's trajectory: they launched investigations, ruined careers, even righted the occasional wrong.

Once she'd started working for the I-team, Candace began finding the articles that filled the paper—the steady hum of the city's scandal and strife—less and less interesting. Not that she disapproved of its content: the *Journal*, though a tabloid, was nevertheless a real newspaper: it steered clear of the cheap-shot partisan politics and focus on celebrity shenanigans that defined its competition in the city. To the extent that the paper had a discernible ideology it was populist: a blue-collar paper in an increasingly white-collar city, it was a defender of cops, firefighters, and unions. The older generation in the newsroom were themselves authentically blue-collar, guys who'd gone to CUNY or a state school if they'd gone to college at all, while most of the reporters of Candace's generation had fancier backgrounds, often including the master's degrees in journalism that the old guard found ridiculous.

There were two news meetings each day. The noon meeting was tentative: an overview of major stories that were developing or in progress. The five-o'clock meeting was where decisions were made about the next day's paper, the lead stories decided on, the news holes filled. Candace's role was just to listen, see if anything jumped out at her as potentially having legs.

It was twenty minutes in when something did. Kevin Bigman, the police beat editor, was doing the roll call of the day's crimes. "We got a murder came over after we'd put the paper to bed last night. A private security guard from Darryl Loomis's outfit was shot at the Jacob Riis projects in Alphabet City. They made a quick arrest, pulled somebody in last night, arraigned him this afternoon. Looks like they got a tight case on the shooter, a project teenager named Nazario who had a beef with the security guard. Life-in-the-projects stuff is all, except the victim's an ex-cop. He was watching over all the new construction."

"Simon Roth's project," Candace interjected, having snapped to attention. Bigman glanced at her, then down at his notes, before shrugging. Seated at the head of the table, the paper's editor in chief, Henry Tacy, a British transplant who'd brought over a particularly ruthless view of the urban tabloid, leaned back in his chair in order to have a clear view of Candace.

"Riis is the public housing that's getting the makeover, right?" Tacy asked. He was about fifty, openly dissipated in a way American newspaper folk no longer allowed themselves, his scratchy whiskey voice and foul mouth contrasting with the aristocratic timbre of his Oxbridge enunciation.

Candace nodded. "Turning it into mixed-income," she said. "It's the biggest thing to hit the city's public housing since the original projects went up, and Roth Properties is overseeing it, which I'm guessing means the security guard was on their dime. What was the beef between the teenager and the rent-a-cop?"

"The security guy'd busted Nazario for smoking pot a couple months ago," Bigman said. "Apparently they're actually arresting people for hitting a joint in the East Village now. Anyway, Nazario's family is getting thrown out of their apartment because of it. So it's looking like a revenge thing."

"Nothing to connect it with the changes going on there?" Candace said, losing interest if the murder didn't have any possible connection to Roth.

"Doesn't look like it," Bigman said. "It'd be a roundup graph in a blotter story except the vic used to be on the job. Right now I've just got Costello on it, and he's working the ex-cop angle more than the murder, since it ain't exactly a whodunit."

"We get a react quote from the kid's public defender?" Tacy asked.

Bigman again looked down at his notes before shaking his head. "Didn't have a public defender at arraignment," he said. "Private-practice lawyer."

"Teen from the projects?" Tacy asked, tilting his head. "Is it anybody we have a relationship with?"

"I never heard of him," Bigman said. "Duncan Riley's the name."

"You're fucking kidding me," Candace said.

"How was that a joke?" Bigman responded.

"You know Riley?" Tacy asked her.

"This paper does have a relationship with him," Candace said. "He's suing us. On behalf of Simon Roth."

"SO WHAT do you think it means?" Nugent asked.

"I don't know, Bill," Candace said. "What do you think it means?"

They were in Nugent's office in the immediate wake of the news meeting. It was full to bursting with mementos spanning Bill's quarter century at the paper, from his time as a Bronx crime reporter, to his glory days as an investigative reporter with the inside scoop into the NYPD, to his brief and never-talked-about stint as an op-ed columnist, followed by his present position as the paper's deputy managing editor in charge of the I-team.

"It could easily not mean anything," Nugent said. "Lawyers represent all sorts of clients."

"Wasn't this how Woodward and Bernstein got hold of the first thread of Watergate?" Candace retorted. "A too expensive lawyer at a nickel-and-dime arraignment?"

"I don't think it follows that every time an expensive lawyer takes a two-bit case a grand conspiracy is afoot. The world does contain coincidence, you know."

"A lawyer who represents Simon Roth also representing somebody who's committed murder at the site of Roth's new development?" Candace said. "That doesn't strike me as a coincidence."

"But I don't see any natural connection either. Why the hell would Roth want to protect some guy from the projects who shot one of his own security guards?"

"I don't have a clue," Candace said. "I'm a reporter, not a psychic."

"Even reporters generally try to start with a theory that makes sense," Nugent said. "Or that's not something they teach at Columbia's j-school?"

"What doesn't make any sense is this being meaningless," Candace countered. "How would this kid possibly afford the same law firm Roth uses? Plus, even if you had that kind of money, this guy Riley isn't who you'd hire in a murder—he's a corporate fancy-pants, not a street fighter."

"What do we know about the vic?"

Candace glanced down at her notepad. "Just that he was an ex-cop, worked for a security company run by somebody named Darryl Loomis."

The name meant nothing to Candace, but she could tell at once that it meant something to Nugent. "It was one of Loomis's guys who got shot?" he said. "That could take this in all sorts of directions."

"How's that?"

"The story was before your time here—must've been, as I was the reporter who broke it. You know about the hip-hop cops?"

While Candace had heard of the controversial hip-hop task force, it wasn't something she'd ever paid much attention to. "Only vaguely," she said.

"The NYPD still doesn't officially admit it exists. They formed it back during the East Coast–West Coast rap wars of the nineties, after Biggie Smalls was killed. Loomis was the guy who created it, working out of gang intel."

Candace got a kick out of the idea that her boss even knew who Biggie Smalls was. "And you broke the story?"

Nugent nodded. "In 2002 the head of First Degree Records was charged with laundering money for the biggest drug dealer in the Bronx. I was covering it, and got it leaked to me that this secret task force had made the case. It was a juicy story—accusations of racial profiling, that kind of noise. Loomis took his pension a month or so later, but has always kept his mouth shut about the task force. Given that he's black, he took some serious Uncle Tom heat at the time."

"And now he's doing security work for Simon Roth?" Candace asked. "Seems like a leap."

"Loomis started a security firm right after he left the NYPD. He originally marketed himself to clubs and the music industry. This was the guy who'd written the police's playbook on how to deal with these guys—it was like having the head of the KGB defect in the middle of the cold war. Within six months his people were doing the doors at every major club, providing bodyguards for Puffy or whatever the hell he's called now."

"Sounds like a tough racket."

"Indeed. You want intimidation, Loomis is your man. Rumor is he's untouchable as far as the NYPD's concerned. If he ever decided to rat out the department, God knows who he could bring down."

"Must be a useful marketing tool for a private security company."

"Last time I heard of Loomis was maybe two years ago. One of his security guys shot and killed somebody outside the 40/40 Club. The dead guy was part of a ring that was robbing celebrities of high-end jewelry, and he had a gun on him. The security guard wasn't charged."

Candace vaguely recalled that shooting, but there was a steady stream of nightlife violence in the city, and it all blurred together for her. "You saying Loomis's guys can get away with murder?"

"I'm saying people might wonder if they can."

"That why he's on Simon Roth's payroll?"

Nugent shrugged, leaning back in his chair. "Loomis runs a full-service shop now—the nightclub work was how they got big, but they do all sorts of security and investigation stuff these days. Being able to survive the rap world and the club world gets you street cred anywhere in this city. Security work at construction sites is as much about keeping an eye on the unions as it is anything else. There aren't many people who even the Teamsters don't want to fuck with."

"So you're saying this security guard could have been mixed up in something?"

Nugent waved his hand, not wanting to go that far. "Could mean he had some enemies, sure. But none of this establishes that the shooting isn't just what it looks like."

"Worth digging into, don't you think?"

Nugent looked skeptical. "Loomis is running a legitimate operation, however hardball it might be. There's nothing suspicious about Simon Roth putting him on the payroll."

"I'd like to poke around, see what I see."

"Even if there is something there in terms of Simon Roth—big if, mind—do you really think you can cover it? The guy's suing you, Candace."

Candace had expected Nugent to raise this. "The whole reason he's suing us is so we don't keep going after him. You keep me off this because of that, you're letting him win."

Nelson snorted out a laugh. "How I miss being a wild-eyed reporter who didn't have to worry about nothing other than chasing the lead. Free advice: when they offer you a promotion that means you're actually going to have to think about the best interests of the paper, don't fucking take it."

A FRIEND from work, Brock Anders, had invited Candace over for dinner. Brock had started at the paper around the same time as Candace, covering gossip and entertainment news. He was the only reporter on staff whom Candace was good friends with, largely because their separate turfs meant there was no competition between them.

"I thought I would make us a little shrimp scampi," Brock said, kissing her cheek in greeting as he let her into his apartment, a one-bedroom walk-up in Chelsea. "There's an open bottle of sauvignon blanc," he added. Brock had his own wineglass, half-empty, by the stove.

"What did I do to deserve all this?" Candace asked.

"You didn't seem like you were having the best week," Brock said. "I thought a nice meal, a couple of drinks, then hit the town."

Brock was right: her nerves felt jangled, had all week. First with uneasiness at the prospect of being deposed, then simmering anger during the deposition, followed today by the puzzling news that this same lawyer who'd deposed her was also involved in a murder case that was connected to a Roth Properties development.

Candace understood it was hypocritical, or at least ironic, to have such a negative reaction to being deposed when she asked people tough questions for a living herself. But the idea that someone could poke and prod at her reporting, peer behind the curtain of her professional self, had felt profoundly invasive. She realized that this must be how many of her own subjects felt upon viewing their actions through the prism of her stories, how unrecognizable they probably appeared to themselves. After all, nobody ever saw themselves as the bad guy. The human brain didn't permit it.

Candace knew she'd responded to the invasiveness of the deposition in some childish ways. Maybe even worse than the memory of calling the lawyer an asshole—and she knew he was right for protesting that he was just doing his job—was the memory of telling him to refer to her as Mrs. Snow. She'd never liked being referred to as Mrs., and Snow was her maiden name, which she'd never changed. Given that her legal separation would in a couple months turn into a divorce, the time for her to be called Mrs. was pretty much at an end. It'd been a petty, embarrassing impulse, insisting the lawyer call her Mrs. like that. She'd done it only because she'd caught him checking out her breasts.

Candace poured herself a glass of wine. "Sorry I was such a drama queen the other night."

"Drama's my second-favorite kind of queen," Brock replied. "And besides, you've been known to put up with my shit. So seriously, if you want to go out, I told Dan and Kyle I'd probably meet up with them later."

"I don't think I'm up for a long night's journey into the next day with those two," Candace replied. "But thanks."

"You going to hook up with Gabriel later?"

Candace had met Gabriel a month ago, gone out with him a handful of times. He was only the most recent of what had unexpectedly become a string of men since separating from her husband. Candace guessed she'd gone to bed with more guys in the past ten months than she had in the three years before she'd gotten involved with Ben. She wasn't old enough to call it a midlife crisis, but she wasn't comfortable thinking of it as just sleeping around either. "I'm not exactly sure that Gabriel is meant to be a, you know . . ."

"Keeper?"

"Exactly."

"You're throwing him back in the lake already? Did you two have a fight?"

"I don't think you can have a fight with Gabriel," Candace said. "It'd be like trying to have a fight with the wind."

Brock smiled. "That actually sounds kind of ideal."

"He's a twenty-six-year-old aspiring musician who works at the Bowcry Bar. I didn't even know that place still existed until I met him."

"You haven't dissuaded me yet. And is your problem with him really that he doesn't work in a trendy enough bar?"

"Of course not. But at some point I have to, you know, snap out of all this, and I don't see Gabriel being my lifeline back to adulthood."

"I thought you were trying to escape from adulthood, not find it."

"I was trying to take a little vacation from it is all," Candace said. "I didn't realize there wasn't a return ticket."

· 8 ·

STEVEN BLAKE occupied a lavish and thoroughly modern corner office: abstract paintings on the walls, modular and sleek designer furniture, matching glass worktable and desk. But the main thing that always struck Duncan about Blake's office was its lack of paper. Duncan's own office was always overflowing with paper: cases he'd printed off Lexis, battered Redwelds stuffed to overflowing with discovery documents or drafts of briefs. There were frequently papers stacked on his floor, an obstacle course that had to be navigated just to get to his chair.

But Blake's office was virtually devoid of any visible trace of paper. There were binders lining the built-in bookshelves that filled one wall, a yellow legal pad on his desk, occasionally a copy of a brief or letter if Blake was in the middle of revising it. But generally his office was minimalist to the point of austerity; it had a cool modernist gloss that gave little sense of its occupant. Duncan thought the whole place could be a showroom, some high-end interior designer showing off his wares. The only personal touches were a couple of framed photos of Blake's third wife and his kids from marriages one and two. The pictures were angled so that visitors to the office generally couldn't see them.

Although the firm had always been business casual, Blake was almost always in a suit, in part because he had court appearances or client meetings virtually every day. He was tall and still trim, his gray hair swept back from a widow's peak, possessing the effortless authority of a man who'd been at the top of his profession for twenty years, although he was a good deal less formal than many other lawyers his age.

Blake generally had two senior associates who served as his lieutenants. Although being a so-called Blake baby was not a guarantee of partnership, the majority of associates who'd filled the role had gone on to make partner, and very few litigators whom Blake had not anointed ever made that cut. A couple of the more talented associates in Duncan's class had left the firm once it was clear that Blake was not going to select them, figuring it signaled the end of their future at the firm.

Like virtually all the associates in his department, Duncan had joined the firm with the goal of becoming a Blake protégé. He'd been assigned to a couple of cases with Blake as a junior and then midlevel associate, working around the clock each time, triple-checking everything, doing his best to be indispensable. By his fifth year at the firm he was spending the majority of his time on Blake's cases, and a year later that was virtually all he worked on.

Despite the countless hours they'd worked together over the past few years, they'd never socialized outside of firm functions, and Blake had virtually never asked Duncan a personal question about himself. The only real feedback Blake gave any associates was through work assignments: if you impressed him, he gave you more; if you didn't, you never heard from him again. Duncan sometimes wished he had a mentor who was actually interested in mentoring, but he wasn't going to complain.

Blake was on the phone when Duncan arrived, barely glancing up as Duncan came in and sat down. Duncan knew to bring work with him when coming to Blake's office, as phone calls and other interruptions were a constant. He spent ten minutes reviewing a memo Neil had written about wrongful-death damages while waiting for Blake's call to wind down.

"So the firm's had a chance to review your memo on Nazario," Blake said after he'd finally hung up. Duncan had met with him the day of Rafael's arrest, updating him on what had happened and making his halfhearted request for keeping the case. Blake, distracted and dismissive, had told him to write a memo on it for the partnership to review. No surprise there: the firm wanted a detailed paper trail now that the case involved a murder. "While it's obviously not what we signed up for, the firm doesn't feel we can desert this client at what's obviously the moment of his greatest need. I'll be supervising the case. At least for now I don't think we need to rope anyone else in, since it doesn't seem like this one's destined for trial."

Duncan hadn't been paying much attention at first, assuming Blake was just launching into a vague explanation of why he couldn't keep the case. Usually when a partner referred to "the firm" as having made a decision, it was to convey bad news while avoiding direct accountability. He tried to conceal his astonishment that Blake was telling him they were keeping it. "What about the fact that the victim was working for Roth Properties?" Duncan asked.

"He wasn't an actual employee. In any event, I've spoken with them—you don't have to worry about it."

Duncan tried to process how he was possibly going to actually handle the demands of the case, something he hadn't bothered to consider when making his feeble pitch for it. "It's going to take up a lot of my time," he said. "My plate's pretty full with the Roth stuff."

"I thought you wanted to keep this," Blake said irritably.

Duncan realized that he did want it. The idea of working on something like a murder would be exciting, a new challenge. It was intimidating, sure, but so was anything that gave you a chance to spread your wings. "I'm just a little surprised is all."

Blake nodded brusquely, not a believer in a lawyer showing surprise. "So I should at least meet our client. Any chance of getting him out of jail?"

"Judge remanded him."

"I guess I'll have to go to Rikers with you then. Set something up for us to go talk to him."

"Will do," Duncan said, understanding he was dismissed.

THAT EVENING Blake and Wolcott was having a party for its summer associates. Their summer class was smaller than those of the more established firms—this year they had fourteen students who were between their second and third years of law school. The firm did less wining and dining of its summers than their competition, offering instead a more realistic and substantive experience (although it still bore scant resemblance to the reality of life as a junior associate). But the summer class still expected a certain amount of frills beyond just being taken out to expensive lunches.

As he was approaching his partnership vote, Duncan couldn't afford to miss such events—recruiting was part of his job duties. He did permit himself to skip most of the predinner cocktail hour, working until about seven thirty before walking up Sixth Avenue to Rockefeller Center.

The party was at the Rainbow Room. Sixty-five stories up, the restaurant offered one of the best views in all of Manhattan. It wasn't Duncan's kind of place: it was ostentatious in an old-fashioned way, full of glittering chandeliers, an aura that seemed like the height of elegance circa 1963. But he liked looking out its windows.

Duncan waded through the crowd and made his way toward the bar. Waiters in black vests and bow ties worked the room, offering appetizers on silver trays. Duncan accepted a shrimp spring roll as he crossed over to the bar, then ordered a vodka tonic once he got there.

He hadn't much bothered to get to know any of the firm's summers this year. A couple of them had done some spot research assignments for him, but it was too much effort to really get the summers up to speed on a complicated case when they were going to be gone in three months. He'd gone to the occasional lunch, but generally hadn't done more than go through the motions of interacting with the firm's prospective future lawyers.

Duncan leaned against the bar, scanning the room, which was stuffed with well over a hundred of his colleagues, and wondered how many of them took events like this for granted, didn't think twice about being plied with free booze and expensive food in ornate surroundings. Duncan imagined he wasn't the only one who was occasionally baffled to find himself in such situations, although by now he'd largely gotten used to the perks of his profession.

"So is it true?" Neil Levine said, materializing next to Duncan. "You're keeping the murder case?"

Word had gotten around quickly, Duncan thought. "I don't much get it either," he replied.

"Are you going to be bringing anyone else on?" Neil asked.

Duncan wasn't surprised that Neil, who was clearly utterly bored with the life of a junior associate, was angling to join the case. "We're probably looking at a quick plea," he said. "Besides, you need to concentrate on not fucking up the Roth stuff."

"You already took me to the woodshed on that," Neil said, not quite as defensively as Duncan would've liked. "Organizational shit isn't my strong suit."

"Organizational shit's a big chunk of the job."

"If your guy's just going to plead out right away, why bother to take the case?"

Duncan shrugged. "My guess is the partners decided it wouldn't look good to drop Rafael when he was on the ropes. Maybe they thought doing the case as pro bono would be good publicity."

"It's got to be exciting, a murder. Compared to the shit we usually do."

Duncan glanced around before frowning at Neil. "You do realize that we're at a firm event, right?"

Neil grinned. "It's not like I'm ever going to be up for partner here," he said. "But I guess you need to keep up a good attitude."

They were summoned to dinner, the entire dining room reserved for the firm's party. Duncan sat down next to Neil at one of the round tables, a summer associate from the corporate department sitting on his other side and locking Duncan into tedious small talk throughout much of the meal.

After dinner Oliver Wolcott made a brief speech, the usual mix of stale jokes and platitudes about how the firm was a family. Duncan could feel Neil glancing over at him as Wolcott spoke, no doubt wanting to share a smirk, but Duncan ignored him. Wolcott had his name on the door because he had been the only other Davis Polk partner to leave with Blake, making him the firm's cofounder, though he had nowhere near Blake's profile. His value to the firm came less from his skills as a litigator (he had a solid but unspectacular niche in antitrust) than from the depths of his Rolodex—Wolcott's family had long been entrenched in the East Coast elite. Duncan had worked on only one of Wolcott's cases—defending against a class-action allegation of price collusion among airlines—and had found him to be a pompous jerk.

After dinner was another round of cocktails, although most of the partners—many of whom lived in affluent suburbs outside the city—left right after Wolcott's speech. There was always a lot of alcohol at summer associate outings, although the summers who had any sense avoided getting drunk. There was no better way to end up not getting an offer of permanent employment than getting shit-faced and acting out at a firm function.

As he made his way back into the bar area Duncan spotted Blake, who had a half dozen summers and junior associates circled tightly around him, hanging on every word. No doubt Blake was relating one of his many war stories. Duncan thought he'd probably heard it before, and continued on until he was buttonholed by a summer associate who'd written a memo for him last month and whose name he was completely blanking on. Duncan chatted with the woman, trying to get through it without revealing he'd forgotten who she was.

Duncan spotted Lily getting a glass of wine at the bar and excused himself to go say hello to her. Back when they were dating they'd kept it a secret at the firm, so Duncan had always been careful about how he interacted with her around coworkers. Even though they no longer had anything to hide, Duncan still felt instinctively on guard when talking with her in public view.

As he greeted her, Duncan could tell that Lily was pissed about something. She wasn't trying to let it show, and Duncan doubted anyone else would notice, but he knew her too well not to spot it. "Everything okay?" he said, getting another vodka from the bartender.

Lily tilted her head in the direction of a secluded corner of the room, and Duncan followed her over. "It's that prick Wolcott," she said. "I was sitting next to him at dinner, and when my salmon came he made some crack about how he was sorry they'd cooked it, offered to see if they had any still raw for me. It was so fucking racist, and I just had to sit here and take it."

Duncan understood why Lily was offended, but he also knew Wolcott offended people on a pretty regular basis. "I don't think he was being racist so much as, you know, stupid. He's a not-funny person trying to be funny, and that's what happens. And besides, it doesn't even make sense—the Japanese cook fish. Remember that awesome miso-glazed cod we had at Nobu?"

Lily clearly was not accepting Duncan's attempt at distraction. "Then he asked if I wanted sticks to eat with."

Duncan frowned. "Okay, well, that's not good, but—"

"*Sticks*," Lily hissed.

"The guy's like sixty-five years old; he'd probably never met an attorney who was a woman of color for the first twenty-five years of his career—"

"Why are you defending him?" Lily said angrily.

"I'm not," Duncan said quickly. "It was a total prick move for him to say stupid things like that. But in five years he'll be retired and you'll be a partner. Just wait the bastard out."

"So I just shut up and take it in the meantime? I bite my tongue about this crap my whole life, and I'm not going to make a scene now, but it's ridiculous and I shouldn't have to deal with it. However long it took for him to meet a female lawyer with nonwhite skin, he's had plenty of time to get used to the idea by now."

"You're right, and it sucks, but he's just an asshole, and you can't take the existence of assholes personally."

Lily fixed him with a sour look. "We don't all have your luxury, Duncan."

"What's that supposed to mean?" Duncan said, giving her a look of his own.

"You know exactly what it means," Lily said. "I know you think you understand, that it's the same for you and me, but you don't get it, not really. Somebody like Wolcott looks at you and he sees a white guy. He looks at me and he thinks the mongrel hordes are pillaging."

Duncan glanced around, checking whether their increasingly heated conversation was attracting notice. Instead of being about Wolcott, this had somehow become part of an ongoing argument between them. Duncan was angry himself now, but this wasn't the time or the place. "I can't change any of it," he said. "So what the fuck do you want from me?"

"Sometimes, Duncan, it's about choosing sides," Lily said. "You can't always be both, or neither, or whatever it is you think you are."

DUNCAN'S APARTMENT was easy walking distance from Rockefeller Center, so he set out west on Fiftieth Street, still stewing over his fight with Lily. It wasn't a new fight, but rather the renewal of an ongoing battle from which their relationship had never recovered. A fight that had started over the firm's attorneys-of-color group.

Like most of the big firms, Blake and Wolcott had created several affinity groups as part of its attempt to attract and retain a more diverse workforce. There was a women's group, one for gays and lesbians, and another for attorneys of color. Duncan found such things a rather dreary reminder of collegiate political correctness. Lily, on the other hand, was active in the attorneys-of-color group, and once they'd started dating she'd encouraged him to join. When Duncan had declined, Lily had accused him of passing. He'd angrily denied it, retorting that on the contrary the reason he didn't join such a group was that he didn't want to worry about having to justify to the group itself whether he belonged. Things had escalated from there, and it had opened up a chasm between them that had never fully closed. Their both being biracial had not actually led to common ground, and what had started out as a rather abstract argument about the value of affinity groups in a corporate context had ended up going to the heart of their respective identities.

And somehow it was a fight they were still having. Duncan hadn't intended to defend Wolcott, had just been trying to calm Lily down, but clearly he'd gone about it the wrong way, become the target of her anger himself. He understood it in part: understood that she was right that he didn't have to put up with the kind of nonsense that she'd had to with Wolcott. Maybe she was right: maybe he was passing simply by not being louder about who he was.

It was nearly ten by the time Duncan made it back to his apartment, buzzed, angry, and at loose ends. Home was a one-bedroom condo in Clinton, the neighborhood formerly known as Hell's Kitchen. Duncan had bought it a little over a year ago, not long after breaking up with Lily. He hadn't really planned on buying an apartment, but after a few years at the firm he'd paid off the worst of his student loans, set up a basic investment plan, bought himself a high-definition TV and all the other electronic gadgets he desired, but as his salary steadily increased he found himself accumulating more savings than he'd known what to do with. A six-figure down payment for the apartment had taken care of that.

In a way it'd seemed like a sort of admission of defeat, buying an apartment for himself in his early thirties. He'd dated a lot when he'd first gotten to New York, but had had only a couple of serious relationships in his eight years in the city. At first Duncan had blamed his job— the seventy-hour workweeks, the travel, the daily unpredictability as to when he'd be able to leave the office. The demands certainly did make sustaining a relationship more difficult, but there were plenty of big-firm lawyers in New York, and at least some of them managed to pull off domesticity.

It was easy to blame your upbringing for the failures of your adulthood. Duncan had been raised by a single mother: his parents had split when he was four and his mother had never remarried. His father had remarried and had two children, forming a new family that Duncan had never felt much part of, for reasons that were both obvious and difficult to acknowledge.

His dad's second wife was black. Duncan's relationship with his stepmother and half siblings would undoubtedly have been plenty complicated without race coming into play; he never knew how much of the awkwardness between them was related to his white mother and Caucasian appearance, and how much was simply due to his being the offspring of a prior marriage.

This reminded Duncan that he owed his mother a phone call. She'd left a message last week and he'd never gotten around to calling her back. Duncan talked to her only every few weeks, generally saw her twice a year at most, some years not at all. He generally went back to Michigan for either Thanksgiving or Christmas, work permitting, but it hadn't last year.

Duncan's mother, Sylvia Connell, had been born in Mason, a small town in mid-Michigan. She'd been the first person in her family to go to college, coming to Detroit to study social work at Wayne State just as the city's white flight had really started kicking in. After graduation she'd taken a job as a caseworker in the state's Child Protective Services, investigating claims of abuse and neglect.

It was a tough, sometimes even dangerous, thankless job, and whatever idealism had originally prompted his mother to do it had burned away a long time ago, replaced by steely anger. She was fearless, frequently putting herself into situations that Duncan suspected a cop would hesitate to step into. Sylvia had once been followed home by a biker gang after she'd taken away a member's kids. More than once she'd been threatened seriously enough that the police had gotten involved.

But the case that had marked her the most had undoubtedly been the death of Shawna Wynn. Shawna, at fourteen months old, had been the first child (but not the last) to die under Sylvia's watch. Shawna's parents had split up, and her mother had complained to protective services that her father was abusing Shawna on weekend visitations, though without any proof to support it. Complaints arising out of joint custody were common, and were generally taken with a grain of salt, as often they were motivated by battles between the parents.

Sylvia had interviewed the father, paid an unannounced visit to his home on a weekend. She hadn't observed everything suspicious, but had planned to do a follow-up a month later.

Two weeks later Shawna was dead, her skull fractured after she'd been shaken and then thrown against a wall. No one could really blame Sylvia for Shawna's death: there hadn't been any obvious red flags, nothing to prevent the father from having partial custody. She'd done her job, but Shawna had died anyway. Duncan had been around six years old, too young at the time to understand what was happening, but looking back he suspected that most people who did his mother's job had a Shawna Wynn haunting them. He suspected that many of them quit right after: most of the field workers in Sylvia's office lasted only two or three years.

His mother had never been the same after Shawna's death, but rather than make her give up, it had made her relentless. While she'd worked hard before, now she was possessed about it, following up on everything. She'd become a hard-ass, not just to the parents she investigated, but to all the other members of the bureaucracy she had to work within.

Doing Child Protective Services meant you were criticized no matter which way you turned: if you tried to keep families together, you were exposing children to abuse; if you tried to save kids, you were a jackbooted government thug breaking up families. Indeed, the next child who had died on his mother's watch had done so after having been placed into foster care. The foster mother had taped a two-year-old's mouth shut with duct tape during the little girl's temper tantrum, asphyxiating her. Duncan had no idea how his mother had kept at it after that.

Sylvia hadn't been a bad parent, but she'd often been an absent presence, physically there but otherwise elsewhere. Maybe that wasn't fair, Duncan thought now: she'd been a single working mother, after all. He couldn't even keep a plant alive unless he brought it to his office and instructed his secretary to water it. But Duncan had always been aware how silly his own childhood problems sounded to his mother, could hear from her the unspoken retort that he had no idea what real trouble was.

Now their relationship was polite but distant. Better than his relationship with his father, sure, but Duncan could easily go a month without talking to either of his parents and think nothing of it. His Michigan upbringing was like a skin he had long shed; like many New Yorkers, he was now the person he had made himself into.

Duncan picked up his cordless phone and dialed his mother's number. Sylvia answered right away, sounding pleasantly surprised to hear from him. She still lived in the house he'd grown up in, a compact two-bedroom in Troy—one of a string of small cities that ringed Detroit.

Duncan apologized for not calling her back earlier, a routine they went through virtually every time they talked. He asked her about how things were going at her job, which prompted a familiar litany of complaints. "How about you?" his mother asked. "What're you working on?"

"Ninety percent of my time is still working on Roth Properties cases," Duncan said. "Stuff coming out of that construction accident I told you about. But actually there is sort of a crazy thing that just happened. I had this pro bono family that I was helping out with this eviction?"

"I remember."

"Yeah, well, the grandson just got arrested for murder, and it looks like I'm keeping the case."

"Really?" his mother said. "I didn't know your firm handled cases like that."

"I didn't either," Duncan replied. "It's a surprise. But it's nice to get a chance to help somebody who's not a robber baron."

"I'm sure," Sylvia said blandly. Duncan tried to fight off the disappointment he felt. Without fully realizing it, he'd been hoping for some recognition from her that by helping Nazario he was doing something she approved of. Neither of his parents had ever come out and criticized Duncan for how he made his living, but he'd always assumed there was some disappointment that he was fighting on the side of those with all the power. Duncan thought his mother would be happy that he was helping the disadvantaged for a change. He should've known better by now than to expect such validation from her—it wasn't in her nature.

They talked for a while longer, and when Duncan hung up he felt melancholy, as he usually did after talking to either of his parents. He lived in a different world than they did, and his attempts to explain his life to them always fell flat. Duncan supposed that was part of the price to be paid for his elite education and high-paying job. Being born to parents of different races played a role too: his perspective on the world was at a different angle from either of theirs.

Duncan pushed away self-pity. He valued his background, the view it gave him, the ability to see past privilege's assumptions. The reason he was disappointed that his mother hadn't reacted more to his representing Nazario was because it felt important to him: he was glad of an opportunity to give something back. He'd seen some of himself in Rafael, which made him want his client to make it past the limitations of his circumstances. The murder charges had changed that: now the question was whether Rafael was going to even get a chance to try to have a successful life. Duncan wanted to give him that chance.

·9·

"So is this a dunker or what?" ADA Danielle Castelluccio asked. Detectives Jaworski and Gomez exchanged a quick glance before Jaworski answered. "It's pretty much a dunker," he said.

Castelluccio and her second chair, Andrew Bream, were meeting in her office with the detectives on the Fowler shooting. Castelluccio was a rising star in the DA's Homicide Division, boasting an undefeated trial record going back to her five years in sex crimes. She wasn't a favorite among cops, with a rep as an arrogant and abrasive micromanager and second-guesser, but she prepared for a trial like an elite marathoner for a race, and her winning percentage earned her grudging respect.

"I've gone through the file," Castelluccio said. "Solid eyewitness, forensics on shooting the gun. That's enough to make the case, but there's also some things I expected to see that I didn't."

Jaworski held her gaze, keeping his expression neutral. This was the kind of crap you got with Castelluccio: you brought her a gift; she bitched about the wrapping paper. "Like what?"

"Where's the gun?"

"The gun's a puzzler," Jaworski said evenly. "We took the kid's apartment apart; we did three different canvasses of the area."

"What's your theory on where it went?"

Jaworski shrugged; he wasn't much concerned about the gun. "I can give you a few, but they're just guesses. Could be he dropped it right near the scene, some joker from the neighborhood snatched it up before our canvass. If so, it might surface, but no way to know until it does or it doesn't. Could be Nazario stashed it somewhere that we missed. Could be he threw it down a sewer, something like that. Guns go missing; guns get found."

"What about video?"

"The shooting itself was in a dead zone in terms of cameras," Jaworski replied. "There's video from the perp's building, but it basically just shows Nazario walking through the lobby. It gives us when he got home, shows he had time to do the shoot, but nothing else."

"How's he look on the video?"

Jaworski shrugged. "It's grainy as hell, not going to get the look in his eyes."

"He's not running or anything," Gomez added. "Just looks like anybody else coming home from work."

"The Housing Bureau has cameras all over the projects," Castelluccio said. "How'd Nazario know where to shoot Fowler so it wouldn't be on tape?"

"The cameras are focused on the buildings more than the surrounding area," Jaworski said. "Don't think he had to be a criminal mastermind not to get caught on tape."

"Did the construction crew have cameras posted?"

Jaworski nodded. "The security company uses cameras, but again they're pointed in at the construction, not out at the street. The head of the security company, Darryl Loomis, was in gang intel on the job before he took his twenty. He reached out to us first thing, sent us over everything they had, but nothing that helps."

"I never met Loomis, though I know the legend. Either of you guys have dealings?"

"Haven't ever met him," Jaworski said. "But I've heard the stories, sure."

"What about other witnesses?" Castelluccio asked. "I know it was fairly late, but this is the East Village we're talking about. There had to be some people still up and about."

"The uniforms who were first on the scene hooked a couple of project touts who were outside Tower Four at the time of the shoot. They saw it as snitching and refused to say anything about seeing anybody. We leaned on them, kept them at our house overnight, but they didn't budge."

Castelluccio leaned forward, her interest sparked. "The dealers would've seen Nazario running from the scene?"

"They were in place to, and assuming they were on duty they would've had their eyes open for somebody running past. But these aren't citizens we're talking about."

Castelluccio was not ready to let it go. "They have jackets?"

"Juvie stuff," Jaworski said. "Nothing pending."

"Any point in leaning on them again?"

Jaworski shrugged, restraining his desire to tell her that if he'd seen any point in leaning on the dealer kids again he would've done so without prompting from the DA's office. "Even if we get an ID from them now, it'll be compromised by their earlier lack of cooperation. We can brace them, see if anything spills, but we don't have much in the way of carrots or sticks."

"An additional witness or two wouldn't hurt. We have anything we need to turn over from the initial interviews?"

Jaworski glanced over at Gomez, whose mouth offered the slightest flicker. "We didn't get a statement from either of them," Jaworski said carefully. It was bad enough that the dealer kids weren't helping to make the case; he had no interest in having them actively hurt it. "One of them denied seeing anybody run past, but it's surrounded with this stop-snitching bullshit."

Castelluccio frowned, not liking this. "You're telling me he didn't make a statement?"

Jaworski got that the ADA was establishing her own plausible deniability, but decided he'd have to live with it. He met her stare with his own. "That's what I'm telling you."

Castelluccio held the look for a moment before nodding. "Anything else I should know?"

Jaworski hesitated; Castelluccio caught it and raised an eyebrow. Jaworski looked to his partner, the ADA following his gaze. Gomez looked unhappy at the attention. "It's nothing," he said. "Nothing solid anyway. It's just that I heard some talk about Fowler a little bit back when he was on the job."

Castelluccio was not liking where this was going. "You heard Fowler was dirty?"

As she'd expected, Gomez immediately started backpedaling, shaking his head and putting a hand up. "Dirty I'm not saying. He was talked about is all."

Castelluccio was irritated by Gomez's vagueness, though she was plenty familiar with a cop's reluctance to talk any kind of shit about another cop. "So what was said when he was talked about?"

"That he didn't live on a cop's salary. But this is just word 'round the campfire."

"Any reason we should go down this road?" Castelluccio asked, her focus shifting back to Jaworski.

"Fowler left the department years ago," Jaworski said. "Even if we knew he'd been dirty, which we don't, there wouldn't be a reason to think it'd gotten him shot."

"Then let's not make a simple case complicated," Castelluccio said.

·10·

I T TOOK Duncan and Blake about an hour to make their way through the bureaucracy at Rikers Island to the claustrophobic interview room where they were to meet with their client, then another fifteen minutes waiting for Rafael to be brought in. Duncan could see Blake's rising frustration at all the wasted time that he could be billing to any number of paying clients, and wondered anew why Blake was making the trip in the first place.

Finally Rafael was brought in. The prison jumpsuit dangled loosely from his spindly frame; his body was hunched, tense, as if bracing for a blow. Duncan performed introductions, feeling a little irrationally disappointed at Rafael's lack of reaction: in the circles in which Duncan generally traveled Blake was a rock star.

"So Duncan has given me an overview of your case," Blake said. "But it's best if I hear everything from you. Tell me about your initial run-in with the security guard."

Even though he'd gone over all this when he'd first taken on the eviction, Duncan paid careful attention: often new details emerged when a client repeated a story; plus the stakes were obviously much higher now that Rafael faced life in prison. If he'd missed anything before, now was the time to catch it.

Rafael told them he'd been coming home from work a couple of months ago when Fowler had accosted him about fifty feet from his building. The security guard had bent down and picked up a half-smoked joint off the ground near Rafael's feet, claimed to have seen Rafael drop it. Rafael didn't take it seriously until two Housing Authority cops had appeared on the scene. Rafael tried to figure out if Fowler was lying or crazy, but the cops took the guard at his word, and the next thing Rafael knew he'd been arrested.

After stewing in a holding cell for about twenty-four hours, Rafael had finally met with a public defender. Clearly not believing Rafael's version of events, the lawyer had encouraged him to plead out to disorderly conduct, saying that time served and a small fine would be his only punishment. Exhausted, and not wanting to risk a real criminal record if he fought it, Rafael took the plea.

Rafael thought the whole stupid mess was over with, but then the following week the Housing Authority issued an eviction notice against him and his grandmother. Rafael's grandmother had gone to a legal services organization seeking help, which was how they'd come to be referred to Duncan.

When instructed by the firm to devote some time to pro bono, Duncan had picked an eviction case because it seemed like a straightforward option, one that would potentially get him on his feet in court. When he'd first heard the facts of the case Duncan had thought he'd at least be able to keep Dolores Nazario in her home, but that confidence had quickly dissipated once he familiarized himself with the relevant law. Just a few years earlier the Supreme Court had ruled that an entire household could be evicted from public housing if any one of them was caught with drugs on or near the property. So if the city could make a case against Rafael, it followed that Dolores too would be on the street.

Rafael had insisted that he'd been set up, claiming that the security guards had pulled the same stunt on other residents. This would have been a promising lead to pursue at the start of the case, but it was basically irrelevant once Rafael had entered his guilty plea in criminal court. Which meant that Duncan didn't really have a legal or factual leg to stand on, other than a long shot like attempting to vacate the plea. That would have been nearly impossible even before Rafael was arrested for Fowler's murder.

After going through the initial run-in with Fowler, Blake turned to the shooting, asking Rafael to take them through what had happened that night. Rafael, who worked in the kitchen of an East Village restaurant called Alchemy, had been there until just past eleven. After his shift he'd walked home, not seeing anyone he knew. He was home listening to music when the cops had arrived less than an hour later, his headphones cranked so loud he didn't even hear them knocking. They'd first brought him to the Housing Authority station on Avenue C, had a man in a security guard's uniform take a look at him through the window while Rafael was handcuffed in the back of the police car. After that he'd been brought to the precinct, where the cops tested his hands for GSR; then the detectives had questioned him briefly before Rafael had asked for a lawyer, at which point they'd put him into the system, sent him down to Central Booking.

"Let's go back over a few things," Blake said when Rafael was finished. "Did you hear the gunshots?"

Rafael nodded. "I wasn't sure it was somebody shooting, but I thought it was."

"Where were you when you heard the shots?"

"I was walking on Avenue D. I thought maybe it was just a car, but I couldn't really tell where it was coming from, thought it was from behind me."

"You didn't see anything? Didn't see Fowler or the shooter?"

"Like I said, I wasn't even sure it was a gun. And not like I'm going to go check it out. I got enough sense to just keep moving."

"What did you tell the police that night?" Blake asked.

"Just that I didn't do nothing."

"Did you tell them you knew Fowler?"

"They already knew about how we were getting thrown out 'cause of him."

Duncan wondered how the police had put that together so quickly. It was a straightforward motive, though he certainly didn't think that Rafael would believe that shooting Fowler would make the eviction case go away. But revenge had its appeal, and he'd certainly heard his client call Fowler all sorts of names.

"Did the police ask you about the eviction?" Blake asked.

"Just to say that was why I'd capped Fowler."

"Did they tell you about the gunshot residue?"

"They come out with that right before I say I wasn't gonna talk to them no more. I thought they were just playing with me, didn't take it for real until Mr. R tells me they're really saying that."

"Did you touch a gun at any point that night?"

"I work in a kitchen," Rafael said. "If I was going to take somebody out, I'd get a butcher knife."

Duncan laughed at this; Blake did not. "Mr. Nazario," Blake said, "I assure you the question of whether you handled a gun that night is no joke."

"Course I didn't," Rafael said angrily. "I've never shot a gun, don't have nothing to do with guns."

"The security guard who's the eyewitness against you," Blake said after a moment. "You ever seen him before that night?"

"I don't think so. Not that I noticed anyway."

"Any idea how or why he ID'd you as the shooter?"

"Either he's wrong or he's lying. All them security dudes are straight-up motherfuckers."

"What's the problem?"

Rafael's lip curled. "They treat us like a bunch of dogs. Course, people are nice to dogs, so maybe like we were rats."

"So other people in the project had problems with them?"

"Hell, yeah."

"You know of anything with Fowler specifically? Anybody else who might have had a motive for shooting him?"

Rafael shrugged. "I don't know nothing like that. But I got an easy time believing somebody else wanted that asshole dead."

THEY SPENT a couple of hours with Rafael, going back over his initial encounter with Fowler as well as the night of the murder. Blake asked virtually all of the questions, methodically covering the bases in a way Duncan had seen him do dozens of times before in different circumstances, though Duncan still felt confounded at the sight of his boss in a Rikers interview room.

"So what did you think?" Duncan asked, once the interview was over and they were out in the prison parking lot making their way to Blake's car. He hadn't realized how tense he'd felt inside the jail until he was back out under the sky.

"He's got a motive and nothing much in the way of an alibi. The eyewitness and gunshot evidence are strong, and even in his version he was walking right by the shooting when it happened."

"That bad?" Duncan said, looking over at his boss as he opened the car door.

"You see a defense here? I'm not saying he did it, but if not, he must've stepped in the world's unluckiest dog shit on his way home that night."

"But he doesn't have a motive, really. Killing the guy isn't going to make the eviction go away. And he had confidence that I was going to win that case. Too much confidence, if anything. He was pissed at Fowler, obviously, but I don't see how he was pissed enough to shoot the guy."

Blake shrugged. "Rule of thumb, criminals don't have an especially good reason to do what they did. That's why we call it crime."

"Sure," Duncan said. "But what I'm saying is, I don't actually think Rafael is a criminal."

"This isn't one to try to make your bones on," Blake said dismissively. "You're not doing your client any favors riding in on a white horse here. Part of winning is defining a realistic goal. Getting him a plea that doesn't mean jail for the rest of his life—that's what a win looks like here."

"The first-degree murder charge seems pretty weak," Duncan said. Generally in New York, first-degree murder was reserved for special cases, like the killing of police officers, but it also applied when the victim was killed in retaliation for giving testimony in a previous criminal case. If Rafael was convicted on first-degree murder, he would face life in prison without the possibility of parole. Duncan wasn't convinced that the DA could make it stick here; he suspected they'd only filed it because Fowler was an ex-cop.

"So then the goal is to get him a decent deal on murder two," Blake replied.

Duncan understood that Blake was giving instructions, not asking for debate. He was surprised at himself for feeling disappointed—he didn't want to write the case off as a loser quite so quickly. "It's a little soon to go looking for a deal, isn't it?" he said. "I mean, they haven't really nailed him yet."

Blake looked over at Duncan, then shrugged. "From where I'm sitting, he looks to be hanging on the cross," he said.

DUNCAN WAS eating the best soup he'd ever had, a rich and meaty crab bisque spiced with a mild curry. Marco Mucci, the soup's creator, was seated across from him. Mucci, a few years older than Duncan, was fast becoming one of the most acclaimed chefs in the city. The *Times* had given Alchemy three stars last year—previously unheard-of for a restaurant on Avenue B.

Alchemy was open only for dinner, so the dining room was empty except for a hostess who was handling the phone. The kitchen seemed active; Duncan could hear music blasting and the occasional raised voice. The hostess had let Duncan in, seated him at a table in the middle of the restaurant, and then gone in the back to get Mucci.

The first thing Marco'd asked was whether Duncan had eaten lunch. Duncan, who generally missed lunch at least once a week, and other times didn't get to it until late afternoon, admitted that he hadn't, and Marco had immediately retreated back to the kitchen, returning a minute later with two bowls of soup expertly cradled in his arm.

It'd been Blake's idea for Duncan to reach out to the restaurant where Rafael worked, see if he could get a character witness. Duncan wasn't happy about it: to him it smacked of giving up. But Blake had instructed him to concentrate on positioning Rafael for a decent plea. While Duncan wasn't comfortable with Blake's focus on making a quick deal, at the same time he prided himself on being nobody's fool. Rafael's story about the security guard planting the weed had never really added up. Rafael had no explanation for how he'd come to be accused of drug possession and now murder. Duncan wasn't sure anyone was actually that unlucky.

"Thanks for taking the time," Duncan said. "I'm sure you're very busy."

Marco waved his hand dismissively. "I'm just glad that Rafa's got a good lawyer on this," he said. "We were talking about taking up a collection here, but I doubt that would've been realistic. We're trying to set something up to make sure people get out to visit him. Are you doing this as a volunteer?"

"Essentially, yeah. That's great that people are supporting him."

"Rafa's been here for over a year. We're going to have his back as much as we can."

Duncan was surprised at this, considering what Rafael was accused of. "Are you always this supportive of your dishwashers?"

Marco frowned at the question, despite Duncan's attempt to ask it lightly. "Rafael wasn't just a dishwasher here anymore. He was doing dinner prep work on a regular basis. I don't define the people in my kitchen by how much training they have or where they apprenticed. At the end of the day, a restaurant's an art form—it's a piece of theater, what we do every night. I look for energy, creativity, enthusiasm—and Rafa had all those things in spades. He actually *liked* coming to work, you know? I think he enjoyed hanging in the restaurant, being part of something."

"He never had any problems here with anyone?"

"Not at all," Marco said. "He found a home here, I think. A kitchen can be that for people. And it wasn't just enthusiasm either—he's a good cook. That's why I got him into classes at the CIA."

"The CIA?"

Marco smiled. "Sorry—kitchen shorthand. The Culinary Institute."

"Other than that he's a great employee," Duncan asked, "what's your sense of him as a person?"

Marco seemed surprised by the question. "Are you asking me if I think Rafa could kill somebody?"

Duncan shrugged. "Now that you mention it . . ."

"I know where Rafa comes from," Marco said. "I grew up on Fourteenth Street. This is my neighborhood. Rafa's not the first person from the Avenue D projects I've hired. A few have worked out; a few couldn't hack basic responsibility. He's one of the good ones. Whatever is going on with that shooting, I'm sure that Rafa didn't have anything to do with it."

"You're convinced he's innocent?"

"Of course," Marco said, looking at Duncan curiously. "Aren't you?"

THE QUESTION lingered as Duncan headed back to his office. Although he didn't have the first idea how to explain away the evidence, he also didn't see his client as a killer. Duncan just wasn't ready to stop trying to prove Rafael's innocence. He could imagine how disappointed Rafael himself would be if he knew that his lawyers were already focused on a plea. It seemed like a betrayal to give up so quickly on the idea of winning his freedom.

He'd have to go back to Blake, try to convince him that they needed to take a closer look at the DA's case. Blake would listen to him, especially if he had a solid plan of attack.

Back at his office, Duncan took off his jacket and loosened his tie, unbuttoning the top button of his starched blue shirt. He'd put on a suit that morning only because he wanted to look like a lawyer when he went to talk to Mucci. Nonlawyers were always surprised to learn that Duncan only rarely wore a suit and tie; something about a casually dressed lawyer seemed to disappoint them.

The rest of his day was to be taken up with preparing to defend Preston Thomas's deposition. Thomas, the CFO of Roth Properties, had drawn the short stick and was to be the first defense witness deposed in the wrongful-death lawsuit. Coming up right after Preston was Tommy Nelson, the general contractor's site supervisor at the Aurora, and a key witness in the case. Omni had its own lawyers who'd be defending Nelson's depo, although Lily was going to attend.

Duncan was culling out what he considered to be the most significant documents and indexing them into a three-inch binder. Thomas, whose deposition was next week, was scheduled to come in tomorrow for a prep session. Duncan's plan for the rest of the day was to make an outline that would serve as his guide to take Thomas through the documents.

Thomas had been the developer's main negotiator in working out the various contracts for the Aurora Tower, both on the investment end and on the construction end. In order to prepare Thomas for the deposition, Duncan was going through the paper trail from the various negotiations, all the e-mails and letters and drafts of contracts through which the assorted deals had been worked out.

Which amounted to a hell of a lot of paper. A hedge fund had been the biggest lender; there were also several investment banks involved in the financing, each of which drove its own separate bargain. Duncan was only skimming the financing documents; his focus was on the negotiations with the site's general contractor, Omni Construction. If the plaintiffs were going to somehow make Roth liable for the accident, they'd presumably have to do so by showing how the developer had exerted pressure on Omni to cut corners.

As he quickly paged through the assorted financing material, Duncan noticed that at least a couple hundred million in construction loans was soon coming due. He knew that the banks were tightening up on big commercial loans, and given that high-end real estate's luster had dimmed quite a bit recently, he suspected the lenders might be looking to take advantage of a moment when they could pull out. Duncan wondered idly if Roth Properties had all that money on hand if the loans didn't get extended.

He was still a little disappointed that their client had to submit to discovery: Duncan had thought they'd had a good shot on their motion to dismiss. He'd drafted the motion, and had in the process thoroughly convinced himself of its merits. But judges generally didn't grant motions to dismiss; it was very hard to get out of a civil lawsuit prior to submitting to discovery. What this meant as a practical matter was that even utterly meritless cases would often drag on for years, costing the defendants millions in legal bills. It also meant that the bulk of Duncan's time, like that of every other big-firm litigator, was spent trudging through discovery, spanning everything from reviewing documents to conducting depositions. Discovery was the lifeblood of large litigation departments, its massive—and massively tedious—document churn the source of millions of dollars' worth of billable hours each year.

Duncan spent the rest of the afternoon and into the evening writing the depo outline. He took a dinner break, realizing as he did so that he was only about two-thirds of the way through.

He was eating sashimi while reading *Above the Law* on his computer when Lily appeared in his doorway. They hadn't talked since their fight at the Rainbow Room, but Duncan was fine pretending it had never happened. "Hey," he said. "You want something to eat? I ordered two appetizers, an entrée, and a dessert. And the fish isn't cooked," he couldn't resist adding.

"Trying to change weight classes?" Lily asked, ignoring Duncan's dig while taking a stack of papers off one of his chairs and sitting down.

"I keep in fighting trim. I just eat half of everything, save the rest for tomorrow's lunch. I mean, it's not like I'm paying for it."

"Fight the power," Lily said. "Anyway, I'm eating at home, or at least I'm hoping I am."

"Depending on what?"

"You," Lily said. "The Blake asked me to make sure you didn't need help on the Thomas depo. He said you've been a little tied up with your murder thing."

Duncan tried to camouflage his reaction. This was not something Blake generally did. Blake assumed his associates were getting their work done without his checking in. "The Blake sent you to check up on me?"

"That's certainly one way to look at it," Lily said.

"If I needed your help I would've asked for it."

"No, you wouldn't have."

"True. So what are the odds I'd do so when you come asking?"

"Pretty much zero. Like I said, I'm hoping to go home."

"Go already," Duncan said.

Lily stayed put, looking at Duncan, who deliberately looked over at his food. "You're really doing a murder case?"

"Rafael was an existing client. Leaving him in the lurch might not have looked great. We have to worry about PR."

Lily was obviously not buying it. "We're defending a murderer as PR? That explains a lot about this firm's reputation."

"PR's the only reason we're doing pro bono generally. The partners got tired of hearing about Karen Cleary's lawsuit."

"And they think throwing in a little pro bono is going to make us girls forget about our oppression?"

"You didn't even *like* Karen Cleary," Duncan said. "You didn't have any sympathy for her when she didn't make partner."

"I didn't think she deserved to make partner, but the fact I didn't like her had nothing to do with that. And I have to be concerned with her lawsuit, because like it or not it affects my career. On the one hand it helps me, because now all the partners are paranoid about pissing off the women; on the other it hurts me, because now all the partners resent that they've got to worry about pissing off the women."

"What would you expect?" Duncan asked.

"Right. It's not like I expect to be judged by my own merits or anything."

"We don't make the rules."

"And sometimes we don't even play by them," Lily replied. After a moment she stood and pushed his office door closed, Duncan tensing up as she did so. "So, listen, Dunk, about the other night."

"Don't call me Dunk."

"I know I flew off the handle at you a little, and I'm sorry."

"Okay," Duncan said neutrally, skittish about getting into this.

"It wasn't you I was mad at. And I'm in no position to judge you for how you deal with who you are, especially in the workplace. Especially in this workplace."

Duncan smiled. "You've judged me for that as long as I've known you."

"It was different when we were together. Then it was at least sort of my business. If I looked like you do in terms of passing, if I didn't have to deal with the bullshit, why would I? It's not fair for me to expect you to make your life more difficult than it needs to be."

"I'm not passing any more than I'm a tragic fucking mulatto," Duncan snapped. "This isn't *Imitation of Life.*"

"I didn't— Shit. I don't know why I'm fucking this up with you. It's hard for me, you know? I look at you, and I see the person I was intimate with, not the guy I'm trying to make partner over."

"I'd imagine you're capable of seeing both those things at the same time," Duncan replied. "It's not like we didn't go into it knowing the risk this was where it'd end up."

"We knew. But then you throw the race thing in there, and it just gets . . . It's not fair for me to expect you to be some kind of double agent or whatever."

"Double agent?" Duncan said with a laugh, pretending he didn't know exactly what she meant. He'd spent his entire life on the outside looking in, one way or another, even if he had grown pretty good at disguising it.

Lily gave him a look, leaving Duncan no doubt that she saw right through him. "Do you know what you said to me once?" she asked, Duncan's stomach clenching at her expression. "You remember that time I was late—you know, *late*. And I'm freaking out a little, and what you said was that our kid would come out looking like America's future. Did I ever love you when you said that, even though it was pretty clear that the last thing you wanted was to have some kind of crazy tri-racial baby with me. I was weak at the knees, kiddo. I was ready to sign on the dotted line."

Duncan, uncomfortable, tried to derail her. "And then I said I'd put *Golf Digest* in the crib," he said. "Just in case that Tiger Woods thing turned out to be genetic."

Lily brushed off his attempt to change the mood. "I'm serious."

Duncan sighed and rubbed at his face, not understanding why Lily wanted to revisit all this. "Look, yes, sure, I remember."

"You remember what?" Lily demanded, her eyes cloudy.

"I remember saying that to you, about our theoretical kid. I remember the look you gave me, hearing it. I remember all of it, okay? And we came close, damn close, you and I, but we didn't get there, not all the way. And I don't quite know why not, and I don't think you know either, but here we are."

Lily swiped at her eyes. "So it wasn't fair of me, the other night, saying you don't understand what my version of this is like. Because I can't understand what your version of it is like either. But okay, you're right, that bridge is underwater. There's no right way to do any of this, and I'm sorry if I've acted like there is."

Duncan smiled at her, mostly out of relief that they'd finally been able to talk about this without it turning into a fight. "I appreciate your blessing," he said.

·12·

NUGENT WAS giving Candace only a small amount of rope. Her editor wasn't convinced that she'd find a story in a Roth Properties lawyer representing a teenager accused of murder. But he at least trusted her instincts enough to let her look.

Candace didn't know exactly what she was looking for. Whatever it was, it wasn't apparent in the murder case itself. The only thing that linked Fowler to Roth Properties was that he was doing construction security for them at the time he was killed. The only link between the accused and Roth was the lawyer, Riley.

Candace had done due diligence on Blake and Wolcott back when the libel suit had been filed against her; she still had the research folder on her computer. She went through it, looking to see if anything popped out differently in the context of the Fowler murder.

The firm had been founded about a decade ago, and had already grown to nearly two hundred attorneys—small for a major law firm, but large considering the firm's youth. Its undisputed star was Steven Blake, who'd been a corner-office partner at Davis Polk & Wardwell—one of the city's most prestigious law firms, whose own white-shoe history dated back well into the nineteenth century. Blake had been a standout—at a firm whose culture was not known for having standouts—before going off on his own, leaving behind the millions a year he'd been making as Davis Polk's leading litigator and announcing plans to start a small trial-oriented boutique. His new firm had taken off with a bang, cementing Blake's place as one of the country's leading trial lawyers while attracting dozens of lateral attorneys to his firm.

But after years of explosive growth and a high-profile winning streak, the firm had come back down to earth in the last year or two. Part of this was no doubt the inevitable backlash to the firm's quick success, but the glow had nevertheless faded a bit.

Her review of the firm's history didn't tell her much of use to her now. There were a couple of references to Simon Roth being a long-standing client of Blake's, and the libel suit itself had triggered a fair amount of press, but she didn't see anything that connected the firm to the changes at Jacob Riis. She turned to the specific lawyer, Duncan Riley, Googling him to see what popped. The first hit was from the firm Web site, a brief professional bio and head shot. The bio informed her that Riley had an undergraduate degree from Michigan and a law degree from Harvard, and that he'd clerked for a federal judge in Manhattan before joining Blake's firm as an associate in the fall of 2001, back when it was only a few years old. It was an impressive pedigree, but probably little different from most of Blake and Wolcott's associates. Duncan did look like an up-and-comer at the firm: his bio listed a number of cases he'd worked on, and Candace had heard of several of them. Including, of course, the one in which she was a defendant.

She studied his picture, a professional studio shot, Duncan in a suit, smiling, clearly striving to look welcoming and competent. His tie and shirt echoed each other, matching baby blue. His smile was slightly self-conscious, or ironic maybe, perhaps an awareness of the fact that he was presenting himself as a white-shoe lawyer. There was something about his face she couldn't quite put her finger on—his dark green eyes seemed out of place against his almost Latin complexion. His dark hair was cut quite short, little more than a buzz cut. Candace couldn't place him in terms of background—she thought maybe Mediterranean or Jewish or even light-skinned Hispanic by his looks, though his name didn't support any of those.

He was good-looking, Candace reluctantly conceded, and she'd had to admit that he'd been an adroit questioner, listening carefully to her answers, following up on any evasion or ambiguity, politely but persistently pressing her, always on the lookout for an opening. She'd recognized his skill, even as she'd hated being on the receiving end.

The fact that Riley was fast approaching a partnership vote, and appeared from the outside at least to have a decent shot at making it, only made his representation of Rafael Nazario more baffling. She logged onto a search engine for New York's courts and ran a search for cases in which Duncan was a lawyer of record.

She found that a couple of months before Rafael Nazario had been accused of killing Sean Fowler, the city's public housing authority had launched eviction proceedings against him, along with a woman who Candace guessed must be Rafael's mother. There was only one filing available electronically: an opinion from the trial court dated a week before the murder. Candace downloaded a pdf.

To her surprise, the order was granting a motion to dismiss the eviction. It appeared to be on a technicality of some kind, and was without prejudice, which Candace, a lawyer's daughter, knew meant the city could refile its case. But still, it seemed like a good start for the defense.

Then why the hell would Nazario shoot the security guard a week later?

The Internet wasn't going to answer that question, so Candace turned her attention to what was happening at Jacob Riis generally. She pulled up all the articles her paper had written on the changes to Riis, the plans for which had been announced a couple of years ago. The idea was to eventually demolish all of the existing Jacob Riis buildings— which, like most public housing in New York, consisted of a sprawling cluster of towering high-rises that had increasingly become dilapidated self-enclosed war zones—while simultaneously replacing them with mixed-income apartments. The new buildings would include public housing, subsidized units for working-class families, and market-rate apartments, all thrown together in roughly equal percentages. The idea was to end the isolation of the projects, and in doing so to make public housing safer while better integrating its residents into the surrounding community. It was an idea that had been tried with some success in other cities, and the plan's boosters—from Simon Roth to the mayor—had consistently declared it an idea especially well suited to New York.

Candace saw their point: in no other city in the country did the lives of rich and poor intersect more than New York. There were pockets of the city where one faction had completely taken over—Park Avenue for the rich, East New York for the poor—but in large swaths of the city you had only to walk a few blocks to go from lavish to desolate and back again. In addition, entire neighborhoods had been transformed in recent years as New York had become safer and awash in money: the East Village of squats and drugs and anarchists that Candace remembered from her own teenage years seemed like a myth in light of what the neighborhood had now become.

And so what better place to experiment with transforming the city's public housing than Jacob Riis? The project stretched from Thirteenth Street down to Sixth between Avenue D and FDR Drive. It'd been built in the wake of World War II, had originally been home primarily to veterans who couldn't afford market housing. Alphabet City had been largely a white ethnic neighborhood—Jews and Italians—back then. Working-class and insular, but a community too. By the seventies the neighborhood and the projects had transformed: the East Village becoming a dangerous bohemia, while the projects became almost entirely black and Hispanic and increasingly isolated from the surrounding neighborhood.

Then the nineties came, and New York found itself in a period of wealth so extravagant and sustained that even the East Village turned flush. Streets once dominated by drug addicts and the homeless were now home to indie film actresses and the more adventurous yuppies. The East Village increasingly turning into New York's version of the French Quarter, less an actual bohemia than a theme-park simulacrum of one. Only Avenue D resisted gentrification's pull, the sprawling projects that lined the entire east side of the street keeping development at bay.

Anyone with money who chose to live in the East Village presumably did so at least in part for the frisson of the neighborhood's outlaw roots. It was relatively easy to imagine East Villagers, even fairly prosperous ones, moving in alongside public housing residents, especially for a bargain apartment. People did more extreme things in the quest for Manhattan real estate.

As extensive as the Riis redevelopment project was—it involved over seventeen hundred apartments in the existing projects—that was nothing compared to the full scale of what was contemplated. If the reinvention of Riis was successful, the city would potentially pursue similar developments, starting with the projects immediately south of it. On lower Manhattan's far east side, projects stretched along the East River from Thirteenth Street all the way down to Delancey. If the city was able to transform them all, the entire Lower East Side would be hugely affected, not to mention enhancing the potential of similar transformation in other parts of the city.

Unsurprisingly, the articles about the plan also included considerable opposition. A neighborhood organization called the Alphabet City Community Coalition appeared to be spearheading it, led by a community organizer named Keisha Dewberry. Candace was a little fuzzy on what exactly the group stood for, but it was quite apparent from the articles what it was against: rich white developers, yuppies, gentrification, the displacement of project residents from their existing homes. Dewberry also asked the obvious question: How were all the existing residents going to be brought back, given that only about a third of the rebuilt housing was intended for them?

Candace went onto the secretary of state's Web site, downloaded all the publicly available information about the ACCC. As a registered nonprofit, it had extensive filing obligations with the state, and that material was available online. Candace printed out the tax forms that would show the group's directors, its board, and the main sources of its financing.

To Candace's surprise, the vast majority of the ACCC's money seemed to come from the city, specifically from the Housing Authority, which had apparently given the organization a half-million-dollar grant. Why was the city giving money to an organization whose sole purpose was to oppose a city-run initiative?

She'd have to speak to someone in the agency. Her most likely in might be through her soon-to-be ex-husband, Ben Cutler, an academic in urban planning. Ben had left her a message at home the other night, and she had yet to return his call. She decided to try him, dialing her old home number.

Ben sounded happy to hear from her. "I was calling because of your mother's birthday this Sunday," he said. "I was going to send her a note, but didn't know if you'd think that was weird or whatever."

"I'm sure she'd appreciate it," Candace said distractedly, panicking at the thought that she'd almost spaced her own mother's birthday. She wasn't going to say it, but of course it *was* weird that Ben wanted to write her mom. But Candace knew her mother wouldn't feel that way: she'd always been fond of Ben. There was no doubt in Candace's mind that her mother would like nothing more than for the two of them to call off their divorce and get back together. She wondered if Ben had an ulterior motive for staying in touch with her family, if what he was really seeking to do was join forces, conspire with them as to how he could win Candace back. But she didn't really believe it: that wasn't how Ben's mind worked; he was lacking in guile and ulterior motives. Perhaps to his detriment, or at least that of their marriage.

"I'm not trying to, you know . . . It's not that I think it means anything," Ben said, reading her thoughts, an uncomfortable reminder to Candace of how well he knew her. "She sent me an e-mail on my birthday last month."

Candace winced, her eyes squeezing shut. Not only was this news to her, but she'd deliberately ignored Ben's birthday herself. She wondered why her mother had never mentioned it. "Mom always liked you," she said, her eyes still closed. "You know that. She thought of you as part of the family."

"But she doesn't really get a vote, does she?"

"Ben—"

"I know, I'm just— How are you, anyway?"

"I'm fine," Candace said. "Busy, as always. Doing a little digging into something you might know about—the city's rebuilding of the housing projects in the East Village?"

"Sure," Ben said, his voice brightening. Candace had never been able to quite get a handle on what aspects of the surrounding world Ben would deem worthy of his attention. There were huge swaths of modern life that he just let pass him by, while he had depths of knowledge on anything that struck his intellectual interest, with little in between. His own work was much more abstract and theoretical than something as practical as changing a housing project. "I mean, for the irony alone," he continued. "It's hard to resist Jacob Riis. Naming a giant tenement-style project after the city's most legendary chronicler of the evils of tenement life. You couldn't find a better way to piss on the guy's legacy if you devoted your life to it."

"You hear about the murder that just happened there?"

"Doesn't ring a bell. You're investigating a murder?"

"Not really," Candace said. "But it led me to what's happening at Riis—I take it you know about how they're changing it over to mixed-income housing?"

"It's about time too. It's embarrassing that New York's behind the curve on this. If Atlanta can have mixed-income public housing, then God knows we can."

"Even brought to you by a private real estate developer?"

"Who wants to see the Housing Authority try to put up market-rate apartments? You want to spend three grand a month for something they build? Having private developers involved is a necessary evil."

"Putting the profit motive into public housing," Candace said skeptically. "They actually let you have ideas like that on the faculty of NYU?"

"I did use the word 'evil,'" Ben rejoined. "Can't be too careful. But if you think about it, the basic idea—mixing people of different social classes together, and in doing so exposing those who live in public housing to other sides of life—is a hell of a lot more progressive than dumping poor people into giant buildings that are walled off from the rest of the city."

Candace was losing interest in debating the big picture of changing Riis. "Anyway," she said, "I was digging around into what's going on there, and I came across something I didn't understand. There's this neighborhood opposition group, the Alphabet City Community Coalition it's called, claiming to represent the interests of the current Riis tenants. I was looking around in its finances, and I noticed that most of its funding not only came from the city, but specifically from the Housing Authority. The city is behind the new and improved Riis, right?"

"Of course. The mayor campaigned on this idea."

"And if the city likes it, and the mayor likes it, doesn't that pretty much mean the Housing Authority has to like it too? So why the hell are they funding the opposition?"

"Now you're getting way too practical for me."

"Do you know anyone there who would talk to me about it?"

Her question was greeted by a noticeable silence. "Are you at work?" Ben asked, his voice gone stiff.

Candace hesitated, realizing that she was letting Ben down. "I am still, yeah."

"And this is why you were calling?"

"I was returning your call."

"From two days ago, and you do it from work, when you want information," Ben said, his voice disappointed, not angry.

"I was going to call you back when I had a minute," Candace protested.

"Uh-huh. Anyway, yeah, I do know somebody high up there. Forrest Garber. I forget his exact title, but he's a policy guy. We've been on some panels together, and I could see if he'd talk to you."

"That'd be awesome," Candace said, wanting to change the subject. "How's the book coming?"

"Don't get me started, Candy Cane," Ben replied. For nearly five years Ben had been working on turning his dissertation into a book. Despite dozens of conversations, its precise subject matter had never been entirely clear to Candace: some sort of mix of New York City history, abstruse urban theory, and semiotics. It'd sounded to Candace like he'd just stuck the entire Brown University syllabus into a blender. She'd said this to Ben once. He hadn't found it funny.

"I don't think you can call me that anymore," Candace said, keeping her voice light but at the same time needing to say it, because the offhand intimacy between them was more than she could bear.

"Sure I can," Ben said, his voice soft with sorrow. "For six more weeks."

Ben said he'd get back to her after reaching out to Forrest, and they said their good-byes. One reason Candace had called from work was that she thought talking to Ben might hurt less if she did it from there. It hadn't worked; she was seized with the familiar sadness that speaking with him caused her now. On top of it she felt guilty for calling him when she was on the prowl for information, using him like he was just another source.

Candace tried to shake free of it, to get her mind back on Jacob Riis. She still didn't get what was in this for Simon Roth. He'd made his name on high-end construction, luxury buildings: getting involved with public housing seemed like diluting the brand. But there was the scale of the thing, she supposed: a New York real estate developer rarely got this large a chunk of the city to play with. And maybe he did see it as part of his legacy, as he'd claimed in the press clippings, a late-innings good deed to make people forget all the greed that had come before.

By the time she was finished with her initial research it was a little after nine o'clock. All the other reporters who weren't on deadline were long gone. She'd gotten as far as she was going to get while sitting on her ass in the newsroom. Next would be hitting the pavement, talking to people at Riis and in the city government.

Candace liked the newsroom at night, the energy riding high as the final editorial decisions were made, the home-stretch scramble of putting the next day's paper to bed. She was in no hurry to return to her lonely one-bedroom in Brooklyn's Boerum Hill. However free leaving Ben had originally made her feel, loneliness nagged at her now. She missed the fundamental comfort of having someone to come home to.

·13·

So how'd Preston do?" Blake asked Duncan, the two of them in Blake's office.

Duncan had spent the previous day in a firm conference room, defending the deposition of Preston Thomas, the CFO of Roth Properties. "Very well," he said.

"What were they looking for?" Blake asked.

"They asked a lot of questions about the structure of the deal with the contractor, the guaranteed maximum price provision on the cost-plus contract. Their idea seemed to be that by capping the costs, Roth was creating an incentive for Omni to cut corners."

"There's a basic logic to that, isn't there?" Blake asked, playing devil's advocate.

"Sure. But capped cost-plus contracts are one of the most common deals out there between developers and general contractors. And a fixed-price contract would create the same situation. It's not like this is something Roth invented. As long as the judge understands that, I don't see how it gets them a thing."

"And Preston came across well?"

"He was great," Duncan said. "Completely unruffled."

Blake nodded. "So where are we on your guy in the murder?"

Duncan took a second to make the mental shift, though he'd been hoping to discuss the case with Blake. "I talked to people who know him in terms of painting a picture of a good kid for the DA. They all say the same thing, which is that they don't think there's any way Rafael shot somebody."

Blake waved a hand at this. "That's not the point."

"It is if he didn't do it," Duncan rejoined, smiling to take the edge off it.

"Are they saying he didn't do it because they can offer him alibis?" Blake said, going into cross-examination mode, a clear indication that he was skeptical.

"No."

"So what, then? They have *instincts*? They know he's not *capable*? That's going to get us exactly nowhere."

Duncan didn't understand why Blake was being so negative. "I understand that, Steven," he said. "But knowing Rafael some myself, I have a really hard time seeing him as guilty here."

"That and two bucks will get you on the subway," Blake said. "You have an actual hole in the DA's case?"

"Their case is two things. First the ID, which is a problem, but there're lots of ways to attack it. Single witness, at night, from a fair distance, cross-racial ID, et cetera. It could well be an honest mistake; it's certainly not foolproof.

"Second's the gunshot residue. I'd like to at least run it by somebody who's got the science to evaluate it, tell me whether there's a weakness."

"You're what, Nancy Drew all of a sudden?" Blake said. Duncan was surprised by Blake's irritation—he was just doing due diligence, the sort of thing he'd automatically do in any case. "Look, I get it. It's fun, cops and robbers. Plus you want to believe—it's human nature. But I need you to keep your eye on the ball."

"You want me to focus on getting him the best deal we can. But we knock out a big piece of the state's evidence, that's going to get the DA to make a good offer more than any character reference will."

Blake's eyes narrowed slightly, his way of acknowledging a point scored. After a moment he nodded curtly. "So let's say you talk with somebody about the residue. You take that, go to the DA and see what they'll put on the table, save everybody the trouble of litigating it. How's that for a plan?"

Duncan nodded quickly, feeling both pleased and relieved. "I think it's the way to go. It gives everybody a little bit of uncertainty, which is generally the best place to make a deal from."

"All right then," Blake said. "You can retain an expert to look at the GSR. Shouldn't be more than a few hours of his time. But remember, they've also got the witness; they've got motive. You're not trying to win the game here, just get the score closer."

"Understood."

"And I need you focused on all this Roth discovery. It's a cluster fuck of cases, and you need to be on top of all the moving parts."

"I'm on it," Duncan said. "Speaking of which, Leah Roth invited me to her father's birthday party this weekend."

Blake arched an eyebrow. "You trying to poach my client?"

Duncan forced a laugh. He hadn't been looking forward to raising the Roth party with his boss, but had felt obligated to do so. "She said she wants us to be allies."

Blake looked serious, leaning forward a little in his chair. "Leah will probably run the company when Simon retires. She'd be a good ally for you to have. But remember that the silver spoon she was born with was made out of platinum. We're little more than family butlers."

Lily knocked on Blake's open office door before stepping in. The three of them had a meeting at the district attorney's office in a little less than an hour, the goal of which was to get an agreement limiting the scope of the prosecutor's subpoena of Roth Properties' files.

"I won't forget my place," Duncan said to Blake as Lily sat down.

"People who do often have a hard time finding it again," Blake replied.

THE ADA in charge of the Aurora Tower investigation, Desmond Sullivan, met the three of them in a conference room in the DA's office on Hogan Place, an aging Art Deco building whose facade was presently marred by extensive repair work, steps from the main criminal courthouse on Centre Street.

Sullivan was the chief of the Rackets Bureau. Because of the long-standing influence of organized crime in New York's construction industry, Rackets handled all investigations into accidents at building sites. Sullivan was fiftyish, a DA lifer, with close-cropped gray hair and piercing blue eyes. After introductions had been performed, hands shaken, and the offer of coffee declined, they settled in to business.

Blake began by handing out their white paper, which Lily and Duncan had drafted and Blake had revised. The white paper's purpose was to make the case why the DA should agree to either limit or withdraw the subpoena, which it did over fifty densely argued pages. It'd taken a lot of hours to put together; Duncan was skeptical that anyone in the DA's office would even bother to read it.

"As you know," Blake began, "Roth Properties has already turned over roughly one hundred thousand pages of its files to your office. It has cost Roth in the neighborhood of a quarter million dollars to do so. We have produced at least some documents in each category of the subpoena request where Roth has responsive documents. It would probably cost the company another half million dollars to finish producing every possible document. We believe that Roth Properties has made a good-faith showing here, and there's simply no value in its files for what you're investigating. Roth is merely the developer; they were not involved in day-to-day discussions or decisions concerning safety issues."

"I appreciate your position," Sullivan said. Duncan was surprised by how subdued the ADA seemed; he'd expected someone distinctly feistier to be running the DA's bureau that focused on organized crime. "As you can imagine, we are still fairly early in the process of reviewing the files your client has turned over. I don't have an army of associates at my disposal to do such things."

"Of course," Blake said. "Our white paper provides a summary of what we've turned over so far, for your convenience. Nothing that we've given you from Roth's files is relevant to what you're investigating."

"How do you know precisely what we're investigating?" Sullivan said, his voice still neutral.

Blake took a moment, his version of registering surprise. "I assumed the sole focus of your investigation was whether there had been either negligent or deliberate failures in the construction techniques or in the safety precautions that led to the accident. Does your case go beyond that?"

"You know what I have had a chance to review?" Sullivan said casually, like he was merely sharing an interesting cocktail party anecdote. "Invoices. There sure are a lot of invoices on a big construction project. But one thing I noticed is that the failure to provide secondary support for the concrete while it settled? It was all billed by Pellettieri, even though the work was never performed. Indeed, we're finding a whole host of things that Pellettieri was paid for, but which appear never to have been done."

"You're saying that Pellettieri was robbing my client?" Blake asked.

Sullivan offered something between a shrug and a nod. "We don't have a final number yet, but it looks to me to be at least three million dollars' worth of man hours and materials that were bought and paid for but never delivered."

Blake allowed himself a quick look over at Lily, whose own expression indicated that this was coming as a surprise to her as well. Duncan, on the other side of Lily from Blake, offered a slight shake of his head, but Blake didn't glance in his direction. "I don't know anything about that," Blake said. "But I don't see how Roth's files would be relevant."

"We can probably agree to limit the scope of the subpoena a little," Sullivan said. "But we're certainly going to need every financial document, and every communication between anyone at Roth and anyone at Pellettieri. Because if the invoices were paid and the work wasn't done, where did the money go?"

BLAKE WAITED until they were packed into the back of a cab before turning on his two associates. "How the fuck didn't we know about this?" he demanded.

Lily was in the middle seat, between Duncan and Blake, which meant that she was largely blocking Duncan's view of their boss. "We wouldn't be able to see it from Roth's files," she said. "Not unless somebody there had caught it. We can't tell from a paid invoice that the work wasn't done."

Blake seemed at least partially mollified. "Sounds to me like Sullivan is gearing up for a good old-fashioned organized-crime prosecution," he said. "This sort of skimming from construction is usually a mob thing. Wasn't there something with the concrete company a couple of years ago?"

Duncan nodded. "Pellettieri's brother went to jail on a racketeering charge. I gather most of the concrete industry in the city was connected twenty years ago, though there've been a lot of prosecutions since then."

"I guess the good news for our client is, sounds like this guy Pellettieri owes them some money," Blake said. "Gives me a way to spin it when I call and tell them they've been ripped off."

·14·

LEAH ARRIVED an hour before her father's seventieth birthday party was scheduled to begin. The house she'd grown up in—a four-story town house on East Seventy-second, between Madison and Park avenues—usually felt ghostly when she returned to it, but this evening it was already bustling with the catering crew setting up.

Leah ignored the swirl of preparation as she searched the house for her father. She was dressed for the party in a backless Dior dress. She preferred business attire, the anonymity it gave her, but she also recognized that one advantage of her thin frame was that it was well suited to cocktail dresses.

She finally found her father in the back garden, where he was smoking a cigar. He was wearing a dress shirt and blazer with no tie, his version of party casual.

"Happy birthday, Daddy," Leah said, kissing him in greeting.

"Where's your brother?" Simon asked.

"God knows I actually am my brother's keeper," Leah replied. "But that doesn't mean I always know his whereabouts."

"The mayor canceled," Simon said grimly. Leah could tell he was in a foul mood, which didn't come as a surprise. Her father had been cajoled into throwing the party, despite protesting that no birthday after thirty was cause for celebration.

"I'm sure a person or two worth talking to will show up."

"I actually enjoyed socializing back when your mother was alive," Simon said, giving his town house a puzzled look, as though he were seeing it for the first time. "She was a gifted hostess."

"I remember," Leah said softly, looking at her father. While most men his age of comparable wealth and position had helped themselves to second or even third wives by now, usually younger versions of their predecessors, Simon had been married to Leah's mother for nearly twenty-five years, only her death from cancer during Leah's senior year of high school separating them. Although he'd had the occasional involvement over the past decade or so, as best Leah could tell her father had never come close to remarrying. While she was fully aware that Simon was often calculating and even brutal in his treatment of others in business, as far as she knew he'd been a good and faithful husband. A fundamentally conservative man, Simon believed in marriage, in its civilizing influence. He made no secret of his disappointment that both his children had entered their thirties without wedding rings.

Leah dutifully stood by her father's side as the first guests arrived, shrugging aside her own discomfort at filling her mother's role. Stripped of his customary bluster, Simon was visibly ill at ease in the role of jovial host.

Jeremy didn't show up until the party was well under way. Leah made a beeline over. Jeremy saw her coming and offered a fuzzy smile. "Dad's already pissed at you," Leah said. "So don't act too stoned in front of him."

"I'm not stoned," Jeremy said, some vague approximation of offense on his face.

Leah did not even pause to consider whether she bought his denial. "You know, this might be a good time in your life to maybe take stock of some things. Perhaps learning something from recent events might not be a bad idea for you."

Jeremy pretended he thought she was kidding, offering her a toothy grin. "But then what would you do all day?" he asked.

Leah didn't feel like the usual banter with her brother. She spotted Duncan Riley over at the bar, glass in hand, looking alone and uncomfortable. "I've got to go talk to someone," she said.

Jeremy leered at her. "I heard you were bringing a date here tonight. Very brave."

Leah ignored this—Jeremy teased her about boys like they were still in high school. She hadn't met anyone her brother was involved with in as long as she could remember. "Stay away from Dad and try not to cause any trouble," she said.

DUNCAN WAS doing his best not to gawk at his surroundings. He felt the same way he had during his first week at Harvard, wandering around the campus like a tourist rather than a student, staring at the ornate buildings, trying to grasp all the accumulated power and influence they carried. Duncan was now used to being around millionaires: many of his firm's partners cleared a couple million a year. But this was on a different level: he guessed a town house like this must be worth tens of millions, not to mention the lavish furnishings and high-priced art on the walls.

"You don't look like you're enjoying yourself."

Duncan turned to the voice of Leah Roth. She looked different; her hair was down, and she was wearing a sleeveless dress that hugged her willowy frame. There was a softness to her, a femininity that Duncan hadn't previously seen. For the first time Duncan allowed himself to entertain the thought of going to bed with her. Over Leah's shoulder he saw Jeremy Roth staring at him, his upper lip curled slightly.

"Actually, I was just plotting how to steal that painting," Duncan replied, nodding to the late-period Picasso on the wall behind the bar.

"It's wired," Leah said. "To an alarm, I mean. You'd better cut the power or wait until the next blackout."

Duncan, who had mainly been looking at the painting because he didn't know what else to do with himself, turned back to it. It was a portrait of a couple, their complexions baby blue in color, the man holding a sword. Duncan guessed it was a riff on one of the old masters, perhaps Rembrandt, a musketeer channeled through abstraction. "Do you think someone would stop me if I just grabbed it off the wall and made a sprint for the door?"

"Well, there're at least three people in the room carrying concealed weapons."

Duncan laughed; Leah's expression didn't change. "You're serious?" he asked.

"I'm not sure they'd actually shoot you if you tried to make off with the painting—as you probably know, New York's got pretty stringent laws on the justified use of deadly force—but I can't promise they wouldn't."

Duncan had understood that this was a different sort of party from those he was used to; he hadn't expected that to include armed guards. "Any particular reason for the show of force?"

"It's not a party without firearms."

A black man in his late forties came over and greeted Leah. He was tall—easily six-three—in a perfectly tailored suit, with a shaved head and a trimmed goatee. Duncan had noticed the man earlier—he was one of the few nonwhite people at the party.

"We were just discussing whether Duncan here would get shot if he made a dash for the exits with our Picasso. Darryl, would you shoot?"

The man turned to Duncan. "You actually want that, or you're just thinking about what it's worth translated into money?"

"I like it," Duncan said. "Though I can see why not everybody would."

"Actually, Darryl," Leah said, "this is the lawyer I mentioned to you the other day."

Duncan didn't understand what was going on, but he saw the man stiffen, giving him an abrupt once-over. He looked at Leah questioningly. She looked back at him with a slight smile that he couldn't read. Not sure what else to do, Duncan extended his hand to the man, introducing himself.

Darryl looked at Duncan's hand, holding the pause just long enough for it to be awkward before shaking it.

"So are you finding your pro bono work livelier these days?" Leah asked.

Duncan put it together: this was Darryl Loomis, the man who ran the security firm that Fowler had worked for. He felt blindsided. "I take it Blake talked to you?" he said to Leah.

"And I in turn ran it by Darryl."

Duncan looked back at the grim-faced Darryl, doing his best to appear contrite. "I'm sorry about Mr. Fowler," he said. "And sorry we're on opposite sides of the case, as it were."

"You got a job to do," Darryl said.

"I appreciate that."

Darryl smiled, viciously. "Course, Sean was just doing his job too. In fact, doing his job was the last thing he ever did."

SIMON ROTH was in the midst of quietly scolding his son when a heavy hand fell on his shoulder. Simon turned, found himself looking down into the raised red face of Sam Friedman. "You're too short for that gesture, Sam," Simon said.

"You've got a lot of fucking nerve," Friedman said.

"Thank you," Simon said. "You do too. But what're you talking about?"

"Inviting me to your birthday party while you're suing me for a hundred and fifty million."

After making his fortune in real estate, Samuel Friedman had bought the *New York Journal* fifteen years ago, back when a newspaper was still considered a trophy worth owning. Friedman was Roth's age, the two men encountering each other at board meetings, benefits, and cocktail parties a few times a year. They were too alike to ever be anything more than brusquely cordial to each other.

"The lawyers came up with the numbers; you know that," Simon said. "And it's not like I'm suing *you*."

"Sure it is," Friedman said. "Whose pocket do you think the money comes out of?"

"Your insurance company's," Simon said with a laugh. "In any event, I'm pleased to see it didn't keep you from coming tonight."

"I came to tell you you've got a lot of fucking nerve."

"That's what everyone comes for," Simon said. "But they stay for the crab cakes."

"Seriously, thirty years we've known each other, and you don't even call before unleashing the dogs?"

"What were you going to do? The article had already run. And besides, I thought you didn't interfere with the content of the paper."

"Interfere, no, but my guidance is certainly listened to. You know what's happening to the newspaper business? The *Journal* lost twelve million dollars last quarter. Last fucking quarter! You put our ad revenue on a chart, it looks like a guy jumping off a cliff. That paper needs legal bills like it needed that asshole Craig to come up with free Internet listings."

"You didn't buy a newspaper to get rich, Sam."

"I didn't buy it to piss money away either. We can't resolve this thing like gentlemen?"

Simon smiled, his attention caught as Steven Blake approached them. Blake saw who Simon was talking to, and immediately turned on his heel. "Perhaps we can," Simon said. "But not here. My wife strictly forbid me from doing business at a party we were hosting."

"Your wife's dead, Simon," Friedman said, not unkindly.

"But I still follow her rules," Simon replied.

OBEYING HIS father's hissed order, Jeremy Roth sought out Mattar Al-Falasi. To his surprise, he found Mattar smoking a cigarette in the garden, a glass of whiskey in his hand.

"I didn't know you drank," Jeremy blurted, before wondering whether pointing out that a Muslim was drinking alcohol was some kind of faux pas.

"I don't in front of my father," Mattar said. His English was very fluent, crisp, his accent a slight variation on an upper-class Englishman's. Mattar was tall and thin, with a beard he kept trimmed to stubble. He combed his dark hair forward, giving him a boyish look, though he was just a couple of years younger than Jeremy. "He knows I drink occasionally."

"Me either," Jeremy said. "In front of your father, I mean, not mine."

Mattar smiled before taking a drag of his cigarette. "The other night at the restaurant, yes. My father appreciated the gesture, I am sure. He can seem old-fashioned, especially when in a city like this. But then I suppose fathers always seem old-fashioned to their sons."

"He couldn't make it tonight?" Jeremy said, struggling to keep his wandering mind on the topic at hand.

"He and my brother had to go to Washington."

"Business?"

"We like to think we have friends in your country as well, not just people interested in our business."

"Of course," Jeremy said, offering up a smile, worried again that he'd just offended Mattar.

"Many of our friends live in your capital, of course."

"Makes sense," Jeremy said, wondering how many American politicians this Middle Eastern family had in its pocket.

"But my father wanted me to stay in New York so that I could come here tonight."

"Just for our party? You certainly didn't have to stay for this."

Mattar took a sip of his whiskey. "Birthdays are important. Seventy years—a milestone, yes? My father thought it important that someone from our family be here."

"We certainly would have understood, especially if you were all out of town," Jeremy said, finding the whole thing somewhat ridiculous. There were a couple hundred people at the party; one less wouldn't have been missed. Then again, his father was precisely the sort of person who would stew over who hadn't come, ignoring all of those who had, so maybe Mattar had a point.

"Just as you did not drink wine at dinner the other night, so it was important for one of us to be here tonight. There can be no business without respect."

"Sounds like something my father would say."

Mattar nodded solemnly, as if he and Jeremy had just agreed on a matter of grave concern. "The traditions are important, of course, but men like you and I know the world has changed. When I am in Dubai, I act according to what is expected of me there. But when in New York, I like to enjoy those things that New York offers."

Mattar looked at him meaningfully as he spoke. Jeremy's present state of mind was working against him; he was too fucked up to get a clear read on Mattar. The guy was clearly not one to come out and say anything in a straightforward way. But Jeremy was pretty sure he understood what Mattar was getting at. "New York can certainly be a lively place," he said. "Especially after dark. I can show you around sometime—a night on the town."

"If it would not be an imposition," Mattar said immediately, smiling, letting Jeremy know he'd understood correctly.

Jeremy grinned back. Let's see his father or, God forbid, his sister fill this role. But then again, presumably neither of them had any interest in being the company pimp.

"A LOVELY party, Simon," Steven Blake said.

"Is it?" Simon replied. "I haven't really noticed."

"And what a wonderful assortment of people you've gathered."

"How many business cards have you handed out?"

"I assure you I'm well past the point where I come to parties to drum up business."

"The truth is, I haven't enjoyed a party since Rachel died," Simon said. "She was the social one. Not like that's a secret."

"Michele complains that she never sees you," Blake said.

"Why isn't she here tonight?"

"I can't seem to drag her out to the city anymore. She's out in Amagansett pretty much year-round," Blake said. His third marriage was to a woman fifteen years his junior. Although still in her forties, Michele had seemingly tired of city life, spending even the winter months in the Hamptons. It was a white lie that Michele complained about not seeing Simon; as soon as they'd married Michele had lost all pretense of interest in Blake's business friends.

"Leah tells me she invited a young lawyer from your firm here tonight," Simon said. "The one you brought to the meeting the other week."

"He mentioned it," Blake said. "I was a tad surprised, I'll admit, but he's one of our real up-and-comers. Who knows, he might even be the next Steven Blake."

"I certainly didn't raise Leah to fraternize with the help."

Blake wasn't entirely sure of the extent to which this was a joke. "Like it or not, the next generation is knocking at the door for both of us. I hope my firm will continue to represent Roth Properties for decades to come."

Leah came over, the two men falling silent at her approach. "You two better not be plotting business," she said. "Have you talked to anyone you don't already know tonight?" Leah asked her father.

"If I don't know them, the fuck are they doing at my party?"

Leah rolled her eyes before turning to Blake. "Was he always like this, and I was just too young to remember?"

"Simon used to respond to prodding better," Blake replied. "But I don't think his fundamental nature's changed."

"I saw that Jeremy was off making friends with Mattar," Leah said to her father. "Surely if he can mingle you can."

"But he won't even remember doing so when he wakes up tomorrow."

"Don't exaggerate," Leah said.

"Don't cover for him," Simon replied.

Duncan had approached the three just in time to overhear Simon's last remark. "Excuse me," he said apologetically. "Sorry to interrupt. I just wanted to say good night."

"Going back to the office, I hope," Blake said in a flat attempt at banter, while Simon Roth looked at Duncan like he'd never seen him before.

"Leaving so soon?" Leah said, just as the pause was growing uncomfortable. "But we've hardly had a chance to talk. Come, we'll go for a quick stroll before you go."

"A stroll?" Duncan asked.

"In our garden."

Duncan followed Leah out the back. The garden space was about eight hundred square feet, slightly larger than Duncan's entire apartment. Other than a couple of stray smokers near the doorway, it was unoccupied. A slatted wooden fence enclosed the yard, only the top windows of the neighboring apartment building visible. Leah led the way to the outer edge, which Duncan realized was likely the only place at the party where they could actually be alone.

"So I'm sorry you didn't have a good time tonight," she said.

Duncan forced a smile, looking over at Leah, whose own gaze was fastened up at the night sky. "Who said I didn't have a good time?"

"People who are having a good time at a party don't generally leave in less than an hour."

"I don't know anyone here other than you and my boss," Duncan said. "And you have hostessing duties, and my boss is my boss."

"I'm sorry if I've put you out. I realize you probably felt like you couldn't say no when I invited you."

"I wanted to come," Duncan said quickly.

"Really? And why was that?"

Duncan didn't have an answer handy, as Leah had obviously suspected. But he was quick on his feet, which was what she was presumably testing. "I figured this was part of the process by which we become allies."

Leah smiled at this; Duncan thought it the most genuine smile he'd seen from her. "That was exactly my intention," she said. "But I'm afraid I fell short on the execution. You have my apologies for that."

"You have nothing to apologize for."

"Blindsiding you with Darryl like that. It was incredibly rude of me."

Duncan wondered if Darryl was at this party as a guest or if he was working, or some combination of the two, but it wasn't a question he was going to ask. "I'm sure you didn't mean to blindside me," he said.

"Oh, but I did," Leah exclaimed, smiling and touching Duncan's arm. "It was absolutely premeditated."

Duncan was unsure whether Leah was actually trying to start a fight, or if this was more in the way of a display of power. He guessed the latter: she must know he wouldn't fight back. Perhaps she was just again putting him in his place. "If there was a moral to the story, I may have missed it."

"It seemed important somehow for the two of you to meet. You do similar work for us, though I don't know if you see it that way, and I think it's helpful if everybody has a human face. Sometimes it's easier to do your job when you forget there are people on the other end; I get that. But we want both you and Darryl on *our* side at the end of the day, not opposed to each other."

Duncan didn't like where this was going. "Listen," he said. "If you guys aren't comfortable with our handling the Nazario case, just let me know and I'll bring it to Blake's attention."

"Don't be silly, Duncan," Leah said. "I've spoken to Blake about it myself. And Darryl understands too."

"He didn't seem all that understanding."

"Understanding and liking are two different things," Leah said. "So you're not going to tell me why you didn't have a good time tonight?"

"It's not that I didn't," Duncan said. "But this isn't my part of town, if you know what I mean."

"Are you sure? Harvard Law, Blake and Wolcott—aren't those just means to an end?"

"To what end?"

"To be here," Leah said. "This is inside. This is behind the magic curtain."

Duncan looked up at the brightly lit house, the shadowy figures moving around inside, as if expecting to see Leah's metaphor somehow brought to life. "Maybe I'm not inside yet."

"Of course you're not. I don't blame you for feeling aware of that, but I'm surprised it registers as flight rather than fight with you."

"Sorry to disappoint. Though I'm not exactly sure what fighting would look like in this context."

Leah studied him, looking vaguely disappointed. It was clear that he'd let her down somehow, but Duncan didn't understand what it was she'd been expecting. "Is this all just work to you?" she asked.

Duncan was still trying to read her and not having any luck. "I'm not sure I know what you're asking," he finally said.

"Right now. Standing here with me in my garden, is this just you being a good soldier for your firm?"

Duncan looked away, smiling, then back at Leah, whose own expression hadn't changed. "If you're asking whether I enjoy talking to you, yes, I do. Do I think you're maybe having some fun keeping me on my toes? Yes again."

"Point taken," Leah said. "If I promise to be on best behavior, would you like to get dinner sometime? And don't say yes just because I'm a client. Although of course I am."

"I'd like that," Duncan said.

"Good. Well, then, I guess you're free to go," Leah said.

·15·

HAVING GROWN up in a housing project, Rafael found many aspects of Rikers Island familiar. He was used to harsh institutional surroundings. Jail was worse, of course: the brutal, numbing fact of confinement, the claustrophobia that came with knowing you were stuck, barely seeing the light of day, the constant hum of menace from both fellow prisoners and the guards. At least you could leave the project when things got to be too much, just head out the door and keep walking.

Rafael was doing his best to keep to himself, head down, not draw any attention. The place was too crowded and intrusive to allow someone to go unnoticed, but Rafael could carry himself hard enough that nobody was looking to punk him.

The one good thing coming out of facing a murder charge was that it got Rafael his own cell. For his first week at the jail, he had been housed in what was known as the projects, large open bullpens with fifty or so bunk beds. But then he'd been moved to maximum security, where every inmate got his own cell.

Rafael had been placed in a block of seventy-five prisoners. It was split roughly evenly between blacks and Hispanics, plus a handful of white guys. During the afternoon their individual cells were unlocked and they were allowed to hang out in the common area, which was basically a stretch of brightly colored plastic chairs, with a small wall-mounted TV on either end. People generally clustered around the tables near the TVs, blacks around one, Hispanics the other. There were four phones in the common area, which were also divided up by race. A white guy who wanted to use the phone had to pick his spots, and make it quick.

There was a delicate balance of power between the black gangs and the Latino gangs; from the phones to the cafeteria tables, pretty much everything was controlled by one group or the other. Segregation was virtually complete: everyone stuck with their own kind; doing otherwise risked violence. The racial hostility was far worse than anything Rafael had ever experienced.

Rafael got the bitter joke that what was keeping him relatively safe in jail was that as an accused murderer he was considered too dangerous to be put in the general population. But on the other hand most of the people in his cell block were facing charges on a violent crime, and the peace that endured was tenuous and uneasy.

The man in the cell next to his, Luis Gutierrez, was also Puerto Rican. Luis was in for armed robbery. He was a few years older than Rafael, short, but with a wrestler's build, a spiderweb tattoo on the side of his neck. Luis clearly wasn't someone that anyone with any sense would ever want to fuck with.

At first glance Rafael had been worried about Luis, but instead the man was friendly from the jump, calling Rafael his brother, introducing him to other Puerto Ricans on the cell block. Rafael couldn't help but appreciate it, but he also knew not to let his guard down.

Other than meals, showers, and exercise, the only time Rafael left the cell block was to work in the jail's laundry room. He'd been hoping to get assigned to work in the kitchen, but no dice. Nobody accused of a violent crime was allowed to work there; the kitchen had more actual and potential weapons than anywhere else in the jail. Instead he spent most of his time preparing the setups for new prisoners. These consisted of a blanket, sheet, towel, soap, toothbrush, and toothpaste. He wrapped everything together in the blanket, creating a little bundle, which he then piled on carts.

He'd spent the morning in the laundry room, his shift ending at noon. From there he went straight to the cafeteria. Like most of Rikers, the dining area was full of bright primary colors—the pastel greens and yellows making Rafael feel like he was stuck in some sadistic version of a preschool. He'd managed to find a seat at the far edge of a table, nobody right near him.

Lunch was a meat loaf so brutally awful Rafael suspected the kitchen of deliberate sabotage. It crumbled, dry as burned toast, and tasted like it had been made out of cardboard mixed with cigarette ash. Rafael was halfway finished eating, forcing the food down, chewing as little as possible to keep actually tasting it to a minimum, when a man sat down directly across from him, looking right at him as he did so. He was a compact Hispanic man, mid-thirties, with buzz-cut hair and a small goatee, a prison tattoo on his right hand. But the striking thing was his direct, friendly look: eye contact with strangers was a rare and potentially dangerous thing at Rikers.

"*Buenos días*," the man said.

"What's up?" Rafael replied, instinct telling him to reply in English. He didn't know who this guy was or what he wanted, which meant he wasn't to be trusted. Answering in Spanish would have created some slight bond between them that he was not willing to concede.

"You don't speak Spanish?" the man asked, looking surprised. His English was good, but with a heavy accent, not that of a native speaker. "You Rafael, right?"

Rafael didn't like it that the man knew who he was. He nodded curtly.

"I'm Armando. Where you come from, Rafael?"

"The Alphabet projects."

Armando cocked his head. He hadn't touched the food on his plate. "No, *amigo*, I mean where you come from."

"I'm Puerto Rican."

Armando waved his hand dismissively, apparently finding that only a statement of the obvious. "Where in Puerto Rico?"

"Vieques," Rafael said. It was basically just a name to him, not a place he had any real sense of connection to.

"My people are in San Juan," Armando said. "We keep track of our own up in here, you know."

"You keep track of all the Ricans in here?" Rafael said. "Must be a busy man."

Armando looked surprised for a moment, then chose to laugh. "It's true they got a lot of us in here, but that's not no joke. You're in here for shooting a white man."

His lawyer had told him not to talk to anyone about his case. Rafael didn't understand how Armando knew so much about him, how he'd come to be on the man's radar. "What you in for?" Rafael said, adding some street to his voice.

"Because I'm a brown man who knows our people got to do for themselves. That makes me a threat to them who run this country."

Rafael tilted his head, not wanting to show too much skepticism, but not buying this either. "They got you in here for representing?"

"They got me in for something they want to call racketeering," Armando said. "But that's just their way of making it into something they know how to deal with. You come up from nowhere, try to get your own for you and your people, they call you a criminal. You go to one of them Ivy League schools and do it, they gonna call you a businessman."

"Got that right," Rafael said. He was pretty sure he saw where this was going, and was confident Armando posed no immediate threat. But that didn't mean Rafael wanted to make an enemy out of him.

"You recognize that we're a people with our own country, right?"

"I grew up here in New York," Rafael said.

"Look around you, yo, you see *America* here? You think this is what America look like to the white boys with all the money? Who you think they put in here? We're the people they don't want out in the street. That includes you, *amigo*, because you're sitting here same as me. A man's gotta know where he's from, because it's only your own people who'll have your back. Not too many can get through this place by themselves."

"I been okay in here. Don't take no shit, don't give no shit—same as out on the street."

"Same game as the street, sure, but motherfuckers play it harder up in here. And it ain't just being safe. It's about doing together with your people."

"I hear you," Rafael said.

"That's all I'm talking, my brother, just listening. Maybe you can learn something about where you belong in this world."

Rafael knew the worst mistake he could make in jail was to get on the bad side of his own. Word would spread that he was unprotected, and the black gangs and the skinheads and every other racist dumb ass would want to take a shot. But he also knew that this was all a sales pitch, and that what Armando really wanted was to recruit him. "I'm doing all right on my own in here," Rafael said. "Going to keep my head down, do my time."

Armando smiled slightly, although his eyes didn't change. "You're going to need your brothers here," he said. "Everybody does."

·16·

YOU HAVE a lovely home," Candace said to Dolores Nazario. This wasn't quite true: all the careful decoration couldn't disguise the fact that the building itself was falling apart. She'd accepted Dolores's offer of coffee; the two of them were seated in the living room.

"I live here for fifteen years," Dolores said. "I make it the best place I can."

Candace was talking to Dolores because her initial research into Jacob Riis had failed to uncover any hook between the transformation of the project and the murder of the security guard. She had the lawyer, Riley, but that was clearly nowhere near enough, as her editor had made clear. The obvious place to look for the connection was the murder itself. She knew Riley wouldn't talk to her, and getting in to see Rafael at Rikers was going to be a long shot at best. That left the grandmother.

"So as I said on the phone," Candace said, "my focus isn't on the shooting that happened, but on what's going on with all the changes they're making around here. How did you and Rafael end up facing eviction?"

Dolores told the story of the security guard, Fowler, claiming to catch her grandson with a joint, and Rafael's arrest and guilty plea, which then led to the eviction. Candace tried not to show her skepticism, but the story didn't quite add up. "I know how it sound to you," Dolores said. "But I raised Rafa not to lie. He tells me something, swears it's true, then I believe him."

"How did you end up with Duncan Riley as your lawyer?"

"Through my church, they told me to go to this place that helps people with free lawyers. They say they have volunteer lawyers who are helping people. They got us to Mr. Riley."

"Did Mr. Riley tell you that he's also the lawyer for Roth Properties, the developer who's behind all the changes here?"

Dolores looked uncomfortable with the question. "He tells us that he do work for Roth, yes, but Mr. Riley say that is no problem because it is the city who is against us."

Candace wasn't going to pretend she understood the nuances of legal ethics, but Riley's involvement with the Nazarios still felt wrong to her. "Roth is one of his firm's biggest clients."

"Mr. Riley, he been working hard for us, taking our side. He went to court, got the case thrown out. Now he trying to get my *nieto* out of jail, doing that for no money."

Candace got the message: she wasn't going to get between Dolores and the lawyer who was trying to get her grandson off a murder charge and herself from being kicked out of her home. Candace was still skeptical that was what Riley was actually doing. "What about the Alphabet City Community Coalition?" Candace asked. "Did you reach out to them about the eviction?"

"I know other people who have gone to them, but nothing happens. I needed a lawyer to help us, not someone to make a protest."

"Other people who were getting evicted had told you the coalition wasn't helpful?" Candace asked, Dolores nodding. "Do you know a lot of other residents who are facing eviction?"

"These security guards, they like to bother people here. Rafa's not the only one."

"What do you think of the idea of what they're doing to Jacob Riis more generally? Mixing market-rate and affordable housing? Couldn't it make things better for the people who live here?"

"It could be good, sure, less crime," Dolores said. "For those of us who get to come back maybe, though how many that will be I don't know."

"You don't think they'll bring everybody back?" Candace asked, not surprised that such rumors would be running rampant at the project.

"They need to make room for the new people, the ones with money. That's why they're getting rid of people like us."

This got Candace's attention. "What do you mean?"

"Like how they're doing with Rafa and me. The security guards, always making up reasons to throw people out of their homes."

Candace leaned forward, unsure what Dolores was getting at. "Are you saying that the security guards are planting drugs on people so they can evict them?"

"Like they did with Rafa, yes. I hear there are many others."

"Do you have proof that this is happening?"

Dolores shrugged. "Me and Rafa, we are proof, yes?"

·17·

DUNCAN FOUND himself buying Professor Nathan Cole an expensive meal. He hadn't been intending to do so, had thought he was just coming to the professor's office, but when he'd arrived Cole had immediately suggested they talk over lunch.

Duncan had obediently followed Cole off of the John Jay campus and over to Eighth Avenue, at which point they'd cut down a few blocks, then over to Gallagher's, one of the city's better steak houses. "I'm not sure we can just get in here," Duncan said.

"I made us a reservation," Cole said. He was a short man with a bad comb-over, wearing corduroys and a blazer, looking like he dressed to ensure that everyone who saw him made him for an academic. "Lunch was the only time I could fit you in."

Duncan understood what Cole was up to: sticking the firm for an expensive meal, the professor taking a little perk from his position as expert. Although he didn't like being taken advantage of, Duncan couldn't get too worked up: the bill would be coming out of the firm's pocket, not his. He'd seen other experts pull similar stunts, snatch every fringe benefit they could get while moonlighting in a lawsuit. Besides, Duncan liked a good steak as much as the next guy.

"So," Duncan asked, after they'd ordered—a filet for Duncan, a rib eye for Cole. "Have you had a chance to look over the gunshot residue report I sent?"

Cole nodded, taking a deep sip from the glass of California old-vine zinfandel he'd ordered. He'd suggested sharing a bottle but Duncan had demurred, citing work. "Do you understand what gunshot residue is?"

Duncan grinned. "For purposes of this conversation, let's pretend I don't."

"Gunshot residue is distinct because it's a fusion of three elements that otherwise don't have occasion to meet: lead, barium, and antimony. When you fire a gun you're essentially making a little explosion that sends the bullet on its merry way. That explosion fuses those three elements and sends a microscopic cloud of them out onto the hand of the person holding the gun. You grab somebody right after he shoots a gun and he's going to have hundreds of these particles on his hand. The thing about those *CSI* shows is all that home-run forensic shit might be true if you caught the guy five seconds after the murder and he was still standing at the crime scene. But once time and distance come into play it's a different story."

"They arrested Rafael about an hour after the shooting," Duncan said. "Are you saying that all the gunshot residue would've worn off?"

"That's one way to look at it. The stuff we're talking about is like talcum powder—it's dust. If you wash your hands thoroughly you might get rid of it."

"What jumped out at me was that the report said the particles were found on Rafael's left hand. He's right-handed."

"That's actually not as significant as you might think. Most people have both hands on or near a gun when firing. Plus it could easily get transferred from one hand to another, or if he held the gun in his non-dominant hand for a second after it'd been fired, like while opening a door or something."

"The report says they found six particles on his hand. Given the time and distance, is that a lot, or a little, or what you'd expect?"

"It's not a lot under any circumstance. The point is that a handful of particles—that could well be incidental contact. Was your guy ever in the back of a police car after he was arrested?"

"Yeah."

"You ran the back of the typical NYPD squad car, you'd easily find a few particles of gunshot residue sitting around in the carpet fibers. With a handful of particles your guy could have picked them up from letting his hand touch the seat cushion just as easily as he could've from shooting a gun. Police stations are also highly likely to have gunshot residue floating around. There've been several instances in which the GSR testing room itself was shown to be contaminated."

"So would your view be that this amount of GSR is inconclusive in terms of showing that my client had actually held a gun?"

"If they'd found a hundred particles, then no way, he'd almost certainly been in contact with a fired gun. But the few particles they found? It could easily be contamination."

"That's great," Duncan said.

"What you need to get is the actual lab notes," Cole said. "They're going to tell you a lot more than the final report does."

Duncan nodded. "So you're saying we really have legit grounds to challenge the GSR evidence?"

"I've learned never to underestimate the extent to which judges are in the DA's pocket. But with anybody who's actually doing their job, then yeah, we've got a fighting chance."

"You think the DA's office realizes that it's weak?"

Cole laughed at the question. "You're at Steven Blake's firm, right?"

"You know Steven?"

"I've seen his name in the paper. I know you guys do all that clash-of-the-corporate-titans stuff. This is what, pro bono for you?"

Duncan stiffened at what he took to be condescension. "We're putting the same resources toward this case as we would any other."

"That wasn't my point," Cole said pedantically. "What I'm saying is, how often do you think a defendant like yours gets to have somebody like me double-check the forensics? What happens is, the DA says they've got gunshot residue on the guy's hands, his public defender tells him he should plead out; plead out he does, and everybody goes home. The reason they don't worry about getting this stuff right is because nine times out of ten nobody checks whether or not they do."

"And you think we can really keep them from bringing it in?"

"Give me a fair-minded judge with an IQ over ninety and I like my chances," Cole said. "So in the New York criminal courts, I'd put it at fifty-fifty."

ALTHOUGH HE'D done his best not to show it over lunch with Cole, Duncan was buzzing from what he'd learned. He was a practitioner of massive, slow-moving, often tedious cases in which success was generally measured by victories so incremental and complex that even other lawyers could scarcely be bothered to understand them.

This was something else. Eliminating the key physical evidence in a murder case—there was something viscerally exciting about it. Of course, even if Cole was right and they could get the gunshot residue thrown out, the police would still have an ex-cop eyewitness and a clear motive. It wouldn't mean in itself that Rafael would walk, not even close, but it would change the momentum, and it would certainly change plea-bargain negotiations.

At a minimum, it was enough for Duncan to go back to Blake with, tell him he needed to keep working the case for a while, at least through the motion to suppress. Duncan hadn't realized how much he'd already come to want to stay on it. Part of it was that everybody went to law school wanting to be Perry Mason. Then there was the undeniable fact that a murder case was much more exciting than what he spent most of his time doing. But there was also the sense that he was actually accomplishing something here, getting a result for his client that another lawyer—one with fewer resources, one who was going through the motions—wouldn't have gotten.

Plus he'd almost blown it. If he hadn't pushed back against Blake, if he'd worried only about finding some character witness in aid of a plea, if he hadn't gone to see Cole, Duncan wouldn't have discovered the weakness in the DA's forensic evidence. He'd almost allowed himself not to do the work, to take a gigantic shortcut he wouldn't have dreamed of taking with a paying client, and as a result he'd almost missed his first break in the case. Duncan felt like he'd betrayed the lawyer's version of the Hippocratic oath: to leave no stone unturned in advancing your client's side. He had Rafael's life in his hands—his actual life—and he'd almost let himself be talked into doing less than everything there was to do. In Duncan's eyes, that wasn't just a mistake; it was a professional sin.

Duncan e-mailed Blake from his BlackBerry as he walked through crowded Midtown streets back to his office, asking for a few minutes of his time when available. He didn't get an immediate reply, which wasn't unusual: getting hold of Blake during business hours generally ranged somewhere between difficult and impossible.

Back at his office, Duncan turned to the libel suit against the *Journal.* The case was a little neglected, nobody at the firm having much enthusiasm for it, the unspoken agreement being that it couldn't be won. Duncan's next task was seeking to uncover Candace's confidential source. He wasn't entirely sure why: doing so probably wouldn't help their case. It would be very helpful if the source repudiated the article, or admitted to lying to the reporter, or had some obvious reason to be bad-mouthing the Aurora. But those were unlikely, and if the source turned out to be someone credible who stood by what Candace had written, then uncovering that person would make winning virtually impossible. The paper didn't have to prove the truth of what they'd printed, only that they hadn't done so with actual malice, and a credible source would provide them with that cover.

Duncan had raised all this, but Blake simply replied that the client wanted them to uncover the source. There weren't that many likely suspects—the information had almost certainly come from an insider in the investigation. The logical assumption was that someone at the DOB had talked in frustration after Durant declined to refer it to the DA's office.

Duncan was finalizing a half dozen deposition subpoenas of the people he considered the most likely. He wanted to prioritize the potential culprits, so he decided to issue the first subpoena to William Stanton, the investigator who'd been in charge of the DOB's probe of the Aurora accident. If anybody was likely to have felt burned by the decision to shut down the investigation it was Stanton.

It was almost eight when Blake finally summoned Duncan to his office. "So I met with Dr. Cole today," Duncan said as he sat down.

Blake frowned slightly. "Who's that?"

"The forensics guy," Duncan said. "About the gunshot residue."

"Did you get closure, or whatever you were looking for?"

"Cole thinks we've got a real shot at tossing the GSR."

Blake started to say something, but caught himself and leaned back in his chair, looking away from Duncan. "Even so," he said after a moment. "They'd still have what, an eyewitness, motive."

"I just don't know if he did it," Duncan couldn't resist saying.

Blake gave him a puzzled look, as if Duncan had just asked him the meaning of life. "Is somebody asking you to know?"

"I understand our focus has been on leveraging a deal, and I under-stand why, but if he's actually innocent shouldn't our focus be on that?"

Blake's annoyance won out. "Jesus, what, you've discovered your *calling* all of a sudden? I let you keep this guy because I could tell you felt sorry for the jam he was in, and I was pretty sure we'd get him a better deal than some public defender. I wasn't looking for you to go searching for the Holy Grail."

"I'm just following the case where it's taking me," Duncan protested, unsure why Blake was reacting this way. "Like I would any other. You want me to take the first halfway decent deal I can get for him, even if I think we can maybe take the state's case apart?"

"Yes," Blake said without hesitation. Duncan looked at him, suspecting he was being fucked with. But Blake's expression did not support that theory.

"But, Steven, I can't just . . . I mean, I'm his *lawyer*."

"And if you had something real—an alibi, a way to get rid of the eyewitness—something that really said he didn't do it—then I'd say go to the wall. But all you've got is that the DA thinks they've got your guy three different ways and you think they've only got him two. It doesn't mean the rest of their case isn't solid. Besides, you've got a lot on your plate here. You know how much our bill to Roth was, just last month? Almost half a million. You know how much of that was you?"

Duncan wasn't comfortable with Blake's sudden shift of direction. "I spent most of my time on their cases."

"Twenty percent. Leah Roth is inviting you to parties, going on walks with you in her old man's yard, for Christ's sake. Having someone like that in your corner when your partnership vote comes up—I don't need to explain that, do I? One of the firm's anchor clients wants you to be a partner here, then you're a lock. Last time I checked, that was what you wanted, right?"

"Of course," Duncan said quickly. Blake had never directly raised partnership like this with him before.

"We play a team sport around here, and I need you on the team. Clear?"

Duncan cleared his throat before he trusted himself to speak. "As a bell," he said.

DUNCAN WAS trying to figure out just how bad this was. He understood what his marching orders were, but he wasn't sure he could follow them. He'd been asked to do a couple of ethically questionable things in the course of his legal career (as had every other firm lawyer he knew), but this was the first time he was being asked not to put his client's interests first. It felt like crossing a different sort of line.

But then again, it wasn't like Blake was asking him to take a dive on the case. Most criminal cases ended with a guilty plea, after all. Blake was just trying to make sure he kept his eye on the ball, that he should take what he had and go to the DA and see where they were.

Much as he wanted to believe it, Duncan wasn't sure that was true. He needed a second opinion, somebody who knew Blake but who wasn't involved in the murder case.

Duncan walked down to Lily's office. They'd been through the wars together, and he trusted that he could talk to her about such things.

Lily was in her office, some obscure trip-hop playing on her Bose iPod dock as she typed away on her computer. "Can I interrupt?" Duncan asked.

"You just did," Lily replied, but she leaned back in her chair, giving Duncan permission.

He closed her door and sat down. Duncan knew the broad outline would be enough for Lily to get the picture. It took him only a couple of minutes to get her up to speed. "So what do you think?" Duncan asked once he was finished.

Lily hadn't looked at him while he was talking, which was typical for her when concentrating. Now she looked over, twisting up one side of her mouth. "You sound pretty fucked," Lily said.

Not exactly what Duncan wanted to hear, though he wasn't sure how serious she was being. "I hear what Blake's telling me. But I have a job to do. I don't romanticize being a lawyer—God, I hope I don't—but I do believe in it. I mean, it's something more than just being a whore in a suit."

"First I'm hearing of it."

Duncan ignored Lily's reflexive sarcasm. "Loyalty. To our clients. That's the difference. You say you're somebody's lawyer, that *means* something. You fight for them, even when you know full fucking well that they don't deserve to win. That's the job, right? I don't do that, I don't follow through for Rafael because it's a pro bono case and I've got work to do—then what am I?"

"I have no idea what you can live with," Lily said. "But Blake's telling you to cut bait. If you really think that goes against your client's interest, then you're basically fucked."

"But if I figure out a way to really win it, don't you think Blake will come around?"

"Maybe what he's telling you is it was good for the firm to help this guy out when he first got indicted and his name was in the paper, but it's not good for the firm to take the case to trial."

Duncan had wondered if it could be something like that. He hoped that wasn't it, because that would mean the firm was putting its own interests above those of its client. While he didn't think himself naive about the fundamentally mercenary nature of his employer, he wasn't willing to accept that they would take it that far. "You really think the Blake would do that?"

Lily shrugged. "We don't have a sight line on all the angles here."

"So what would you do if it was you?"

Lily looked uncomfortable with the question. "Play out the string as long as you can. Get the best possible deal for your guy—it's obviously up to the client whether to take it or not. At the end of the day he's a nonpaying client who's going to be in your life for one case. You and me, the Blake babies—you know what partnership here brings."

"Don't question, follow orders, that's your advice?"

Lily shrugged. "That's why they call it work."

·18·

DUNCAN TOOK Leah to Jean Georges, a serious contender for the title of the city's best restaurant. It wasn't his normal idea of a first-date place—if this was, in fact, a date. But he figured Leah was used to the finer things, and he felt obligated to take her to the nicest place he could get a table at, although he wasn't able to get a reservation until nine forty-five.

"Tell me," Leah said as they were seated, "do you always eat dinner so late?"

"Best I could do," Duncan replied.

"Did you have trouble getting a reservation? You should have told me; I could've taken care of it."

Duncan didn't know whether Leah was once again being purposely provocative or simply condescending. He decided that by now he had license to ask. "Was that deliberate?"

"Was what deliberate?" Leah said innocently, though Duncan wasn't buying it.

"Your putting me in my place."

Leah tilted her head, but with the ghost of a smile. "I did no such thing."

"So it wasn't deliberate?"

"My point was simply that you should avail yourself of whatever shortcuts I could provide."

Duncan smiled, though he knew his patience for this would quickly wear thin. "Hey, I'm a modern man," he said. "You want to make any future dinner reservations that the two of us may need, by all means be my guest."

"I've offended you again, haven't I?"

"I'm a lawyer," Duncan said. "People say mean things to me all the time."

"And yet here I am, constantly on your wrong side," Leah said. "Let's talk about something more pleasant. Do you have siblings?"

"I have a half sister and brother, but nobody full."

"Are you close to them?"

Duncan was uncomfortable with the topic, but not inclined to lie. "Not really, to be honest."

"Are they still in Michigan?"

Duncan nodded, a little surprised that Leah remembered where he was from.

"You ever go back?"

"Not really," Duncan said with a shrug. "Christmas maybe."

"Never thought of returning to your home state after law school?" Candace asked. "They must need lawyers in Michigan."

"I'm sure they do," Duncan said. "But they don't need me."

"Too small-time for you?" Leah said with a smile.

"I doubt that surprises you."

"Some people like where they're from."

"Sure," Duncan said. "Though they don't tend to be people from Michigan."

The waiter brought them their first course, fluke with a frozen wasabi sauce that unleashed its flavor as it melted. The restaurant ran like clockwork, the service flawless yet unobtrusive. It'd taken Duncan about five years of living an expensive life in New York to get used to places like this; he assumed Leah took them for granted.

"Family is important, of course," Leah said. "But there are times when I would love nothing more than to be on the other side of the country from mine. What do you think of my brother?"

"I don't know him," Duncan replied, relieved that he didn't, since it wasn't a question he would be inclined to answer. "I've only met him the one time at your office."

"Jeremy is very weak," Leah said gravely. She was looking closely at Duncan. "It gives me no pleasure to admit that, but it's impossible to deny. The truth is, that's probably the real reason my father came around on my joining the business. At some point he realized my brother wasn't going to have what it takes to run it, at least not without a lot of help."

Duncan was surprised that Leah was confiding in him about this, but tried not to show it. "Weak how?"

"My brother's a prisoner of his appetites. He's got no control over them. He's been that way since we were growing up. Sometimes I think I'm as much his parent as his sister."

"Does it interfere with his work?" Duncan asked, probing for why Leah was telling him.

"It interferes with everything, unfortunately. But I do what I have to do. As you probably realize, my family *is* Roth Properties. What's bad for our family is bad for the company, and vice versa. So protecting my brother from himself isn't just about protecting him; it's about protecting everything we have."

Duncan wasn't sure if this was a personal or professional confession. "I understand."

"Do you?" Leah asked, and in the look she gave him Duncan realized that he wasn't at all sure he did.

"I think so," Duncan said. One waiter removed their empty plates as another poured them more wine. Duncan leaned back, muttering thanks to the waiters while waiting for them to leave. Was Leah saying that her brother needed his help? Was he in some kind of legal jam she was trying to work her way up to discussing? "Is there something specific?" he asked Leah once they were alone again.

"Not just now," Leah said dismissively. Whatever she'd been getting at, she clearly didn't want to articulate it more than she already had. "So what's going on with your murder? You still think it's going to plead out quickly?"

Duncan was getting used to Leah's abrupt changes of subject. "I'm not sure," he said, instinctively not forthcoming when talking about a case with someone other than the client.

"What's changed?"

"We're challenging the forensics. It's not enough to win the case for us, but obviously it could weaken it."

"Are you challenging the science just to be doing something, or are you challenging it because there's something wrong with it?"

Duncan was surprised by Leah's interest in the murder, but then again he supposed everybody found such cases interesting, at least on some level. "It's for real. It doesn't exonerate my guy, but it's something."

"You seem like you're enjoying it," Leah said, leaning back as a waiter put another course, this one some elaborate duck confit, before them, Duncan only half listening as the waiter detailed what he was serving them.

"Honestly?" Duncan said, before digging in. "It's the scariest thing I've ever done as a lawyer. But I suppose I enjoy that aspect of it."

"Fear's the great motivator, after all."

"Indeed," Duncan said. "It either blankets you like a fog or it charges you up. Me it charges."

Leah was again giving him her openly evaluating look, though this time it seemed more clearly tinged with approval. "So, Duncan," she asked, "are you ever going to get comfortable with me?"

Duncan smiled, meeting her calm gaze. "How do you know this isn't my version of comfortable?"

"Is it because I'm a client, or because I'm rich?"

"Is both an option?" Duncan said.

"I hope it's not because of my tendency to be blunt."

"If we're being serious, it's mainly about your being a client. I'm not used to socializing with my clients."

"Blake socializes with my father."

"That's not the same."

"Why?" Leah said, smiling at him, but with some challenge in her look. "Because I'm a girl and you're a boy?"

The fact that he'd half expected this conversation didn't make having it any more comfortable. "What do you want me to say?"

"I'm aware that you're a boy. I assume you're aware that I'm a girl."

"Do you want me to be aware that you're a girl?"

"Now you're just trying to get me to do your work for you," Leah said.

Duncan offered a smile and a mock salute; any ambiguity as to whether they were on a date pretty much dissipated. "Blake might not be too happy if he knew we were having dinner," he said.

"Why would he care?"

"I can think of a few different reasons," Duncan said. "None of which does it strike me as wise to articulate."

"I fail to see how our having dinner is going to affect the institutional relationship between my family's business and your law firm."

"Me either," Duncan said. "But that doesn't mean I'm going to tell Blake about it."

AFTER DINNER the two of them stood outside the Trump building where Jean Georges made its home. "It didn't occur to me that I was taking you to eat inside one of your competitor's buildings," Duncan said. "Is that bad form?"

"He's not our competition," Leah said dismissively. "The Donald's a haircut and a franchising plan, not a real developer."

"I guess that answers that," Duncan said. "Anyway, I enjoyed having dinner with you."

"And I you," Leah said. "So perhaps we shall have to do it again sometime."

"Perhaps we shall," Duncan said with a smile. "Should I get you a cab?"

Leah glanced over at a parked Town Car. "I believe that's my ride," she said. "Can I drop you?"

Duncan wondered how long the driver had been sitting there. He took Town Cars to go to the airport and such, but he'd never had one pick him up after dinner. "It's a short walk," he said.

On his way home Duncan tried to sort out how he felt about Leah, and just what she might be up to. He'd been too on his guard to fully enjoy dinner; her blatant manipulation was equal parts maddening and alluring. It was hard to believe that someone as wealthy and powerful as she was would have any interest in him. While Harvard Law and a job at an elite law firm had given Duncan some access to the corridors of power, he was still very much a minor leaguer compared to the sort of Upper East Side society that Leah had grown up in. And the difference in status between them was only heightened by the fact that his firm did work for her company.

He suspected that these power differentials fed into Leah's interest, that she liked having the control they gave her. Which in turn heightened Duncan's being on his guard with her, not trusting her motives. But Duncan also saw the appeal in distrust, felt the seduction of the way that Leah wielded her power, as well as the lure of what being with someone like her could mean for him, both personally and professionally.

But the fact that she was the heir apparent at a major firm client certainly complicated matters. There was no hard-and-fast rule against a lawyer getting involved with a client, other than for divorce lawyers, but it was generally frowned upon, and Duncan had no doubt that Blake would be pissed. Mixing law firm business and personal romantic pleasure was a dangerous game, one that Duncan knew a more cautious lawyer wouldn't even be contemplating. Perhaps that was why he found himself intrigued.

·19·

AFTER TALKING with Dolores Nazario, Candace had begun looking into other evictions at Jacob Riis. She started out by having the paper's research librarian help her compile a list of recent and pending evictions at the housing project. There turned out to be over two dozen, which struck Candace as a lot, though she didn't really have anything to compare it to. Candace went through the court dockets that were available online, but there was little there that was especially helpful, nothing she saw where anyone was alleging that the evictions were trumped-up.

She put together a list of all the families facing eviction, began working the phone. After a couple of days of making calls and pounding the pavement, she'd come up with a handful of people who claimed that their evictions were a result of drugs being planted on someone—almost always a teenager—by the private security guards. The stories were fundamentally the same, which was the main thing that made Candace believe they were true.

Candace wasn't necessarily looking to establish that the evictions were based on planted drugs, but simply that there were consistent and credible allegations of such frame-ups. But even for that, she needed to get the security guards' side of the story, as well as a better sense of what might actually be behind the evictions.

She thought the best place to start was digging into the murdered guard, Fowler. The shooting was obviously the story's biggest hook. The reporter who was covering the murder, Alex Costello, had quoted Fowler's ex-wife in a story. Candace walked across the newsroom to the metro section, tracking down Costello.

Costello was loudly chewing gum while writing an e-mail. He wore a loose tie, the top button of his shirt was unbuttoned, and his hair looked like it hadn't been touched since he'd gotten out of bed that morning. His cubicle was a complete mess, filled with a variety of odd objects, including what looked to be some kind of miniature fish tank.

"What the hell is that?" Candace asked.

"Sea-Monkeys," Costello said. "Apparently the birthday gift for the man who has everything."

"It just looks like a jar of dirty water," Candace said, leaning down. Looking closer, she could see tiny buglike creatures twitching through the murk. "Gross. Anyway, I'm looking into a piece for the I-team that may have a little overlap with a story you covered."

"Let me guess, the Fowler murder?"

Candace was surprised that Costello had figured it out. Because she could tell Costello wanted her to ask how he had, she resisted doing so. "I thought it might be helpful to touch base with Fowler's ex. You have contact info for her?"

"I'll call her and set it up," Costello said.

"That's nice of you," Candace said, a little surprised, given how territorial reporters tended to be.

"Sure," Costello said. "When do you want us to go see her?"

"And by 'us' you mean . . . ?"

"The Fowler murder's mine. And I've got the relationship with the weeping widow."

"I'm not interested in the murder itself."

"Then why do you want to talk to her?"

"I'm digging into a broad piece on Jacob Riis," Candace said, not for a second considering a more truthful answer. "Looking at the changes in the projects, who wins and who loses."

"Because it's a Simon Roth thing? The same Roth who's presently suing you, and the rest of the paper, for—what was it? One hundred and fifty million dollars?"

Candace rolled her eyes. "That's just some number they made up to get attention."

"How's that working out for them?"

"Apparently it's doing something," Candace said, "given that you can quote it off the top of your head."

"And you're doing another Roth story?" Costello asked skeptically,

Candace now understanding why he'd assumed she'd come over to talk about the Fowler murder.

"The libel lawsuit has no legs. Nobody's worried about it."

"Even winning it won't be cheap, though. Last I heard, this paper was broke. I heard there's going to be another round of buyouts next month."

"So what, we don't do any more stories about anyone who's rich enough to sue us?" Candace asked. "Because we've got a word for people like that: newsmakers."

"We've also got a word for a reporter who becomes part of the story," Costello said.

Candace was getting tired of this. "We do?"

Costello took a beat. "Actually, no, I guess we don't. But it seems like we should."

"Just give me the damn number," Candace said.

"Not going to happen," Costello said. "She and I have a rapport. You want her, we go together."

CANDACE BARELY knew Alex Costello, but she knew by reputation that he was a gunner. Which likely meant he was either angling to join the I-team or to make the switch over to an editor's desk. It also meant he was going to be a territorial pain in the ass about anything relating to the Fowler murder. Of course, the move he was pulling now to try to latch onto her story wasn't different from what Candace would've done if their positions were reversed. Newsrooms were always competitive places, even more so now that the threat of layoffs was always in the air. Everyone wanted to make themselves indispensable (or they wanted to escape).

None of which meant Candace wouldn't cut Costello out the first chance she got. This was her story, and she didn't plan to share any more than she absolutely had to.

Candace drove them out to Staten Island, which took forever, first navigating Manhattan traffic, then winding their way out to the Verrazano Bridge. Liz Pierce lived in a small house on the South Shore, a neighborhood so suburban it was hard to believe they were still in the city.

Liz was a pale woman in her late forties, gray streaking her hair and lines beginning to spread across the edges of her face. Candace tried to take in the room without being obvious about it, noticing pictures of children, school trophies on the wall, barely restrained clutter. There was the sound of a video game being played somewhere in the house, the occasional taunting of kids' voices.

As agreed, Costello did the talking to start with, catching up with Liz, doing his best to make it seem like they were old friends, rather than a reporter and the ex-wife of a murder victim. Candace sat next to Costello on the living room couch, trying to look pleasantly sympathetic. She was fairly used to barging in on complete strangers at their times of crisis. But it felt much more awkward to be sitting here passively while Costello ran the show than when she was the one working the source.

"So the reason we're bothering you again is, my colleague here, Candace, is doing a broader piece on the changes at Jacob Riis."

"I wouldn't know anything about that," Liz said. "Sean and I've been divorced for a couple of years, and even when we were married he didn't tell me much about his work, going back to when he was a cop."

"People often know more than they realize," Candace said, something she'd said dozens of times before in interviews. "Right now, even basic background is helpful. Do you know when Sean started working security at Jacob Riis?"

"Six months ago, maybe. He was brought over when they first started putting up the new buildings."

"What was he doing before that?"

"The same sort of stuff for the security company. Not always construction security, but that was part of it."

"Had he been on other Roth Properties sites?"

"I think so. Is that who was doing the building in SoHo? The one with the accident?"

SoHo: the Aurora Tower. Candace hadn't had any idea Fowler had worked there, though it made sense that the same private security company would cover multiple Roth construction sites. "Was Sean working there when the accident happened?"

Liz nodded. "I remember him talking about it."

"What did he say?"

"We're divorced," Liz said with a shrug. "I didn't really listen anymore when Sean complained."

Candace saw a way in. "I'm in the middle of a divorce myself," she said. "Not having to listen is definitely one of the bright sides."

"Not that I have an option now anyway," Liz said flatly, looking right at Candace. "Sean being dead."

Candace, caught off guard, sat back in her seat. "Do you remember anything he said about the accident?" she said after a moment.

Liz looked uncomfortable, her eyes losing focus. Candace was not sure if it was that this was dredging up painful memories, or that Liz had a sense she shouldn't be sharing it. "Just that one night when he'd been drinking—as compared to when, I don't know—we were on the phone, arguing about money—our daughter's developing expensive taste in clothes—and he said something about how they could've done something to stop it."

"Who could've done something?"

Liz looked back in the direction of the video game noise, as if hoping her children would provide an interruption. "I just thought he was feeling sorry for himself, trying to find a way to be the victim in something that had nothing to do with him. I wasn't exactly asking follow-up questions. I was pretty much just waiting until he'd talk himself out and I could get off the phone. It took Sean a long time to realize that he and I really weren't together anymore."

"I know how that goes," Candace said, hesitant to try another round of divorce-based bonding. Out of the corner of her eye she caught Costello looking at her, but ignored it. "But he was saying someone at the Aurora could've prevented the accident?"

"I think so, yeah."

It was all she was going to get about the Aurora, Candace realized, but it was potentially quite a lot. She shifted back to what she'd originally come here to ask. "Did Sean ever say anything to you about catching Nazario smoking pot?"

"Sean was a cop for a long time. It would take something a lot bigger than catching a kid smoking a joint for him to brag about it."

"You ever hear him mention Rafael Nazario at all?"

"No."

"What about evictions at Riis? Did he mention anything about families getting thrown out?"

Liz shook her head, frowning. "Why would he?"

Candace ignored the question. "Sean ever talk about any problems he was having at Riis? Any sign of trouble?"

"Nothing like that. He actually seemed pretty happy, at least to the extent that was a possibility for him."

"Was there something in particular that had him feeling good?"

"He'd straightened himself out financially, which made things easier for everybody. He'd gotten behind on child support—this is going back to last year—and he was able to get that back on track. He was picking up stuff he didn't have to—a Wii for Sean Junior, things like that."

"Had he come into some money?"

"He was working a lot of overtime," Liz said. "Apparently there was as much as he wanted, and he was getting time and a half for it. Sean said he'd never had it so good."

"YOU GOT something, didn't you?" Costello asked, once they were back in Candace's car.

Candace shrugged, looking out at the road. "Maybe a lead or two. Nothing direct."

"I want in."

"There is no in," Candace said dismissively, glancing quickly over at Costello.

"What is there then?"

"There's just me looking around is all."

"I'm a good reporter," Costello protested.

"That's great," Candace said. "Best of luck with that."

"If it ties into the Fowler murder, then I should have a role."

"If what ties into the Fowler murder?"

"You're investigating the vic. You must think there's a connection."

"Right now I'm just wandering around in the dark with my hands in front of my face."

Costello was not mollified. "If you get to where it connects to the murder, I need to know," he said. "I'm still working that story."

"Fine," Candace said. "As long as you'll loop me in if anything in the murder shows a connection to Roth, or to evictions at Riis."

"You think there's something wrong with the Nazario eviction, is that it?"

Candace shrugged. "I think there's something wrong somewhere," she said. "Finding out what is the trick of the thing."

·20·

DUNCAN WAS deposing William Stanton, the Department of Buildings' lead investigator into the Aurora Tower accident, in his search for Candace Snow's confidential source. Stanton brought a city lawyer with him to the depo, Grant Sawyer from the Corporation Counsel's office. Duncan was surprised the lawyer hadn't at least tried to quash the subpoena. The *Journal*'s lawyer, Daniel Rosenstein, was present as well.

Duncan planned to get straight to the point, not wanting to spend a lot of time on this depo if Stanton wasn't Candace's source. "Mr. Stanton," he began, after the witness had been sworn in. "You were the primary investigator for the Department of Buildings of the Aurora Tower accident, correct?"

"I was."

"And as the primary investigator, you were charged with drawing conclusions as to the cause of the accident?"

"That's right."

"What were your conclusions?"

"The reinforcing steel that was supposed to support the floor while the concrete was setting wasn't properly anchored," Stanton said in the practiced tone of someone with technical expertise who was used to explaining things to people who lacked it. "Plus they didn't put in the temporary supports to give the concrete time to set. Members of the construction crew had pointed these things out, and that there were visible cracks in the concrete, which meant it was showing the strain of anchoring the structure before setting. Any construction professional who understood the basics of what they were doing would've understood there was a significant risk of collapse. To me it was clearly willful neglect, if not worse."

"In fact, you thought it was potentially criminal, didn't you?"

"I did recommend that it be referred for a criminal investigation, yes. Which is now what's happened."

"You made that recommendation to the DOB at the conclusion of your investigation?"

"I did."

"And initially, did the DOB follow your recommendation?"

"They did not."

"Did they follow your recommendations regarding finding that the safety violations were willful?"

Stanton seemed a little annoyed; whether at what he considered the obviousness of the question, or at the memory of his inability to push his recommendations through, Duncan couldn't say. "No," he said tartly.

"Did you have any conversations with your superiors regarding why your recommendations weren't being followed?"

"My bosses don't explain their decisions to me. Basically the first I learned about it was when I saw the final report."

"Did it bother you that the DOB elected not to follow your recommended findings?"

Stanton smiled slightly. "Anytime someone disagrees with me it bothers me some. It comes from thinking you're always right."

Duncan decided it was time to get to the crux of the matter. "Do you know who Candace Snow is?"

"She's the reporter who wrote a story on the Aurora Tower accident."

"Have you met her?"

"Yes."

Duncan could feel the atmosphere in the room change with Stanton's answer. "Did you talk to her regarding the Aurora Tower accident?"

"Yes," Stanton said without hesitation.

Duncan was a little thrown by how easily Stanton had given it up, but tried not to show it. He took a moment, wanting to be careful and precise with how he phrased the next few questions. "Were you a confidential source on Candace Snow's article in the *New York Journal* regarding the partial collapse of the Aurora Tower?"

"I guess so."

"You guess so? Are you saying you don't know?"

" 'Confidential source' isn't a term I use in my everyday life. I'm not sure exactly what it means. But I told her things on the condition she not use my name. If that's what it takes for me to be a confidential source, then I was."

"Did you ever tell your employer that you were a source for Ms. Snow's articles?"

"No," Stanton said, looking over at Sawyer, who was busy writing on a yellow legal pad. "But something tells me they've pretty much figured it out right about now."

Duncan hadn't given any thought to the possibility that this deposition might get Stanton in trouble with the DOB. Not that it was his problem—collateral damage was part of most lawsuits. "What precisely did you tell Ms. Snow?"

"I'm sure you've read the article."

"I'm asking for your own recollection of what you actually said, not what appeared in the article."

Stanton glared at Duncan, who looked back impassively. "I told her my view of the accident, that it called for a finding of willfulness, which would've led to substantial fines and a referral to the DA for a possible criminal prosecution. I told her that Ron Durant apparently saw it differently. I told her that a month or so later Durant left the agency and joined the Arps Keener architecture firm."

Duncan didn't want to go too far with this, as it could backfire on his client. He knew that Durant was in fact now doing work for Roth Properties, and he understood that it looked bad, despite Roth's insistence that there'd never been any quid pro quo.

"Did you indicate to Ms. Snow that Mr. Durant's conclusions had been influenced by some kind of arrangement whereby Roth Properties would retain him as an architect when he left the DOB?"

"I don't have any evidence that there was some kind of arrangement."

"Were you Ms. Snow's only source within DOB for her article?"

Stanton shrugged. "Didn't ask, and I'm sure she wouldn't have told."

"How many times have you spoken with Ms. Snow?"

"Four, I think."

"Was that four different interviews for her article?"

Stanton shifted in his seat, looking uncomfortable. "Only one real interview," he said. "When she called me the first time I said I'd think about whether I'd speak to her. Then I called her and we talked. Then she called me once more for a quick follow-up as they were getting ready to run the story."

"And the fourth time?"

Stanton paused, glancing at first Sawyer, then Rosenstein. "I called her after I found out I was going to be doing this."

"You called Ms. Snow to tell her you were being deposed?"

"Yes."

"Why?"

Stanton's hesitation was growing. "I didn't want it to come out that I'd talked to her for her story. The whole idea was she was supposed to leave my name out of it. I was hoping maybe her lawyer would be able to keep me from having to do this."

Over the course of his answer Stanton's attention had shifted to Rosenstein, until by the end he was openly glaring at the paper's lawyer, who pretended not to notice.

"Did Ms. Snow ever ask you whether you thought the developer of the Aurora, Roth Properties, had a role in causing the accident?"

"She may have; I don't recall for sure."

"Do you believe that Roth Properties played any role?"

"I couldn't say."

Duncan was a little surprised by this. "Why not?"

"DOB looks at what causes an accident from a physical point of view. A developer would pretty much never play a direct part in that sense."

"So you didn't investigate whether Roth Properties possibly had a role in the accident?"

"That's something the DA would look into, if anyone."

"I take it then that you never suggested to Ms. Snow that Roth Properties was responsible for the accident?"

"No," Stanton said. "And I don't think any of the quotes in the article suggest otherwise."

"If Roth Properties wasn't responsible, why would they seek to derail the investigation?"

"Objection," Sawyer said. "Calls for speculation."

"An investigation generally slows down work at the construction site, which in turn costs the developer money," Stanton said. "So there's that."

Duncan figured he'd pretty much gotten what he was going to get. All that was left was due diligence, making sure Stanton wouldn't make some kind of surprise concession regarding the article's accuracy. Duncan entered a copy of the *Journal* article as an exhibit and proceeded to walk Stanton through it, checking whether there was anything in it he'd disown. As expected, there wasn't: Stanton agreed that he was the unnamed source for the most damning quotes, and that they were accurate statements of his view of the accident.

After Duncan was finished asking questions, Rosenstein took his turn, devoting his time to gilding the lily—establishing that Stanton considered the article to be accurate based on his inside knowledge of the investigation into the accident. As Duncan had feared, uncovering Candace's confidential source had come at the cost of that source fully backing up her article.

Duncan went back to his office after the deposition, unable to cast off a feeling of failure. Blake had understood that outing the reporter's source would likely tank their case, but had instructed him to go ahead regardless. Why? Duncan couldn't answer. He couldn't see the whole picture; that much was clear. It was a feeling he was having more and more.

·21·

DUNCAN WAS back at the DA's office on Hogan Place, this time waiting for a meeting with the ADAs handling Rafael Nazario's case. He was no stranger to negotiating with opposing lawyers, but this felt different: Duncan was used to fighting about money, not over a person's freedom. These ADAs, Danielle Castelluccio and Andrew Bream, pled out criminal cases as their bread and butter; they would be fully aware that this was their world and not his.

Duncan's only previous encounter with the prosecutors had been with ADA Bream at the arraignment. He'd never met the lead prosecutor, but he'd done his due diligence on her. A couple of years older than Duncan, Castelluccio, a Columbia Law grad, had gone straight to the DA after graduation, and had been prosecuting homicides for a few years, already having handled a couple of the office's highest-profile cases.

Bream came and got Duncan from the front waiting area, leading him to a conference room where Castelluccio was already at the head of the table. She rose to shake Duncan's hand. Castelluccio was tall, with a rangy, athletic look. She had long dark hair, matched by a black suit with the jacket buttoned over a white shirt. She didn't smile as they said hello.

"How's life at Blake and Wolcott?" she asked.

"Can't complain," Duncan said, sitting down on one side of the table as Bream sat on the other.

"A couple of people I know from law school went there," Castelluccio said. "Including a good friend. Karen Cleary. Did you know her?"

Duncan hoped his face hadn't betrayed his response. "Yeah, I knew Karen. How's she doing?"

Castelluccio shrugged. "The corporate law thing was never for me, but Karen was one of those people, that's really what she wanted. What happened with the firm wasn't easy for her. Though I think she feels good about standing up for herself with the lawsuit."

"I probably shouldn't really talk about it," Duncan said, pretty much positive that Castelluccio had brought up Cleary just to fuck with him. "The case is still pending and all."

"I guess you want to talk about Rafael Nazario, then," Castelluccio said.

Her tactic had worked; Duncan felt off balance. She was going to be a worthy opponent. "Indeed. I'm going to challenge the gunshot residue."

"Based on what?"

Duncan wasn't about to give Castelluccio a full preview of what he had to attack the GSR, but he'd come to the meeting expecting to give her a thumbnail. "The police stuck Rafael in the back of a cop car without bagging his hands, then checked for gunshot residue a couple of hours later, found just a handful of particles," he said. "He could've picked it up from the backseat just as easily as he could've from firing a gun."

Castelluccio frowned, glancing quickly over at Bream. "We get this sort of GSR evidence admitted all the time," she said. "This doesn't sound like an issue to me."

"My expert feels differently. I'm going to need to get the lab notes underlying the GSR report," Duncan said, taking a letter out of his Kenneth Cole attaché case. "I've put it in writing, just to, you know, put it in writing."

"I don't think we have the notes," Castelluccio said, looking a question at Bream, who nodded. "We just get the report, same as you."

Duncan was in the habit of getting as much of the other side's experts' underlying material as he could; it was always a mistake to take an expert report at face value. "My guy wants the notes," Duncan said. "They're *Brady* material. I'm happy to take this to the Court if it's going to be a problem getting them turned over."

"We don't need to fight about the lab notes," Castelluccio said irritably. "We'll collect them and turn them over."

"Great," Duncan said. "So listen, you don't know me personally, and I'm sure you deal with some defense lawyers who'll file frivolous motions they know they're not going to win. But I'm not filing this just to file it. Before I do, maybe get a different kind of light shining on this case, I thought I'd see what you were inclined to put on the table."

"Your client wasn't arrested because of the GSR. We have motive, an eyewitness. Far as I'm concerned, though, even if your motion was a winner, all it does is knock your guy's conviction chances down to ninety-seven percent from ninety-nine."

"Which is why I'm not asking you to drop the charges," Duncan said with a smile. "I'm asking what your offer is."

Castelluccio made a show of thinking, though Duncan suspected that it was only a show, and that whatever she was about to say was what she'd planned on before he'd walked into the room. "I'll take life without parole off the table, give him twenty-five years."

While Duncan knew little about the practice of criminal law, he knew a thing or two about negotiating with opposing counsel. "This was always really murder two—that's what you were going to offer if I'd just said Rafael was a nice kid."

"No," Castelluccio said. "Good kid doesn't take life without off the table. Your client killed Fowler because of his role in the previous case, which makes this textbook murder one. I'm a straight shooter too—ask around, if you haven't. Way I figure it, Blake and Wolcott can make my life miserable with two years of pretrial motions if you want to. You won't win them but you'll keep me away from all my other cases, so I'm willing to go twenty-five as a reward for your coming to me early. You make me go through a hearing, the deal is off the table."

"I think we understand each other," Duncan said. "Sounds like we both have a little work to do; then we can see where we are."

Castelluccio leaned back in her chair. "So," she said, something between a smile and a sneer on her face, "how are you enjoying slumming so far?"

"Excuse me?" Duncan said, a verbal placeholder as he adjusted to what she'd said.

"Isn't this what this is for you?"

"Rafael's my client," Duncan finally said. He was angrier than he could ever remember being with an opposing lawyer, because as far as he was concerned Castelluccio was challenging his fundamental professional legitimacy. He spoke slowly, his voice low, but was unable to keep the tremor out of it. "It was supposed to be an eviction case; now it's something else. But he's still my client. This isn't what I do, as such, but I'm a lawyer and he's my client and this is the job. You can think of me as a dilettante as much as you like, but I know how to do my job."

"I'm sure you do know how to do your job, Mr. Riley. I'm just not sure that what you're doing here now *is* your job."

"The law's the law," Duncan said, glaring at the ADA.

Castelluccio offered a thin smile. "Is that what they teach at Harvard?" she said.

·22·

T HE MAIN office for the city's Housing Authority was on lower Broadway, steps from City Hall. Candace waited in the ninth-floor lobby for fifteen minutes before Forrest Garber came out to get her, apologizing for keeping her waiting.

"So how's Ben doing?" Forrest asked as he gestured her to a seat across from his desk.

"I don't actually much know," Candace replied.

Forrest looked at her, puzzled. Candace wondered why the hell Ben hadn't told him. "We're separated," she added, not seeing that she had a choice.

Forrest looked even more uncomfortable than Candace felt. "Shit, I'm sorry," he said.

"Not your fault," Candace said, looking around Forrest's office, which was utilitarian in that grim way that only government bureaucracies ever managed.

"So anyway," Forrest said awkwardly, "Ben told me you were interested in the switch to mixed-income over at Riis."

Candace nodded, noticing as she did so that Forrest appeared to be checking her out. She pulled out her digital recorder, showed it to Forrest, who gestured his approval. Candace pressed the record button, then placed the recorder on the edge of his desk. "Right. What's your title here?"

"I'm the deputy manager for policy planning and management analysis. So yes, that does translate into having an active role in the changes to our public housing."

"I understand the general idea of mixed-income housing, and I understand its appeal to your office. But I guess I'm a little surprised that the Authority chose to partner with a private for-profit developer in putting the plan into place."

"That's easy to explain. In a word, money. The Authority is facing a huge budget shortfall, largely because so much of the federal funding for public housing has dried up. Most of our buildings were put up after World War Two, and they were never intended to last forever, or even for as long as they already have. You combine those two things and it becomes impossible for us to do this without the private sector."

Candace was skeptical. "So we end up with for-profit public housing in this country, just like we have for-profit jails and private military contractors?"

Forrest smiled, not taking the bait. "I assure you there're easier ways for a New York City developer to make a buck than this. Only a third of the housing will be market-rate, after all."

"But I assume it's a lot less risky for the developer than conventional commercial development."

"Sure," Forrest said. "But developers are happy making gambles, or they wouldn't be in real estate."

Candace nodded, conceding the point. "So I was mainly curious why your office was funding the Alphabet City Community Coalition, given that the point of their organization seems to be to protest the changes at Riis."

Forrest nodded crisply. "Ben mentioned that, so I looked it up. The money is going through us, but it's actually been designated by a city councilwoman. The way it works is, the council's allocations for this sort of nonprofit funding are then administered by the relevant city agency, depending what kind of project it is. The agency has oversight over the nonprofit, making sure the money is used the way it's supposed to be. But who actually gets the funding isn't our call."

"Who on the council allocated the money to the ACCC?"

"Karla Serran. She chairs the committee on public housing, so she's active on these issues."

Candace understood, but it still didn't quite add up to her. "Here's what I don't get," she said. "You basically have the city agency that's in charge of remaking Jacob Riis also funding a community group whose sole purpose seems to be to protest those changes."

"I see the irony, or whatever you want to call it. But like I said, we didn't actually have any role in deciding that the ACCC got the money, and the money doesn't come out of our operating budget. It's essentially just funneled through us. This is how all of the council's nonprofit funding allocations work."

"Got it," Candace said. "I don't suppose you have any role in overseeing the ACCC?"

"None whatsoever. My only day-to-day involvement in what's going on at Riis took place in the early planning stages. But as far as I know, everything with the ACCC has checked out fine."

"Okay. The funding was really the part I was curious about."

"I understand it probably looks a little strange from the outside, but it really is quite common. Anything else I can do for you, Candace?"

"I don't think so," Candace said, smiling as she picked up her recorder and turned it off.

Forrest pulled open a desk drawer and took out a business card. "Here's my info if you want to follow up about anything. And again, sorry to hear about you and Ben. Must be tough, being separated."

Candace didn't react, though she was pretty sure she wasn't imagining that Forrest was trying to see if she'd show any interest. "It depends what you're comparing it to, I suppose," she said. "Being married, for example."

Forrest laughed, Candace noting his wedding ring as he did so. "Like I said, if there's anything else I can do . . ."

Candace took his card, offering a little salute with it. "I'll be sure to tell Ben just how helpful you were," she replied.

BACK AT her office, Candace turned to looking into councilwoman Karla Serran, curious whether her support of the ACCC was part of a larger opposition to the changes to Riis. The first-term councilwoman had actually grown up in Jacob Riis, something her political biography stressed. She'd gone to Stuyvesant, and from there to Cornell and Fordham Law. She'd spent most of her career working for the city, first as a lawyer, then in policy jobs, before getting elected to the council.

Candace couldn't find anything linking the councilwoman and the ACCC. On the contrary, Serran was a public supporter of the Riis redevelopment, speaking out on its behalf, talking about the poor condition of the existing project and the dangers of living there when she'd been growing up. So by supporting the ACCC she appeared to be playing both sides of the street.

Candace went back to what she had on the ACCC, looking for something that would connect the agency and the councilwoman. After a few minutes she spotted it: one of the members of the ACCC's board of directors was named Antonio Serran. Candace pegged the odds of the overlapping last names' being a coincidence at pretty much zero.

Assuming Antonio was a family member, it was worth noting but hardly shocking that Karla Serran was funding his organization. Even if it was only for the appearance of the thing, a politician's funneling money to a community group where a spouse or relative was on the board didn't seem like a great idea. But of course such things happened all the time in politics. It probably wasn't enough in itself for a story, but it made Candace want to know more about the ACCC. Something wasn't quite right here; she could feel it.

·23·

IT'S NOT a terrible deal," Duncan said, though he made no effort to show enthusiasm for it. He was alone with his client in a Rikers interview room. The room was small, Duncan's knees almost touching Rafael's as they sat across from each other. One wall was reinforced fiberglass, allowing the guards to keep an eye on them.

Duncan knew he was supposed to be trying to get Rafael to take the plea, but his heart wasn't in it. While he wasn't going to discourage Rafael from taking it, he wasn't going to do a hard sell either.

"Twenty-five years?" Rafael said incredulously. "You saying twenty-five years?"

"That's the offer," Duncan said. "Doesn't mean you'd actually serve all of that, with good behavior and parole."

"What's a bad deal look like? They gonna drag me on out to the yard and shoot me in the head?"

"It's a murder charge, Rafael. Any plea on this is going to be serious time."

Rafael was still incredulous at the thought of agreeing to spend twenty-five years in jail. "Serious time for what? Tell me what I've done that I'm going to do time for."

"I've got an obligation to let you know when the DA makes you an offer. I've got to tell you too how it looks compared to what could happen if you get convicted at trial. It doesn't mean you have to take it; it doesn't mean we can't keep going with the case. But you have to understand that most murder prosecutions don't have happy endings for the guy on the hook."

"But you said you can tell the judge how I hadn't shot a gun, right?"

Duncan was well aware that Rafael placed too much confidence in the idea that the case was some sort of misunderstanding that could just be straightened out. "I hope so, but it's far from a lock. You can't believe that I'm just going to be able to get you out of this. I mean, I'm going to do everything I can, but you need to know that there's nothing that I'm promising you in terms of a result."

Rafael shook his head, leaning back in his seat, his anger making the tiny interview room feel even smaller. "So you telling me I should spend twenty-five years in the hole for something I didn't even do?"

Duncan knew what his marching orders from Blake were, but he also believed that his primary duty was to his client. And on some level, he didn't want Rafael to plead out so easily. "Listen, you don't want to take the deal, then don't take the deal. Just remember I'm not Superman. Even if I get the gunshot residue thrown out, the DA's still got a witness; they've still got a motive. The reason they're not offering very much is because losing the gunshot evidence doesn't scare them that much. I can't promise this will reach a moment where it's better than it is right now."

Rafael looked at Duncan carefully, studying him. "I say fight," he said after a moment. "You gonna fight?"

Duncan held Rafael's gaze. "Fight, yes," he said. "That I can promise."

"And it don't matter that I can't pay?"

Duncan felt offended by the question, but quickly realized he couldn't blame Rafael for wondering that. "That's not what this is about. I get paid to do my job, Rafael. Defending you is part of my job. I'm doing what I'd do, saying what I would say, whether you were paying or not."

"Then let's go to war," Rafael said.

DUNCAN HAD rented a car for the trip out to Rikers. As he drove back to Manhattan he thought about how he was going to spin this to Blake, who was doubtless going to be displeased.

It also meant figuring out how to go forward with the case. The obvious thing was the hearing on the gunshot residue, see if he could get that thrown out. Despite what Castelluccio had said, doing so would likely get a much better deal offer, which could potentially end it.

But it was also time to make a real effort to establish Rafael's innocence. Duncan wouldn't necessarily communicate that part of the plan to Blake, but he didn't see how he could avoid at least making some effort in this direction. It was a one-witness case; the obvious thing was to take a hard look at Chris Driscoll.

Duncan couldn't shake the uneasy feeling he'd had ever since Blake had told him he'd be keeping the case. There was something going on he didn't understand, a hidden agenda. Duncan had a lingering suspicion that he was being used in some way, but why and by whom he couldn't tell. Then again, Blake was never exactly forthcoming, and the last couple of weeks had been generally disorienting, particularly with Leah Roth's entrance into his life. He didn't see his way to figuring it out, so Duncan resolved to just do what was in front of him to do. If something else was going on, it would reveal itself eventually. With any luck he would see it coming in time.

·24·

WELCOME TO our cave," Jeremy said to Mattar Al-Falasi. They were at the Buddha Lounge, a subterranean nightclub in the Meatpacking District, tucked into a private VIP room that was indeed styled as a cave.

Alena, after some protest, had furnished a friend, Ivy, to be Mattar's date. Ivy was Asian, still modeling, although not as much as she used to. She was beautiful and aloof; Jeremy was unsure if her blankness was a form of superiority, or just the expression of her essential dullness.

Mattar was dressed in a suit, though without a tie. Jeremy had yet to see the guy without a suit jacket on. Jeremy was dressed more casually, though no less expensively, in a long-sleeved Armani polo shirt, not wanting to look like he'd just stepped out of a business meeting when hitting a club. Both Alena and Ivy looked great, of course: Ivy in the standard little black dress, a sleeveless number with slits to midthigh, Alena in a scoop-necked turquoise dress that was one of Jeremy's favorites.

Private rooms at the Buddha required bottle service, Jeremy shelling out $350 for a fifth of Grey Goose that he could buy at a liquor store for less than forty bucks. Not that he gave a shit: being out with Mattar made tonight a business expense; his bar tab would be on the company. His father still kept him on what Jeremy considered a tight financial leash, essentially forcing him to live on his salary while all the real money was tied up in long-term trusts and property he wasn't allowed to touch.

Jeremy had never been able to live within his means, going all the way back to high school. It wasn't his fault: everyone knew how rich his family was, so people had certain assumptions about his lifestyle. It wasn't like he could explain that his father had him on an allowance that made his wealth a fraction of what people assumed.

The blond bartender had made them all martinis, showing off her cleavage as she did so. She left the bottle chilling in a gold-plated ice tray. It was Jeremy's first drink of the night: this was a business outing, after all, and Jeremy wanted to stay at least somewhat on his toes around Mattar. "Cheers," he said. "To new friends."

They all clinked glasses, but the moment felt forced, nobody but Jeremy even bothering to try to act happy about being there. Jeremy did not understand why Mattar seemed so distracted; the whole evening had been constructed for him, Jeremy thinking he'd put together exactly what Mattar had requested.

"Is your family back in the city?" he asked Mattar.

"My father is in Dubai; my brother has gone to Los Angeles," Mattar said.

Jeremy knew better than to explicitly bring up business, but without that he was at a loss as to what to talk about. "Ivy just got back from Paris," he said, the first thing that popped into his head.

Mattar turned to her, his expression blankly polite. "Is that so? It is a beautiful city, of course, but for me I find the relationship between the French and the Arabs too difficult."

"More than with Americans?" Alena asked, Jeremy not at all liking where this was going.

"It can be difficult with the Americans as well, of course. Iraq, the support for Israel."

"I was actually thinking 9/11," Alena replied.

Mattar paused and nodded his head slightly in concession. "Yes, of course. But some Americans seem to think that 9/11 was the first time that America encountered the Arab world."

"*Encountered?*" Alena said.

This was heading off the rails, Jeremy thought. "Let's not," he said.

"It was of course a completely horrible tragedy," Mattar said, ignoring Jeremy's interjection. "But my point was that, even so, the Americans, the New Yorkers especially, they still see me as a person when I am here, not as an Arab terrorist. In Paris I'm simply an Arab, nothing else."

"We're the new world," Jeremy said, talking just so that Alena was not.

Alena stood abruptly, saying she wanted to dance. Ivy stood up immediately. "Not for me," Mattar said. "But please go; it's fine."

"I'll keep Mattar company," Jeremy said. "You two have fun."

Alena and Ivy made their way out to the dance floor. Jeremy smiled at Mattar, then took a sip of his drink. "I hope this place is okay?"

"It's nice," Mattar said, glancing around as if he'd neglected to actually notice his surroundings.

"And the company is satisfactory?"

Mattar hesitated, but it seemed to be more out of politesse than actual uncertainty. "Actually, if you want to know the truth, I prefer the other one."

Jeremy made no effort to hide his surprise. "You mean Alena?"

"If you will forgive my being blunt, it is the white girls I prefer," Mattar said with a slight smile. "And perhaps it is also true that I like the difficult women also."

"I didn't realize," Jeremy said, laughing because he didn't know what else to do.

"If the Asian one is attractive to you, then perhaps . . ." Mattar trailed off.

Jeremy's smile was straining, but he held it. "No, but . . . Alena's with me."

Mattar flushed. "She's your girlfriend?"

"Maybe that's not quite the right word, but we're seeing each other, yes."

"I thought— Please excuse me," Mattar said.

"A simple misunderstanding," Jeremy said quickly, finishing off his martini. "Don't think twice."

"You must think me a crude man. Where I am from, it's very different with men and women. When I see women advertising their bodies, perhaps I make assumptions I should not make. But that is no excuse for offending you."

"It's fine. No big deal," Jeremy said. He told himself that was true. Jeremy decided to find the whole thing funny. Hell, it *was* funny, when you looked at it from a certain angle. Not that Alena would think so. She just wouldn't have the right point of view.

·25·

RAFAEL HADN'T known his mother was coming to New York until she showed up at the jail. Yara had come alone, which surprised Rafael: he would've expected her to hide behind his grandmother.

Yara had given birth to Rafael when she was little older than he was now. His parents had never been legally married, though they'd lived together in Vieques for the first few years of his life. When Rafael was about three his father had come up to New York, looking for work. The idea had been for Yara and Rafael to follow a month or so later, but that month had somehow turned into a year of waiting to be summoned north.

So Yara had finally taken matters into her own hands, bringing Rafael with her on an unannounced trip. Rafael was too young to remember any of it himself, but what Yara had discovered in New York was that his father was living with another woman.

Looking back, Rafael understood that his mother must have suspected what she was going to find. Nevertheless, she'd decided to stay in New York. A short time later Yara's mother had come up from Vieques and moved in with them. In Rafael's earliest memories, he was already living in Jacob Riis with his mother and grandmother. He had never seen his father again, had no actual memory of the man, wouldn't recognize him if they passed on the street.

When Rafael was twelve his mother had been arrested and sent to prison, and his grandmother had brought him up on her own from there. Rafael gave her most of the credit for seeing that he came up right: she'd been stuck with the hard years, when the temptations of drugs and gangs claimed so many of his classmates from the projects. Rafael had stayed in school, graduating from high school last spring, been working full-time at Alchemy ever since. He loved it at the restaurant, was taking classes so that he could one day become a proper chef, maybe even open a restaurant of his own.

But those dreams were distant now. It was hard to imagine any kind of future at all while in the harsh confines of Rikers. So Rafael focused on the present, and the surprising sight of his mother in the visiting room.

This was the first time Rafael had seen Yara in almost a year. It'd been nearly seven years since they'd last lived together, since her arrest. She'd been caught in her then-boyfriend's apartment in a raid, charged with possession of cocaine with intent to distribute. Yara had insisted she wasn't involved, resisted taking a plea till the last possible second, and even then she'd refused to testify against her boyfriend. She'd ended up being sentenced to eight to twelve years and doing over five. Upon her release Yara had decided to return to Vieques. Rafael hadn't considered going with her: he'd grown up in New York, it was home, and by then his grandmother felt more like his parent than his mother did.

Rafael had gone down to Puerto Rico the last two Christmases, but other than that he hadn't seen his mother since right after she got out of prison. She hadn't previously come up to New York since moving back to Vieques: Yara blamed the city for what had happened to her, though Rafael thought that bullshit, just a way of making excuses for herself.

"You didn't need to come up here," Rafael said in Spanish as she sat across from him in the visiting room.

"Of course I did," Yara replied, also in Spanish. Her eyes were already welling with tears. She'd just turned forty, although Rafael thought she looked older: she'd grown heavy, her hair fast turning gray. "My only son in jail."

"I didn't do anything wrong."

"I should've made you come back home with me," Yara said, a tear escaping. She made no effort to wipe it away, as though she didn't even know it was there. "It's this city; it just eats our people up."

"Don't cry, Mom," Rafael said. "I don't want to see you cry."

"You were always so good. I know I disappointed you, but I tried."

Rafael's own vulnerability came out in anger. "How could you try from a jail cell?" he said.

Yara looked stung; he could see her fighting her own anger down. "I held you in my heart every day I spent in jail," she said. "I said a prayer for you first thing when I woke up and last thing before I went to sleep."

Rafael didn't know why he'd brought it up, why they were rehashing all of this again. But now that it was there it was hard to let it go. "You could have made a deal right away; you could have testified against Emilio. You didn't have to end up spending all that time in prison."

Yara finally took out a tissue to wipe the tears off her face, Rafael feeling bloated with guilt and shame for making her suffer more than she already was just by seeing him like this. "It was nothing but hard choices back then," Yara said. "If I could make things come out different I would."

"I know, Mom," Rafael said, trying to make peace.

"I wish you'd come back with me after I'd got out. Things can be hard in Vieques too, but people stick together there."

"I thought New York was where I belonged," Rafael said, realizing as he said it that he was no longer sure it was true. "One thing I've learned in here—I'll always be a Puerto Rican, not an American."

"When this case gets cleared up, maybe you can think about coming down to Vieques to live. What does your lawyer say?"

"The DA offered a plea if I'd do twenty-five years. Turned that down, so now we got to fight it."

"I don't understand why they can't just clear this up."

Rafael had felt the same way when he'd first been arrested, but not anymore. Now he found it naive. "Nobody cares what really happened," he said. "Just find the first Puerto Rican who might have a reason to shoot the white guy, put him in jail for it. How it's always been."

Yara started crying again, more fiercely this time. "I know I messed things up with you. This city, I just couldn't live here anymore. I haven't been there for you when you needed me."

"You didn't need to come back here," Rafael said, coldness seeping back into his voice. He wasn't going to trust his mother to be there for him, wasn't going to open up to her. She couldn't help him here—she'd never helped him, and he didn't need to be let down right now. "I'm going to get through this same way I have everything else—on my own."

·26·

DUNCAN HADN'T bothered to try to talk to the eyewitness to Fowler's shooting while he'd been assuming the case would reach a quick plea. Chris Driscoll, like Fowler, was an ex-cop, which presumably meant both that he'd be a good eyewitness and that he'd do what he could to see Fowler's alleged killer put down. The point in talking to him was to see if there were any flaws in his story, anything that could be exploited down the road, and also to get a sense of how the man came across. There were established methods for attacking eyewitness identifications—the unreliability of interracial IDs, the weapons-focus effect—but at the end of the day a believable witness was just that.

Unsure whether Driscoll would agree to meet, Duncan decided to go over to Jacob Riis unannounced in the evening and try to find him there. He left the office around seven, took a cab to Twelfth Street and Avenue D, since Alphabet City was largely off the subway grid, a relic of its tenement past.

This wasn't his part of town, and Duncan had no doubt it showed. He kept his pace brisk, walking purposefully even though he wasn't exactly certain where he was going, wanting to seem sure of himself. Not that he was worried: while daylight was fading, the time was long past where the lettered avenues of Alphabet City had been said to stand for Attention, Beware, Caution, and Death. Avenue D still lagged far beyond the others in terms of gentrification, but you no longer took your life in your hands by walking down it.

This was particularly true because the transformation of Jacob Riis was already well under way. The city was tearing down the existing buildings one block at a time, putting residents in another project as they were displaced, or else giving them federal Section 8 vouchers that they could use to cover rent at private residences. They'd taken out two square blocks so far—from Thirteenth Street to Eleventh. That was where the security guards were concentrated; it was where Duncan eventually found his way to Chris Driscoll.

Driscoll was in his late forties, burly but fit, with sandy brown hair and pale blue eyes that gave him a ghostly look. Duncan had found him walking along the edge of the new buildings, where they met the remaining project. When he'd introduced himself as Rafael's lawyer, Driscoll hadn't seemed surprised.

"Do you mind if I ask you a few questions about that night?" Duncan asked, he and Driscoll standing somewhat awkwardly next to a plywood wall blocking off the construction site. Duncan realized they were less than a block from where Fowler had been shot.

"I was expecting someone from his side," Driscoll said. "But nothing I know is going to help your guy."

"How long have you been working for Darryl Loomis?"

"Almost two years now."

"Did you know Sean Fowler well?"

"I saw Sean pretty much every day once we were both detailed to Riis. Can't really help but get to know a man you work with that closely."

"What exactly do you guys do here on site?"

"It's a mix of foot patrol and manning the booths we set up by the equipment. Main thing is to make sure you don't get people sneaking into the construction site and making off with stuff. Because nobody's actually living there now, people see it as an easy target."

"Had there been any trouble before the shooting?"

"Some kids trying to climb the fence for kicks, that sort of thing, but in my line of work we don't call that trouble."

"Did Fowler ever have problems with anybody around here?"

"You mean other than your client?"

Duncan didn't take the bait, grinning instead. "That's exactly what I mean."

One side of Driscoll's mouth curled into something like a smile. "We've busted some people around here on some minor stuff. There were things that people got used to getting away with 'cause cops don't give a fuck what happens on Avenue D unless a body drops. Now they got us writing it up. You don't make a place like this ready for civilians without skimming the scum off the top. That's what we're doing, and we're getting it done, but it don't make us any friends. Actually it probably does, 'cause there's some perfectly decent people stuck in this shithole, but they're never going to tell us thanks."

Against his better judgment Duncan found himself liking Driscoll. "You guys ever break anything up that might've made you enemies?"

"The drug boys weren't exactly putting out a welcome mat. You transform this into someplace livable, you take down the neighborhood dealers as collateral damage."

"Drug dealing was pretty entrenched here?"

Driscoll shrugged. "Same as any other project like this."

"But they didn't ever give you any problems?"

"Dealers are like cockroaches. You shine a light somewhere, they know to avoid it. They just go somewhere else."

"That doesn't mean they liked the disruption."

"What it does mean is, they're generally going to know better than to do battle with the keepers of the peace. They don't need the attention. We never had any problems with the dealers here."

"How much actual dealing is there?"

"Fair amount. Used to be everything from Avenue B on over was pretty much little Amsterdam. Back when you had squats and abandoned buildings everywhere, there were guys on every corner. Now you got an East Village yuppie with a jones, he lives on Avenue A, but his condo development chased out the corner dealer. So he hits the projects."

"Do you guys go after them?"

Driscoll laughed. "You kidding? We're here to provide security to the construction site. We're not here to be cops."

"But Fowler allegedly busted my client for smoking a joint."

"Somebody wants to shove it in our face, sure, we make a citizen's, call in the NYPD Housing Bureau, hand it off. Get rid of the people who won't be able to live in a civilized version of this place."

"But drug dealers don't fall into that category?"

"Hey, in a perfect world, right? But we're not in a position to take down a real crew, and plus my guess is those guys will take themselves out of the mix anyway. They can't operate in a functioning environment. Once this place is livable they'll be moving on."

"You're sure of that?"

Driscoll shrugged. "I'm just the hired help," he said. "What do you want from me?"

Duncan figured that was as much big picture as it was useful to get. "Can you walk me through what happened that night?" he asked.

"There's not a whole lot to walk through. Sean had been on a patrol. I was coming over to sub him out for his break. When I saw him he was arguing with someone. They were standing under a streetlight on Tenth, Sean with his back to me while the kid, your client, was facing me. I was less than a block away when your client drew down and shot him. It happened real quick; I didn't see it coming, so I didn't react like I would've in my prime, twenty years ago when I was a uniform walking a beat. I yelled; he took off, cut into the project. I wanted to go after him but I needed to check on Sean first. A couple of cops from the housing unit showed up a minute or so later."

"So you never went chasing after the shooter?"

Driscoll shook his head. "I stayed with Sean. By the time the cops got there I was pretty sure he was gone, but I wasn't going to leave him. But once the ambulance arrived we wanted to work quickly to try and make an ID. The Housing Authority has photos of every resident, so I went down to the station and they showed me pictures of everybody who was about the right age and description. It only took about five minutes before I found him."

"Then what?"

"They went and picked him up, had me take a look in person. I made the ID, and here we are."

"And you were sure of your ID? Even though you'd never seen Rafael before that night?"

Driscoll laughed off the suggestion. "I've been doing this since you were in middle school. Making somebody is second nature to me."

"Sure, but they brought him to you in the back of a squad car. Obviously the police were letting you know they thought this was the guy."

"They thought he was the guy; I thought he was the guy. We all thought he was the guy. That's because he was the guy."

CANDACE WAS making her way east on Tenth Street, heading back to Jacob Riis, when she saw them. It was only the lawyer, Riley, whom she recognized, but she figured it had to be Driscoll that he was talking to, the two of them up the block on the far side of Avenue D. Driscoll, the very guy she herself had come down here looking for.

Instinct told her to hang back, and so Candace dawdled on the sidewalk, moving around slowly without going anywhere. Her first reaction had been to assume there was something sinister in spotting the two of them together, but as she thought it through Candace realized that she had nothing but her gut to back that up. If confronted, Duncan could simply say that he was interviewing the eyewitness in the murder case against his client. And for all she knew, that was what he was actually doing.

But she didn't for a second believe it. Both these men served the same master. Whatever they were talking about right now, it was in Simon Roth's interest. The fix was in. She didn't have the pieces, but she could feel it.

This Riley was fairly young, still getting himself established. He was quite possibly in over his head on this. Maybe he'd talk. Hell, maybe he'd want to talk. She decided to take a swing, see where it got her. If she had something to lose, she couldn't see what it was.

Finally the two men went their separate ways, Duncan heading south on D, walking right toward her. Candace stood still on the corner, looking straight at him, waiting for him to notice.

He was still across the street, waiting for the light to change, when he did. Duncan quickly looked away, pretending he hadn't seen her. As he crossed Avenue D, Candace realized he was planning to walk right past. Even people with something to hide weren't usually this obvious about it.

She sidestepped directly into Duncan's path, giving him no choice but to look up. "Remember me?" Candace said.

"I can't talk to you," Duncan said. He'd stopped, but wasn't looking at her.

"What's that supposed to mean?"

"It means you're a represented party on the other side of a case. I'm not allowed to talk to you. You know, ethically."

"I'm not here to talk about the libel suit."

This didn't appear to make Duncan any more comfortable. "Look, I'm not just making this up. If Rosenstein found out I was talking to you without him around, he'd bring me up before the bar."

"Whatever it is, I hereby waive it, okay? I'm the one who came up to you."

"Did you want to call me an asshole again?"

Candace felt herself flush. "I'm sorry I called you an asshole. I know you were just doing your job. If it's any consolation, I've been called worse things in the line of duty myself."

"I don't find that so difficult to believe," Duncan said. "Moving on, just for a second, are you following me?"

"Why would I be doing that?"

"I have no idea. Is there some other reason you're standing here?"

"You and I should talk."

"About what?"

"Simon Roth," Candace said.

"That's not something that you and I are going to talk about."

"Why not?"

Duncan made a face. "I'm not allowed to talk *to* you, and I'm also not allowed to talk *about* him. So talking to you about him is pretty much out of the picture."

"Rafael Nazario then."

Duncan's surprise was visible, as Candace had hoped it would be. "How do you know about Rafael Nazario?"

"It's not a secret that he's your client, is it?"

"Of course not. But I don't know why it's of interest to you."

"Let's go talk about it. I'll buy you a drink."

Duncan was looking away from her, as though mapping out an escape route. "I'm still working," he said.

"So I'll buy you a latte. There's gotta be a Starbucks on Avenue B by now."

DUNCAN MADE Candace send her lawyer an e-mail from her BlackBerry before he'd talk. Duncan dictated the e-mail while Candace wrote, the two of them huddled in the street. He felt stupid, certain he was further convincing Candace what a lawyerly douche bag he was, but talking to a represented adversary in the absence of her lawyer really was the kind of thing that could get him hauled before the disciplinary committee. He also declared their conversation off the record; he wasn't going to give her a quote on anything until he'd had a chance to run it past Blake.

No Starbucks in sight, they ended up at Life Café on Tenth and B. "I have to admit, I only know of this place because of *Rent*," Candace said as they sat down at a small and rickety wooden table with their coffees in tow.

"Because of rent?" Duncan asked, not following.

"You know—the show? You never saw *Rent*?"

"Not really my thing," Duncan said, looking around the cramped café. "Seems like a hard place to do a song-and-dance number."

"Not onstage, it wasn't," Candace said. "I think a bunch of it was actually written here."

"Those were the days, huh?"

"I can't say I've liked watching the whole of Manhattan turned into a habitat for the hedge-fund crowd."

"On the list of things that killed off the edgy version of the East Village," Duncan said, "*Rent* must make the top five."

"What about tearing down the Jacob Riis projects?"

"What about it?"

"What's that going to do to the neighborhood?"

"I don't know, make it safer maybe. But that's bad for the drug dealers and the muggers, so there goes the neighborhood, right?"

Candace didn't disagree; she'd never really understood people who treated gentrification as a categorical evil. "I don't have a problem with the idea of changing housing projects into livable places, but last time I checked, Simon Roth wasn't a humanitarian."

"If you bought me a latte to get me talking about Simon Roth, you wasted five dollars."

"I'll just ask about you, then. You do know that Roth's developing the new and improved Jacob Riis, right?"

"Sure," Duncan said readily. "That's public knowledge."

"And you know that Sean Fowler was working security for Roth's company, right?"

"Are you cross-examining me?"

"What I'm doing is wondering how you can represent Simon Roth on the one hand, and represent someone accused of killing his employee on the other. You've been talking a lot about ethics; isn't that a conflict of interest?"

"It's not, actually. Rafael's being prosecuted by the State of New York, not by Simon Roth. There's no legal conflict."

This didn't seem quite right to Candace, but she wasn't versed in the finer points of legal ethics. "But how can you represent Nazario when the victim worked for your client, the eyewitness works for your client? Roth can't want you to be helping a guy who shot someone who worked for him."

Duncan was trying to figure out the balance between not telling her anything about internal firm discussions while talking her down from assuming he was masterminding some kind of conspiracy. "I'm not going to discuss any privileged conversations that may have taken place, but I will assure you that there are no concerns from any of our clients regarding anything that might be perceived as a conflict here," Duncan said, clearly choosing his words with care. "So if that's why you were stalking me, I'm afraid you had the wrong idea."

Candace felt herself losing ground. "What about the fact that they were throwing people like Nazario out of Jacob Riis on fake drug charges?"

Duncan tilted his head. "What are you talking about?"

"The eviction proceeding against your client and his family. You really don't know that Fowler and the rest of the security crew had racked up over a dozen of those?"

Duncan didn't hide his surprise. "All on drug possession?"

"That's right. And yes, I know that drugs are a part of a housing project, but even at Jacob Riis there can't really be that many people who stand around smoking joints in front of security guards."

Duncan was intrigued, though he didn't know quite what to make of it, or whether it could help his case. Dolores Nazario had told him that there were a lot of other recent evictions at Riis, but he hadn't paid much attention, not finding it surprising that the city would be aggressive in throwing lawbreakers out of public housing. And while he'd gone along with Rafael's protestations that he hadn't actually been caught smoking pot, Duncan had never fully believed it. "So what are you saying?" he asked.

"It looks to me like the security guards are faking drug busts to kick people out of Jacob Riis, empty the place so that they can refill it with yuppies. You should know more about this than I do."

"Why should I know about it?" Duncan asked defensively.

"You're defending somebody who's a victim of it, and the obvious suspect in terms of being behind it is also a client of yours. Now's your chance to get in front of this, Duncan."

Duncan looked at her incredulously, his mouth open, eventually forming some forced approximation of a smile. "You're serious? You think I'm involved in some sort of setup?"

"It's a bit much to all be a coincidence. Listen, my dad's a big-firm lawyer; I know a thing or two about how they operate. You must be up for partner soon, right? You're not at a point yet where you make the calls; you've still got to follow orders. Somebody comes to you, says Roth wants this done, you might think it's weird, but you don't really have a choice but to do it. Maybe you didn't piece it together. Maybe you didn't ask questions that you didn't want the answers to. But now you're in the middle of it, and I'm your way out."

Duncan's smile grew broader, more genuine. "Wow," he said. "It must be really exciting to live in your version of the world. Conspiracies, dirty tricks. I'm sorry to say that I'm not in the middle of anything.

When I took on Rafael's case it was just a straightforward eviction, nothing else. His family was being evicted by the New York Housing Authority, not by Simon Roth. Look, I understand you've got it in for Roth; he sued you, and I get that you might not like me after I deposed you, but I haven't done anything wrong, or unethical, or that I'd be ashamed to read about in the newspaper, provided it was accurately told."

Candace didn't know what to make of it. She didn't get the feeling Duncan was lying. But that wasn't enough to convince her that she was wrong. "Something's not right," Candace insisted. "Maybe you're not part of it, but I know something's wrong with these evictions."

"If what you're saying about evictions is true, I want to know about it. It might help my client."

"What if Roth's behind it?"

Duncan didn't have an answer for that, and made no effort to act like he did. "I don't even know that there's actually an 'it' for Roth to be behind. I just have what you're telling me."

"Why should I trust you with anything I know?" Candace asked.

"Why should I trust you with anything I know?" Duncan retorted.

"I'm not connected with Simon Roth."

"You're one of his enemies. That can be a pretty close connection."

"My only goal here is to find out the truth."

"Yeah, 'cause that's all that reporters are ever worried about. You're just the world's referees, right? If we're going to talk to each other, let's do better than that."

"Are we?" Candace said.

"Are we what?"

"Going to talk to each other?"

"I don't know," Duncan said. "I've tried to convince you that I'm not the Antichrist. And I'm interested in the evictions at Jacob Riis."

"You have to promise me something."

"I don't think I do, but what is it you want me to promise you?"

"That if what I tell you can help Rafael Nazario, you'll use it. No matter who it hurts."

Duncan paused, clearly not liking the idea of making a promise of any kind, lawyers being creatures of contingencies. "I promise that if you tell me something that can help Rafael, I'll make sure it does."

Candace thought about it. "How do I know you're not going to take everything I tell you right back to Roth and let him know what I've got?"

Duncan smiled, leaning back in his seat. "If you're asking me why we should trust each other, I can't really think of much in the way of a reason."

"So if the eviction thing helps you, what do I get back?"

"I'll give you the inside track on the Nazario case. Anything happens that's newsworthy, I'll give it to you."

Candace figured this really could be worth something—not necessarily to her, but to the paper. She could pass it off to Costello, maybe get him off her back. "Like what?"

"Okay, how about this? You might have read, say in your newspaper, that the cops found gunshot residue on Nazario's hand?"

"Rings a bell."

"It wasn't because he'd fired a gun. The particles were almost certainly picked up while he was sitting in the back of the police car. Your paper can be the first to print it."

"I'm not sure that's enough for a story, but I guess it's a start."

"Think of it as a peace offering then, or a sign of good faith."

Candace considered it for a moment, then nodded. "On the evictions, I'm not going to lay it out for you, in terms of telling you who specifically I've talked to or anything. You'll have to read that in the paper. But I can tell you that there're enough people telling the same story that there must be something to it. I think the security guards are targeting teenagers on minor drug charges, then kicking out their families. Just like they're doing to your client."

"And they're doing this why?" Duncan asked.

"If I answered that question honestly, you'd probably add it as a count in Roth's libel suit against me," Candace said. "So I'm afraid you're going to have to draw your own conclusions."

"You think Fowler and Driscoll, specifically, were planting drugs on teenagers in order to evict families from Jacob Riis?"

"Look, if you don't know how to add one plus one by now, I'm not here to teach you," Candace said.

"So Rafael's story about that can be backed up?"

"Do you want me to just wait until you catch up, then we can talk?"

"I'm stating the obvious," Duncan conceded.

"You just did it again."

Duncan smiled at her despite himself. "The DA wouldn't see this as exculpatory necessarily. I bet they'll say it just gives Rafael more of a motive if Fowler had set him up."

"But what about Driscoll? This would suggest he wasn't exactly the impartial observer he presented himself as. Presumably he's lied to the police about something here."

She had a point, Duncan thought. Showing Driscoll was involved with planting drugs could be very useful. "If he's had some practice framing people, that would certainly call his ID into question," he said.

"That leads down an interesting road, now, doesn't it?"

"Driscoll and Fowler wouldn't be throwing people out of Jacob Riis just for their own amusement," Duncan said carefully.

"So who stands to benefit from having fewer poor people to fit back into the new and improved Jacob Riis? Who had the ability to give Driscoll and Fowler marching orders to do this?"

Duncan wasn't going to say it; there wasn't even a chance of that. Studying Candace, he saw she wasn't going to either. It didn't matter whether it was spoken, anyway. Clearly they both knew there was only one person who met the criteria Candace had suggested.

Simon Roth.

·PART·
TWO

·28·

THE ALPHABET City Community Coalition operated out of a tiny storefront on the west side of Avenue D, across the street from Jacob Riis. There were a half dozen desks jammed haphazardly around the main front room, only two of which were occupied when Candace arrived for her meeting with Keisha Dewberry, the organization's executive director. One of the two people in the front was talking on the phone; the other was playing online Scrabble on Facebook.

Candace had expected the head of an activist nonprofit that was going up against the city and a billionaire developer to be falling over herself to talk to a reporter. Instead it'd taken three days for Dewberry to return her call. It might mean nothing—for all she knew Dewberry had been out of town—but it made Candace wonder.

Dewberry was in her mid-forties, with short dreadlocks, dressed in an African print shirt. She had the sole private office, in what looked to be a converted storage space. It was cramped, with barely enough room for the desk and chair.

"So you're doing some kind of thing on the switch over to mixed-income at Riis?" Dewberry asked.

Candace nodded. "How did you come to be involved in the issue?"

"I've been active in public housing for a long time," Dewberry said. "I'd been at ACORN for about a decade before taking this position. What's your angle here?"

"I don't know that I have one," Candace said. "I've done prior reporting on the developer, Roth Properties, particularly the accident at the Aurora Tower last year. What's your organization's view on the transition to mixed-income?"

"We're not actually categorically opposed to it. For one thing, once you have middle-class tenants in these buildings, they're not going to stand for the crap that goes on in this city's public housing these days. Elevators that don't work, graffiti in the hallways, vermin. Not to mention that the buildings themselves are falling apart. So if transitioning to mixed-income means better conditions for everyone, great. The concern, of course, is how you make the change without completely disrupting the lives of existing residents. Is this just a smoke screen to displace them, move them out to less desirable neighborhoods?"

Candace thought that a good question. "Is it?"

"That's certainly something we're keeping an eye on," Dewberry said. "It's in the developer's interest to get as much market-rate housing into the new buildings as possible. Our priority is protecting the existing tenants."

"Do you oppose having private companies involved?"

"Trying to stop the current plan isn't really an option at this point—the construction's already under way. So our focus is on doing what we can to ensure that the process is as fair as possible to the current tenants."

"Inevitably there will be some displacement of existing residents, won't there?"

"The city claims not, but common sense says yes. We'll fight it every step."

"What about all the drug evictions? Are you involved in fighting those?"

Candace was surprised to see confusion cross Dewberry's face. "Drug use is an unfortunate fact of life in public housing," Dewberry said, falling into rehearsed patter. "That's what happens when you take away opportunity, take away hope."

"I'm sure there is drug use at Riis," Candace replied. "But that's not what I'm talking about. Have you heard accusations from people about the private security companies planting drugs on kids as a way to evict their families?"

"It certainly sounds like something we should look into," Dewberry replied after a moment. "We don't have lawyers on staff, so we don't have direct involvement with any legal issues involving residents."

This didn't add up to Candace. The eviction issue would be gold for an organization like the ACCC, and if they had their ear to the ground in the project they should've at least heard rumors about it. There was something so fly-by-night about the whole operation that Candace wondered if it was actually doing anything at all.

"You haven't heard about the private security guards causing problems?" Candace asked.

"I'll definitely ask around," Dewberry said. Rather than trying to make her case through Candace, Dewberry was clearly counting the seconds until the interview was over. "Glad you brought it to my attention."

Candace didn't want to be giving Dewberry information; it was supposed to be the other way around. "I assume you're familiar with the recent shooting of the security guard?"

"A tragic situation," Dewberry said blandly.

"I understand that the young man charged with the shooting is accusing the guards of previously planting drugs on him. Has your organization had any dealings with the Nazarios?"

"Not that I know of."

Candace, growing frustrated, decided there was no reason to keep things friendly. "I noticed that one of your directors was named Antonio Serran. He wouldn't happen to be related to Karla Serran, the city councilwoman, would he?"

Dewberry frowned, fixing Candace with a suspicious look. "Why does it matter if Antonio is related to a councilwoman?"

"I'm not saying it does. But it looked from your last year's tax filing like most of your funding came from the city, specifically from the Housing Authority."

Dewberry, already tense, turned actively hostile. "How did you get our tax forms?" she demanded.

Candace was amazed how frequently people failed to realize what you could dig out on the Internet these days. "Your filings as a registered nonprofit are available on the state AG's Web site," she said.

"And why were you looking at them?"

Candace offered a smile, wanting to defuse at least a little of the tension. The small room was a claustrophobic setting for the conversation they were having. "Following the money is pretty much Journalism 101."

Dewberry was clearly not appeased. "Most nonprofits get significant funding from the government," she said tartly.

"Of course. But I was curious about how your funding came from the Housing Authority, given that they're the city agency running the changes to Riis. So I spoke to someone there, who explained to me that the money isn't really coming from the Authority, that it's actually city council discretionary spending, which then passes through the most relevant agency when it's allocated out. So my understanding is that Karla Serran is your actual rabbi, in terms of funding."

Dewberry looked about ready to throw Candace out of her office. "There's nothing wrong with that."

"I didn't say there was," Candace said calmly. "Are you denying that Councilwoman Serran is who directed the money your way?"

"It sounded like you were suggesting something improper, in terms of Antonio and his sister."

Progress, Candace thought. Baby steps, but progress. "So they are brother and sister?"

"Is that what you're really here about? Trying to suggest there's something wrong about our funding?"

"Not at all," Candace protested, but she could tell that Dewberry had already shut down.

"I'm afraid that's all the time I have, Ms. Snow," Dewberry said.

CANDACE SPENT the subway ride back to the newsroom trying to figure out how she could nail this down. She'd been suspicious of the funding even before her meeting with Dewberry—ever since she'd noticed Antonio Serran on the organization's staff. But Dewberry's defensive response—coupled with her lack of even basic knowledge of what was going on at Riis, and the bare-bones nature of the ACCC's office—made Candace wonder about the organization's legitimacy.

Back in the newsroom, Candace opened the folder of material she'd assembled on the ACCC. She always went back and reviewed everything in her files after an interview; often connections appeared that had been missed the first time.

Nothing leaped out at a glance. But Candace felt sure there was something she wasn't seeing, something that Dewberry was worried about.

She pulled up a list of Serran's political contributors, information that was available online for all city politicians. What she'd said to Dewberry about following the money was true; it was something she always looked at, especially when dealing with politics. She skimmed the list, not looking for anything in particular.

The first thing that caught her eye was a two-thousand-dollar donation from Antonio Serran. Most of Serran's donors gave a good deal less than that, so his contribution stood out. Of course, there was nothing suspicious about a family member giving money to a politician.

But there was something about the donation that nagged at her. She turned back to the ACCC's tax form, checking the date on which the Housing Authority's money had been dispersed to the agency. The brother's donation had been made the following week.

And not just his: there were a whole cluster of donations made that week, probably close to a hundred thousand dollars' worth, far more money than Karla Serran had received in the surrounding weeks. Keisha Dewberry had given a maximum donation the day after Antonio Serran.

Candace made a list of everyone who had given Karla Serran money that month, planning to dig into each one of them, see if she found a connection to the ACCC. Was this how Simon Roth had arranged to buy the councilwoman's support? Candace had that feeling she got maybe once or twice a year, a tightness in her chest that made it hard to breathe. It was the feeling of being on the verge of breaking open a big story.

·29·

"THANKS FOR seeing me, Mr. Loomis," Duncan said.

From across his desk Darryl Loomis fixed Duncan with a level gaze. After a moment he offered a slight shrug. "You've got friends in high places," he said.

Duncan smiled in response, though doing so didn't cause Darryl's expression to change. "We've got friends in common, yes," Duncan said. "And in that spirit, let me tell you exactly why I'm here."

Darryl gestured for Duncan to continue. The two of them were in Loomis's corner office eighteen stories up in an Avenue of the Americas skyscraper just a few blocks from Duncan's firm. It was filled with plaques and photos of its occupant with a wide range of boldfaced names, from the mayor and the chief of police to business moguls and hip-hop stars. Duncan thought it looked more like the office of the head of a record label than the mental image he had of a private investigator's workplace.

But nothing about Darryl was in keeping with the stereotype of a down-at-the-heels private eye, and as Duncan understood it, actual detective work was only a small part of what the company did. Darryl employed over one hundred people, many of them ex-cops. They did a mix of corporate investigations, security work for clubs, celebrities, and VIPs, as well as more prosaic security work, such as on construction sites.

"As I'm sure you understand, part of my firm's defending Rafael Nazario involves looking into the victim, Mr. Fowler, and the witness, Mr. Driscoll, both of whom work for you. Were the two of them friends?"

"They were friendly enough, far as I know."

"Was Fowler having any problems with anybody that you know of?"

"He had some back-and-forth with his ex, but just the usual nonsense."

"Meaning what?"

Darryl shrugged. "He was divorced with kids. Weekend visitations, vacations out of state, alimony—shit never ends."

"How long ago did he get divorced?"

"Couple of years. Probably past the point where Liz would shoot him. Plus I don't think Chris would ID her as a teenage male Hispanic."

Under the circumstances, Duncan viewed Darryl's sarcasm as progress, and so pretended to be amused by it. "What about problems at Jacob Riis?"

"Nothing that ended up on my desk. Chris would've been the person for you to ask that."

Duncan had expected Darryl would know that he'd already spoken to Driscoll. He also wasn't surprised by Darryl's sullen attitude: he couldn't blame the guy for not wanting to help him. Leah Roth's intercession was no doubt the only reason Darryl was speaking to him at all. "I assume you know that Sean Fowler had allegedly caught my client smoking pot, which is what led to his eviction?"

"I do now, yeah. It wasn't anything I paid attention to when it happened. The eviction part didn't have anything to do with my people."

Now or never, Duncan thought. "What about all the other evictions?" he asked.

Darryl shifted slightly in his seat, but his gaze didn't leave Duncan. "Evictions are done by the city," he said.

Duncan studied Darryl, looking for signs of unease. "But your guys have caught at least a dozen different people at Riis with drugs, and those all led to the city seeking to evict their families."

"And your point?" Darryl said brusquely.

Duncan wasn't getting a read on Darryl's response one way or another. It could just be vexation at hearing the accusation, or it could be something else. "Word on the street is that the drug busts are a way of getting the Riis numbers down, so the city doesn't have to move everyone back."

"You here to teach me something about word on the street?" Darryl said, smiling but not in a way that took the edge off. "Word on the street is conspiracy shit, way to keep people from owning their fuckups. You got any proof?"

"Do you?" Duncan said immediately, smiling as he said it, though that didn't blunt Darryl's angry response.

"I was a cop for twenty years," Darryl said, speaking slowly. "I've dealt with a lot of lawyers. I know what a defense lawyer does—tries to put together some kind of story out of whatever rumors they can find."

"I'm not talking about rumors. I'm talking about the fact that there's a consistent story out there that your guys are planting drugs on people and busting them, with an eye toward evictions."

Darryl's expression turned harsh. "You're accusing my people of a crime? Based on what some project kids they caught with drugs are claiming? Negro, *please*."

Duncan was caught off guard by the last bit, Darryl catching it and smiling. "I don't think even I would've have been able to tell," he said.

Duncan wondered if there was any way he'd misunderstood. "Tell what?"

"If I hadn't seen a picture of your dad."

So much for any misunderstanding, Duncan thought. He tried to tamp down his reaction, not wanting to give Darryl too much of an upper hand. It wasn't that Darryl had discovered something Duncan tried to keep hidden—although the man seemed to think he had—it was just that Duncan didn't understand why Darryl had been poking into his personal life. "Why were you looking at a picture of my father?" he asked.

"We run background on anybody before they set foot in my office. Can't be too careful, know what I'm saying? And you never know what you're going to find out, not until you find it. Don't worry, my brother; your secret's safe with me."

AS SOON as the lawyer had left, Darryl picked up his phone and called Chris Driscoll at home, summoning him to his office. Driscoll arrived forty-five minutes later, looking bleary-eyed. He worked nights, had sounded like he'd been sleeping when Darryl called. Not that Darryl gave a shit.

"That lawyer handling Nazario was just here," he said as Driscoll sat down across from him. "He's claiming that you and Fowler were planting drugs on kids at Riis."

Driscoll's gaze didn't waver, but Darryl could see the effort behind it. "We were doing like you told us Roth wanted, keeping an eye out for criminal stuff we could turn over to the housing cops, helping trim down how many people they had to bring back."

"I know what I told you to do," Darryl said. "That's not what I'm talking about. Were you guys actually planting shit on folks?"

Driscoll hesitated, but he knew better than to lie to his boss. "It was Sean's idea," he said. "You know he was always on the make for extra money. He said since Roth was going to throw us a couple grand for anybody we got rid of, we shouldn't wait for the opportunity to present itself."

Darryl couldn't believe the stupidity of it, the unnecessary risk. "And you went along with this nonsense? And then you didn't tell me, even once we had problems with that motherfucker?"

"I didn't see how it would ever come out. We weren't going crazy with it, and we were focusing on teenagers, so it's not like anybody would believe them."

"You don't make that call," Darryl said. "You follow orders here, my orders. This shit's trouble enough without you keeping something like that from me."

Driscoll nodded, his gaze downcast. "I fucked up; I'm sorry. What can we do about it?"

"Nothing we can do now but gut it out," Darryl said. "And know that the only reason I'm not firing your ass is because I can't."

"Got it," Driscoll said.

· 30 ·

DAYS STARTED early at Rikers: breakfast was usually served in Rafael's cell block around six a.m. Rafael had gotten used to falling asleep by ten o'clock at night; when he'd been free he'd routinely stayed up until two in the morning or later. He'd usually worked in the restaurant until at least eleven, then often hung out with people from the kitchen after his shift, so it hadn't been unusual for it to be past one by the time he got home on a typical workday, even if he wasn't partying.

He was woken at around five thirty by noise outside his cell. Yawning and barely awake, Rafael dutifully got out of bed, assuming it was the breakfast crew coming a little early. But instead it was the tactical unit, charging in full force for a spot search.

Surprise cell searches were a part of life at Rikers, but that didn't make them any less jarring. It was like some sort of military invasion; the tactical guards came in full gear: helmets with protective visors down, shields that could deliver an electric jolt severe enough to temporarily incapacitate a prisoner.

They searched the cells a dozen at a time, the prisoners lining up for a body-cavity search while their cells were gone through. This was done through a special chair that was wheeled in, the BOSS. It was a clunky device, gunmetal gray, with a scanner that could detect metal or other contraband that was hidden in the body.

When his cell door was opened Rafael stepped out, getting into line for his turn on the BOSS. He was standing there, still mostly asleep, when he heard raised voices from behind him. Rafael glanced over his shoulder, knowing the guards wouldn't like it if he actually turned around. An inmate a few cells down from his was refusing to come out, though Rafael couldn't hear why. It was a newbie on the cell block, a middle-aged white guy with stringy long hair and missing front teeth. Everyone had given him a wide berth: the guy was jittery, talked to himself, seemed to be seeing things the rest of them weren't. A crackhead, Rafael was pretty certain, though it also seemed like the miswiring of the guy's mind was more fundamental than that.

A half dozen of the tactical guards had quickly flanked out around the cell door, their electric shields at the ready. Another guard turned on a video camera to film the forced extraction. The prisoner was yelling something from inside his cell, but Rafael couldn't make out the words. There was an edge to everybody now, prisoners who'd been sound asleep five minutes ago tensing up. The tang of imminent violence was in the air, like the moment before a thunderstorm breaks. "Stay in line, stay cool," a guard next to Rafael said, his voice sharp.

Then the tactical unit moved into the cell, which hardly seemed big enough to contain them all. There was a loud scream, then nothing but the sound of moving feet in heavy boots as the guards carried the prisoner, who even from a distance was clearly unconscious, out of the cell. He'd been hit with an electric shield; Rafael could smell it, like burning plastic. There was muttering from other prisoners, vague noises of protest at seeing one of them treated this way, but Rafael thought it a little halfhearted. This was a white guy, a crazy dude: he had no allies on the block; nobody really wanted to stand up for him. Rafael guessed the man's refusal to leave his cell hadn't even been because he had something to hide, but was just a reflection of his crumbled mental state.

Once the unconscious prisoner had been taken out of the block, the guards began moving back into cells while prisoners were placed on the BOSS. There was still tension in the air, the energy flowing from the proximity to violence, but it felt contained.

Rafael made his way to the front of the line. Once there, he first had to place his chin on the back of the BOSS, the machine working its magic on his mouth. Then he sat in the chair, the scanner looking for something hidden up his ass. That was the most common hiding place on the body in Rikers, and Rafael had heard some pretty unbelievable stories about things that had gotten smuggled in that way—cell phones and the like. He couldn't even think about it without squirming.

Once cleared through the BOSS, Rafael went to stand in front of his cell, which a corrections officer was still inside of. His bedding had been removed and was being scanned by another CO with a wand like those used at airports.

He noticed that a guard was waving a scanner around the common areas. Rafael felt his nerves tighten as the guard held the scanner up to the air-conditioning vent that ran above the top of the cells and then began walking in his direction. Rafael knew something was in that vent right above his cell, but he didn't know what, or if the scanner would detect it.

A few days ago he had seen Luis Gutierrez fiddling with the vent. Rafael had been fifteen feet away, watching TV. He hadn't been able to tell what exactly Luis was doing, but had assumed he was hiding something. Rafael had wanted to tell Luis to put whatever it was somewhere else, but hadn't had the nerve.

The CO with the scanner was now waving it right above Rafael's cell. There was a high-pitched whine as the device reacted to something. A couple of other guards came over, and one started unscrewing the vent's grille.

Rafael watched nervously as the guard gingerly reached up into the opened vent. The CO pulled out a homemade shiv, a thin piece of metal that had been sharpened at one end, the other end wrapped in duct tape. Other guards quickly gathered around. Rafael could sense movement behind him, and he tensed, trying to keep himself still, not wanting to give the guards any excuse to take out their leftover adrenaline from the forced extraction on him.

"What you got?" a CO called out as he approached. His uniform had officer's stripes on the sleeve; Rafael assumed he was in charge.

"We found a shank hidden in the vent right above this cell," the guard holding the scanner said.

The head guy nodded brusquely, then turned to the gathered prisoners. "Who's cell is this?"

There wasn't any point in denying it, so Rafael stepped forward. "That blade's not mine," he said.

"Never heard that one," the CO holding the shiv said.

The head guy's eyes were locked onto Rafael. He had the hood of his visor lifted, the rest of him cloaked in the riot gear the entire tactical team was wearing. All Rafael could tell was that he was a middle-aged white guy with a graying mustache. "I'm Deputy Warden Ward. You're who?"

"Rafael Nazario."

"Nazario—you're that kid who killed a cop?"

Rafael was surprised that Ward knew who he was. "I didn't kill nobody," he replied. "And he wasn't a cop anymore."

"You mouthing off to me?" Ward barked, taking two quick steps forward, so that he was fully in Rafael's face. They were about the same height, but Rafael reckoned Ward had nearly fifty pounds on him.

Rafael hadn't been mouthing off, didn't think Ward really thought otherwise. The CO was just trying to provoke him. "No, sir," Rafael said, casting his eyes down, trying to appear subservient, just get through this.

"You affiliated, Nazario?"

Rafael shook his head, keeping his gaze on the floor. "I'm not in no gang," he said.

"You going to fess up that this is your blade?"

Rafael shook his head. "I never seen that before."

"What's it doing in the vent right above your cell? If you didn't put it there, you must've seen who did."

Ward was staring at him, awaiting a response, but Rafael knew that fingering Luis would lead to far worse problems than taking the blame himself. Whatever the guards could do to him was nothing compared to what prisoners would do if they considered him a snitch. Especially if he crossed Luis, who was with a gang. "I didn't see nobody messing around with that vent," he said.

"You planning to take out a guard here like you did that cop?"

"I never seen that blade before," Rafael said again, trying to keep his voice calm.

Ward sneered at him, moving still closer, their faces just inches apart. Rafael forced himself to meet the man's stare, his whole body braced for a blow. "Cuff him," Ward said to the COs behind Rafael. "We'll write him up for the shank."

"It's not mine," Rafael protested.

"You going to tell me whose it is, then?" Ward said. When Rafael didn't respond, Ward nodded to the guards. "Then looks like it's yours now."

CANDACE HAD arranged to meet Councilwoman Serran at her East Village office and speak to her on the walk to a school board meeting in the neighborhood. Candace had been as vague as possible about what she wanted to discuss, saying only that she was reporting on the changes to Riis. She figured there was a good chance that Serran already knew about her meeting with Dewberry, but that wouldn't necessarily be enough to make the councilwoman nervous.

Serran was a short, stocky Hispanic woman in her early forties, dressed in a light cotton business suit. She was wearing tennis shoes and carrying both a formal attaché case and a rumpled shopping bag.

"Hope you don't mind walking," Serran said as she shook Candace's hand. "The school's about fifteen minutes away."

Candace was wearing flats, as she usually did when working. "No problem," she said.

The heat of day was just starting to cool, and although it was too early for the East Village's nightlife to have kicked in, there were already plenty of people crowding the streets: the teenage punk rockers whose look hadn't changed since Candace's own teenage years in the city, the newer yuppies, heading home to their condos in buildings that twenty years ago had been squats, the Ukrainians and Puerto Ricans who still claimed dwindling slices of the neighborhood.

Serran turned out to be a quick walker, Candace having to increase her own pace as they headed up Avenue A. Candace wondered if it was a conscious effort on Serran's part to make their time as short as possible. "So I understand you're doing a piece on the changeover to mixed-income at Riis," Serran said.

Candace nodded. She was planning on doing her best Columbo impression today, not wanting Serran's guard up. People who spoke with her often failed to realize how much prep she did prior to any interview, all the time on the computer she logged before actually sitting down with someone. Information was power, never more so than when asking someone questions that you knew they weren't going to want to answer. Candace was confident Serran was going to be pretty unhappy by the time they were done.

"One basic thing I haven't been able to figure out is why Riis was chosen as the guinea pig, if you'll pardon the expression."

"First I heard of the proposal, it was already attached to Riis. That's how it was brought to the council's housing committee."

Given that Serran chaired the city council's committee on public housing, Candace's guess was that Riis had been chosen to sweeten the pot for Serran, ensure her support for the development. "Was it the mayor who brought it to you?"

"Actually it was Speaker Markowitz."

David Markowitz, the council's speaker, was young and preppy and photogenic, widely considered the most promising and ambitious city politician of his generation. Candace guessed, perhaps unfairly, that Serran must hate his guts.

"But you don't know why the speaker wanted it to be Riis?"

Serran shrugged. "I don't think he has any public housing in his own district," she said, before adding quickly: "That's off the record."

An interview subject couldn't place something off the record after saying it, which Candace certainly expected any politician to know. But she wasn't looking to work up a snarky quote (though perhaps accurate: Markowitz's district was in the Upper East Side) into anything—she was after bigger game. "How did Roth Properties come to be the developer on the Riis project?"

"There was a bidding process, but that was handled by the Housing Authority. The council didn't have a direct role."

"You probably know the Riis project better than anyone else in city politics," Candace said, intending it as flattery but also thinking it could well be true. "What do you really make of the idea of changing it to mixed-income?"

Serran glanced at her, Candace guessing the politician was gauging how honest she wanted to be. "I had some concerns, sure. I didn't want it to just end up being an excuse for dispersing poor people out of the neighborhood so that the city could do to the East Village what it just did to Times Square. Tourists own enough of this city as it is. But I'm a realist, and I can't pretend to much nostalgia for the Jacob Riis I grew up in. Avenue D wasn't pretty back then. I know some people in the community are opposed to anything that can be called gentrification, but it's not that simple. My constituents who live or work near the project—the people who own stores over there—I can tell you they supported this one hundred percent."

They turned onto First Avenue, just a few blocks below P.S. 19. Candace was already running out of time. But she still didn't think an all-out attack was the way to go. "I assume you've been following the recent murder case at Riis?"

Serran's face went dutifully somber. "The security guard? A terrible thing—not just for the victim, but for the community. But it didn't have anything to do with the changes to Riis, did it?"

"The family of the accused, the Nazarios, are getting evicted because of the private security guards. Have you heard anything about problems between the private security and residents, or issues concerning evictions?"

Serran shook her head. "There're always evictions going on at Riis, unfortunately."

"I've got sources telling me that the security guards are setting people up on minor drug charges, then using that to evict the families."

Candace watched Serran for a reaction, but saw nothing other than surprise. "If people have claims about that, you should have them call my office."

Candace nodded noncommittally. She was generally reluctant to broker such contacts, not wanting to take an active role in a story she was reporting, even when doing so might help her subjects. She decided instead to throw a curve. "Your brother Antonio hasn't told you anything about it?"

It worked: Serran's gaze darted toward Candace, then quickly away. "You mean because of his work at the ACCC," she said after a moment.

"Right," Candace said.

"I don't recall him mentioning it."

"I assume you follow the ACCC's work carefully," Candace said, studying Serran as she spoke. "Not just because of your brother. Most of their funding comes from you, doesn't it?"

Candace had expected Serran to be on guard for the question, but the councilwoman appeared unnerved. An ambulance with its siren on went screaming by, giving Serran an opportunity to pause for a long moment before answering. "I've helped them secure some funding from the city, yes," Serran said once the noise had died down. "There's nothing surprising about that. Riis is in my district, and I'm very active with public housing issues through chairing the council's committee."

"But aren't you then essentially helping both sides? I mean in that you're supporting the redevelopment, while also financing its opposition?"

"The existing community at Riis deserves protection. That's what the ACCC is doing. My focus was on helping to ensure that the existing residents had a voice."

Bombs away, Candace thought. She wasn't getting anywhere interesting playing nice, and she lacked the time for a subtle approach. "What about the fact that you allocated a half million dollars to the ACCC, and a short time later you got a few dozen donations from people who were in some way connected to the organization? It looks to me like in the month or so after they got the city's money, you must've received at least a couple hundred thousand dollars in contributions linked to the ACCC. And that's just what I've been able to track down so far."

"What are you suggesting?" Serran said. She'd stopped walking right in the middle of the sidewalk, so Candace stopped too, looking the councilwoman in the eye.

"I'm not suggesting anything. But it is a fact that those two things happened in quick succession. You arranged for a lot of city money to go to the ACCC, and people connected to the ACCC then gave a lot of money to your reelection campaign."

"I haven't done anything wrong," Serran protested, but it sounded feeble to Candace. Serran looked thoroughly rattled; she looked, Candace thought, like somebody who'd just been caught. "What's your agenda here?"

"I'm simply going where the story takes me," Candace said. "I was just trying to get a handle on the redevelopment, which brought me to the ACCC. That organization appears to consist of a storefront, a telephone number, and a couple of desks. If they've made good use of a half million dollars in city funds, it's not readily apparent. Perhaps that's because a lot of that money just passed through them on its way to your reelection campaign."

"Jesus," Serran said, the councilwoman appearing so shaken that Candace found herself momentarily entertaining the possibility that she really hadn't known. "To the best of my knowledge, all campaign contributions I've received are legitimate. It isn't illegal for employees of a nonprofit that receives city funding to donate to a city politician."

"There's probably something illegal about it if they were simply laundering the city's payments to the ACCC back to your campaign," Candace said.

Serran flushed, but held her anger in check. "If they were contributing taxpayer money, I'll certainly return it. But I don't know that's true."

"Your position is that you had no idea that so many people connected to the ACCC were donating to you?"

"Maybe my brother was encouraging people," Serran said. "There's nothing wrong with that."

Candace wasn't going to argue the point, though she didn't find it convincing. "You want me not to focus on you, what you need to do is put the focus somewhere else."

"And how would I do that?" Serran asked. They were still planted in the middle of the sidewalk, people giving them dirty looks as they walked by.

"You're the council's point person on public housing. I'm assuming Simon Roth wanted you on his side in terms of becoming the developer on Riis. Did somebody suggest to you setting up the ACCC, getting it established as the visible opposition to the transition to mixed-income; you could fund it with one hand and take the money for your campaign with the other? Was that your reward for supporting the project?"

"Is that what you want me to say?" Serran said, studying Candace carefully.

Candace realized she'd overplayed her hand. "I want you to tell me the truth," she replied.

"What you just said would mean I was taking a bribe for my support of Riis."

"I was speculating is all," Candace said. "My point is just that if there's a larger context you want to put this in, I'm listening."

"Nobody bribed me to support the changes to Riis," Serran said after a moment. "I believe in what's happening there."

Candace was irritated with herself for feeling disappointment; she shouldn't have come into the interview with preconceptions that Serran would lead her to Simon Roth. "So how did your brother come to be working for the ACCC?"

"Can you keep Antonio out of it?" Serran pleaded, her voice strained. She looked on the verge of tears. "My brother's not a public figure. I understand that I'm fair game, but my brother's just a regular guy, trying to get through the day. He doesn't need you destroying him on the front page of a newspaper."

"I'm not out to destroy anyone," Candace protested, a little taken aback. Anger in a subject she could deal with, but pleading was hard, and unexpected from a politician. "But you see how this looks from my angle on it."

"I see how you can make it look if you choose to," Serran replied.

Candace didn't like the sound of that: it wasn't a matter of her using insinuation to manufacture a scandal. "I think things usually look like what they actually are," she said. "And this looks like taxpayer money being funneled into your campaign coffers. If you want to get back to me with a different story, by all means, but you have very little time."

WHEN SHE returned to the newsroom, Candace left a voice mail for Nugent, giving her editor a heads-up that she thought she was well on her way to breaking a significant story. Next she turned to David Markowitz, wanting to see if she could find anything indicating why he would be leading the charge on having Roth Properties transform Jacob Riis. She started by reading through some archived articles from her paper from when Markowitz had been elected speaker, reminding her of his privileged upbringing on the Upper East Side (not so different from her own); college at Princeton followed by law school at Yale, a handful of years as a staffer for Senator Schumer, then a couple of years with the state attorney general's office before winning a council seat his first time in the race, followed by becoming speaker four years later. Term limits were going to force the current mayor out at the next election, and Markowitz was among the names rumored to be running.

Candace searched for connections between Markowitz and the Riis development. She came across references to his support for the project, but nothing that explained its origins. Next she searched for links between Markowitz and the Roth family. She didn't find anything other than some passing mentions.

She went on the Secretary of State's site, printing out a list of Markowitz's donors. The first thing she noticed going through them was that he had a lot more contributors than Serran, and that they'd generally given a lot more money. Many of his donations were for the maximum allowed, a couple thousand a pop. And while virtually all of Serran's donors had been individuals, with Markowitz many were companies.

Candace noticed that many of the business donations were from corporations she'd never heard of. She circled a number of them, then searched for their registrations with the Department of State.

On her third try, a limited liability corporation with the unrevealing name MTS LLC, the listed address for the business rang a bell. Candace couldn't actually place it until she saw that it matched the address of the company's registered service agent: the law firm Blake and Wolcott.

·32·

DUNCAN WAS sitting in on the deposition of Jack Pellettieri, the head of the concrete company at the Aurora Tower. Pellettieri had his own lawyer defending him; Duncan was just there to observe, see if the guy said anything that would harm Roth Properties.

They were in the office of Pellettieri's lawyer, Harvey Peters, who practiced a good deal farther down the legal hierarchy than Blake and Wolcott. His office was in a nondescript building just off Madison Avenue. The conference room was small, stuffy, and windowless: a depressing place to spend a day.

Duncan had arrived a little before nine, everyone else already in place. Although usually the mood in the room before a deposition was at least polite, the tension here was palpable, especially coming from Pellettieri. The plaintiffs' lawyer, Isaac Marcus, was also more withdrawn than usual, going through his papers and barely looking up to acknowledge Duncan's entrance.

The tension was understandable: Duncan figured this was the most important deposition of the case. He didn't see any way Pellettieri himself wiggled out of liability; the question was more whether he was going to take anyone else down with him.

Marcus came out swinging from his opening questions, going straight to the failure to support the concrete as it set. Peters began objecting strenuously and loudly, lecturing Marcus about his questions while the plaintiffs' lawyer snapped back at him. Duncan leaned back, aloof from the squabbling, his focus on Pellettieri, who also seemed to be ignoring the skirmishes.

It quickly became clear that Pellettieri was taking the hit all by himself. He agreed that the pouring had fallen behind schedule. He conceded that the steel rebar that was supposed to undergird the concrete

while it settled had not been properly anchored. He further admitted
that the temporary supports that were supposed to be in place to provide
backup while the concrete hardened had not been correctly installed,
and that as a result they'd collapsed as soon as the rebar had given out.
Pellettieri had no real choice but to concede that all of this violated
established construction techniques.

Marcus followed up on these concessions by introducing a number
of Pellettieri's invoices into evidence. With little fight, Pellettieri agreed
that his company had billed for safety work that it had never actually
performed.

Not that Pellettieri took personal responsibility for any of it. On the
contrary, he denied knowing that corners were being cut. Duncan didn't
believe him, didn't think anybody in the room did. Not that it mattered,
anyway: Pellettieri's company would be on the hook regardless.

Even though he was nailing Pellettieri to the wall, Marcus did not
appear satisfied. The plaintiffs' lawyer went on to ask a series of questions about whether anyone at Omni, the general contractor, had
pressed Pellettieri not to do the safety work, or had known he wasn't
doing so. Pellettieri flatly denied it, not taking anyone down with him. If
the plaintiffs couldn't get to Omni, that pretty much ensured they
couldn't get to the developers either. Roth Properties was entitled to
rely on the general contractor for updates on the construction; if Omni
didn't know about problems, there was no reason to think that Roth did.

Pellettieri clearly was not enjoying his battering at Marcus's hands.
He was big, with a sloping gut and a receding hairline. There was a suggestion of violence about him; he was the kind of guy you could picture
getting into a bar fight. His beefy face was flushed, sweat beading his
temples, which he angrily stabbed at with his fingertips. Duncan hoped
Pellettieri wasn't about to have a heart attack on them.

By the time they broke for lunch Duncan thought the end of the
case was pretty much in sight. Pellettieri would have little choice but to
offer a generous settlement—Duncan guessing the case would close out
at ten million tops, maybe as low as four or five. One of the dead guys
was an illegal, which put his future earnings into question, dragging the
number down.

Duncan joined Peters and Pellettieri for lunch, the three of them
going to a bar and grill down the street, Pellettieri not talking the entire

way, still pissed. Once they were seated and the waitress came over, Pellettieri ordered a Glenlivet on the rocks. "That's really not a good idea," Peters said, putting a hand on his client's arm. Pellettieri jerked away, the movement so violent the waitress took an instinctive step away from the table.

"What's it matter?" Pellettieri demanded, his voice shaking. "The whole thing's over now anyway."

Peters leaned in toward Pellettieri, speaking softly into his ear while Duncan looked away, feeling something like embarrassment. Finally they were at least able to get through ordering, though Pellettieri still insisted on having his whiskey.

Duncan was a bit thrown by the extent of Pellettieri's anger: the guy must've seen this day coming, and he had no one but himself to blame. Peters was still trying to calm Pellettieri down, telling him that the worst of the deposition was over. Pellettieri didn't pretend to listen, looking around the restaurant like he was alone at the table. Only when the waitress brought his drink did his focus return; he downed half of it in a gulp before turning his baleful glare on Duncan. "You tell that fucker I held up my end," he said.

Duncan was thrown for a loss. "Excuse me?" he said.

"That drunk creep," Pellettieri said. "You tell him."

"I have no idea what you're talking about," Duncan protested. His first thought had been Blake, but "drunk creep" didn't fit.

"Don't bullshit me," Pellettieri said. "That's why you're here, isn't it?"

Duncan still wasn't putting this together for sure, though his guess was that Pellettieri was referring to someone connected to the Roths. "I'm not bullshitting," he said, feeling himself acting guilty as a nervous reaction.

"Jack," Harvey said. "Come on now. Let's drop it."

Pellettieri held his glare on Duncan a moment longer. "Maybe you don't know anything. Probably makes it easier for you."

Duncan looked to Harvey, but the other lawyer wouldn't meet his eyes. "What's this about?" Duncan asked.

"Ask your own people," Pellettieri said, "you really want to know."

Duncan hesitated, unsure what his next move was. If Pellettieri's deposition testimony was untruthful, Duncan didn't want to hear about it. Knowing would ethically obligate him to do something, and that would be a mess. His instinctive curiosity battled against his lawyer's training, and his training won out.

"I'm sorry you're upset," he said blandly, closing the door on the subject.

"You just tell him," Pellettieri said. "Tell him I gave it up like I was supposed to."

DUNCAN WAS still trying to figure out what to make of it when he met Neil Levine for a drink that night at the Royalton. He asked Neil if he'd come across anything about Jack Pellettieri when reviewing Roth Properties' files on the Aurora.

"The concrete guy? I remember there was some back-and-forth with Jeremy Roth telling Omni he didn't like something about the company that had made the lowest bid, wanted to go with Pellettieri instead. But that was way early, obviously."

"You never saw anything about any problems with Pellettieri? In terms of billing, or not getting work done properly, anything like that?"

Neil shook his head before taking a sip of his Manhattan. "Why, what's up?"

Duncan didn't think Neil needed to know the full story. "Pellettieri was acting weird today at his depo, is all. You ever see any direct communication between him and anyone at Roth?"

Neil thought for a moment. "Don't think so. Nobody at Roth was really dealing with the subs, far as I know."

No surprise, Duncan thought: normally a developer wouldn't be directly communicating with the subcontractors. "Do me a favor," he said. "Have the staff attorneys tag any communication involving Pellettieri, or even where his name comes up, and make sure you take a look at it."

"Sure," Neil said. "But what am I looking for?"

"Beats me," Duncan replied. "Just anything that doesn't seem right."

"I can't believe how many documents we still have to look through. None of them have anything to do with the accident."

"The DA's casting a wide net."

"It's still a little hard for me to get my mind around how much of our time is spent dealing with this stuff that's just categorically irrelevant," Neil said.

Duncan had once spent twenty-five straight days in a warehouse in suburban New Jersey, digging through lab notes in a patent dispute, most of what he was looking at way too technical for him to have any sense of what it meant. He didn't need Neil to tell him how mind-numbingly tedious document review could be. "There're dues to be paid, is all," he said. "You'll get to more interesting stuff if you're patient."

"Like a murder case? What's going on with that, anyway?"

Duncan told Neil about turning down the plea; his recent consultation with Professor Cole about challenging the GSR. He could see Neil's eyes light up, feel his envy of the case. On some level it didn't make sense: Neil could have become a criminal defense attorney if he'd wanted to. Of course, any such job would pay a fraction of what Blake and Wolcott did.

"You need any help on it?" Neil asked. "Working with the expert or anything?"

"We're keeping staffing light, since it's pro bono," Duncan replied. In truth, he felt territorial about the case, was enjoying having it to himself.

Neil finished his drink, looked around for the waitress. He seemed to be fighting back a smile. "So I heard a rumor about you," he said.

Duncan's first thought was something to do with his upcoming partnership vote, though on reflection Neil seemed unlikely to have the inside track on that kind of office gossip. "What's that?" he asked.

"I heard you and Lily were an item."

Duncan had long been braced for this to make the rounds, though he didn't understand why it was happening so long after they'd broken up. "We went out a couple of times like a year ago," he said, as much of a concession as he was willing to make. "But it's old news, and we were never really an item."

Neil looked disappointed. "I heard you guys broke up or something at the Rainbow Room party."

Duncan didn't like the idea that this was being gossiped about, but if it was he preferred to know about it. "Lily was pissed about something at the party, but it wasn't me. And we certainly couldn't have broken up that night, since we weren't together."

"You one of those white boys with yellow fever?" Neil asked.

Duncan tried not to react. People said things like this; they didn't mean anything by it. He'd never mentioned his background to Neil, couldn't expect the guy to have picked it up on his own. It wouldn't be fair to Neil to make a thing out of it, Duncan thought. "Like I said, we only went out a couple of times," he said.

"Not that you'd need an Asian fetish to go out with Lily," Neil said quickly, clearly sensing that Duncan wasn't going along. "She's pretty, though she cracks the whip a little when dealing with junior associates."

"Lily could teach you a thing or two," Duncan replied.

Neil arched his brows. "I'll bet she could."

Duncan was a little pissed, but trying not to show it. "About practicing law, asshole," he said.

"That too," Neil agreed.

·33·

"**M**R. SPEAKER,**"** Simon Roth said, gesturing David Markowitz to a seat. "What can we do for you?"

Leah sat in the chair next to Markowitz, facing her father's desk,
while their general counsel, Roger Carrington, was seated on a couch off
to the side. Markowitz had not only come to them, he'd come alone:
clear signs that he was worried about something and trying to keep a lid
on it.

"This reporter who's out to get you, Snow from the *Journal*, she's
calling my office, trying to come in to see me," Markowitz said. He was
looking only at Simon. "She's dug up all the LLC contributions to my
campaign, seems to have figured out they're companies controlled by
you."

"Did you confirm that we own them?"

"I haven't talked to her directly, just had my staff say they'll look into
it, and that LLC contributions are perfectly legal."

"Which they are," Carrington said, from his perch on the couch
behind them. "The campaign contribution limits only apply to individual businesses. If someone happens to own fifty LLCs, each one still has
its separate contribution limit."

Markowitz shook his head impatiently. Leah assumed Carrington
hadn't been talking for the speaker's benefit anyway, but rather to assure
her father that the company wasn't exposed. "Legal doesn't cut it in my
line of work," Markowitz said. "How it looks is the question."

"What is it you want me to do, David?" Simon asked, Leah noting
how her father spoke as though there wasn't a company at all, like she
wasn't even in the room.

"You're the one she's after," Markowitz said. "My political career is
just collateral damage, far as she's concerned."

"Your political career is not in any danger," Simon said. "This is widely done, even if not widely known. We'll get in front of it, put it in context, and also see about getting this little vendetta of hers tamped down."

"It sounds like she's trying to make it connect to Riis, look like quid pro quo between you getting the project and the contributions."

Leah could tell that her father was struggling to keep his patience. "She can look all she wants for that," he said. "Seeing as there's nothing to find. We know better than to put something like that in writing, don't we?"

Markowitz looked aghast, even after he realized Simon was joking. "It's not funny," he said. "Somebody puts two things next to each other in a newspaper article, people jump to conclusions. I've seen federal pay-to-play cases get started on less."

"There's nothing here that isn't politics as usual," Simon said.

"I also hear she's poking around about evictions at Riis, with your security guys. Is there a problem there?"

Leah was surprised to see an uncomfortable look from her father. She wondered if he was noticing the same thing about her. "What kind of problem?" he asked.

"From what I'm hearing, she's looking into whether they are involved in getting people evicted, something so you wouldn't have to move people back in."

"There're nearly five thousand residents at Riis," Simon said. "She think we're going to pick them off one at a time?"

"All I know is, she's after blood," Markowitz said. "What did you do to this woman?"

"Called her a liar," Leah said.

"THIS IS going to take some navigating," Simon said to Leah after Markowitz had left, Roger Carrington showing the speaker out.

"I told you not to file the libel suit," Leah said. "You flashed the red cape at her, and now she's on the rampage. What's this eviction thing she's gotten hold of?"

Simon hesitated. "For mixed-income to work over there, we have to get rid of the bad apples."

Leah wasn't letting him off that easy. "Get rid of them how, exactly?"

"Every apartment we don't have to rent back to an existing resident brings in about twenty-five grand a year more in revenue," Simon said, ignoring her question. "We reduce who we have to bring back by even forty households, that's a million a year in additional market-rate money coming in. Play that kind of reduction out over a few years, you're talking serious money."

Leah couldn't believe what she was hearing. All developers did a lot of give and take with the city over building some below-market-rate units as part of getting permission to build, and a certain amount of gamesmanship was expected in fulfilling such obligations. But this was public housing, for Christ's sake. Bad publicity could jeopardize the entire project, if not worse. "So you're having the security guards throw people out?"

"We're not throwing people out for no reason. I simply told Loomis's people to be on the lookout for bad behavior. The Housing Authority understands that eliminating the dregs before bringing in market-rate tenants is a necessary step for this thing to work. Getting rid of people who aren't going to fit into the new version makes sense for everybody."

Leah didn't think this was the whole story. "Did you give Loomis's crew an incentive to do this?"

Simon refused to look embarrassed. "What if I did?"

"Well, then, Jesus, Dad, did it ever occur to you that maybe they'd cut some corners on who they kicked out?"

"Darryl's guys know better than to set people up."

Leah didn't share her father's optimism in this regard, but there was no point in arguing. "The reporter's digging into it now, and we know she's going to paint a dark picture. How do we cut that off?"

Simon looked away, Leah wondering if he was still uncomfortable plotting strategy with her. "I'm going to tell Darryl to turn it up a notch on her."

"That could just add fuel."

Simon shrugged, clearly not interested in an extensive discussion. "She's used to Marquess of Queensberry rules," he said. "Let's see how she likes a street fight."

"You really think Darryl can scare her off the story?"

"That's only a step in the dance. I'm going to reach out to Friedman, who's trying to stop the bleeding over there. But we've also got to get in front of the LLC thing, for our own sake as well as David's. We're going to have to respond to the reporter on that front—we can't leave David to take the hit. Why don't you grab the reins? Talk to Roger, make sure you're up to speed on the LLC issue, and give the PR girl a call to go over things."

Their outside public relations person was a brassy woman in her fifties who was nobody's idea of a girl, but Leah wasn't in the mood to confront her father's provocations. "Anything else?" she said, shifting in her chair.

"What's going on with the Aurora wrongful death?"

Leah didn't want to talk to her father about the Aurora case, but if she wasn't forthcoming her father would eventually hear it all from Blake. "Depos are under way," she said. "They just did the concrete contractor. Sounds like he's facing liability, though the rest of us are clear."

"Why is the contractor on the hook?"

Leah hesitated, wanting to limit the extent that she had to get into this as much as possible. "He didn't do the safety work."

For a moment Simon just looked at her, frowning. "And nobody caught this?" he said.

"Doesn't look like it," Leah said. "We certainly wouldn't have."

"Did we pay him for it?"

"He was overbilling generally, is how it looks. But it's not like he was going to submit invoices saying he wasn't performing work."

Simon was full into a slow boil. "How much did he take us for?"

"That can't be our priority right now, Dad," Leah said. "Let's get the lawsuit taken care of, then worry about it."

Simon did not react well to being told what to worry about, and he fixed his daughter with a skeptical look. "What are you not telling me?"

"What do you mean?"

"Don't play dumb with me, Leah," Simon said. "I've seen all your report cards."

"I'm sparing you the details, is all. Everything's under control," Leah said, doing her best to hold her father's gaze. She never had been good at lying to him.

·34·

LEAH WAS making Duncan dinner. They'd been e-mailing every day or so since dinner at Jean Georges, but it'd taken a while for their schedules to mesh for meeting up again. Duncan hadn't been in any hurry; whatever was going on here, he needed to proceed slowly and very carefully. But then Leah had complicated that by proposing Friday-night dinner at her apartment.

She lived in a penthouse loft in Tribeca, walking distance from where the Aurora Tower was under construction. While considerably smaller and less ostentatious than her father's town house, Leah's loft was far more stylish, with muted colors, exposed brick, and hardwood floors.

Only the bedroom and bathroom were walled off; the rest of the apartment was open space. Like most New Yorkers, Duncan was an old hand at eyeballing the size of an apartment: he put this one at over three thousand square feet, which he guessed in this neighborhood put the price around six million. It was a rich person's apartment without a doubt, but Stephen Blake's lavish Westchester mansion was probably worth nearly the same.

"This place is amazing," Duncan said.

"I feel a little weird living like this. Me without an artistic bone in my body."

"I'm sure your family has sold plenty of downtown lofts to people who weren't artists."

"That doesn't mean I'm not part of the problem. Drink?"

"Sure."

"I've got both colors of wine, vodka, gin, scotch, brandy, and port."

"Cigars?" Duncan said, arching an eyebrow.

Leah smiled: "I know, I'm a sixty-something man trapped in a thirty-something woman's body."

"I'll have what you're having," Duncan said. "So long as you're not having port."

Leah headed to the kitchen, instructing Duncan to sit, so he went over to the couch. He looked around the room, his attention caught by a large piece of contemporary art, two shadowy figures enveloped in an abstract red landscape, like they were emerging from flames.

Leah returned with two glasses of white wine. She handed one to Duncan and settled onto the couch beside him. She was dressed casually, in a dark skirt and a short-sleeved cream-colored shirt. Her hair was loose, unlike whenever Duncan had seen her in a professional context.

"So there's something I need to talk to you about," Duncan said.

"That's your business voice, isn't it?"

"I'm afraid so."

Leah shook her head. "It's Friday night, Duncan, and I just poured us wine. Are you one of those lawyers without an off switch?"

"I wouldn't have brought it up if it wasn't important," Duncan said, though he was already having second thoughts.

"Is it something that you want me to do something about tonight?"

"It's not urgent in that sense, no."

"Well, then, shut up and drink," Leah said with a smile.

"Will do," Duncan said, feeling chagrined. He still wasn't sure where the line was between business and personal stuff between him and Leah, but clearly being in her apartment on a Friday night was not on the business side of it.

"Dinner will be ready in about twenty minutes," Leah said, clearly talking to fill the dead air.

"You really didn't have to cook, you know."

"Of course I didn't have to. But I thought it would be nice. Plus I get to show you that I'm actually capable of doing it, which I thought would impress you."

"I never had any doubt that you could fend for yourself," Duncan said. "Though I certainly feel honored that you'd go to such trouble on my account."

"You didn't answer my question before," Leah said. "About whether you have an off switch."

"From being a lawyer? Not as much as I would like. It becomes harder to turn off with each passing year."

"That was one of the reasons I never practiced," Leah said. "I thought law school was useful in terms of learning some methods of thought, but ultimately the lawyer's view of the world always struck me as a little parched."

"Parched?"

"Yeah, you know, dry. Desert-like. I worried that it appealed to the side of me that I didn't want to give myself over to."

"What side is that?"

"The side that plays my life like a chess game," Leah said, putting her wineglass down on a coaster on the coffee table before standing up. "I've got to step back into the kitchen. Why don't you put some music on?"

"Sure," Duncan said. He made his way over to the iPod that was plugged into Leah's stereo receiver. Duncan shuffled around on it for a couple of minutes, checking out Leah's taste, before selecting an old Sade album he hadn't heard in over a dozen years, Leah giving him a bemused look as it came on.

"Is this what you played to seduce girls in college?"

"No," Duncan said. "But come to think of it, I think maybe a girl played it once when she wanted to seduce me."

Dinner was broiled swordfish with a rice pilaf, simple but well pre-pared. Leah dimmed the track lighting over the dining room table, which served to accentuate the extent to which "Smooth Operator" was indeed booty music.

"You're smiling to yourself," Leah said.

"Was I?"

"Can I take that as a sign that you're finally relaxing a little?"

"It's probably the wine," Duncan said.

"Then by all means keep drinking if that's what it's going to take."

"Take to do what?"

"For you to forget you're my lawyer."

Duncan forced a smile, feeling uncomfortable with the subject. "The swordfish is terrific," he said after a moment.

"You sound surprised."

"Not at all. I'm sure you succeed at everything you try."

"Right," Leah said dryly. "I'll never know where I would've ended up without the running start of my family. That's the trade-off of being born with money: you never really get to take your own measure."

After dinner Leah poured them both glasses of port. Duncan took it in the spirit offered. "This is mad tasty, actually," he said, after sipping.

"Port is underrated," Leah said. "Even without cigars. So should I give you the tour?"

"The tour?" Duncan said, gesturing out at the room. "Can't we do that from here?"

"You can't see everything from here. The bedroom, for example."

"By all means, then," Duncan said. "Give me the tour."

LEAH KEPT her eyes open while making love. Duncan found it disconcerting: it added a different level of intimacy—almost too much, at least for the first time. Leah had a pale, thin body, the arc of her rib cage visible as she lay on her back. Duncan worked his way down her body, tasting her, then slowly back up, kissing her neck as she guided him in. He took his time, moving slowly, catching her gaze, then kissing her small breasts as a way to avoid eye contact. Leah was quiet in bed, hard to read. Duncan lasted as long as he could, unable to detect any approach of an orgasm in her, and finally let himself go. She kissed his neck as he subsided, her hand stroking his hair.

"I have to tell you," Duncan said, settling in beside her, "you give great tour."

"So what was it you wanted to talk to me about before?"

Duncan laughed. "We couldn't talk business before dinner, but we can in bed?"

"I didn't want our evening to turn into work," Leah replied. "Now I'm not so much worried about that."

"It can wait."

"What was the topic?"

"Honestly, this isn't the time."

"Just tell me what it's about," Leah said, her voice playful, though Duncan thought that might be a front.

"If I tell you what it's about, we're just going to end up talking about it."

"But now I'm all curious."

Duncan rubbed his eyes and sat up a little in bed. He could tell Leah wasn't going to let it go. "I was at Jack Pellettieri's deposition," he said.

"And something kinda strange happened at lunch. Pellettieri was pissed, and he told me to tell my boss that he'd done like he was supposed to, meaning taking the rap for the accident."

"Did you tell Blake this?"

"Pellettieri wasn't talking about Blake," Duncan said. "I think he was talking about either your brother or your father."

Duncan could feel Leah stiffen beside him. "What makes you say that?"

"I could be wrong," Duncan said quickly. "Pellettieri wasn't exactly a model of clarity. But he was talking about somebody inside your shop, not mine; I'm pretty sure of that."

"What're you saying?"

"I don't know what exactly's going on, but I know enough to know that I probably don't want to know. And I have no idea what if anything you know about it. But it's a dangerous game to be playing, that's all. Pellettieri didn't strike me as so in control."

"We're not playing any game," Leah said angrily.

"Look, I'm not—this is me as your lawyer—as your *ally*. I can't protect you from things I don't know anything about. I'm not going to try to figure out what it is, and we can never talk about it again, but I thought I should tell somebody that Pellettieri gave me a message to pass on."

"I've never even met Jack Pellettieri," Leah said.

"Let's forget it," Duncan said.

"Sorry if I was snappish just now," Leah said after a moment. "It's a dreary business, is all. The accident, I mean."

"Can we adjourn the meeting?" Duncan said, putting his hand on Leah's hip.

"By all means," Leah said as she turned toward him.

DUNCAN HAD left his BlackBerry at home when he'd come over to Leah's apartment—a rare indulgence, even on a Friday. He and Leah ended up going out for brunch in the morning, and it was well into the afternoon by the time Duncan got back to his apartment.

The first thing he did upon getting in was pick up his BlackBerry. It was pathetic, Duncan thought, how completely tethered to the fucking thing he was. Unless he was asleep or in court he rarely went much more than an hour without checking his e-mail, and sure enough he had a dozen new messages since yesterday evening, as well as a voice mail. He skimmed the messages, not seeing anything that couldn't wait until Monday, then checked the phone message.

He was surprised to hear his father's voice. Max rarely called him; they hadn't spoken in a month. His father's message was from eleven last night, asking Duncan to call back as soon as he could, his voice tight and muted.

Duncan returned the call. "Something wrong?" Duncan said, after his father picked up on the second ring.

"It's your mother," Max said.

"Is she okay?" Duncan asked, but he already knew she wasn't, that it was bad, though just how bad he didn't know, not until he heard his father say the impossible words, tell him that his mother was dead.

·35·

From the August 9, 2008, edition of the New York Journal:

AS HOUSING PROJECT PREPARES FOR TRANSFORMATION, CONTROVERSY SWIRLS AROUND RECENT EVICTIONS
By Candace Snow

Seventeen-year-old LaShonda Jennings thought the security guard who she claims planted marijuana on her was playing some kind of prank. But it's no laughing matter now that her entire family is facing eviction because of her arrest.

The Jennings family is not alone. The city's Housing Authority is evicting at least a dozen families from a housing project based on accusations of drug possession that are allegedly fabricated.

The Jacob Riis project is being transformed into mixed-income housing in a pilot program. Critics of the plan have long pointed to a problem of simple mathematics: in order to include all of the new residents, there would not be room to return many of the existing ones.

Indeed, city records show that over the past six months the Housing Authority has commenced over two dozen eviction proceedings involving more than 75 existing Riis residents—a far greater number than at any other public housing complex of similar size. In 2006, before the transformation of Riis began, the city instituted just 7 eviction proceedings there.

In at least a dozen of the recent cases, private security guards employed by the developer behind the project have claimed to catch young project residents—usually teenagers—openly possessing or smoking marijuana. If one member of a household in public housing is arrested for drug use, the entire family can be evicted. But many of the teens tell the same story: that they were framed by the security guards, and then pled guilty to disorderly conduct—a mere violation, not a crime—simply to avoid the hassle and risk of fighting a misdemeanor charge, not realizing that such a plea would potentially open the door to their families getting evicted.

LaShonda's story is typical. She claims that she was chatting with a friend on a bench outside her building when she was approached by a security guard who claimed to have just seen the two of them rolling a joint. "He just straight-up planted drugs on us," LaShonda said. "It was crazy. I didn't understand why he would do that, not until we got a letter saying we were being evicted."

Another teenager who was allegedly caught by the private security guards is Rafael Nazario, 19. Nazario was supposedly busted smoking pot by a policeman turned security guard named Sean Fowler. After pleading guilty to disorderly conduct, Rafael and his grandmother found themselves facing eviction. Nazario has since been arrested for fatally shooting Fowler.

Darryl Loomis, a former police lieutenant and the head of the security company involved, did not respond to repeated requests for comment. A spokesman for the Housing Authority said that while eviction decisions were made on a case-by-case basis, generally any drug-related arrest of a public housing resident leads to the eviction of their entire household. "Nobody ever told me that we'd get thrown out of our home because of the guilty plea," LaShonda Jennings rejoined. "I only took the plea because my lawyer said if I fought it I could end up with a real criminal record."

According to LaShonda's mother, if they are evicted from public housing the family will not be able to afford to stay in New York, and will instead move in with relatives down south. "This project may not be much," her mother said. "But it's where I raised my children, and it's my home. The city is trying to take that away from me, based on a lie."

THE SIGHT of Henry Tacy—her paper's bellicose editor in chief—bearing down on her in the newsroom struck fear in Candace, as it did in every reporter at the paper. Her first thought was that there was a problem with the story she'd published that day, or else with the Serran story that she was now finishing up. Not even the fact that Tacy was smiling mitigated her rush of nerves.

"I come bearing glad tidings," Tacy announced in his booming voice. Everyone within thirty feet who hadn't already been watching his approach now turned to him. "You, my dear, are no longer a defendant in a lawsuit."

It took a moment to sink in. "The libel suit's over? What happened?"

"Roth agreed to drop it. I guess he saw the error of his ways."

The idea of Simon Roth simply walking away from a lawsuit seemed completely out of character. "I didn't see that coming," Candace said.

"Maybe his lawyers convinced him he couldn't win. Maybe he thought he'd made his point, such as it was."

"Gift horses, I guess. That's really great news. It's a weight off."

Tacy nodded. "Of course, we were never worried about actually losing, but it could have dragged on for a couple more years, cost us God knows what in legal bills."

"I'm just happy I can go back to concentrating on doing my job."

"By all means," Tacy said, offering her a slight bow. "Be my guest."

CANDACE WAS still buzzing with relief a couple of hours later when Brock Anders came over to her cubicle. "I just heard," he said, kissing her cheek in greeting. "Congratulations, ex-defendant."

Candace thanked him, allowing herself to express some of the relief she felt at not having the lawsuit hanging over her. It'd felt like a black mark next to her name, an unresolved accusation that she'd fucked up a story.

"We must celebrate, darling. Tonight?"

Candace hesitated. It wasn't like she was going to be fielding any other offers for her evening. She'd never even properly broken things off with Gabriel; she'd simply stopped calling, and he'd either taken the hint or been equally indifferent. "Only if you promise not to keep me out too late," she said.

"I'm absolutely not going to promise that," Brock replied. "You deserve a late night. I want you crawling in here at noon tomorrow, wearing sunglasses."

"I'm too old for midweek hangovers."

Brock shook his head. "I swear, it's like this isn't even a newsroom anymore. Where are all the drunks?"

"Laid off," Candace replied.

"It'll be work too, tonight. I've got a de la Renta event we can start off at, over in the Meatpacking District."

"Why are they always *events*, these things you go to?"

"That's not true," Brock said. "Sometimes they're premieres."

Candace's phone rang. "I'll get back to you," she said to Brock, before answering.

The caller turned out to be William Stanton, who demanded to see her right away. Stanton refused to talk on the phone, or even explain what was so urgent. Candace didn't feel like dealing with him right now, but it was obvious that William was upset: there was a tremor in his voice, an edge to his insistence.

Stanton had last called her a couple of weeks ago, right after he'd gotten a deposition subpoena from Duncan's firm. It hadn't been a pleasant conversation, Stanton insisting that she do something to prevent him from being deposed. Candace had promised she'd talk to her lawyer, but she'd already been virtually certain there wouldn't be any way to stop it. Stanton had lost his temper, raising his voice at her, reminding her that she'd promised to keep his identity confidential.

Candace had spoken to Rosenstein about it, but he'd told her there was nothing he could do. Rosenstein had called her after the deposition, so she knew that Stanton had outed himself. She had little doubt that he was even angrier with her now, but Stanton had been a good source and she felt an obligation to at least go meet with him, even if it just meant letting him vent.

She met Stanton at a diner on Ninth Avenue in the Forties, a short walk from the *Journal*'s office, which was a little west of Madison Square Garden. Stanton was already there when Candace arrived, a cup of coffee in front of him on the table. "So what's up, William?" she asked.

"I just got through meeting with a lawyer," Stanton replied, his voice worn and scratchy.

"What do you need a lawyer for?" Candace said.

"They fired me," Stanton said flatly.

"The DOB fired you? Why?"

Stanton barked out a failed laugh, then coughed. "Insubordination."

Although she found it hard to believe Stanton had been fired for any reason, insubordination did at least sound somewhat plausible. "What happened?"

"What happened is I talked to you."

Candace winced. "They told you that?"

"They didn't need to. They benched me months ago, back when they suspected but couldn't prove I was your source. Now that they knew for sure, it was time to get rid of me."

Candace was dubious that the city would really fire Stanton just for talking to a reporter, but maybe she simply didn't want to believe it. "It never occurred to me the department would retaliate against you for talking to me," she said. "Why would they?"

"I embarrassed the DOB. I called out Durant, who certainly has more powerful friends than I do."

"And they said this?"

"Lack of discretion, they said. The point was pretty fucking clear."

"It's bullshit, obviously," Candace said, wanting to soothe Stanton a little, offer him some support. "So you were meeting with a lawyer about suing?"

"He said that I didn't have a case. I can't claim they fired me out of some kind of discrimination, so I'd have to say it was retaliation for being a whistle-blower. But as far as the lawyer was concerned, talking anonymously to the press doesn't count as blowing the whistle. At least, not in a way that gives me any rights."

"So there's nothing you can do?"

"You told me that nobody would ever know I'd talked to you," Stanton said accusingly.

Candace shifted in her seat, feeling defensive but understanding that Stanton had a right to be pissed. "I said I would keep your identity a secret, which I did. When they deposed me I refused to answer any questions about my sources. If there was anything else I could have done I would've done it. I never for a moment thought Roth would sue me over an accurate story."

"What's going on with the case? Am I going to have to testify at a trial?"

"Actually, I just got word that Roth's dropping it," Candace said, careful to keep any enthusiasm out of her voice, sure this news would only further inflame Stanton.

He looked stunned. "They find out I was your source, I get fired, and then that's game over? Was the whole thing just a witch-hunt to get me?"

Candace didn't blame the man for his paranoia under the circumstances, but she also didn't see any reason to encourage it. "I can't imagine that this was all done just to uncover you," Candace said. "Besides, it's not like it was Simon Roth who fired you."

"He could be behind it," Stanton said. "Of course he could."

The fact was, Candace didn't have any idea why Roth had suddenly dropped the lawsuit, any more than she understood why he'd brought it in the first place. She didn't have a better explanation than that the whole thing had just been to make an example of Stanton.

"Even for Roth, a lawsuit is a lot of money and trouble to go to just to out you as my source," Candace said. "But I can't tell you what his plan was here, and I don't know whether he had a role in your losing your job."

"What about the role you had?" Stanton said. "I'd still be an investigator if I'd never talked to you."

He was right, and Candace knew it. "I'm sorry, William," she said. "I did everything I could to protect you. This is the first time in my career that I've had a source get outed; believe me, I feel like shit about it. But we did do some good, didn't we?"

Stanton nodded reluctantly. "Word around the DOB campfire before I got shit-canned was that there're indictments coming down out of the Aurora investigation. You heard that?"

Candace had been hoping to hear of a criminal prosecution arising from her reporting on the Aurora. She tried to tamp down her excitement, wanting to make sure she didn't push too hard, keep Stanton from telling her what he knew. "I hadn't heard that. What kind of charges?"

She clearly hadn't been subtle enough; Stanton glared at her balefully. "Christ, is that all you can ever think about? Getting the damn story in your paper? It was just rumors, nothing solid."

Candace wasn't going to press it, but made a mental note to follow up, though she didn't have any immediate thoughts about how she'd do so. She also knew there was no point in continuing to defend herself, that Stanton had gotten screwed over and that nothing was going to change that. "I don't know what to say, William. If there was anything I could've done to protect you, I would've done it. But there would never have been any indictments coming down if you hadn't talked to me."

"Well," Stanton said, "doesn't that make me feel better."

CANDACE LET Stanton talk out his anger, feeling like he'd earned that, even though it was clear there was nothing she could do. When he was done she headed back down Ninth Avenue toward the newsroom. Her earlier good mood was a dim memory: so much for her story in today's paper and the end of the libel suit; both were trumped by how bad she felt about what had happened to Stanton.

Lost in thought, Candace registered the steps of someone running up behind her only when they were fast approaching. She started to turn, but before she could she found herself falling to the ground.

She was on her hands and knees before she had any idea what was happening. Someone had gone charging into her full speed, and now that same man was grabbing at her shoulder. Candace's arm gave way and she collapsed to the sidewalk.

He was stealing her purse, Candace realized. He'd plowed right into her, then snatched away her purse while she was down. By the time she looked up, the man was sprinting away. Candace picked up jeans and a baseball cap but nothing of the actual person.

Candace's pants were torn at one knee; both her palms were scraped and bleeding from breaking her fall. A couple of people had stopped, one of them helping her to her feet while another called 911. But the thief was well in the wind.

TWO BLOCKS away, Darryl Loomis was in the driver's seat of a battered and idling Ford Taurus. He saw Asante Webber as soon as he came running around the corner toward the car. Asante had been a confidential informant of Darryl's for a number of years, during which Darryl had rescued him from three separate collars: two B and Es and a purse snatching. Asante wasn't quite finished paying off his debt.

He was sprinting down the sidewalk, a red purse slung over his shoulder. Darryl looked past Asante to see if anybody was chasing. When he'd run halfway down the block with nobody coming after him, Darryl gunned the engine, the signal for Asante to get in the car. Once he was in, Darryl started driving, turning south on Eleventh Avenue, planning to double back onto the West Side Highway, but for now taking it nice and slow. There was no reason to hurry; it was already clear to Darryl that they'd gotten away with it.

·36·

DUNCAN'S FATHER was waiting for him at the airport, hugging him in greeting, holding it longer than any hug Duncan could remember the two of them exchanging. Max Riley was just past sixty, with thinning gray hair and a thick gray beard. Nobody ever pegged them as father and son on sight; Duncan himself couldn't really see it.

He had agreed to stay at his father's house for the few days he would be back in Michigan. Duncan hadn't really wanted to, would've preferred a hotel, but he could tell it was important to his dad. It seemed forced, Max wanting to be there for him now. They weren't really close; since his parents' divorce, Duncan had never spent more than a long weekend in his father's house.

It was impossible for him to say whether race had anything to do with it, not in any clear way, anyway. But his father lived in an almost completely black neighborhood in Detroit, and even as a child Duncan had been aware that he stood out there. There'd been one bad incident, back when Duncan was twelve or so. He'd gone to a corner store by himself in the middle of the afternoon, a group of neighborhood kids surrounding him, calling him honky (the only time Duncan could remember actually hearing that word used as a racial insult), a few hard punches thrown before they'd taken his money, leaving Duncan bleeding from his nose and mouth.

Duncan had been old enough to understand why it'd happened, but neither his father, when Duncan returned to the house, nor his mother, when she heard the story upon coming to pick him up the next night, ever acknowledged that he'd been beaten up and robbed because he was a white-looking kid in a black neighborhood.

He'd been left to think it through on his own. He didn't blame the kids, really. He hadn't been seriously hurt—though it was the only time in his life that he'd been beaten up—and he understood that they considered the neighborhood theirs and him an interloper. But that was just it: the clear message was that he didn't belong. When people looked at him they saw a white person, and so a white person was what he was. America simply didn't have biracial people, not really: your skin put you on one side of the racial line or another.

Neither of his parents had ever been inclined to explain themselves to Duncan, so his understanding of how they'd come to be together was as fuzzy as his understanding of how they'd come apart. Nor did he understand why his mother would go from an interracial Detroit marriage to raising her biracial son in Troy, a small city whose population was virtually entirely white. Given that both his parents had essentially retreated to their separate racial corners after divorcing, Duncan had often wondered if their relationship had been based on some leftover sixties idealism that they'd carried through the seventies but couldn't ultimately sustain.

Duncan had never thought of what he did growing up as passing: he'd never lied about his racial background, and anybody he'd ever been close to knew about it. But growing up in a white neighborhood and being raised by a white woman, Duncan felt his identity was in many respects no different from that of any other white person.

It still hadn't really sunk in that his mother was dead, and he had no idea when it would. The woman who raised him—that phrase kept floating through his mind. His mother never remarried, his father had been distant, and so she'd pretty much done it all herself.

And yet in so many ways she was still a mystery. On the one hand was the bleeding-heart social worker who'd married across the color line; on the other was Duncan's bland and provincial suburban upbringing, his mother's apparent indifference to Duncan's own inchoate ambitions.

Her death had come without warning: a stroke. As far as Duncan knew, she'd been perfectly healthy right up until it happened. He wished it hadn't been something so out of the blue, that he'd had a chance to prepare, to say good-bye, to achieve whatever kind of closure was possible with your mother at the end of her life. But every way death happened probably seemed like the wrong way, and you never ended up saying everything you wished.

He and his father barely spoke on the drive from the airport, Duncan staring out the window. All the familiar Michigan scenery seemed different now. It was such a strange feeling, Duncan thought, to see a place that had once been home.

It wasn't home anymore, hadn't been for some time. It wasn't just that he'd moved; it was that the world he now occupied was so different from the one in which he'd been raised. Ever since the day he'd gotten the acceptance letter from Harvard Law, Duncan had known that his adult life was going to have scant resemblance to his upbringing.

It'd been a bumpy transition: Duncan had felt less like he'd been accepted to Harvard and more like he'd infiltrated it. He remembered when he'd first started there, trying to explain to his mother what it was like, the hothouse atmosphere full of privileged overachievers. But it'd proven impossible to really put into words.

Duncan had gone to law school with some vague idea of doing good. But at the same time, neither of his parents was exactly inspiring in that regard. Harvard had a subculture of public-interest types bent on using the law to change the world, and it had taken Duncan a while to realize that the vast majority of them had one thing in common: family money. It hadn't been easy to figure out; at Harvard, hiding your money had become more fashionable than flaunting it.

But he'd eventually realized that the more self-righteous a classmate was about using their law degree to help the disadvantaged, the more likely that do-gooder streak was subsidized by inherited wealth. Unlike those trust-fund Marxists, Duncan didn't think he could afford the luxury of using a Harvard law degree to earn forty thousand dollars a year in some quixotic effort to change the world. He had never been able to tell if his joining a corporate law firm had been a disappointment to his mother. But he'd seen what a life on the front lines had done to her, and that wasn't the life he wanted.

His father's house was small and tidy, the neighborhood mostly residential, a once middle-class neighborhood fighting a losing battle to stay that way. With each passing year there were more houses with plywood in the windows, and each vacant house dragged the neighborhood down a little farther. The city had simply shrunk too much for outer neighborhoods like Conant Gardens to make much sense; most of Detroit's middle class had left the city limits some time ago.

Duncan followed his father inside, hearing noises coming from the kitchen. Beverly, his stepmother, called out a greeting before stepping into the living room, wiping her hands on a dish towel before enfolding Duncan in a hug.

Feeling suffocated by all this solicitude, Duncan wished again that he was checking into a hotel, getting room service and watching TV. He and Beverly had never been comfortable with each other. As with everything else to do with his family, Duncan was never able to be sure what role race played in it—whether Beverly simply wished her husband didn't have a son from a previous marriage, or if it was that Max had a Caucasian-looking son that was the problem.

Beverly was followed out by Kaleena, the youngest of their two children, a full decade younger than Duncan. He was closer to her than any of them, probably, or at least somehow it had always been simpler with Kaleena.

"So sorry about your mom," Kaleena said as they embraced.

"Is Antoine around?" Duncan, referring to Kaleena's older brother. As soon as he said it he felt Kaleena wilt beside him, then caught the sharp look from Beverly to his father.

"Antoine's back in the system," Max said after a moment.

"Shit," Duncan said, though his surprise was more that nobody'd told him than that it'd happened. His half brother had been in trouble on and off since he was a teenager, culminating in the felony plea. "What happened?"

"He had this parole officer who was all on his back," Kaleena said. "Kept threatening to violate him for one thing after another, finally did a couple of weeks ago."

Duncan turned to his father. "And you didn't tell me?"

Max's face was grim. "I hadn't talked to you since it happened, other than to tell you about your mom. That didn't seem like the right time. Besides, there's nothing you could've done."

Duncan couldn't quite get his head around it. Antoine had been raised by good people in a stable home, yet somehow he'd ended up in thrall to the thug life, carrying himself like he'd been raised in inner-city Detroit. Whenever Duncan wondered how different his own life would be if his skin had come out a darker shade, his thoughts always went to Antoine, with his GED, his rap sheet, and his stunted future.

Duncan's emotional state was already on the verge of collapse, and this news threatened to sink him entirely. He felt tears coming, though he couldn't really say if they were for Antoine. Making matters worse, they'd put him in his half brother's old room. Antoine hadn't lived here for years, and it'd been redone into a guest room, little trace of Duncan's half brother remaining. Duncan remembered the huge Tupac poster that had hung on a wall, how the room had always smelled faintly of weed.

Duncan unpacked his bags as much as he needed to, then lay down on the bed. He was staying through the weekend, longer than he wanted to be back, but there was much to do.

His mother would be buried tomorrow afternoon. It was still impossible for him to believe. Duncan had to call his aunt Marie tonight. They were supposed to meet up at his mother's house first thing in the morning. It would be put up for sale once they'd cleared everything out. Marie had already started organizing things there, but she needed Duncan to say what he wanted to keep. He planned to donate most of what was in there; he didn't think there was much he'd hold on to.

He somehow fell into something like sleep, woken by his father when dinner was ready. Duncan felt groggy, even more ill at ease. Conversation lagged, Duncan deciding the circumstances freed him from making any effort. After eating, Kaleena went out to meet a friend and Beverly retreated to her bedroom, leaving Duncan alone with his father.

They ended up in the living room, his dad fetching a couple of beers. The moment felt stage-managed to Duncan, self-conscious, more obligatory than anything else. They simply weren't close in a way that allowed for this.

"I really am very sorry about your mom," Max said. "Sylvia was a good woman."

"We don't need to do a whole thing about that," Duncan said. "I'm well aware of how long it's been since you two got along."

"You're old enough to know it's not that simple," his father protested. "We couldn't make it work for the long haul, but that doesn't mean I didn't still care for her a great deal. When you've loved someone for years, made a child with them, that never goes away."

"You two always seemed to have done a good job burying it," Duncan said. "I mean, I'm sure you loved each other at some point, but it's not something I have any memory of."

His father studied him for a moment, Duncan not sure what he was looking for. Duncan wasn't trying to start a fight, wasn't angry, really, but if he and his dad were going to talk about this, he was going to be honest. "We were in love when we had you," Max said.

"But you didn't mean to have me," Duncan replied, the words out before he'd realized what he was about to say. His mother had been five months pregnant when his parents had wed. He hadn't said anything about this since he was a teenager, thought it was something he was long past. "It's okay, Dad. There's no shame in it, and I'm glad you guys decided to keep me."

Max looked like he was struggling to keep his own composure. "We made a decision to have you," he said after a moment, speaking slowly. "And we were always glad we did, even in the tough times. And look what you've become, Duncan."

Duncan laughed harshly, the feel of it like chalk in the back of his throat. "What is it exactly I've become? I help the rich get richer—hell, that's what I do on a good day. Mostly I help them get away with it. I don't think that's exactly what Mom had in mind for me."

Max shook his head. "Your mother was proud of you becoming a lawyer, getting into Harvard. We gave you opportunities that we didn't have, and that's your best goal as a parent."

"I know you did. It's just . . . what am I doing, really? I'm making money, which is nice, but then after that?"

Max looked pained, the conversation clearly not going as he'd anticipated. He took a long sip of his beer, then peeled the edge of the label off. "I didn't know you were unhappy with your job," he said.

"I'm not saying I am," Duncan said. "But if you'd asked me fifteen years ago what I was going to do with my life, this certainly wouldn't have been what I'd have said."

"I remember you when you were a teenager," Max said. "If I were you I wouldn't put a whole lot of stock in what you thought back then."

Duncan managed a smile. "I wanted to be the lead guitarist in a band, so yeah, I'm not saying that was the right answer. But I thought I'd be doing something that felt more meaningful than this."

"What, like represent a union? You know how fucked we are? We're on a sinking ship, and everybody knows it, yet we can't make any concessions because we're too afraid of looking weak. I spend most of my time fighting over people GM wants to fire, but they have to go through me to get rid of them. Some of these people—I mean, it's probably dangerous to have them in the plant, yet I've got to fight to keep them on. They show up drunk at nine in the morning, they steal things, but they're in the union, so we protect them."

Duncan had never heard his father be so open about the downside of his job, though as he'd risen through the union ranks to shop steward, Duncan had gotten the sense of a growing cynicism. "Mom never really felt that way about what she did, far as I could tell. I mean, look at the horrible shit she had to deal with all day—beaten-up kids, lying parents—and she just kept at it."

"You know why your mother never stopped being a street-level social worker? Because she was such a pain in the ass with everyone she worked with. She got in fights with her bosses all the time, going all the way back to when she started there. You just never saw that side of her. It's one thing you inherited from me, Duncan, your ability to work within a system."

"That can be a mixed blessing."

"No doubt," Max said. "But not having it was part of why your mother could never get ahead. Though she made her peace with that a long time ago, I suppose. She cared about helping people. You do too, Duncan. Isn't that why you became a lawyer?"

"I became a lawyer without the slightest idea of what being a lawyer actually was," Duncan replied.

"You might not see through your own cynicism, Duncan, but I do," his father said. "You're more your mother's son than you think."

·37·

CANDACE FOUND Tommy Nelson at McGee's, an Irish bar in the West Fifties. She'd met him there last year, when he'd spoken to her on background while she was digging into the Aurora accident. He'd been on a first-name basis with the bartender, so Candace had pegged him as a regular.

Nelson was the site supervisor for Omni at the Aurora, making sure the various moving parts were not colliding. He had talked to Candace off the record a couple of times when she'd been doing her original investigation into the accident. It hadn't been especially fruitful. Nelson had pinned the blame for the accident on Pellettieri, focusing on what the subcontractor had done wrong while making excuses for why he hadn't caught it. Candace assumed Nelson had talked to her with the blessing of his employer, trying to make sure that Omni wasn't the focus of her story. She'd ended up using almost nothing he'd told her, finding it too self-serving, but she'd thought Nelson a decent enough sort.

Nelson was standing at the bar, talking with a couple of other men. Candace sat down a few feet away, ordered a beer she had no intention of drinking, looked over at Nelson until she caught his eye. He said something to the men he was with, then picked up his drink and came over to her.

"The hell do you want?" he said in greeting. He was tall, with white hair and a red face, broken capillaries crawling along his cheeks.

"Good to see you too," Candace replied, lifting her glass in a pretend toast that Tommy, ever the Irish gentleman, turned into an actual one.

"Haven't you already used me up and spit me out?"

"Now, Tommy. You're not even half used up."

"The Aurora Tower must be ancient history as far as you're concerned."

"I think the Aurora's about to be back in the headlines."

"Is that so?" Nelson said neutrally, taking a sip of his whiskey and holding the liquor in his mouth for a moment before swallowing.

"I hear an indictment's in the cards. The DA's saying that it wasn't just negligence that caused the accident, but deliberate misconduct. I get you another Jameson?"

"You remember your whiskey," Nelson said with a half smile.

"Of course, you already know about this," Candace said as she attempted to flag down the bartender.

Nelson looked taken aback, but Candace didn't buy it. "I do?" he asked.

"The DA must've talked to you," Candace said. "Unless of course you're a target."

This got a reaction, Nelson leaning back and away from her, offering an exaggerated shake of his head. With a quick glance Nelson secured the bartender's attention and ordered another drink. "We're off the record," he said.

"Do we have to be?"

"You're the one who came to me," Nelson said. "I was perfectly happy with the idea of never seeing you again, my dear."

"Fine, off the record," Candace said.

Nelson's fresh whiskey arrived, and he bantered with the bartender for a moment and took a sip before turning back to Candace. As he did so he noticed the bandages on both of her palms. "What happened to your hands?" he asked.

"I was mugged the other day," Candace said. "Broad daylight."

"You okay?"

"Fine—I was knocked down is all, and got scraped on the pavement. All for like forty bucks too," Candace said. To her surprise, the cops had found her purse about an hour after it'd been stolen: it'd been dumped in a trash can on Eleventh Avenue, the cash removed but everything important—her driver's license, credit cards, even her BlackBerry—intact. "Anyway—you were saying?"

Nelson glanced around, then leaned slightly toward Candace. "I've gone before the grand jury," he said quietly.

"Who are they looking to indict?"

Nelson leaned closer to Candace, their shoulders touching. "Pellettieri," he said quietly.

"Just him?" Candace said, lowering her own voice, though it seemed silly in the crowded bar.

"Far as I know."

"They don't normally prosecute for this sort of thing, do they?"

"If it was only negligence, then possibly not. But this was clearly deliberate."

"How so?"

"Pellettieri created a paper trail for work he didn't actually perform."

"Are they looking to get him for fraud?"

Nelson shrugged, using the little red straw to stir the ice in his drink. "Three people are dead, Candace."

Candace felt her heart skip a beat. "They're going to charge him on some kind of homicide?"

"Wouldn't you?" Nelson said.

"And you really didn't know anything about this at the time?"

Nelson's discomfort was visible, and Candace knew her instinct was right: the guy was too sharp for something like this to be going on under his nose without him knowing anything about it. "Look, I'm basically middle management. That's all a site supervisor is. I spend my days taking shit from above and below."

"But you knew something was wrong with Pellettieri," Candace said, suddenly sure of it. "And you would've done something to stop it if it'd been up to you. So something made you let it go."

"I certainly didn't say any of that," Nelson replied, but he couldn't look her in the eye.

"We're off the record, Tommy, and if you want we can make it hypothetical too. Let's say that you had known something was wrong with Pellettieri; what would've made you not do anything about it?"

"I didn't know that Pellettieri was cutting corners on safety. I wouldn't have stood for that, no matter what. But let's say I did know he was overbilling, had ghost employees, that sort of shit. If I knew about that, and I didn't do anything, that would probably be because the people I report to already knew about it as well."

"Who are we talking about, Tommy?"

"I was talking hypothetically."

"So hypothetically, Simon Roth knew what Pellettieri was doing?"

Nelson shook his head with a slight smile. "Simon Roth had nothing to do with the Aurora," he said. "His son was managing it."

Candace leaned back, her mind whirling. She'd known that the Aurora was officially Jeremy Roth's project, though she'd always assumed that was more for show. Candace didn't know much about Jeremy; had never suspected that he might have a significant role in what'd happened.

"Why would Jeremy Roth turn a blind eye to a contractor who was ripping him off?" Candace said, less as a question than as a way of thinking it through. Nelson took a sip of his drink, not bothering to offer an answer. "So Jeremy was embezzling from his own construction project through Pellettieri."

"That would seem to explain it, now, wouldn't it?" Nelson said.

"Did you tell the grand jury that Jeremy Roth knew what Pellettieri was up to?"

Nelson looked uncomfortable, his gaze losing focus. "I wasn't asked," he said.

"The DA isn't looking at Jeremy Roth?" Candace said, surprised.

"ADA Sullivan didn't show me his playbook. But as far as I know, the grand jury was only looking at Pellettieri."

"And you didn't tell this to Sullivan?"

"Like I said, he didn't ask. And I'm telling you this off the record, which is a hell of a lot different from testifying about it in court. That I'm not going to do. If you're going to strike the king you'd better be able to kill the king, right? I rat out the Roth family, I'm never working in this town again. An ADA takes a shot at them and misses, he's never working in this town again. Same goes for you if you try and write this story."

Candace shrugged off the warning. "Somebody had to be between Jeremy and Pellettieri," she said. "I mean, they weren't sitting in a room together, counting out hundred-dollar bills."

Nelson smiled. "There was this private security company Roth used on site. There's always security on the lot—not just to make sure equipment doesn't go walking off, but also keeping an eye on the unions and so forth. There's a lot of sausage making on a big construction site, and those are the guys that do the stuff people like me don't want to know about."

Candace was doing her best to read between the lines, getting that Nelson wasn't going to spell out any more than he had to. "So Loomis's guys, they were the bagmen?"

Nelson registered a flicker of surprise that Candace knew Loomis's name. "There was one of them, yeah, who things went through. He's not going to talk to you, though, so don't get your hopes up."

"How do you know he won't want to confess?"

"Because he's dead," Nelson said.

It came to Candace right away, and with it a feeling like her body had suddenly been doused in ice. "This is Sean Fowler we're talking about?" she said.

Nelson again showed surprise. "May he rest in peace," he said after a moment. "The prick."

·38·

GETTING A hug from Leah Roth in a public place made Duncan nervous. They were at the Algonquin Hotel's bar, just a couple blocks from his office, and he was skittish about their being spotted by someone from the firm.

They hadn't seen each other since Duncan had spent the night at Leah's apartment. Duncan didn't particularly want to see her now: he felt numb and worn and nowhere near up to dealing with her. It was almost like the flu, the way that grief left him not just exhausted but with a dull ache in his body.

Duncan had gotten back to town a few days ago. His aunt was handling things with his mother's house, for which Duncan was grateful. He'd been in a hurry to get out of Michigan, had found his whole stay there almost unbearable.

A Catholic priest had done the funeral service, though Duncan was virtually certain his mother hadn't set foot inside a church since taking him to his first Communion. Despite his mother having worked the same job her entire professional life, only a couple of her coworkers had shown up. Duncan had come with his father's family, although he felt sure they all resented the imposition. His mother, who had spent her life trying to help the helpless, had fewer than twenty people at her funeral.

Duncan had spoken after the priest, his grief mixed with bitterness. It was a mixture that he still felt, and he was nursing it by interacting with as few people as possible.

But when Leah e-mailed suggesting a drink, Duncan had felt like he couldn't really say no. Part of it was the lack of a line between business and personal between them. There was also the fact that Jeremy Roth's deposition was fast approaching in the wrongful-death case, and based on their prep session the day before, Duncan had serious concerns about how Jeremy would fare.

"I'm just so sorry about your mom," Leah said as they sat down at a small table. "I lost my mother when I was still in my teens. She'd been the family glue. I don't think any of us realized the extent of that until she was gone. Are you okay?"

Duncan shrugged. "I honestly don't know. It was so completely out of the blue that it's still just sinking in."

A waiter came over; they ordered drinks. Duncan felt like he needed one. "But you're back to work already?" Leah said, after the waiter had left. "I'm sure Steven would've given you more time."

"What would I do? It's not going to help just sitting around my apartment feeling tragic. I'd rather keep busy."

"Mourning is healthy, you know. It may not feel like it, but it is."

"I'm mourning, don't worry," Duncan said. "I just don't want to do it twenty-four/seven."

"Work can be a consolation, or at least a distraction, sure."

Duncan wanted to change the subject. "But I hear I'm not going to have the libel suit to occupy my time any longer," he said, nodding thanks as the waiter placed a Manhattan before him.

"I tried to keep Dad from ever filing that damn case," Leah said, surprising Duncan by how bitterly she said it. "All it did was make that awful reporter even more obsessed with going after us. And Dad made his point, I think, about people telling tales about our business to reporters."

Duncan wasn't sure what she meant by that, but decided not to ask. He picked up his drink but didn't sip from it. "She confronted me, actually," he said instead. "The reporter."

Worry passed across Leah's face. "Candace Snow did?"

"She came up to me out of the blue on the street a couple of weeks ago. She had some crazy conspiracy theory about the Nazario case."

Duncan had thought this a minor anecdote, but he could tell Leah was taking it far more seriously. "What do you mean?" she asked.

"She was suspicious that I was defending Nazario when you guys were doing the Riis project. She seemed to think I was part of some cover-up."

"Cover-up of what?"

Duncan was surprised by how agitated Leah seemed. "She basically just thought it was suspicious that I'd be representing somebody who was a Jacob Riis tenant, because you're doing the mixed-income thing. I explained to her how it wasn't a conflict; how you guys had nothing to do with the eviction."

"I don't want you to ever speak to her again," Leah said sharply. "She's on a vendetta against us, and as you said, she's conspiracy-minded. She was doing a story on the murder?"

"I think I was able to talk her down. She wasn't really interested in the murder itself, just on whether she could somehow loop you guys into it."

Leah leaned back, clearly trying to calm herself down. "I don't mean to be melodramatic, but she really is digging into every single thing we do and everybody who we do business with, looking for something she can try to turn into a scandal."

"I don't like talking to reporters anyway," Duncan said. "Though it wouldn't shock me if somebody from her paper is at the Nazario hearing next week."

"What's the hearing?"

"I'm challenging the gunshot residue evidence."

Leah cocked her head. "You really have a basis?"

"My expert seems to think so. We just got the lab notes from the police expert, and they've got my guy jumping up and down."

"What would it mean for the case if you won on the residue?"

"It certainly wouldn't be game-over," Duncan said. "But it'd be big."

Leah smiled thinly, but something still seemed to be troubling her. "How did it go with my brother the other day?"

Duncan hesitated, knowing he was on thin ice.

"Be honest," Leah said.

"How honest?" Duncan replied.

"That bad?"

"It was more that he wasn't interested than anything else," Duncan said, deciding that was as close to the truth as he was comfortable getting. "I'm sure he'll be more focused at the actual depo."

"We've made a settlement offer, you know. Not us, but Pellettieri has. But enough—I didn't mean for us to be talking about any of this tonight. I meant to be talking about you."

"It's better for me to think about work, honestly."

"Did you spend time with your father while you were back?"

Duncan nodded, thinking that this was an opportunity to clue Leah in on his father. It was past time for him to mention his racial background to Leah, but he found himself hesitating. Normally he assumed it wouldn't faze people, at least not cosmopolitan New Yorkers. But in this instance he didn't have that feeling, though he couldn't put his finger on why not. It came out of her wealth somehow, the idea that he didn't belong in her world.

Perhaps he was just being paranoid. Leah was Jewish; her grandfather had immigrated from Eastern Europe: she was far from a conventional blue blood. They'd never spoken of religion either; Duncan had no idea if it mattered to her that he wasn't a Jew. Duncan had navigated these things in other relationships; it'd never been that big a deal, and he had no basis for assuming that it would be here. He was being unfair to Leah. The world had changed enough that he was probably the one guilty of sustaining old prejudices. And yet he didn't say it.

·39·

"SO WHAT can I do for you, Candace?" ADA Sullivan asked.

"You can confirm for me that you're about to indict Jack Pellettieri on homicide charges," Candace replied.

Sullivan's eyes narrowed in surprise. They'd met up at Mustang Sally's, a bar a couple of blocks south of Madison Square Garden. Candace figured Sullivan didn't want her coming anywhere near his own office, risk anyone seeing him talking to a reporter.

Sullivan had already been there when she'd arrived just after seven, seated at a small table in the front corner of the bar, his back against the wall, a glass of clear liquid in front of him. Candace wondered idly whether it was alcohol. Sullivan had found the most isolated spot in the room, a place where he couldn't be overheard and from which he could keep an eye on everyone else. Paranoid, perhaps, but as head of the Manhattan DA's Rackets Bureau, Sullivan no doubt had plenty of enemies in low places.

"Grand jury proceedings are secret, as I'm sure you know," Sullivan finally said.

Candace smiled. "So you're presenting Pellettieri to a grand jury?"

"Did I say that?" Sullivan replied, mock innocent. "We need some ground rules here. No using my name, no direct quotes."

"The Aurora accident would never have been referred to you if it wasn't for my reporting."

Sullivan offered a slight nod. "Why do you think I'm sitting here?" he said.

"I'm hoping you're here to tell me what your game plan is on prosecuting it."

Sullivan smiled dryly, the fingers of his right hand dancing across the table. "And why would I want to do that?"

"I've got things to trade, plus you'd have a forum. You're going up against people who know how to get their voices heard."

"My arena's the courtroom," Sullivan said stubbornly.

"Sure, but I think we both know how the world works," Candace replied. "Is Pellettieri the only person you're looking to indict?"

"I read your article on Councilwoman Serran the other day," Sullivan said. "I hear the attorney general's office is opening an investigation. Think she'll survive?"

"My guess is no," Candace said. "Are you trying to change the subject?"

Sullivan shrugged, looking around the room. "Do we have an understanding as to the terms of our conversation?"

"On background," Candace offered. "Senior law enforcement with knowledge of the investigation."

Sullivan nodded, an old hand at this. "Pellettieri's the first person I'm looking to indict. You build a prosecution one brick at a time, and you start with the case you're sure you can make."

"So you think other people were involved?"

"I think it's worth finding out," Sullivan said. "Especially given past sins."

"Meaning you think his company's still connected?"

"I prosecuted his brother, you know. Back then Pellettieri Concrete was deep into no-shows, skimming, double billing—all the ways the mob likes to bleed the construction industry. All things I'm seeing at the Aurora too."

Candace realized that Sullivan suspected organized crime was behind the Aurora. She thought he was on the wrong track, but she wasn't going to tell him that. "Why'd you leave the company standing the first time?" she asked instead.

"They were a real concrete company too, and we didn't have anything on Jack. Doesn't mean there wasn't anything there, but I didn't find it."

"Are you looking into whether people above Pellettieri at the Aurora knew what he was up to?"

Sullivan seemed surprised by the question. "Pellettieri wasn't the lowest bid on concrete for the Aurora, which was a red flag. But that also just happens—somebody's owed a favor, the contractor doesn't trust the low bidder to get the job done, whatever. There's no reason for Omni to let a sub get away with shit like that. My bigger concern is whether the mob was pulling Pellettieri's strings."

Sullivan gave her a look, Candace guessing he was hoping she'd offer up some confirmation that organized crime had been involved. "Are you're hoping to flip Pellettieri?" she asked.

"Premature to speculate about that," Sullivan said. "So maybe now's a good time for you to tell me something."

Candace didn't like helping law enforcement actually make their case—it put her too close to them—but she also knew sometimes you had to give information to get it. "Has your investigation looked at Sean Fowler at all?"

Candace had half expected Sullivan to already have Sean Fowler in his sights, but the prosecutor looked blank. "Who's that?"

"He was a security guard at the Aurora. He's also been murdered."

Sullivan frowned, the drumming of his fingers increasing in intensity. "He was involved with Pellettieri?"

"I was hoping you could tell me," Candace replied, not wanting to say more than she had to. "But I've heard whispers, yeah."

"Has there been an arrest in his murder?"

Candace nodded. "A project teenager."

Sullivan frowned. "Are you suggesting this Fowler's death connects to the Aurora in some way?"

"I'm nowhere near being able to prove that," Candace said. "But it might not be a bad idea for you to take a look."

"What's the connection between Fowler and Pellettieri?"

"The money that Pellettieri was moving," Candace said. "I'm hearing he didn't keep it all. Fowler may have been the conduit. Have I earned my keep now?"

"You're saying that I've got a dead bagman on my hands?" Sullivan said. "I'm not hearing that."

"Maybe you haven't asked the right questions," Candace replied.

DUNCAN WAS struggling to pay attention. He was defending Jeremy Roth's deposition, and it was taking a lot of effort just to listen to the questions and make objections.

Duncan had spent a frustrating day prepping Jeremy earlier in the week. Jeremy had shown up forty-five minutes late, looking hungover (Duncan thinking that it must be Jeremy, and not his father, that Pellettieri had called a drunken creep) and was completely uninterested in actually preparing. Jeremy seemed outright hostile: Duncan wondered if Jeremy knew about his budding involvement with Leah, and perhaps disapproved of her mingling with the help.

Dealing with Jeremy's depo was the first real work Duncan had done since getting back from his mother's funeral. He hadn't been sleeping well, which at least gave him an excuse for his constant irritability. Duncan had been in no mood to try to make the prep session useful in light of Jeremy's attitude, so they'd ended up going through the motions, the sense of mutual contempt becoming dangerously close to overt.

Jeremy had at least shown up clear-eyed and feisty for his actual deposition. If anything, too feisty: his answers were prolix and arrogant.

Duncan was mildly surprised that this deposition was taking place at all: he'd thought the case would've been settled by now. The plaintiffs had their hooks into Pellettieri, and that was what they were going to get. Pellettieri had made a settlement offer, which the plaintiffs had countered, but Duncan had no direct involvement with the negotiations and only a tenuous sense of where things stood.

"Mr. Roth, did you have a supervisory role in the Aurora Tower construction project?" Isaac Marcus asked. They were a couple of hours into the deposition, Marcus finally making his way into the meat of Jeremy's testimony.

"It depends what you mean," Jeremy replied. "I was supervising it from the developer's perspective. Which is quite different from supervising the construction itself."

"Would it be fair to say that you were the person at Roth Properties who knew the most about the day-to-day operations at the construction site?"

"That would be accurate as far as it goes in terms of our company, but it's still pretty misleading. We're not focused on the construction so much, certainly not on a day-to-day basis. That's the general contractor's job."

"Prior to the accident were you aware that Pellettieri Concrete had submitted bills for what's known as secondary support work—work that is intended to ensure the safety of concrete while it hardens?"

"This is a half-billion-dollar construction project, counsel," Jeremy said condescendingly. "I wouldn't be aware of every small invoice."

"Are you aware as you sit here today that those bills were submitted?"

"Yes, they were."

"And they were paid?"

"Of course. Contractors' bills get paid; otherwise they don't work, put a lien on the property."

"Do you know whether the actual work was performed?"

"I know now it was not."

"When did you first become aware that this work had not been performed?"

"I'm not sure," Jeremy said.

Marcus looked skeptical. "Wasn't this an important piece of information?" he asked.

"What was important was that three people had died at the construction site. Figuring out why came after, and whether we had paid for the work was hardly relevant."

"Were you aware that this safety work had not been performed prior to the accident?"

"How could I have been?" Jeremy said irritably. "I was never on site, not since the groundbreaking. All I knew about the actual construction I learned at the monthly status meetings, and there was never any discussion at those meetings of a problem with the secondary supports, or with anything involving the concrete."

"Do you think your company, as the developers of the building, had a responsibility to know that essential safety work had not been performed?"

"That question shows a basic ignorance of how real estate developers work," Jeremy said, Duncan wishing Jeremy wasn't laying it on quite so thick with the superiority. He'd have to try to find a polite way of conveying that at the break, though he doubted it would be of any use. "The developer isn't hanging around on the site, making sure that everybody's doing their job right. That's the general contractor's job. I'm not an expert on construction safety. We entrust that role to the contractors. I don't really know what else I can tell you."

EVEN BY his standards, Jeremy had been putting it back all night. Alena had asked what was bothering him as they'd sat down for dinner at Chanterelle, but Jeremy hadn't responded, focusing on the two martinis he'd polished off before the arrival of their entrées. He'd finally loosened up around the end of dinner and their shared bottle of Château Haut Brion, getting more talkative, as he usually did a few drinks in. As soon as they'd arrived back at the apartment (Alena still unable to think of it as *her* apartment), Jeremy lit up a joint, Alena taking one hit but otherwise passing. The pot had only made Jeremy petulant and sulky. Alena ended up surfing the tube while he brooded beside her.

Jeremy had been lost in thought for most of the evening. He'd kept his shit together for the deposition, made it through that fine, but once it was over it was like every bad memory in his head had been awakened. The whole thing had been just about the worst experience of his life. As soon as Jeremy had heard about the accident at the Aurora, he'd suspected that Pellettieri was going to be mixed up in it. He should've known that asshole would take advantage of their arrangement.

Their deal had been that the concrete company would overbill Roth Properties, but most of the skimmed money was to make its way to Jeremy, though Pellettieri would get a cut. It would've worked out for everybody, but then Pellettieri had gotten greedy. Putting people at risk had never been part of the deal.

Jeremy had felt like shit about the accident. It wasn't his fault, other than in the sense that it'd started with the skimming. He'd also understood that it created a risk of exposing the missing money. His father had made some calls to Ron Durant at the DOB, not because he was worried about the investigation or had any idea of Jeremy's potential exposure, but just because a protracted probe would push the building further behind schedule. Back then, Jeremy had been confident that all he had to do was wait it out, not do anything to draw any attention. And sure enough, the DOB had levied some small fines and the whole thing had looked like it was going away.

But then the newspaper article had run, stirring everything up again. It'd been a short time later that Sean Fowler had shown up at Jeremy's office. No appointment, no warning: Fowler just strolled into the lobby.

"What're you doing here?" Jeremy had said to Fowler once the two of them were alone in his office, the door closed.

"Nobody's looking," Fowler replied as he sat down across from Jeremy's desk. He was a big guy with a beer belly, still with a cop's swagger.

"We don't know who's going to be looking at what," Jeremy replied. "We've got to be careful."

"I hear the DA's got the case now," Fowler said casually, like he was commenting on the weather, not on a criminal investigation that could land them both in jail.

Jeremy nodded. "Which is why we've got to lie low. You need to make sure Pellettieri's going to keep his mouth shut."

"Opening his mouth's not going to get Jack anything," Fowler said.

Jeremy still wasn't getting what Fowler was doing in his office. He could tell Fowler was enjoying his discomfort. Jeremy tried to tell himself that he was the one here with power: this was his office, he was the vice president of a major development company, the man across from him was just a step up from a janitor. But it didn't feel that way, not with Fowler being the one with some kind of agenda. "So you and me, we shouldn't talk. You shouldn't be here."

To Jeremy's surprise, Fowler smiled at this. He was chewing gum, his mouth open. He looked around Jeremy's office, making a show of taking it in. "Just wanted to tell you that I won't be telling anyone what I know."

Jeremy hadn't needed to be told this, and he was sure Fowler didn't think he had. His bad feeling was getting worse. "Of course," he said.

"But I do think, circumstances having changed, I deserve a little something for staying out of sight."

There it was: his hand was out. Jeremy had been afraid that this was what it was. Fowler had gotten a cut from the skim, never complained that he wasn't getting enough. But maybe greed was contagious.

Jeremy looked at Fowler, who looked right back, still snapping his gum, no hint of shame or even uneasiness with what he was doing. "This is money you want?" Jeremy asked.

Fowler reacted like money was Jeremy's idea. "I'd appreciate that, yeah. A little reward for loyalty."

"I don't have much here," Jeremy said. "A couple hundred bucks, maybe."

Fowler chuckled, like Jeremy had just told a pretty good joke. "I wasn't looking to empty your wallet," he said. "The kind of money I was thinking, you're not going to have lying around your office."

Jeremy had wanted to believe this wasn't full-on blackmail. He was in over his head, wishing he could take a time-out, bring somebody in who knew how to deal with this. "What kind of number were you thinking?"

Fowler shrugged. "Two fifty large, maybe," he said.

Jeremy was stunned. He hadn't known what to expect, but hearing that kind of number overwhelmed him with the reality of what was happening. "You've got the wrong idea," he said. "I don't have that kind of money that I can just grab hold of."

"Way I count it, you took at least a couple of million out of the Aurora," Fowler replied. "I think you can pull together two fifty."

Jeremy felt queasy. "You really want to do this?"

Fowler stood, looking down at Jeremy. "You don't have to answer right now. I'll give you twenty-four hours to think about it. Don't take twenty-five."

Jeremy had suspected Fowler was bluffing, but he couldn't risk it. Just the thought of having that threat hanging over him was more than he could stand. So he'd pulled together a quarter million in cash, hoping it would buy Fowler's silence. When Jeremy had agreed to pay, he'd made it clear it was a onetime thing; Fowler had readily agreed.

It had taken less than six months for Fowler to come back for more. He'd again come unannounced to Jeremy's office. Jeremy had been out in a meeting this time, his secretary giving him the message when he got back. The mere sight of Fowler's name on the little pink slip had caused Jeremy's hands to shake.

Jeremy wasn't willing to spend the rest of his life under Fowler's thumb. He wasn't sure what to do, but knew he had to do something. He needed advice from someone, and his sister seemed like the least wrong choice. He'd gone over to her apartment that night.

"There's a problem with the Aurora," Jeremy had told her.

Leah frowned at him. "If this is a work thing, why aren't we talking about it at work?"

"It's not something we want to talk about in the office. I'm in a jam, Lee."

"With the Aurora? Now? What's going on?"

Jeremy had known she was going to be pissed—beyond pissed, probably. But he didn't think he had a choice but to tell someone. "Pellettieri and I, we had an arrangement. Dad's always so tight with our money still, these stupid trusts, the property we can't sell."

"Life's hard on a couple of million a year, I know," Leah interjected. "But what does that have to do with Pellettieri and the Aurora?"

"Like I said, we came to an arrangement. The concrete company was overbilling the project; I was signing off on it. It wasn't a lot, not for a half-billion-dollar project, nothing that would keep us from making a profit. And it's our money anyway."

Seated beside Jeremy on her couch, Leah's whole body seemed to have clenched together, like her entire being was making a fist. "You were stealing from the Aurora? With Pellettieri?"

"He was just supposed to be overbilling a little, not avoiding doing actual work. That was just him—the safety shit, I didn't have any idea. I wouldn't have let him do that."

"Jesus, Jeremy—you could go to jail for this. What if you get linked up to the accident?"

"That's what I need to talk to you about," Jeremy said. "Somebody knows about it, and they want money to keep quiet."

Leah's eyes narrowed. "Who?"

"A security guard. He was working with us—on taking the money, I mean. A few months after the accident he came to me with his hand out. I told him it was a one-time-only thing, but now he's back."

"How much does he want?"

"Two fifty."

Leah didn't understand. "Two fifty what?"

"A quarter million is what he wants."

Leah frowned slightly at the number. "What does he have on you?"

"More than enough."

"What were you actually doing to take money?"

"It was all under the table, obviously. After we set it up, I never even talked to Pellettieri. That was the security guard, Fowler—he was our middleman."

"If this man Fowler went to the authorities, it wouldn't even matter whether you ended up being prosecuted. The story alone would destroy you. It might destroy our entire business. How could you be so fucking *stupid*?"

"I didn't tell you this just so you could yell at me. I need your help, Lee. I can't just keep paying this guy off. What can I do to get him off my back?"

Leah laughed, harshly. "How the hell should I know? I've never been in a mess like this. What makes you think I can fix it?"

"I needed to tell somebody."

"What about Dad?"

"He'd kill me."

"I'd kind of like to kill you too," Leah said. She closed her eyes for a second, trying to force herself to think. "This security guard, it's not like he wants to turn you in because he has a guilty conscience. What he wants is money. And if you've already paid him once, then if he turns you in now you could do the same to him for blackmail."

Jeremy brightened. "That's true," he said. "We could at least come back at him with mutually assured destruction."

"Except you've got a lot more to lose than he does," Leah said. "I'll talk to Darryl Loomis. Maybe he can fix it. You stall the guy for as long as you can. And, Jeremy?"

"I know."

"You know what?"

"I really fucked up."

Jeremy had thought Fowler's death was the end of it, but it still wasn't over. It was poisoning everything, including this night, the fancy dinner, the beautiful and willing woman lounging bored beside him, all of it soured by the bitter taste of the mess he'd made.

"Nobody was supposed to get hurt," Jeremy said abruptly, breaking the long-standing silence.

Alena looked at him, puzzled. "Who got hurt?" she asked.

"Those three guys," Jeremy said. "They *died*."

"You mean the construction accident?"

"It was my fault," Jeremy said. "Those people would still be alive if it wasn't for me."

Alena was used to Jeremy revealing things in isolated melodramatic bursts, though she was never sure how much of it was exaggerated out of self-pity. "Is that what you're being blackmailed about?"

"That's over with," Jeremy said dismissively, waving his hand like he was shooing the topic out of the conversation. "The thing with the construction guys, I never should've let it happen."

Alena was not sure she was following; not sure she wanted to be. "You're saying you knew the accident was going to happen?"

Jeremy shook his head. "I should've, though. I gave the concrete guys an inch, they ran a fucking mile with it. And now it won't go away."

"Were you just asked about it for the court thing?"

Jeremy again waved his hand, clearly not wanting to answer her questions. "We've got it under control. But it still makes me feel like shit."

"I don't understand," Alena said. "Why did you let it happen?"

"Why does anybody let anything happen?" Jeremy said. "I needed the fucking money."

· 41 ·

CONSTRUCTION AT the Aurora Tower was running about six months behind schedule. The outside of the building was virtually complete, but the interior was almost entirely raw. They'd already been a couple of months behind at the time of the accident; in its wake a stop-work order from the city had been in place for a month while the DOB investigated. They'd just started to make up some of that lost time when the investigation had been reopened. Once the city inspectors had come back, work had again bogged down, the project getting further behind.

Tommy Nelson wasn't usually particularly worried by delays; most large-scale construction projects fell behind schedule sooner or later, especially if there was a serious accident. As the general contractor's on-site superintendent, he was the point man for all the various subcontractors. Most of Nelson's time was spent making peace between the factions that inevitably stepped on one another's toes: the concrete guys hated the rebar guys, who had to finish their work on a floor before the mud could be poured; everybody hated the pipe guys, who acted like they had the toughest job around but whose idea of a disaster was some spilled water.

But delays meant additional expenses, and additional expenses meant more money out of the developer's pocket. Dealing with haranguing developers was part of his duties as site superintendent. The Roths did raise complaining to an art form, full of bluster and threat. But for Nelson's employer the biggest concern with construction delays was the possibility that unforeseen expenses would stretch the developer's money to the breaking point, leaving the project in limbo. This was increasingly a fact of construction life: the money was drying up as the commercial real estate market cooled, banks that were already overextended refusing to go any deeper on developments that were losing ten percent or more of their value even before they were finished being built.

Nelson had the biggest trailer on site, at the back edge of the lot, an area of relative peace and quiet. In addition to his office in the back, it had a conference room where the weekly meeting with the heads of all the subcontractors took place. Those meetings could last half a day, often degenerating into an extensive airing of mutual grievances. Nelson had been forced to break up a fistfight or two in his time as a site super.

He was in his office, on the phone with Omni's corporate headquarters, when two men he'd never seen before walked into his office. Both were in their late forties, big guys in suits, one of them black, the other white. Nelson looked up, equal parts puzzled and angry, wondering how they'd gotten on site. He made them as cops from how they carried themselves. "What's the trouble, gents?" Nelson asked, after hanging up the phone.

"The problem, Tommy, is who you've been talking to," Darryl Loomis said, as Chris Driscoll, his hands in his pockets, stood beside him.

"What're you talking about?"

"The reporter, Snow," Darryl said. "What'd you tell her?"

The two men weren't acting like cops. "Who are you?"

"I'm the motherfucker whose questions you're going to answer," Darryl replied, leaning forward. "Now what'd you tell the reporter?"

"Who said I talked to a reporter?"

"We saw the two of you in the bar," Darryl said. "So stop wasting my time."

Driscoll had come around so that he was standing just to the side of Nelson's desk, blocking him in. Darryl stood directly in front of the desk, both men too close, obviously trying to intimidate him. Nelson wasn't in the habit of being intimidated, especially in his own office. He debated standing up himself, or picking up the phone and calling the police, but neither seemed like quite the right play. He decided instead on bluster.

"What business is it of yours who I talk to?" he demanded.

Darryl smiled in response. "I don't think you're understanding the kind of talk we're having right now," he said.

"I've had enough of this shit," Nelson said. "Either tell me who the fuck you are and what the fuck you want, or get the fuck out of my office."

"We work for people who value discretion," Darryl said. "And your ass needs to start being discreet."

The movement was so sudden that Nelson caught it only out of the corner of his eye, Driscoll taking a step forward, a small length of metal pipe in his hand, which he brought down with a quick swing on Nelson's right knee.

Nelson doubled over from the shock of the pain. In doing so he left himself exposed, and the next swing caught the top of his head, spinning him out of his chair and onto the floor. Nelson, dizzy, the pain so sharp and overwhelming he could scarcely even feel it, instinctively rolled himself into a ball, putting his arms up over his head.

"There's two ways your future can go," Darryl said, his voice unchanged. "Either way, you're never going to see us again. One possible future is you keep your mouth shut, and we stay out of your life. The other is you don't shut up. In that case you just never see us coming, and it's game-over for you. I got your attention?"

Nelson lay still, his eyes squeezed shut. Driscoll swung the pipe one more time, a sharp *thwap* as it broke Nelson's left ankle.

"You really should answer when I ask you something," Darryl said.

"Yes," Nelson managed to rasp, his throat clogged.

"Yes, what?"

"You've got my attention." Nelson forced the words out in a hoarse whisper, fluttering on the edge of passing out. "I won't talk to the reporter again."

"That wasn't so hard," Darryl said. "Now tell me everything you told her."

·42·

DUNCAN HAD come down to court by himself. Blake was no longer pretending to show any interest in the Nazario case; he'd made it clear that the hearing on the gunshot residue was Duncan's to win or lose. Not that Duncan was complaining: he enjoyed having the freedom to operate without a more senior lawyer constantly peering over his shoulder, something he didn't get in cases with hundreds of millions of dollars at stake.

Rafael had been brought down from Rikers for the hearing, the first time Duncan had seen his client in a few weeks. He met with Rafael in the visiting area on the twelfth floor, one of a row of lawyers lined up, their clients brought to sit across from them, reinforced glass in between. It was loud, and Duncan did his best to tune out the grim room, focus on Rafael. If this was the part of imprisonment that the system allowed the lawyers to see, Duncan couldn't imagine what the actual daily reality of incarceration was like. He thought of his half brother, violated on parole and back in prison. There was nothing he could do for Antoine; it was Rafael he could help.

"So is everything okay?" Duncan asked as he sat across from Rafael.

"They got me in hell out there," Rafael said, speaking quickly, his usual enthusiasm taking on a manic edge. "Somebody put a blade in the vent above my cell, so now I'm in solitary for thirty days."

"Shit," Duncan said, feeling once again out of his league. "Did you have a hearing or anything before they moved you to solitary?"

Rafael's administrative hearing had been the same day the shiv had been found. The adjudication captain, a middle-aged black woman, had at least been polite, hearing Rafael out as he insisted that the blade was not his and that he didn't know who had put it in the vent (Rafael feeling like he had no choice but to lie about that). She'd taken notes on a form, rarely looking up, although she'd looked Rafael in the eye when asking if he had any idea who'd hidden the weapon.

He'd been put in the Central Punitive Segregation Unit, what prisoners called the bing. Inmates were kept in lockdown twenty-three hours a day, with one hour for the exercise yard and the shower. Even that hour was basically just another form of solitary: Rafael was not exactly interested in mingling with the hard-core prisoners who made up the CPSU population. There were some freaky people in the bing—the gangbangers had nothing on the guys who were just out of their heads. Rafael had thought life in the cell block had been tedious, but that was nothing compared to solitary. Time crawled when it moved at all, each day an endurance test.

"The hearing was bullshit," Rafael said.

Duncan wanted to offer to do something about it, but he wasn't at all sure he could. He wondered if Rafael was telling the truth about the shiv. Duncan didn't know how much violence there was at Rikers, or how unsafe Rafael might feel. "Is there any way to appeal it?" he asked.

"I don't think so," Rafael said. "Seems like they can do what they want to me out there."

"Were you having some kind of problem before they found the blade?"

"What do you mean?" Rafael asked.

Duncan shrugged, feeling awkward talking about it. "Just, is there a problem you're having in the jail, anything I could maybe help you with?"

Duncan saw the hesitation in Rafael, the flicker of something. "Nah," Rafael said. "I'll get through Rikers. What's going to happen here in court?"

Duncan wondered if he should let it go, but the fact was, he didn't know how to help Rafael with any problems at the jail. He decided to just turn to the task at hand. "I think we've got a real good chance here," he said. "I've got some surprises up my sleeve for the DA's so-called expert."

"I didn't shoot nobody that night, so what that man's saying has got to be a lie," Rafael replied. Duncan understood the logic, even if he knew things were never quite that simple in a court of law.

"We may not find out today how the judge is going to rule," Duncan said. "And even if we win, the case won't be over."

"I hear you," Rafael said. "Least it gets me up out of Rikers for a day."

"Have you heard the news from your grandmother about the eviction?" Duncan asked, wanting to cheer Rafael up.

Rafael shook his head. "She can't talk to me while I'm in the bing."

"There was a newspaper article a little while back raising questions about whether the security guards were planting drugs on people at Riis. It mentioned you, in fact, and Fowler. Anyway, the city has announced it's suspending all eviction proceedings where the security guards played a role while they look into it. So your grandmother doesn't have to worry about losing her home, at least not anytime soon."

Rafael brightened. "So if they know Fowler set me up, what's that mean for the murder charge?"

"Honestly, probably very little," Duncan replied. "My guess is the DA's going to feel like you might even have more of a motive to shoot Fowler if he was lying about you. We'll see, but I wouldn't assume it changes much in this case. But still."

"It's good, though, yeah. I mean, it was crazy that they were trying to kick her out."

"She'll be in court today," Duncan said. "Hopefully you'll get a chance to talk to her. I should go get ready to do this thing. I think we're about to have a good day."

WHEN DUNCAN entered the courtroom fifteen minutes before the scheduled noon hearing, another set of lawyers were arguing a motion before the judge, Jacob Lasky. The judge was red-faced, his voice raised as he berated the defense lawyer. Not a welcoming sight, Duncan thought.

Lasky was in his sixties, had been on the bench for about a decade. Before that, he'd spent most of his career in the district attorney's office. His reputation was for being both prickly and law-and-order, a gruff no-nonsense judge who ran a tight ship. Not a good draw for a criminal defendant, but not the worst one out there either.

Duncan saw Dolores Nazario in the second row—the front row reserved for lawyers and cops—and sat down beside her, smiling hello. He noticed Candace Snow and the other *Journal* reporter as he walked past, but didn't acknowledge them, nervous enough without worrying about the press.

Once the other argument was finally over, the judge took a fifteen-minute recess, so it was well past twelve thirty by the time Lasky returned to the bench. Even though it was the defense's motion, the burden of establishing the evidence's admissibility was on the prosecution, so they would go first. Each side was going to be presenting one witness, Professor Cole for the defense, and for the DA the police lab worker who'd conducted the GSR testing, Kevin Logan. Duncan and Cole had spent much of the weekend together in a firm conference room preparing for the hearing, and Duncan was confident he was ready to go.

Logan was sixty or so, mostly bald, with stray wisps of white hair crossing the top of his head. He was dressed in a sports jacket and tie. ADA Bream handled Logan's questioning. He started with a brief summary of the witness's background and experience, followed by a step-by-step recounting of the process by which he'd tested for gunshot residue using a scanning electron microscope. Duncan listened carefully, taking detailed notes. But the show wouldn't really start until it was his turn to ask the questions.

Judge Lasky made no effort to pretend he was paying attention. The judge had brought some papers to the bench with him; he appeared to be marking up a document, rarely looking up. ADA Bream, perhaps sensing the judge's lack of interest, kept things short, taking only about twenty minutes to run Logan through his paces.

When he was finished Duncan stood, slowly making his way to the podium directly in front of the witness. The courtroom was fairly small, no more than ten feet or so between Duncan and Logan. Duncan was nervous, but a good nervous: he was full of adrenaline, ready to do battle. Dr. Cole had guided him in preparing for his cross, giving him a lot of scientific ammunition. He hoped to be able to pretty much destroy Logan on the stand.

"How many GSR particles did you find on my client's hands, Mr. Logan?"

"Six."

"Were particles found on both of his hands?"

"No, just the left hand."

"Do you know whether my client is left-handed?"

"I have no idea."

"Would it surprise you to learn that he is, in fact, right-handed?"

"Not at all."

"The fact that the GSR was found on my client's nondominant hand, that wouldn't surprise you?" Duncan asked. He'd expected Logan to deny that this was significant, but it was part of the broader picture he intended to paint about the validity of the GSR finding.

"Not really, no," Logan replied, smiling, looking like he was relaxing a little, which was fine with Duncan. He hoped Logan was thinking this was all Duncan had to hit him with.

"Why not?"

"A number of reasons. GSR is easily transferable from one hand to the other, for one thing. If the defendant had touched the gun with his nondominant hand near the time of firing it, that could easily be the cause of the GSR. It's also not uncommon for a gun to be held in both hands when being fired."

"You mentioned that GSR is easily transferable. Is it possible to pick up GSR not from a gun, but from another surface that has GSR on it?"

Logan glanced over at the prosecution's table, as if needing permission to concede even this. "That's possible," he said.

"So, for example, could the back of a police car have GSR in it? Say from someone who's fired a gun having previously been put into the car?"

"It could."

"And someone could then pick up that residue off the seat?" Duncan asked, trying to establish a brisk pace, get Logan in a rhythm of answering his questions.

"I suppose. They'd probably have to rub their hands into the seat cushion."

"If your hands were handcuffed behind your back, they might be rubbing into the seat cushion, right?"

"I don't really know."

"As a matter of common sense, it's certainly possible, right?" Duncan asked with a little smile, no trace of confrontation, wanting to suggest that he was simply asking Logan to admit the obvious. He was totally focused on Logan now, everyone else in the room forgotten.

"It seems possible."

"What about a police station interview room? Is that a place where GSR could be?"

Logan scoffed. "I don't think people generally fire guns in police interview rooms," he said.

Duncan wondered if Logan was purposely being obtuse. "I'm not talking about GSR being there because a gun was actually fired in the room. I'm talking about GSR that someone carries in on their person or clothing, which then comes off in the room."

"That could happen, maybe a single stray particle, but I don't think more than that, not unless someone walked in right after firing a gun."

Duncan had read up enough on GSR to know that what Logan was saying wasn't accurate, though he didn't know if it was out of ignorance or deliberate. "In fact, Mr. Logan, police stations are widely regarded as containing stray GSR particles in the manner I've just described, correct?"

Logan shrugged. "I don't know what you mean by 'widely regarded.'"

"Are you aware that studies have repeatedly found a high level of GSR contamination in police stations?"

"I don't recall seeing such studies."

"Are you aware that in many jurisdictions, a suspect's hands are bagged when he is first taken into custody if the police are planning to perform a GSR test, precisely to avoid such contamination?"

"We encourage the police to bag hands here," Logan said. "But unfortunately it doesn't always happen."

"In your written report, you state that, quote, 'six particles of gunshot powder residue were found on the hands of the subject.' Do you recall writing that?"

"I recall that's in my report, yes."

Duncan was moving in for the kill, but he doubted that anyone in the courtroom could tell. "But in your lab bench notes, you are more specific about the six particles you found, correct?"

Logan frowned, taking a moment. "I don't know what you mean," he said.

"You note that you found one particle that was a fusion of lead, barium, and antimony, and that the other five particles were just a fusion of lead and barium, correct?"

"I'd have to review my notes."

Duncan handed Logan a copy of his lab notes, then gave a copy to Bream, who looked a little uneasy. Duncan suspected the ADAs hadn't taken much of a look at the underlying forensic work behind Logan's report, had assumed it was solid and that Duncan was just using this hearing to draw the case out. If so, they were in for a surprise.

"Yes," Logan said. "That's what I found."

Duncan could feel his nerves grow taut as he got ready to ask the next question. "Are you aware, Mr. Logan, that a fusion of lead and barium is not sufficiently unique to be considered gunshot residue?"

The courtroom was dead silent, Duncan savoring the pause while Logan considered his response. Duncan could tell he had Logan completely off guard. "I believe that particles showing a fusion of lead and barium can accurately be classified as GSR," Logan finally said stiffly. "Especially when found in conjunction with a fused particle of lead, barium, and antimony."

"Are you aware that your belief is not shared by the FBI?" The question hung there for a moment in the silent courtroom. Duncan had them in the palm of his hand; he could feel it. He reminded himself to remain stoic, not let any sense of triumph show.

"I don't know what you're referring to."

"In 2004 you went to a forensics training conference held by the FBI at Quantico, correct?"

Logan was clearly surprised by the change of direction. "I did."

"Do you recall going to a session about GSR?"

"Yes."

"Do you recall whether there was a discussion at that session regarding the fact that the FBI considered only the three-element fusion of lead, barium, and antimony to be sufficiently unique to be called GSR, not the two-element fusion of lead and barium?"

Logan was shrinking on the stand, his shoulders hunching as he leaned into himself. "I don't recall."

"I have a copy of the written materials for that presentation," Duncan said, entering the exhibit into evidence. "Mr. Logan, could you please read the highlighted passage?"

Logan squirmed in his chair as Duncan approached him. "'Because a fusion of lead and barium is not unique to GSR, but can also be found in certain paints, in brake linings, and in other industrial materials, the

FBI considers only a three-element fusion of lead, barium, and anti-mony to be sufficiently unique to be considered gunshot residue.'"

"Does reading that passage refresh your recollection regarding what you learned at that FBI training session?" Duncan asked. He hardly cared how Logan answered: the point was made. He had the state's expert boxed in, and he didn't see the guy coming up with a way out.

"I don't work for the FBI, so even if that's their standard I wouldn't be required to follow it," Logan said, looking over at the prosecutor's table for rescue.

Duncan took a step away from the podium, wanting to draw Logan's attention back to him. "Because you personally view the two-element fusion as being sufficiently unique to be considered GSR?"

"When found in conjunction with three-element particles as well, absolutely," Logan replied, glancing back at Duncan.

"What's your support for this belief?"

"My own professional experience," Logan said, his eyes downcast.

"Are you aware of any secondary sources, any scholarly materials, any law enforcement agencies, or *anything*, for that matter, outside of your own experience, that supports the idea that your view is right and the FBI's view is wrong?"

"I'm a trained expert in this area." Logan was finally showing at least a little bit of fight.

"I see," Duncan said mildly. "Is that because you go to training sessions like the one at Quantico?"

"In part."

"It doesn't seem like you paid a whole lot of attention there, did you?" Duncan said, allowing himself to put some edge into it.

"Objection," Bream said sharply.

"Sustained," Judge Lasky said, but his voice was muted. Duncan glanced at the judge, who had put his papers down and was peering over his glasses at the witness.

"Do you know what Mr. Nazario does for a living, Mr. Logan?"

"I do not."

"So you don't know if he works with industrial materials?"

"I don't."

"So you don't then know whether he might've been exposed to the two-element particles by using, say, a scouring pad in a kitchen, or an industrial-strength dishwashing unit?"

"I have no idea."

"Putting aside the two-element particles you found, you also found one particle of fused lead, barium, and antimony, correct?"

"That's right," Logan said, looking relieved that Duncan was shifting ground.

"Are you aware, Mr. Logan, that according to FBI protocols a finding of one particle of GSR is insufficient to be considered an indication that the person has handled a discharged gun?"

Logan paused, as if waiting for inspiration, or perhaps rescue. "I don't recall being aware of that, no."

"Were you aware that, again according to the FBI, finding one particle is as likely to be caused by contamination as by firing a gun?" Duncan said, trying to stay methodical, keep any reaction out of his questions. He didn't want to seem like he was gloating; Duncan wanted to be gentle about eviscerating Logan—he'd watched Blake do this a number of times, and was trying his best to emulate his boss's technique.

"No," Logan said flatly, the last dregs of resistance draining out of him. Duncan decided he'd gotten everything he could out of Logan. All that was left was to use Cole to nail down the coffin.

"No further questions," Duncan said to the judge, turning to go back to his seat. He walked slowly, wanting to take in the room. Duncan had rarely gotten to actually question a witness in court; he'd never had the chance to really take someone apart on the stand like that. At the DA's table, neither Castelluccio nor Bream was making much effort to hide their frustration with how badly Logan's testimony had gone. He saw that Dolores Nazario looked pleased, and that behind her the reporters were intently engaged in their note taking. Candace glanced up at him, and to Duncan's surprise she smiled. At the defense table Rafael was grinning broadly.

The DA didn't have any other evidence to put on, so Duncan called Cole. The professor had testified dozens of times as an expert; Duncan guessed that Cole made more money from testifying than he did from his day job.

Once Cole was on the stand, Duncan led him through his credentials, which were far better than Logan's. ADA Bream offered to stipulate to Cole's expertise, an offer Duncan declined, wanting to stress the professor's bona fides. He then turned to Logan's report.

"Dr. Cole, have you reviewed the GSR report prepared by Mr. Logan regarding Mr. Nazario?"

"I have," Cole said. The professor was leaning back in his seat, his legs crossed, appearing thoroughly at ease.

"And do you have an opinion on the merits of that report?"

"I do," Cole said. "In my view it is so flawed as to be entirely worthless as a piece of scientific evidence."

"And in coming to that conclusion, are you relying on generally accepted principles in the area of GSR testing?"

"I am applying the standards of the FBI, as well as numerous states that have set formal minimum standards for when GSR results are acceptable."

"After reviewing Mr. Logan's report, were you able to glean the facts on which Mr. Logan's opinion was based?"

"Not from his report, no," Cole said. "I had to review his underlying bench notes in order to clearly see the actual facts and not just Mr. Logan's conclusions."

"And were you able to form your own expert opinion, based on those facts?"

"I was, yes. In my opinion there was only one genuine particle of gunshot residue found on Mr. Nazario's hands. Given that he'd been in a police car and a precinct house, as well as around numerous armed police officers, it is far more likely that he picked up the particle as incidental contamination, rather than from actually handling a recently fired gun himself. In my opinion it would be utterly inappropriate to infer that Mr. Nazario had shot a gun based on these GSR results."

"As to the five other particles, the two-element particles, do you have a theory as to where those came from?"

"It's impossible to determine," Cole answered. "They could also be incidental contamination, say from the police car. They could be · from something Mr. Nazario handled at his job in a restaurant, some industrial product he came into contact with in the kitchen. That's the problem with the two-element particles—nobody can say what their origin is."

"Thank you, Dr. Cole," Duncan said.

Bream and Castelluccio were huddled together at their table, Castelluccio looking furious, Bream like he'd just been kicked in the balls. Duncan offered them a bright smile as he walked to his table.

"Your Honor, if we could just have a short recess to prepare our cross-examination of Dr. Cole," Bream said.

"What's there to cross-examine Dr. Cole about?" Lasky said irritably. "Are you challenging his description of the general scientific consensus in the areas of his expertise?"

Bream, at a loss, looked over to Castelluccio for rescue, but she was glaring at the judge and didn't so much as glance Bream's way. "We would like to confer with Mr. Logan regarding that," Bream finally said.

"Thank you, Dr. Cole," Lasky said to the witness. "You can step down now."

"Your Honor—" Bream protested.

"You just put on the record that you didn't have any basis to cross-examine this witness. I'm an hour behind schedule as it is, Mr. Bream. This hearing is adjourned; I'll reserve my ruling. And I'll see counsel in chambers. Now."

Duncan felt disappointed that the judge had reserved decision; he thought he'd done more than enough for Lasky to rule right from the bench. He had no idea why they were being summoned to chambers, but hoped it would be good news. He was charged up from demolishing Logan, and allowed himself a momentary fantasy that he'd been so effective that the judge was going to propose ending the case, though he knew realistically that wasn't about to happen.

He followed Bream and Castelluccio to the door in the back of the courtroom, which the courtroom deputy was holding open for them. "You know why he wants to see us, Mike?" Castelluccio asked the deputy.

"Who knows?" Mike replied. "The old guy's just full of surprises today."

He ushered them into Judge Lasky's chambers. Rather than going to his desk, the judge had sat at the head of a small table at the front of the room, where he gestured for them to join him. He'd unzipped his robe, underneath which was a rumpled gray polo shirt. Duncan had never seen a judge in a polo shirt before. Duncan sat by himself on one side of the table, the two ADAs on the other.

"How many cases has this Logan testified in for your office?" he asked Castelluccio as soon as they were all seated.

"I've no idea," Castelluccio said after a second, clearly thrown by the question. "Dozens, though, I would think, if not more."

"Don't pretend that you don't see the can of worms this just opened up."

"I'm not sure I understand," Castelluccio said carefully.

"How many other cases you think this joker has found this two-element thing and said it was gunshot residue? I write an opinion in this case, say what really just happened out there, everybody ever convicted where Logan testified is going to be asking for a hearing."

"I don't think his testimony went that badly," Castelluccio protested.

"Give me a break," Lasky said. "The guy ID'd stuff as GSR that wasn't actually GSR. It's as simple as that. And I guarantee you this wasn't the first time."

"I would have to respectfully disagree with your characterization, Your Honor," Castelluccio said. "But I understand that your opinion's the one that counts."

"You're damn right it is. I don't need any more enemies, including your boss. And the district attorney isn't going to like it if I write up what just happened to your witness."

Castelluccio was squeezing her hands together so hard the knuckles were turning white. "So what do you suggest, Your Honor?" Castelluccio said.

"You drop him as a witness," Lasky said. "And your office doesn't use him again, at least not until he's cleaned up his act."

Castelluccio looked aghast, but she kept eye contact with the judge. Duncan couldn't quite believe what was happening, but he understood that there was nothing for him to do but keep out of the way. "But his report—"

"Obviously you can't use his report if you can't use him."

"So you're saying we withdraw our GSR evidence?"

"If you don't, you're just going to make me throw it out," Lasky said. "And believe me, that's going to be far worse for everyone."

DUNCAN STROLLED out of chambers, Castelluccio storming off in front of him with Bream in tow. He followed them down the hall and back to the courtroom, hoping to have a chance to update Rafael on what had just transpired. But the courtroom was now empty, which meant Rafael had likely been shipped back to Rikers. Duncan decided he'd settle for calling his client's grandmother later, filling her in. When he walked out of the courtroom back into the main hallway he found Candace Snow leaning against the wall.

"That was pretty hot," she said.

"Excuse me?" Duncan said after a moment, hoping his reaction wasn't showing.

"I mean, as somebody who asks people questions for a living myself," Candace said. She was smiling at him, looking far warmer than Duncan had previously seen her. Candace was dressed relatively casually, black jeans and a dark purple shirt under a suit jacket that was her sole concession to being in court. Duncan assumed she was aware of being pretty, knew that it let her get away with things she otherwise couldn't. "Once, maybe twice in my whole career I've really gotten somebody like that in an interview. You know, where you've just exposed them for what they are. It's the best high in the world."

Duncan smiled without meaning to, that high still pumping through his blood. "Are you writing a story about the hearing?"

"I'm not, but somebody else from my paper was here. He went back to write it up."

"He didn't even want a quote from me?" Duncan said, intending it as a joke but realizing as he said it that there was some real disappointment there too; he wanted recognition for his knockout of Logan.

"Oh, no, he does," Candace said. "I agreed to stick around to get one. You can talk to me now, right?"

Duncan felt pleasantly surprised that she'd asked without either challenge or sarcasm. "The libel suit is over, so yeah, you're not off-limits anymore."

"Speaking of the libel suit, you hear about William Stanton? The DOB canned him."

"Why, 'cause he talked to you?" Duncan retorted after a moment. He felt bad at hearing that Stanton had lost his job, but he wasn't going to let the reporter guilt him over it.

"That's not fair," Candace protested.

"The city sent along a lawyer when Stanton was deposed. I'm guessing the DOB didn't like him airing its dirty laundry."

"I protected William," Candace said. "He only got outed because you went after him."

"I had nothing against Stanton. Sorry if he got a raw deal, but I had a job to do."

"William thinks the whole point of the libel suit was to get him fired."

Duncan remembered what Leah had said about the libel case as a warning shot about bad-mouthing her family, but pushed it out of his mind. "I don't blame a guy for being self-centered when it comes to losing his job," he said, not wanting to concede anything.

"Can you tell me for a fact that wasn't the point of the case?"

Duncan thought he probably shouldn't be talking to Candace, even without the libel suit. Leah had forbidden him to, for one thing. Duncan also didn't think Blake would like him going around spouting off to the press about the Nazario case, but he decided a single quote about the hearing wouldn't kill him. The judge's decision to bury the larger problem with the GSR evidence hadn't sat well with Duncan; if Logan had given similar testimony in other cases, those defendants should have the chance to challenge it. The judge and the DA might be too invested in keeping the system going to worry about that, but Duncan had no such obligations. He decided to try to come up with something that would put some pressure on the DA to fix the broader mess.

"I don't think we should talk about the libel case. I'll give you a quote on the Nazario hearing, but that's the only on-the-record chat you and I can have."

"If that's how you want it," Candace said.

Duncan looked at Candace, who wasn't holding paper or pen. "You ready?"

"Fire away."

"Give me a second," Duncan said. He closed his eyes, went back into his courtroom mode, let himself take his time. The paper wouldn't print the pause. "Okay, here goes: I have serious concerns that Mr. Logan's scientific testimony was not only inaccurate in this case, but that his larger ability to perform his job duties was also called into question. There can be no doubt that the so-called scientific evidence against my client is nothing of the kind, and I fully expect the district attorney's office to decide not to bring it forward on its own accord. It wouldn't surprise me if they launched their own review of other cases in which Mr. Logan has presented evidence."

"Okay, thanks," Candace said. She was still standing with her hands at her sides. "That's it?"

"You got all that?" Duncan asked skeptically.

"I got it."

"But you didn't write anything down."

"I'm recording."

Duncan frowned at her. "You're tape-recording us right now?"

"Technically it's digital, but yes."

"Are you serious?" Duncan asked, though he realized as he said it that she obviously was. "Is that even legal?"

"Of course it's legal," Candace said. "New York's a one-party-consent state. For recording your own conversations, that is."

"Well stop," Duncan said, not liking the idea of being recorded, even though he wasn't sure what difference it made when speaking to a reporter.

"Sure," Candace said. She reached into the inside pocket of her suit jacket and turned off the recorder. "Now can we go somewhere to talk?"

Duncan hadn't been expecting this. He didn't want to talk to any reporter if he could help it, and Candace least of all. "What do we have to talk about?"

"I want to ask you about a couple of things. One to do with your firm, the other to do with this case."

"What about this case?"

"I want to run a theory by you."

"A theory about what?"

"Why somebody might have wanted Sean Fowler dead."

·43·

CANDACE AND Duncan ended up at the Peking Duck House on Mott Street. Duncan had suggested it: Blake had a thing for the duck, and last year when they'd had a trial in the nearby federal courthouse the team had come here for lunch once a week. The idea of bringing Candace there—of having lunch with her at all—was strange. But he needed to find out what she knew, and he also needed to eat: it was now well past two in the afternoon.

"So," he said, after they'd ordered. "What's this about Fowler?"

"It's not something for nothing," Candace said. "So here's what I want from you: I assume you know who David Markowitz is?"

"The politician? I've heard of him, sure."

"Your firm is the agent of record on numerous campaign contributions made by various shell companies to Markowitz. I'd like to confirm where the money is actually coming from."

Duncan didn't much like the sound of that. "I don't know anything about it," he said. "I can ask around, but no promises. Are you suggesting something illegal's going on?"

"You're the lawyer."

"Can't you just ask Markowitz?"

"He's been avoiding me," Candace said. "Which is not exactly the best way to get off my radar."

"I'll get back to you on it," Duncan said, who had no trouble imagining that dodging Candace was a bad idea. "That's all I can commit to. So what is it you have about Fowler?"

Candace looked at him for a moment. "I assume you know that Sean Fowler worked at the Aurora Tower before he was at Jacob Riis?"

Duncan was surprised by this—not the information itself, but that it could be going somewhere. "I didn't know that, but it doesn't really surprise me. The same security guys do all of Roth's construction security work, from what I understand."

"So you never looked at what Fowler was up to before Riis?"

"I know a thing or two about the Aurora, and I've never heard Fowler's name come up. But security guards had nothing to do with the accident there, if that's what you're getting at."

Candace leaned back, again studying him, her arms folded across her chest. Duncan was not sure what she was looking for. "You remember the first time we talked?" Candace finally said.

Duncan grinned. "When you called me an asshole?" he replied. "How could I forget?"

Candace looked momentarily flustered but quickly recovered. "A deposition isn't a conversation. I'm talking about when I asked whether you could promise that you'd use anything you got that would help Nazario's case."

This confirmed Duncan's suspicion that whatever Candace had regarding Fowler was going to connect to Roth Properties in some way. "I remember," he said neutrally.

"So why don't you know—assuming you really don't—that Fowler was involved in what was happening at the Aurora?"

"This is the first I've heard Fowler's name come up in the context of the Aurora," Duncan said. "And I have no idea what you mean when you say there was something happening there."

"What about Jack Pellettieri?"

"What about him?"

Candace looked annoyed. "Tell me something that'll make me think we're having an actual conversation."

Duncan smiled; Candace didn't smile back. He took a sip of green tea, which was watery and too hot. He considered telling Candace a real secret: that settlement negotiations in the wrongful-death case were nearly complete, the two sides having agreed on a number, now just working out the details of the formal settlement agreement. Roth wasn't paying out, just Pellettieri, so his firm had no direct involvement in the negotiations. But the whole thing was confidential at this point, and Duncan decided it was too big a risk to leak it to a reporter. "Jack Pellettieri's a dick," was what he ultimately said instead.

"I tried to interview him for my story you sued me over," Candace said. "I thought he was going to take a swing at me, right there on the street. But I wasn't really looking for whether you liked the guy."

"Off the record?" Duncan said. After a moment Candace nodded. "Say it out loud, in case you still have that tape recorder of yours running."

"Off the record," Candace said, rolling her eyes.

"You're asking me whether he's in the shit," Duncan said. "The answer is yes."

"And that means what exactly?"

"The Aurora. He's on the hook. He's the bad guy. Clear enough?"

"Clear enough but not good enough."

Now it was Duncan's turn to grow a little frustrated. But he figured he didn't owe Pellettieri any protection. "Pellettieri was running a racket at the Aurora. He was overbilling, he was cutting corners, he didn't do what he was supposed to in terms of safety."

"And you think that's where the buck stops?" Candace said, shaking her head. "I don't think we can do business, Duncan."

Duncan was surprised at his own disappointment. "What's that supposed to mean?"

"You're not stupid, and I don't imagine you're naive. So for you to know as little as you do, it either has to be that you're trying not to, or that you do know, and you're not telling. Either way, it's not going to be a productive interaction for me."

"What is it you're so sure I should know?"

"Why was Pellettieri able to get away with all this, before the accident?"

"You think it went higher up."

"It did go higher up," Candace insisted.

"And you think Fowler came into it somehow?"

"Fowler was in the mix of what was wrong at the Aurora."

The waiter arrived with their duck, which he then commenced to carve tableside. Duncan was grateful for the interruption, trying to play this out. After the waiter left, Duncan, who was starving as well as puzzled, started right in, Candace just looking at him, making no move to touch the food. Duncan was thinking about Pellettieri's outburst at lunch, his message about holding up his end. But that wasn't something he could tell Candace about, not if it pointed where he thought it did.

"It's not adding up to me," Duncan finally said. "You're suggesting Pellettieri had somebody's blessing to be doing what he was doing, but why would a security guard have any role to play in that?"

"You want to move money around without certain people ever actually having to be in the same room, you look for somebody who has a license to roam."

So Candace was suggesting that Fowler'd been a middleman. "Even if Fowler was somehow mixed up with Pellettieri, how does that help Rafael?" he said.

Candace laughed dryly. "Fowler was involved in a scam at the Aurora that led to the deaths of three people. Can't think of any reason somebody who knew too much about that would have something bad happen to them?"

"You have anything but your suspicious mind to support that?"

"You're the lawyer. Shouldn't you be looking for someone other than your client to blame the murder on?"

"Gladly, but as a lawyer, unlike a reporter, I need to worry about things like, you know, actual evidence," Duncan said. Beneath his sarcasm was a thought: if Fowler was a middleman on embezzling at the Aurora, there should be a money trail. He could subpoena Fowler's financial records, see if there was anything out of the ordinary.

"And if you get anywhere with this, you're gonna tell me, right?"

"You'll be the only reporter I talk to, sure," Duncan said. "You really think Fowler's death has something to do with the Aurora?"

"Actually, the only reason I ever had for doubting that Nazario shot him was that you were the kid's lawyer."

The exchanged their first shared smile of the lunch. Duncan found himself actually liking Candace, something he hadn't been sure of before now. "Nice to see you coming at this with an open mind."

"It's not like I'm prejudiced against Roth Properties. It's just that I've seen how they operate."

"That's the thing about being a lawyer; I don't have to pretend that I'm an impartial observer. I get to leave it to the judge to pretend that."

"You think I pretend to be objective?"

"No, actually; I don't think you bother to pretend. You've clearly got an ax to grind here."

Candace shook her head, her expression serious. "There's nothing about this that's personal to me. I thought I'd gotten the whole story when I first covered the Aurora, but now I realize I didn't have the whole thing at all, that it may have spilled out into something else entirely. I just want to get the truth, because that's my job."

Duncan shrugged, not wanting to push them back into confrontation. "If you say so."

"And it's not like I buy that lawyer bullshit about how your only concern is for your client and it's not for you to think beyond that," Candace said. "I know how much my father disapproved of some of the things he had to defend. It didn't keep him from doing his job, but it bothered him. In any event, this is our second conversation where I've given you more than you've given me. That's not how this is supposed to work."

"I'm acting in good faith here," Duncan protested. "I'll look into the Fowler Aurora angle, and if something breaks you'll get the only heads-up."

"Plus you'll get back to me on the LLC thing?"

"Deal," Duncan said.

Candace reached into her purse and pulled out a business card, Duncan doing the same out of his wallet. They handed them across, which proved a somewhat awkward exchange. Duncan noticed that Candace wasn't wearing a wedding ring.

"How come you don't wear a ring?" he asked impulsively. "You seemed pretty adamant about being called Mrs. and all."

To his surprise, Candace promptly started blushing. "Oh, God. I don't know what was wrong with me at that deposition. I'm actually in the middle of getting divorced."

Duncan couldn't resist a smile. "You know you were under oath, right?"

"I'm still technically married," Candace said. "For another few weeks, anyway. I'm sorry I was such a bitch that day, and then when I waylaid you outside Riis."

"Okay, then," Duncan said. "So, truce?"

"If I find out you've been bullshitting me, I'll burn you in print," Candace replied. "Long as we're clear on that, then yeah, truce."

· 44 ·

LEAH WALKED briskly through her office building's lobby and out to a waiting Town Car. She got in the backseat, making eye contact with Darryl Loomis by way of the rearview mirror. It was Darryl's idea for them to meet like this: it was a way for them to hide in plain sight.

Leah recalled the first time she'd met Darryl this way. It'd been only a couple of months ago, although in some ways it felt like a lifetime had passed. Leah had called Darryl the night her brother had told her he was being blackmailed, said they needed to discuss a sensitive matter in person as soon as possible.

They'd arranged for him to drive her to work the following morning. When she'd left her building at eight thirty Darryl had been outside in a parked Town Car. Leah had met him a handful of times over the past couple years, but had never been alone with him before. Darryl had always been polite to the point of deference with her, not showing any of the street swagger on which his reputation was based. But being good at blending into every kind of environment was part of what he brought to the table.

Leah had slept little the night before, her mind wrestling with the prospect of the conversation. She had absolutely no idea how Darryl would react. For all she knew, he was mixed up in what Fowler was doing, and raising the issue with him would only make things worse.

"What can I do for you, Ms. Roth?" Darryl had asked once he'd started driving.

"Leah, please. This is going to be awkward, so I'll just say it. One of your employees has found out something embarrassing about my brother. Worse than embarrassing. He's asked for compensation to keep what he knows to himself. I'm assuming you don't know anything about this?"

It was hard to read Darryl's reaction from the backseat, especially as he navigated rush-hour traffic on Houston Street. "One of my guys is trying to blackmail your brother?" he asked after a moment.

Leah wondered why she'd couched it so weakly. It *was* blackmail, and it was silly to call it anything else. "Right," she said.

As he stopped at a red light Darryl turned in his seat to look at her. "Any way this is some kind of misunderstanding?"

"My brother's already paid him a quarter million dollars," Leah replied, a little sharply. "Now he wants more."

Darryl winced, shaking his head. The car behind them honked, long, the light having gone green. Darryl swore under his breath and continued driving. "Why didn't you tell me about it when it started?" he asked. "I would've put a stop to it real quick. Your brother wouldn't have had to pay out."

"I just found out last night myself."

"Who is it?"

"His name is Sean Fowler," Leah said. "I've never met him, I don't think."

"This something to do with the Aurora?"

Leah's throat felt dry. "Yes," she said, almost choking on the word.

"I'm very sorry this happened," Darryl said. "I've never had a problem like this in my shop. I'll take care of it."

"And how exactly will you do that?"

"That's not a question you want me to answer," Darryl replied without hesitation.

Leah hadn't really let herself think about what she expected Darryl to do. She realized that Darryl hadn't asked what it was that Fowler knew. "We can't have Fowler arrested," she said. "What he knows would come out then, and it would be extremely damaging."

Darryl flicked a quick glance at Leah by way of the rearview. "I wasn't going to have him arrested," he said.

The thought that Fowler was going to be killed had been in Leah's head in some amorphous, nonverbal form, but just then it'd taken definite shape. Not that Darryl had said it. Clearly he was trying to say as little as possible, and Leah understood that might be more to protect her than himself.

But she was already deep in it, as well as her brother, and they'd inevitably run the risk of being linked to whatever happened to Fowler. Closing her eyes to it wasn't going to change that. "Are you going to kill him?" she asked.

Darryl acted like he hadn't heard the question, his eyes now glued to the road.

"Because if Fowler ends up dead," Leah continued after a moment, hearing the tremor in her own voice, "and he was in the middle of blackmailing my brother, that's the kind of thing that could come out in a police investigation, right? Especially with the money he's already gotten."

For a moment Leah thought Darryl was again just not going to respond as he drove north on Hudson Street. "There're ways to keep there from being a protracted investigation," he finally said.

"Such as?"

Darryl could no longer fully contain his frustration. "Look, Ms. Roth—"

"Leah."

"This is what I do, Leah. Due respect, it's not what you do. The reason you pay me is because I possess a skill set the rest of your company doesn't."

"I understand all that," Leah said, a little irritably, feeling that Darryl was condescending to her. "But this situation could destroy my family, and my company too. I need to know what you're going to do."

"There's risks that come with that."

"Then I'll have to take them," Leah had replied.

FOOLISH BRAVADO, she thought now. She hadn't really understood the price that knowledge would extract, or how long the risks involved would linger. She hadn't realized that there'd be no going back. But it was too late now. She needed to focus on the present. She shifted in her seat, making eye contact with Darryl. "What's up?" she asked.

"The reporter, Snow. Our tail on her paid off; we know she's got something on the Aurora."

Leah had known this was a risk for some time, but that didn't make hearing it any easier. The dust had just started to settle on the reporter's article regarding the evictions at Riis, and now she was back poking at the Aurora. "How?"

"Tommy Nelson."

That was a surprise: from what Leah knew of Tommy Nelson, she thought he'd know better. A site supervisor who got on the bad side of a major developer, however unfairly, risked getting blacklisted from his livelihood. "You know what he told her?"

Darryl nodded curtly, his expression unchanged. "He took a little convincing, but once he saw we were for real he gave it all up."

Leah frowned, her gaze darting back to Darryl's, which remained impassive. Originally Leah hadn't wanted to know the details of how Darryl actually went about his tasks, but that had changed after the eviction mess. Darryl had insisted he'd had no idea that Fowler was planting drugs on people at Jacob Riis, but that was scant consolation. Not knowing about it hadn't been acceptable, and the story itself was damaging. Now the city was looking into the evictions, an embarrassment that could bog down the whole project. "Meaning?" she asked.

"Meaning he's on crutches."

"Jesus," Leah said. Hurting Nelson seemed like a foolish risk, but she also knew better than to try to micromanage Darryl's end of things. It wasn't like the man was a sadist; if he'd hurt somebody, it was because he'd deemed doing so necessary, a means to an end. "To find out what?"

"The reporter's got that money was coming out through Pellettieri, and that he's facing charges."

Leah hissed in a breath. "What about my brother?"

"Sounds like she's pretty much there too," Darryl replied. "And it gets worse. She's got that Fowler was in the loop."

"Nelson gave that to her?" Leah said incredulously. "How does he have that?"

"He's supposed to have open eyes around the site. Sean wasn't always the most careful of men, so there's that."

"So she could piece together . . ."

"Pretty much everything, yeah."

"That can't be allowed to happen," Leah said firmly, with a conviction she couldn't support.

"Meaning?" Darryl said, turning around in his seat to look at Leah directly.

"Christ, no, not that," Leah replied immediately. "For a reporter?"

"It works for the Russians."

"We're way too exposed on this as it is," Leah said.

"I can keep raising the pressure on her," Darryl said. "But backfiring's always a possibility with that."

"Dad's already worked the paper," Leah said, calmer now that she'd moved on from absorbing the bad news to trying to deal with it. "He and Friedman go way back."

"But we should assume Pellettieri's going down," Darryl said. "If it's not the reporter, it'll be the DA."

"I've never actually met Pellettieri," Leah said. "What's your sense of whether he'll hold up?"

"I wouldn't much count on it."

Leah sighed heavily; that was not what she'd hoped to hear. "What do you think we should do about him, then?"

"Money's not going to do anything more to get his loyalty than it's already done. I don't think we can scare him worse than going to the big house does. You could buy him a one-way ticket to Buenos Aires."

"What're the odds he'd take it?"

"Given his options, he might be looking for an escape hatch. Want me to ask?"

"Never hurts to ask," Leah said neutrally. She closed her eyes for a moment. "All right, so you make an offer to Pellettieri and keep up pressure on the reporter. Fingerprint-free, of course. But we have to stop just escalating this. Every time we shut one thing down we seem to end up opening two more. That's got to stop."

"That how these things tend to go," Darryl said.

"For the people who get caught," Leah replied.

·45·

UNDER ORDERS from Castelluccio, Detectives Jaworski and Gomez had brought Dwayne Stevenson back in. Dwayne was one of the corner boys who the beat cops had tagged as a possible eyewitness to Nazario's rabbiting from the murder scene. Castelluccio wanted them to take another run at him now that their forensic evidence had gone south.

Because they'd made such a quick arrest the night of the shooting, neither Jaworski nor Gomez had interviewed Dwayne then. Instead he'd been handed off to a couple of other detectives, who'd mainly left him stewing in an interview room all night, the idea being that the best way to get him to talk was by tiring him into it.

"Dwayne Stevenson," Jaworski said, paging through a small file, angling the pages so that Stevenson couldn't see that they were nearly all blank sheets of paper. Stevenson was short and stocky, already seeming hardened beyond repair despite his youth. "See here you've got a possession with intent hanging over you now."

Dwayne crossed his arms in front of his chest. "I'm waiting on my day in court. You want to talk about that, you best be getting me my lawyer."

"You don't need a lawyer here, Dwayne," Gomez said. "We don't want to talk to you about your own not-so-successful ventures into criminal enterprise. We want to talk to you about the shooting of Sean Fowler."

"I don't even know nobody named Sean Fowler."

"The security guard killed outside your project," Jaworski said.

"I didn't have nothing to do with that," Dwayne said. "You all kept me here all night on some bullshit."

"We didn't bring you in, then or now, 'cause we thought you'd done the shoot," Jaworski said. "We know who did it. And after he shot that man, he ran right past you and your friend making his getaway. You know Rafael Nazario, don't you?"

"We was in school together back in the day," Dwayne said. "But not like we tight."

"But you saw him running back to his project after he shot the security guard, didn't you?"

"That's what them other cops were saying back when it happened. All's I saw running that night was the black five-oh."

"We know what's happening with your family, Dwayne," Gomez said, softening his voice, playing good cop.

Dwayne wasn't buying it, curling his lip in response. "You don't know shit about shit," he sneered.

"We know your family's being evicted because of your getting busted for touting rock," Jaworski said. "Putting your own mother out on the street—that's pretty much the definition of ghetto there, Dwayne."

"I got that on me," Dwayne said, showing more shame than Jaworski was expecting. "But that don't have nothing to do with some security guard getting shot."

"No, it doesn't, unless you make it."

Dwayne glared at Jaworski. "Make it how?"

"You know how this works," Jaworski said. "You help us; we help you. You manage to remember what you actually saw that night— Nazario running from the scene, a gun in his hand maybe—then we put in a good word for you, see if we can get this eviction to go away."

Dwayne was openly incredulous. "That's what you drag me here for? Ask me to lie for you, and all you're going to even offer up in return is some shit 'bout how you gonna see if maybe you can help me out? You must be thinking somebody dropped me on my head and never even bothered to pick me back up."

"We can help you out," Gomez said quickly. "The DA's on board with this. It's for real."

"Can I go now?" Dwayne said. "I don't even want to be breathing the same air as you."

"We can help keep your mother in her home," Jaworski said.

"You said I couldn't call my lawyer, so I ain't under arrest. Guess that means I can go, right?"

Jaworski shooed him away with the back of his hand. "Christ, get out of here already."

"YOU NOTICE what he said?" Gomez asked Jaworski. They were back at their desks, which faced each other, in the squad room. They'd switched back to day shifts a couple of weeks ago, right about the same time Gomez's wife had let him move back in, and now he was showing up to work on time and bright-eyed, maybe still drinking some but keeping it under control. The downside for Jaworski was that his partner had become almost hyperactive on the job, a little too full of energy, making him a pain in the ass.

"He didn't really say anything."

"He said we were asking him to lie about seeing Nazario."

"So?"

"We assumed the bangers weren't talking because of some kind of stop-snitching shit," Gomez said. "But if that's all it was, he could've just said he didn't talk to cops, given us the usual on that. But that's not what he said. Instead he told us that he didn't see Nazario running through the courtyard that night."

Jaworski didn't feel like indulging this. "Maybe," he said. "Or maybe he just doesn't want to cooperate. Maybe Nazario snuck behind him, or maybe this Dwayne kid was stoned out of his mind that night. Who the fuck knows? Doesn't mean Nazario didn't run back to his project."

"You sure about that?"

"Where you going with this?"

"Nowhere," Gomez said. "But I'm not pretending I didn't hear it either."

"Meaning what? Now you don't think Nazario's the guy?"

"I'm not saying that. But I'm maybe starting to wonder."

"The case is down," Jaworski said, clearly finished with the conversation.

Gomez gave his partner a look. "So I guess that means we shouldn't worry about whether it's down right," he said.

·46·

E-MAILS REGARDING Candace's article claiming that Jack Pellettieri was facing imminent indictment by a grand jury on manslaughter and fraud charges had started hitting Duncan's BlackBerry before he'd even woken up, and as soon as he'd read the story he got himself in gear to get to the office ASAP.

Blake summoned Duncan as soon as he got in, Lily already in Blake's office when Duncan arrived. "We need to get as close to in front of this as we can," Blake said. "Obviously the concern for our client is whether there's any way this goes higher up the food chain."

"How can Pellettieri blame anyone else?" Lily asked.

"People facing a murder indictment can get real creative."

Pellettieri's behavior at his deposition flashed unbidden to Duncan's mind. Pellettieri knew something that could hurt the Roths; Duncan could feel it. He tried to figure out how to say that to Blake.

"I think maybe we need to ask Jeremy Roth point-blank what Pellettieri has on him," Duncan said.

Blake turned to Duncan, clearly not liking the sound of that. "This is from the depo?"

"Right," Duncan said. He'd told Blake about Pellettieri's outburst the day it happened, Blake remaining poker-faced in response, thanking Duncan for telling him but showing zero interest in discussing what it might mean. Jeremy's name hadn't come up in that initial conversation.

"I'll talk to Jeremy," Blake said. "See if there's something specific we need to be worried about."

LEAH ROTH called Duncan almost as soon as he returned to his desk.

"Why haven't you called me?" Leah demanded, her voice tight. She sounded panicked, Duncan thought. He was surprised she was so quick to show fear—it made him wonder what it was exactly she was afraid of.

"Blake is calling your dad in a minute," Duncan said. "It's not my place to preempt him."

"They're really trying to make this into murder? It was an accident."

"It can be an accident and still be manslaughter," Duncan said. "Like driving drunk. Pellettieri knew he was putting people's lives at risk."

"We can't be dragged into this."

Duncan didn't understand how Leah, a lawyer herself, not to mention a shrewd and coolly reflective businesswoman, could be looking for the sort of assurance that he clearly was not going to be able to provide. "What is it you want us to do, Leah?" he asked.

"It sounds like you're telling me there's nothing you can do," Leah replied, her voice rising.

"We're on it," Duncan said. "But we can't magically make a sitting grand jury disappear."

"I'm not asking for magic; I'm asking for results. And I expect to see some."

"I think you're being a little—"

"I'd be very careful right now if I were you," Leah interrupted, her voice steely. "Don't think our personal relationship affects your firm's representation of my family. Understood?"

"Of course we'll get results," Duncan said after a moment. But he'd said it to an empty room—Leah had already hung up on him.

·47·

"WHY DO I have to come?" Alena protested. She was putting on her makeup in the bathroom with the door open, calling out to Jeremy, who was leaning forward on the couch, rolling a joint.

Jeremy was taking Mattar Al-Falasi out to dinner. The Al-Falasi family had left the country a few weeks ago without anything being decided on going into business together. Simon Roth had met with Mattar's father, Ubayd, right before they'd returned to Dubai, finally making the formal pitch, but without getting much in the way of a clear response. Then a few days ago Mattar had sent Jeremy an e-mail saying he was going to be in New York and proposing dinner. It was less an invitation than it was a summons, Jeremy thought resentfully, though he had dutifully feigned enthusiasm in reply.

"Mattar seemed to like you the last time," he called back to Alena.

"You don't want me to pimp out Ivy again?"

Jeremy resisted the impulse to tell her about Mattar's faux pas at the club. "I got the sense he wasn't so into her," he said instead.

"Don't the two of you need to talk business?"

"It's the dads who will be doing that. I'm just supposed to provide the entertainment."

"And what is it I'm supposed to provide?" Alena asked, strolling into the room. She was dressed for going out, in a wine-colored sleeveless dress. Jeremy felt a stirring of desire just looking at her. Alena had a virtually flawless ability to clothe herself in a way that showed her body off to maximum advantage.

"What's that supposed to mean?"

"It means what it means."

"Jesus, what—are you studying Zen now or something?"

"It means I don't understand why you want me to come."

"It'll make it more comfortable, having you there. I don't really know how to talk to this guy either. He can't just come out and say anything; it's all gotta be in code."

They were due to pick up Mattar at his hotel in ten minutes. Jeremy had a limo waiting for them downstairs. He lit the joint, wanting a quick smoke before going down. They had dinner reservations at Peter Luger, Mattar's idea, the Brooklyn steak house's legend apparently carrying all the way to Dubai.

"What am I going to eat at Peter Luger?" Alena said, shaking off the offered joint as Jeremy exhaled.

"You could eat steak for once in your life."

"You know I don't eat red meat."

"You're not on the runway tomorrow or anything."

"That doesn't mean I've stopped taking care of myself."

"Taking care of yourself is overrated," Jeremy said.

THEY HAD to wait at the bar for fifteen minutes for their table, Peter Luger not being the kind of place where the concept of VIP meant much. Bill Murray was having a drink a few feet away from them, and to Jeremy's surprise this prompted wide-eyed enthusiasm in Mattar, whose recall of the plots of *Ghostbusters* and *Stripes* far exceeded Jeremy's own. Even after they were seated Mattar was still buzzing about seeing the movie star.

Jeremy didn't really understand the purpose of the present outing. His father was having dinner with Mattar's father in a couple of days, which figured to be the do-or-die discussion on the Dubai family's coming on board. Jeremy knew full well that his dad wouldn't want him to be involved in the seduction dance if Simon had felt confident that the deal would close.

An awkward silence descended after they'd ordered, which Jeremy fought to clear. He was feeling talkative, as he often did when high, but he didn't want to babble on, make a fool of himself. Alena had retreated into herself, not making any effort, clearly intending to coast through the evening. Mattar also seemed slightly tense, as if he too was there subject to some larger plan. Jeremy ordered a martini, Mattar doing the same, Jeremy hoping some alcohol would loosen things up.

"So," Jeremy said, "I hope we have many more dinners to come. As business partners, I mean."

"My father, he has some concerns."

Jeremy was irritated but told himself to focus, wondering where the hell this was going. "What sort of concerns?"

"You must, of course, understand that we from the Middle East who are supporters of your country realize that some Americans distrust us. The business with your country's ports, that was most unfortunate. And embarrassing for us too, I must say. Dubai is a friend to America, and we hope to be treated as a friend is treated."

"Absolutely," Jeremy said emphatically, utterly lost as to where Mattar was going with this. Mattar sat ramrod straight in his chair, maintaining eye contact with Jeremy, poised and assured.

"When engaging in business deals here, we need to be very careful about how they are perceived. We need to try to make sure they will not involve us in controversy, because when they do, there is focus on us, the Arabs, which can be most unfortunate. You understand?"

Jeremy didn't. "Sure," he said.

"The accident that happened last year . . . The police are still investigating, is what we understand."

Jeremy was blindsided. He felt hot, a prickle of sweat on his forehead, his tie tight on his neck. He took a sip of his martini, too big, so that he then coughed, needing to reach for his water to wash down the vodka. Alena was staring at him like he was a bug that had just started crawling across the table.

"That's all going to blow over," Jeremy said, trying to force some confidence into his voice. "The accident was tragic, of course, but these things do happen in construction. If anyone was to blame, it was a subcontractor."

"But there has been quite a lot of publicity regarding it, even to this day. You sued the newspaper."

"My father did, yes, for libeling him."

"I understand in this country lawsuits are part of how some people choose to do business. When you have a disagreement, you can choose to fight. But we do not have that luxury."

Jeremy wondered why Mattar was bringing this up with him, before the meeting between their fathers. He was sure that Mattar wasn't acting on his own initiative; this had to be something that the Dubai family had decided on. A warning shot across the bow, perhaps, or a way of setting the stage for walking away from the deal.

"I hear you," Jeremy said, fighting against his indignation at Mattar's presumption. Did he expect Jeremy to pretend that his father was going to change the bare-knuckled way he did business at this stage of the game, just to please some towelheads who had a place at the table only because a perverse God had stuck oil under their otherwise wretched portion of the earth?

"But we bore your friend with this unpleasant talk of business," Mattar said, turning to Alena and offering a wide smile. "Permit me to say you look particularly lovely this evening."

"Thank you," Alena said, with the rote brightness of a woman who'd been complimented on her looks all her life.

"As I'm sure you know, the traditions where I am from do not permit a woman to display her beauty in the ways that are customary here. I must admit, as a man, it is a luxury of coming to this land. I of course mean nothing forward by that," Mattar added quickly, glancing over at Jeremy.

"I took it in the spirit it was intended," Alena said, Jeremy wondering just what the hell she meant by that.

"Excellent," Mattar said. "Is it a cliché to ask whether you were ever a model?"

"Yes," Alena said.

"Yes, it is a cliché, or yes, you were?" Mattar asked with a smile.

"She was a model," Jeremy said, not trusting Alena to answer.

"I still am a model," Alena said.

"In your country, there is such a cult of youth. I think a woman should look like a woman, not a girl."

Jeremy felt his irritation rising—he was sure that Mattar was flirting with Alena, right there in front of him. Then again, he was stoned, and sometimes weed made him paranoid about the intentions of others.

AFTER THEY'D eaten, Mattar suggested a nightcap back in Manhattan. Jeremy agreed, having little choice. When Mattar excused himself for the men's room Alena turned to Jeremy, her look frosty. "Can I plead tired and go home, let the two of you finish this as a boys' night out?" she asked.

"I don't want to be alone with him," Jeremy protested. "Besides, I think he likes you more than he likes me."

"I suspect there's a reason for that," Alena said.

"He's just excited to be around a woman who doesn't have a scarf over her face," Jeremy said. "Who can blame him for that?"

"I know a bit more about spoiled rich men than you do. Well, I suppose that's not precisely true."

Jeremy ignored the insult. "What's gotten into you?"

"I'd just like to go."

"We'll get one drink somewhere back in the city, yawn a couple of times while we're drinking it, say we're tired, and then go home. That's not so bad, right?"

Alena wouldn't meet his gaze. "You're the boss," she said.

THEY WENT for drinks at Plunge, a rooftop bar in the Meatpacking District, not all that far from the apartment where Alena was staying. The bar had enjoyed a vogue a couple of years ago, though the trendsetters had moved on. But Mattar had suggested going somewhere where they could be outside, and Jeremy actually liked the place more now that it'd settled down.

Alena excused herself to use the bathroom as soon as they arrived, telling Jeremy to order her a glass of chardonnay if the waiter came by. When she was gone Mattar turned to Jeremy, smiling. "Since we stay out so late, I take it you are not married?"

Again confused by Mattar's question, Jeremy offered a forced laugh. "To Alena? God, no."

"Not to Alena, no. I meant someone from society? Is that how you would say it here?"

"You mean like a socialite?" Jeremy asked. "I'm not married to anybody."

"You don't have a girlfriend?"

"Nobody besides Alena."

Mattar frowned slightly, hesitating a little before speaking. "But she is not the one you take home to your father, as they say, no?"

"That's true."

"There are women like Alena in Dubai. More than you might think."

"I don't find that so hard to believe. Hopefully I can get over there sometime soon."

"But this one, Alena. She has a fire, wouldn't you say?"

"I would say. Yes, indeed."

"That can be very compelling in a woman. Like you must tame her."

Jeremy, uncomfortable, busied himself flagging down a waiter.

"I can talk to my father," Mattar said. "If I reassure him about working with your family, I think that would help him feel more comfortable."

"That would be great," Jeremy said.

"I am happy to do you this favor," Mattar said. There was something in his voice. Jeremy looked at him, trying to gather focus. Mattar was proposing a trade.

"I appreciate that," Jeremy said as Alena rejoined them. He was distracted, trying to work it through. The sales at the Aurora that had been expected to cover most of the $300 million in short-term construction loans had not materialized, and with the collapse of the credit market their lenders were insisting on getting their money. A year ago getting an extension on construction loans was a matter of course—especially given the high interest such loans carried. But now the money was gone, and if the Al-Falasi family did not step in, the Roths would have to personally come up with the money.

They didn't have it. On paper, his father was a billionaire, easy, but most of their money at any given time was in actual real estate. The only way they could come up with $300 million was to sell an entire skyscraper. Doing so right now would be almost impossible—prices were in free fall, yet nobody was looking to buy, and if they put something on the market priced to sell, people would smell blood in the water. And once weakness was detected, everybody would turn on them, try to take advantage. Everything that had been built over the last sixty years could be potentially destroyed, or at least severely wounded, by one building with terrible timing. The first building where Jeremy had been in charge too—it would be viewed as his fault, proof that he wasn't capable of filling his father's shoes. And their last best chance to stop that from happening was sitting across the table from Jeremy, making a play on his girl.

It'd never been intended as anything permanent, Jeremy thought.

The longer he stayed with Alena, the more risk that he'd forget that, and if he forgot that, the more risk she'd end up hurting him. Sooner or later one of them would betray the other; that was how these things went.

And besides, it wasn't like Alena would sleep with the guy. If Mattar wanted to take his shot in exchange for $300 million, that was his business.

When their drinks arrived Jeremy bolted his down. "Listen," he said. "I've actually got an eight a.m. call tomorrow morning. The government of Singapore. You guys don't need to call it a night on my account, though. I can leave the limo, just grab a cab."

Mattar feigned something like concern.

"I'm pretty much ready to go too," Alena said quickly.

"But you've got an untouched glass of wine before you," Mattar said. "I can at least keep you company until you finish it."

"It's fine if you want to stay," Jeremy said. "With my early morning, I was just going to go home."

Alena looked at him, and rather than anger what Jeremy saw in her eyes was sadness. "Is that what you want, for me to stay?"

"Sure," Jeremy said. "Give Mattar a chance to enjoy the view. We just got here, after all."

"Okay, then," Alena said softly, not looking at either of the men. "I'll let you go."

·48·

DUNCAN WAS finally getting around to looking into Candace's tip about the bogus evictions at Jacob Riis involving the private security guards. He hadn't made it a priority because it was a double-edged sword: while it would potentially call into question Driscoll's honesty if he could establish that the security guys as a group were involved in framing people to set them up for eviction, Fowler's lying to get Rafael evicted gave his client more of a motive to shoot the guy. He thought of just tracking down the girl LaShonda whom Candace had quoted in her article, but he decided instead to start from scratch—there was no point in chasing after what Candace already knew.

Duncan searched the online court database, sifting through all the cases in which the Housing Authority was a plaintiff to find those involving people at Jacob Riis, a tedious task that consumed a few hours. Once he had a list of defendants, he looked for phone numbers, finding listed numbers for only about half.

The first couple of people he tried didn't answer; the next one hung up on him. Then he reached a woman named Betty Stevenson. Duncan explained that he represented Rafael Nazario and was calling regarding evictions at the project.

"My son already got a lawyer," Betty said. "For all the good it done."

"I'm not looking to represent your son," Duncan said. "What I'm looking into is whether the security guards at Jacob Riis are setting people up with drug busts in order to get evictions. The city is claiming that drug possession is the reason they're evicting your family, right?"

"On account of my oldest, Dwayne."

"Were the private security guards involved in Dwayne's arrest?"

"Why are you asking about this?" Betty asked suspiciously.

"I represent Rafael Nazario, who lives in Riis. He's been accused of shooting that security guard a while back. Do you know the Nazarios? Rafael or his grandmother, Dolores?"

"The police just been hassling my boy about that," Betty said. "He don't know nothing about it."

Duncan was doubly surprised: first that the police would be questioning this Dwayne about the murder, and second that they'd done it recently. Clearly the cops were up to something that Duncan knew nothing about. "The police were talking to your son about the shooting of Sean Fowler?" Duncan said carefully, wanting to make sure there was no misunderstanding here, while also trying to make sure he didn't spook Betty.

"I don't know the Spanish boy, but the police want my son to go up in court and lie about seeing him. They took him the other day, saying how they would help keep us from being thrown out of here if he'd say he saw that other boy running away from shooting the security guard."

"I'm sorry, ma'am, but I'm not sure I understand," Duncan said. "The police have tried to get your son to be a witness against Rafael in the shooting?"

"That's what I just got done telling you," Betty said impatiently.

Duncan's mind was racing with what this meant. "What is it they wanted him to say he saw?"

"The Spanish kid running away after he shot that man."

Duncan sucked in his breath. "Is Dwayne home?"

"Last thing my boy needs is to be mixed up in some kind of murder."

"I understand that, but my client is also a young man who lives in Jacob Riis, and he's looking at spending the rest of his life in jail for something he didn't do. I need to talk to your son."

Betty finally relented, saying that Dwayne wasn't home but that if Duncan came by that evening she would try to have her son waiting. So around eight o'clock Duncan took a cab down to Avenue D. Night was falling, and despite himself Duncan felt nervous as he approached Jacob Riis. He was used to housing projects; they were stitched into the city's fabric. But getting used to them really just meant learning to ignore them. A key to successfully living in New York was developing the ability to tune out the depressing aspects of the city.

Duncan found himself fighting against his own instinctive resistance as he headed directly into the project, looking for the Stevensons' building. He had no doubt that anyone glancing his way pegged him as an outsider. He caught a hard look or two from people gathered on the benches along the project's walkways, but nobody said anything to him.

In the lobby of the building was a bored-looking security guard behind bulletproof glass, who asked Duncan for ID before calling up to the Stevenson apartment. It was clear as soon as Duncan walked into the apartment that Dwayne Stevenson didn't want to talk to him. He was sitting stiffly on the ragged living room couch, looking like he was serving detention.

Duncan sat down in a chair across from Dwayne. Betty stood behind him, not joining them but not leaving the room either. The apartment was roughly the same size and condition as the Nazarios' apartment, though it lacked the decorative flair that at least somewhat brightened his clients' home. Dwayne was stocky, hard-looking: Duncan would've been intimidated by him if their paths had crossed on the street. He introduced himself, explained why he was there, the kid dead-eyed the whole time. "The private security guards have been faking drug busts as a way to be able to throw people out of here, so they don't have to move them back when they rebuild the project. When you got arrested, did they have anything to do with it?"

Dwayne shook his head. "It was the housing police that took me in. I don't know shit about the security guards."

"Do you know Rafael Nazario?"

"I know who he is. You're helping him out on the murder beef?"

"That's right. Your mother said the police are trying to get you to be a witness against Rafael."

"They want me to say I saw your boy running away from where he dropped that guy. They brought me in the night of the shooting. I told them I ain't see nobody running except the five-oh, but that wasn't good enough. Then the other day they come and got me again, saying that if I lie for them they'd help us with getting thrown out of here."

"What was it they wanted you to lie about, exactly?"

"Me and my boy Lamar was on a bench outside our project. These two po-po come running up, start asking us did we see somebody go by. We say we didn't see nothing like that. They took us in, kept us all night, trying to get us to say we saw Rafael. I told 'em I'm not no snitch, and besides that I never seen him go past that night."

"Would you have definitely seen Rafael if he had run by?"

Dwayne clearly thought this was a stupid question. "Not going to miss somebody booking past us," he said.

"Got it," Duncan said, getting to his feet. He figured he'd gotten what he'd come for, at least for now. "Thanks for speaking to me, Dwayne. This has been very helpful."

Dwayne didn't seem to like being told he'd been helpful. "But I didn't see nothing," he said.

"Exactly," Duncan said.

·49·

CANDACE WASN'T sure when the feeling she was being followed first came to her. It'd crept up slowly, starting in a far corner
of her awareness. As a woman in the city, she was always at least dimly
aware of strange eyes on her when she was on the street, men checking
her out. At first this feeling just blended with that, but gradually it grew
into something else. She couldn't nail it down, though, couldn't tag a
specific person who was always behind her. But even without that, the
feeling persisted, grew solid, and after a while Candace stopped doubting its basic truth.

She wanted to talk it through with someone, but nobody seemed
right. Her parents would freak out, insist that she call the police. If she
told anyone at the paper, they'd feel obligated to have meetings about it,
maybe even rope in the lawyers. That is, if they believed her—if not,
they'd probably rope in a shrink. She told herself as soon as she had anything concrete she'd take it to Nugent.

She started walking around with her cell phone in hand, set to camera, wanting to be ready if she ever identified someone. After two days of
doing this and not coming up with anything she started feeling stupid
and gave it up. Candace knew that she could be paranoid, feel like people were conspiring against her, but she'd never in her life felt like she
was being spied on before this. If it was actually happening, she had little doubt who was behind it.

After separating from her husband, Candace had rented a one-
bedroom just off Smith Street in Boerum Hill. As soon as she walked
into her apartment that night she knew something was wrong. The first
thing she noticed was that her cat was not at the door to greet her as he
almost always was.

Someone had been here. It was obvious as soon as she started looking around: the apartment was a mess, books dropped on the floor, her television's screen bashed in.

Candace's first impulse was to leave. She stood frozen in the open doorway, straining to hear whether someone was still in the apartment. After a moment her cat came padding out from the bedroom. Candace relaxed a little at the sight: Lazlo was scared of strangers and wouldn't have emerged from under the bed if a burglar was still in the apartment. Candace went to her bedroom, first stopping in the kitchen and grabbing a butcher knife, even though she felt sure she was alone. Her bedroom was also trashed, her dresser drawers open, clothes on the floor, the top mattress of her bed askew. Candace's heart was still pounding; the knife in her hand was quivering like a struck tuning fork.

Candace called 911, reported the break-in. Her nerves were still jangled—first the purse snatching, now this. Life in New York could be tough, but two incidents like this in one summer seemed a little much. She wondered if someone was sending her a message.

Candace pushed the thought out of her mind and set about figuring out what was missing before the police arrived. Her jewelry box had been emptied, although for the most part it held little of actual value. Her iPod was gone, her almost-new bottle of Vera Wang perfume. Only then did it hit her, and she hurried back to the living room to double-check.

It was true: her laptop was gone. As soon as she realized it, everything else missing seemed trivial. She occasionally e-mailed notes and even drafts between her laptop and her office computer. Her home computer was like a second brain. More than that, it was a window into what she was working on, where she was with it.

It was the most valuable thing stolen out of her apartment, and its value to her went well beyond its cost. Her mind quickly went to the question of whether the laptop was what the thieves had come for.

A couple of uniformed cops arrived fairly quickly in response to her 911 call. Candace listed for them everything that was missing, stressing the laptop as the most important. She resisted the urge to tell them that she thought Simon Roth was behind the break-in.

Candace ended up packing a suitcase and taking a cab back into Manhattan to stay at Brock Anders's apartment. She planned to call a locksmith, maybe even get an alarm installed—she wasn't sure what it was going to take for her to feel safe inside her apartment again. Brock told her she could stay as long as she needed. He insisted that she share his king-size bed, rather than sleep on the couch, and though Candace acted reluctant she found comfort in having someone there in the room with her; it made her feel a little safer.

At work the next morning she went straight to Nugent, filling him in. Her editor looked dutifully concerned, but also a little unclear as to why Candace was telling him about it.

"Do you need the day to take care of stuff?" he asked.

Candace shook her head impatiently. "I'm worried about whether what I've been working on has been compromised."

"By a break-in?" Nugent said, frowning as he looked at her.

"They stole my laptop. It had work-in-progress stuff on it—interview notes, some research."

"You're not suggesting this was a targeted thing coming out of your reporting?" Nugent asked.

"I'm saying, yes, that possibility has occurred to me. You think it's so far-fetched?"

"You name sources in your notes?"

"Not full names, but initials sometimes, yeah. Someone who understood what they were reading could probably figure some of it out."

"You should be more careful."

Candace resisted the urge to stand, pick up her chair, and throw it at her editor's head. "I didn't leave the fucking thing in the back of a cab, Bill," she snapped. "Somebody stole it out of my apartment."

Bill held up a hand in silent apology. "What did the police say?"

"They took down a list of the missing stuff, said you never know, sometimes things turn up. But they were just going through the motions."

Nugent nodded, the two of them sharing an awkward gaze. "Why are you looking at me like that?" he finally said.

"Not sure how I'm looking at you, but don't you think it's a little strange that somebody breaks in and steals my laptop while I'm digging into this Roth stuff? They've already shown how willing they are to play hardball."

Nugent cocked his head, making no effort to hide his skepticism. "You think Simon Roth broke into your apartment?"

"Not personally."

"Should I even bother to ask if you have any proof of this?"

Candace tried to force herself to stay calm. She thought Nugent was condescending to her; she wondered if he'd be so dismissive if she were a man. Of course, he didn't know that Candace also thought she was being followed, but she certainly wasn't going to bring that up now. "Look, I understand that break-ins happen, that coincidences happen. But I think you could be underestimating what we're up against in Roth. I'm not saying I know he's behind it, but it certainly doesn't strike me as outside the realm of the possible."

Nugent was still giving Candace a look she didn't like. "You know what I'm wondering?" he said. "I'm wondering if you've been on this story too long."

Candace gave up on Nugent and went back to her desk. She was too angry to think about anything else, though. After a minute an idea came to her and she picked up the phone.

Tommy Nelson's phone at the Aurora construction site was answered by a brusque woman who informed her that Nelson was no longer working on the project. When Candace asked where she could reach him she was told he was out on medical leave.

Candace found herself wondering if Roth had somehow gotten to Nelson. Christ, she thought, maybe Nugent was right: she was getting paranoid.

·50·

"Before la Sombra started our association, he was already very involved with the battle for liberation of our people," Armando Medina said. They were at a corner table in the cafeteria, Armando surrounded by Rafael and three other young Puerto Rican prisoners. "That's what landed him in the *cárcel* in our homeland. When he was there, he realized it was the same system as on the outside, only in the *cárcel* they didn't hide it no more. That's one useful thing about being here, *hermanos*: it shows you real clear what this country thinks of you. 'Cause we all know, it ain't so different in here than it is on the street. How they want to keep us in cages, beat us when they feel like it, keep us away from the good things they keep for themselves.

"La Sombra understood that no one man could stand up against injustice. He formed our association at El Oso Blanco, dedicated it to brotherhood, and to defending against the abuses of the prison. La Sombra was murdered in El Oso Blanco, but the association only grew bigger and more powerful.

"The association is now bigger in *Nueva* York than it is in our homeland. There's hundreds of us here. The warden, the *policía*, they going to call us a gang. If we were white folks with money, they'd call us a political party, *hermanos*, but 'cause we poor and brown, they call us a gang.

"We not no gang. One hundred and fifty percent *corazón*. That's what we have. Heart, my brothers. Heart. Every eye that is closed is not asleep. Every eye that is open is not seeing."

Rafael understood that Armando was offering a well-rehearsed sales pitch. He looked around at the other young men who were listening to Armando's spiel. He was surprised how rapt they all looked, like eager students seeking to impress a favorite teacher. Rafael understood the hunger: for protection, for power, for something to do in the midst of the overwhelming boredom and drudgery of prison.

Armando had approached Rafael a few days ago, right after Rafael had gotten out of the punitive segregation unit. Armando was again sitting down across from him in the cafeteria.

"Luis told me how you got sent to the bing," he'd said. "'Cause of a shank."

"Wasn't my blade," Rafael had said.

"I know it wasn't. I told Luis he can't be getting you in no more trouble like that. I know you could have said something to the CO, that asshole Ward they got running gang intel. But you kept your mouth shut, did the thirty days, and didn't cause no trouble. Took what came at you like a man."

Rafael said nothing, just looked at Armando.

"They got you back working with the laundry, right, doing setups?"

Rafael nodded. "I want to be working in the kitchen, but they won't let me do that."

"You been cooking up sandwiches on the iron? That shit's better than anything they serve us out the kitchen."

Rafael smiled. Making grilled cheese sandwiches by placing them in a brown paper bag and then running a clothes iron over it was a Rikers staple, and indeed they were better than most of what the kitchen offered. "Yeah, we do that. Not exactly like cooking, but it's something."

"Laundry can be like the mail around here, good way to move stuff around. You already did us a solid, though, not snitching out Luis on the shank. I'd like you to hear what we can do for you, *hermano*."

Rafael had been a little surprised that Armando had come back to him, given that Rafael had shrugged off his first approach. But that had been before Rafael had a deputy warden on his back, before he found himself accused of yet another thing he hadn't done.

Armando turned to Rafael now, breaking through his reverie. "How about you?" he asked. "You understand that we are all fruit from the same tree?"

Rafael hesitated, not sure how to answer this. "I'm proud to be Puerto Rican," he said.

"That's something, but not everything. You smoke, *hermano*?"

"Cigarettes?"

Armando laughed, turning to the others. "He smokes something, just not cigarettes. We got that too. The Association provides for the Association. I say it like that because the Association is its members, and we are the Association."

Armando made a quick gesture, his hand palm outward, the index finder crossed in front of the middle finger. The guards were trained to watch out for gang signs; getting caught could get you put in the bing.

"So how we join up?" the young man next to Rafael asked.

"You got to follow the seven steps. You come talk to me later, any of you who wants to have brothers for life."

As Rafael stood to leave, he found Armando standing next to him. "Will I see you later, *hermano*?" Armando asked.

Rafael understood all this talk of brotherhood for what it was. He knew what joining a gang would lead to; the question was whether he still had any choice. "I got to think on it," he said.

"Nobody survives in here without his brothers," Armando said, putting a hand on Rafael's shoulder. "It's important to be part of something beyond yourself."

"I hear you," Rafael said.

Armando smiled. "Struggle, share, progress, and live in harmony," he said.

"Amen," Rafael said.

·51·

A RE YOU listening to me?" Leah demanded.

Jeremy wasn't, not really. Even in the best of times, paying attention to his older sister wasn't his strong suit, and these were far from the best of times. Jeremy hadn't been able to focus for a while now, and it was only getting worse.

He still didn't quite understand what twisted impulse had made him pimp out Alena to Mattar. He'd realized the enormity of his mistake by the time he'd arrived back at his apartment that night. He'd called Alena's cell phone repeatedly, but she hadn't picked up. At his wits' end, Jeremy had gone over to her building and let himself in at three a.m., scared about what he was going to find.

Alena wasn't there; Jeremy decided to wait for her. He'd ended up falling asleep, but there was still no sign of her when he woke up a little before ten the next morning. Distracted and miserable at the office, he'd left a couple more messages during the course of the day, then headed straight back to her apartment after work.

All of Alena's belongings were gone. The furniture remained, the apartment fully reverting back to the elegant sterility it had possessed as a display unit. Jeremy searched in vain for any sign of Alena, anything to indicate she had ever been there at all.

Jeremy didn't have a clue how to track her down. She'd been living with a couple of roommates somewhere on the Lower East Side before moving into the model unit; Jeremy had never gone to that apartment. The only friend of hers he'd ever met was Ivy, and he didn't even know Ivy's last name, let alone how to contact her. All he had was Alena's cell phone, which was now going straight to voice mail without ringing.

Jeremy hadn't been expecting to miss Alena like he was. From the start he'd convinced himself that their relationship was fundamentally transactional in nature, more sexual barter than romance. Because he'd always ascribed mercenary motives to Alena, he'd tried to block himself from falling for her, not wanting to play the fool. That was probably why he had left her with Mattar: he'd figured one of them was bound to burn the other sooner or later, and he didn't want to be the victim.

But what if her betrayal hadn't been inevitable? What if there'd been a real possibility of their building something, and he'd destroyed it? What if he'd acted solely out of paranoia and an inability to trust people's motives? So much of his waste of a life was nothing but one long self-fulfilling prophecy caused by his own preemptive destructiveness.

Jeremy also hadn't seen Mattar since that night, assumed he never would again. The summit meeting between their fathers had taken place a few days later, and by the end of that meeting the Al-Falasi family had officially withdrawn as potential investment partners in the Aurora Tower. Jeremy's father had not offered any details, and Jeremy knew better than to ask.

So whatever his reasons for betraying Alena, doing so hadn't accomplished its supposed goal. Jeremy didn't know where his father was going to turn next for the hundreds of millions of dollars they needed to keep the construction going.

"Jeremy?" Leah said, her voice rising as it always did when she was angry with him. "Please tell me you're not high."

Snapped back to the present, Jeremy rolled his eyes at his sister. They were in her office, a little before noon. "What're you talking about?" he said irritably.

"You're just refusing to pay attention out of principle? This is your mess, remember."

The endless aftermath of the accident: one more thing Jeremy just couldn't bring himself to care about anymore. He wondered if the instinct for self-preservation had simply withered away in him. He knew that the problems relating to the Aurora had spiraled out of control, and that it was far too late to come clean, the sins of the cover-up having by now exceeded those of the original crime.

"It sucks that the DA's going after Pellettieri, but I don't think we can shut that down, not at this point."

"Pellettieri could sink you."

"You want me to talk to him?"

"You can't even be in the same room with him. For all you know he's already flipped."

Jeremy watched as his sister stood up from behind her desk and turned to the window, looking out at a swath of Central Park. "What do you want to do, then?" he asked.

"Darryl thinks we should get him to run."

"Run? You mean like leave the country?"

"Darryl would organize it, do it professionally. He'd disappear."

"Isn't that up to Pellettieri?"

"Not necessarily," Leah said, her voice clipped.

"What does that mean?"

Leah turned back around, but was still too agitated to sit down. "Look, we didn't put Pellettieri in this position; he got there on his own. He's the one who got those people killed."

Jeremy felt a sudden stab of something like compassion. "I'm worried about you, Lee," he said. "You've gotten too deep into this."

"You think I should've just left it to you to handle?" Leah said. "You can't even take care of yourself."

"You're my sister, not my mom."

"Mom told me I was going to have to take care of you," Leah said, before she could stop herself. It was something she'd almost let slip a half dozen times before.

Jeremy was half smiling. "Yeah, right," he said. "When was this?"

"It was just before she died," Leah said quietly, regretting having said it. "Mom told me you were going to need me to look after you."

"I doubt this is what she meant," Jeremy replied sarcastically.

"This isn't some game I'm playing for my own amusement," Leah snapped. "Your greed is what created this mess."

"I never wanted anyone to get hurt."

"You think that matters?" Leah said, feeling anger seep into her as she glared at her brother. "Nobody cares what you wanted to happen. What matters is what did."

"What do you want from me?" Jeremy said angrily. "An apology? I'm totally fucking sorry that any of this happened, okay? I only came to you about Fowler because I didn't know what else to do. All I was look-ing for was *advice*, you know. I didn't know you were going to start run-ning some kind of death squad."

"Don't you dare," Leah said slowly, her face going taut. "Don't you dare put this on me."

"Fine," Jeremy said angrily. "Are we done, then?"

Leah sucked in a breath, willing herself to calm down. "We can't fall apart over all of this, Jeremy. That doesn't do anybody any good. Are you okay?"

Jeremy looked at his sister, puzzled. "What do you mean, am I okay?"

"You haven't seemed okay lately."

"Things have been fucked up ever since the accident at the Aurora."

"Really? Is that when things started to get fucked up?"

Now it was Jeremy's turn to glare. "What's that supposed to mean?"

Leah hesitated, deciding not to say what she was thinking, which was that Jeremy's shit had never been together, certainly not since their mother had died. Their father never should have put Jeremy in charge of the Aurora—it was the sort of mistake Simon never would have made if it hadn't been his son. "Nothing," she said instead. "Just that it seems like a long time now, we've been dealing with this. And you were right before: one thing just keeps leading to another—it keeps getting bigger whenever we try to control it."

"Do you think Dad suspects anything?" Jeremy said.

"I don't think Dad's capable of imagining there's anything going on in this company that he doesn't know about. Certainly not anything like this."

"He'd kill us if he knew," Jeremy said. "Literally, don't you think?"

"It might kill him," Leah said. "But let's not find out."

Now it was Jeremy's turn to study his sister. "How are you holding up?" he asked.

"I'm coping."

"You're fucking that lawyer, aren't you?"

Leah was taken aback, less by the question itself than by the way Jeremy had asked it. "Don't talk to me like that," she said.

"Are you?"

"It's not any of your business," Leah said. "I never ask you about your sordid girls."

"This lawyer, he knows a lot. Why aren't you worried about him?"

"He's on our team. Most of what he knows is privileged, and most of what he suspects he knows better than to think about. Our lawyers get to know our sins. Most of them, anyway."

·52·

AFTER UNCOVERING Dwayne Stevenson, Duncan had immediately put together a motion demanding that the DA turn over all records of the police's contact with their failed witness, as well as asking for sanctions for the DA's failure to comply with the *Brady* requirement to turn over all exculpatory material to the defense. He'd e-mailed a copy to Candace after filing it, and sure enough the other reporter, Alex Costello, had done a brief piece.

He and Candace had been e-mailing on and off for the last week or so, Duncan using his personal Gmail account. It'd started with his e-mail about the LLCs, in which he'd apologetically given her the brush-off, saying that his firm wouldn't comment. Candace had given him a hard time about that, but in a playful way, Duncan pretty sure they were flirting a little now, strange as that seemed under the circumstances. Their uneasy truce was official, anyway, and it could certainly be useful to have the ear of a reporter, particularly for the Nazario case.

To his surprise, Duncan had received a call from Judge Lasky's courtroom deputy just a few days after he'd filed the motion, telling him the judge wanted to see the lawyers in chambers at the end of the week. Duncan thought it good news that the judge wanted to deal with the motion in private rather than publicly in court, since Lasky had already established that he didn't want to embarrass the DA.

When Duncan got to chambers on Friday afternoon ADA Castelluccio was already there, seated in the front room across from the judge's secretary. Duncan greeted her, Castelluccio offering him only a glare in response. He'd known that asking for sanctions wasn't going to improve their relationship, but still thought it childish of her to refuse to even say hello.

The two of them sat in silence for ten minutes before being summoned into the judge's office. Judge Lasky was dressed more formally this time, in a white dress shirt and tie, his judicial robe hanging by the door. He was seated behind his desk, an opened tabloid paper in front of him, peering over his glasses as they approached. After gesturing for them to sit, he looked down at the newspaper and began to read aloud: "'After the hearing, Nazario's attorney, Duncan Riley, said he expected the district attorney's office to drop Logan as a witness. He also predicted that the DA's office might launch an internal review of other cases in which Logan had presented GSR evidence.' Did you say that, Mr. Riley?"

Duncan could tell this wasn't going anywhere good. "I don't recall what I said word for word, but I did say something along those general lines, yes," he said.

"I can only assume it was because you wanted to cause problems," Lasky said, the edge in his voice growing sharper.

"I wasn't trying to cause anything," Duncan protested. "The reporter buttonholed me outside the courtroom; I was just trying to say that I didn't think the DA would be putting forward the GSR evidence."

"Judging from this article, that's not all you said," Lasky said. "Were you trying to get the reporter to dig into Logan's other cases?"

"No, but if there are innocent people in jail—"

"Look, son," Judge Lasky interrupted. "I don't know how they do things at your white-shoe firm and your billion-dollar lawsuits in federal court, but let me just explain to you where you are. You're in New York City's criminal justice system, and it's safe to say I've forgotten more about how this system works than you will ever know."

Duncan resented being condescended to, even by a judge, but he also knew it wasn't in his client's interest for him to further piss Lasky off. "Yes, Your Honor."

"The system is a delicate balance. We process thousands of cases a year, with a new pile of shit getting shoveled on each and every day. We have to keep things going forward, because otherwise the whole goddamn mess is doing to collapse. Do you understand what I'm telling you?"

"I do."

"Then don't go around showboating to the press, and don't try to turn your client's victory into some parade for all humanity. I'm issuing a gag order—there will be no more talking to the press about this case by you or anyone else involved. Failure to obey this order will result in your being held in contempt. Clear?"

"Crystal," Duncan said. He didn't like the idea of being gagged, but it was within the judge's authority to do it, and Lasky clearly wasn't looking for a debate.

"Now, what's being done about Logan?" Lasky asked Castelluccio.

"Mr. Costello from the *Journal* has been looking into other cases in which Mr. Logan has testified," she said, ignoring Duncan and talking only to the judge. "He's called our office about it, reached out to some defense attorneys as well, I understand."

"Sounds like the genie has left the bottle, then," Lasky said. "It wasn't my intention to reopen closed cases, but there's nothing I can do at this point. How's your office going to respond?"

"I'm not sure," Castelluccio said. "But I believe there is serious consideration being given to opening up a review of other GSR testimony from Mr. Logan."

The judge shook his head. "Congratulations, Mr. Riley," he said contemptuously. "With any luck some stone-guilty murderer will get a new trial, thanks to your meddling. Now what fresh trouble are you looking to cause today?"

The judge's anger was real, but Duncan had little choice but to go forward with making his argument, despite the obvious hostility it would face. "I recently uncovered a witness who was between the site of the murder and my client's apartment at the time of the shooting. That young man didn't see my client running away from the crime scene to his home, contrary to what Mr. Driscoll has claimed. This new witness has been interviewed by the police twice, once on the night of the murder, once more recently. Further, at this second interview, he claims that the police offered to assist him with his own legal troubles if he would testify against my client. Yet no record of either of these two interviews was turned over to me as *Brady* material."

Judge Lasky regarded Duncan for a moment before turning to Castelluccio. "Did the police interview someone who contradicted Driscoll?"

"Your Honor, in canvassing the area shortly after the shooting, the police came upon two known drug touts, both of whom said they refused to, quote, 'snitch.' This person was not saying he didn't see the defendant, but rather refusing to say what he did see. The police simply viewed him as uncooperative. They therefore did not consider his interview to be exculpatory."

"Do you have any objection to turning over whatever interview notes exist for this witness?"

"But it's not actually *Brady* material—"

"Then reviewing it will prove to be a waste of Mr. Riley's time," Lasky interrupted. "But if he's so inclined to waste it, I'm not inclined to stop him. Let's moot the motion, agree to turn over the material, and go on from there."

"My concern, Your Honor, is that Mr. Riley plainly intends to suggest that this witness was offered something by the police for his cooperation."

"I'll see to it that Mr. Riley obeys the rules of evidence in my courtroom," Lasky said. "Just as he'll restrict his advocacy to the court and not the press. One warning is all I give, Mr. Riley."

"I'm not somebody who needs to be told twice, Your Honor," Duncan replied.

·53·

PELLETTIERI CONCRETE was on Verona Street, an industrial strip of Red Hook just off the East River in Brooklyn. Jack Pellettieri was in the office by himself, the front door locked. It was a little after ten at night, and he was going through the books, preparing his company for bankruptcy. The ink was barely dry on the wrongful-death settlement, and the plan was for the company to be in Chapter 11 before the plaintiffs could come for their money. His insurance company was first on the hook for paying off the lawsuit, but there was little doubt that they'd refuse to pay, arguing that the accident had been caused by deliberate misconduct.

It'd be a long, tedious fight, and Pellettieri couldn't bring himself to give much of a shit who ultimately won. His company was going under no matter what; there was no bringing it back. It'd been a dead man walking ever since the accident. Their work had completely dried up, and while they had finished doing the Aurora, that had just been a matter of litigation strategy by the developer and the contractor. Omni had been on their ass every step of the way.

So Pellettieri was doing what was left to do: getting the books in order. It was not a task he could leave to anyone else. He was stripping out what assets he could before the company filed Chapter 11. His company's books had always had a tenuous correlation to its actual operation. Their equipment—from the mixers and trucks on down— was all rented from other companies that Pellettieri also owned. Pellettieri paid well over the market rates to rent equipment from himself, an easy way to make some extra money on a job. It was fraud, technically, but everybody did it. The company's assets had always been kept to a minimum, and Pellettieri was making sure that he had as much of them flowing out to his other companies as he possibly could.

Not that Pellettieri expected to be around to enjoy it, not anytime soon. The DA's Rackets Bureau had its knives out for him, and his lawyer had made it clear that real jail time was almost certainly in the cards. Pellettieri was already thinking about a plea—it'd be too risky to go to trial on manslaughter charges.

He was surprised at the extent he'd made his peace with it. But the accident was his fault, ultimately: he'd gotten too greedy, taken unnecessary risks. The skimming and no-show billing and all that were one thing, but putting the people who worked for him in danger was another. Sure, Jeremy Roth had paved the way, but Pellettieri couldn't bring himself to blame Jeremy for what had happened, not anymore. He was a stupid rich kid, somebody born to it who couldn't tie his own shoes. You couldn't blame such a child for a man's mistakes.

Pellettieri was jerked out of his reverie by a noise. He looked up, trying to figure out what it was he'd just heard. A moment later he saw a shadow moving across his open office door.

"Burning the midnight oil, my man," Darryl Loomis said as he stepped into the room.

Pellettieri found himself standing up behind his desk. Back when his brother, Dominic, had been his partner, there'd been a pistol in the drawer, but those days were long gone. "How'd you get in here?"

"I've had a key to this place for weeks," Darryl said.

"You kidding?" Pellettieri said, still standing.

"Don't worry, I didn't steal nothing," Darryl said. He looked at Pellettieri. "Why you all jacked up and shit? Sit down, relax."

"You been spying on me?" Pellettieri said, reluctantly sitting.

Darryl, still standing, smiled thinly, a show of diminishing patience. "Course we have. Thought you'd be taking that for granted."

"I've done everything you guys asked," Pellettieri said. He was looking up at Darryl now, which he suspected was the reason the man had told him to sit. "I haven't caused any trouble."

"But trouble we have, Jack. Has ADA Sullivan come to you about making a deal?"

"Deal? They haven't even arrested me; how's there going to be a deal?" Pellettieri said. If Darryl was here to kill him, Pellettieri thought, he wouldn't bother talking to him first, and wouldn't have come alone. He wasn't sure either of those things was actually true.

"Nothing tests a man's sense of loyalty like looking down the barrel of serious prison time," Darryl said. "I've seen brother turn against brother."

"I've earned a little more respect than this, Darryl," Pellettieri said angrily.

"You can think that," Darryl replied. "But there's a solution for everybody. You run."

Pellettieri couldn't believe what he was hearing. "I'm in my fifties. I've got a wife and kids."

"Your kids are grown," Darryl replied evenly. "And your wife won't much like going to visit you in jail."

"If I run and they find me, things will be a lot worse."

"Not like we're talking about buying you a one-way ticket to Mexico here," Darryl said. "I'll be putting together your plan."

"And what if I say no?" Pellettieri demanded.

Darryl's expression didn't change, his face impassive, his eyes blank. "You think you've been asked a question?"

·54·

SORRY TO keep you waiting, Ms. Snow," Leah said, extending her hand.

Candace, who'd been cooling her heels for nearly half an hour and didn't appreciate it, made a point of hesitating an instant before shaking hands. "Thank you for seeing me, Ms. Roth," Candace replied. "I know your family isn't the biggest fan of my reporting."

Leah feigned confusion as she gestured Candace to follow her back to her office. "I don't think my family has any opinion of you at all, Ms. Snow."

"Call me Candace."

"Call me Ms. Roth," Leah said. Candace turned to her, needing a second before it registered as some form of joke. "An old icebreaker of my father's. Perhaps it works better among men."

"Perhaps," Candace said. "When I said your family wasn't a fan of mine, I didn't mean to imply your family paid that much attention to me, just the lawsuit."

They'd reached Leah's office, which offered a spectacular view of the park. Candace debated ignoring or complimenting it. Given the extent to which they'd already gotten off on the wrong foot, she decided to go for complimenting.

"Wow," she said. "That's quite a view."

"Thanks," Leah said. "I imagine you work out of a cubicle?"

"In the newsroom, sure," Candace said, not rising to the bait.

"I'm sure it helps build a certain esprit de corps," Leah said.

"Most of my work takes place out in the world," Candace said. "You know, uncovering corruption, that sort of thing."

Leah smiled thinly, signaling she was ready to move on from their initial round of territorial pissing. "So, Candace, I understand you were interested in some campaign contributions that were made to Speaker Markowitz?"

"Yes," Candace said, pulling a piece of paper out of her shoulder bag. "I have a list of LLCs that have made donations to him, and I'm wondering if you can confirm whether they are owned by your family."

Leah took the paper from Candace but didn't so much as glance at it. "We do control a number of corporations that have made political contributions, including but not limited to contributions to Speaker Markowitz, who we believe has a very bright future in this city, and perhaps beyond. The limits on political contributions treat every corporation as a separate entity, regardless of who owns it. So there's nothing illegal, or wrong, about various corporations in which we have an ownership stake making political contributions."

"But isn't this just a loophole for you to get around the contribution limits?"

Leah showed no reaction to the challenge. "As I said, under the law, each company is treated as a separate entity, like it was a separate person. So just like a big family can make more contributions than a small family, so can somebody who has an ownership in multiple companies."

"Do these corporations actually conduct any business? As far as I can tell they're just shells, other than the political donations they make."

Leah looked like she was losing patience. "Our tax lawyers handle our various corporate entities," she said. "I can tell you that all of these companies are properly registered with the state and are legitimate corporations."

"Can you confirm for me, then, that all the companies on that list are owned or controlled by your family?"

"I wouldn't know off the top of my head. I'll have someone get back to you on the list. But I can confirm that we operate numerous LLCs that make political contributions. And I want to stress that Mr. Markowitz is by no means the only politician to whom we make such donations. Any article singling him out and implying wrongdoing on his part would be misinformed, if not libelous."

Candace was now getting why Leah was meeting with her at all: this was a favor to Markowitz, to make sure he didn't end up alone in the spotlight. "Could you furnish me with a list of who else you made donations to?"

Leah scoffed. "That's not something I just have here on my desk. I don't really see why it's our obligation to get you that."

Candace figured it was a waste of time to press the point. "There was one other thing I wanted to ask you about," she said instead. "Sean Fowler."

Leah appeared confused, though Candace thought it looked like acting. Interesting, she thought. Had Leah expected to be asked about this?

"What about him?"

"You know who he is?"

"He was working for us when he was murdered," Leah replied tartly. "Of course I know who he was."

"He also worked for you at the Aurora, correct?"

Leah looked slightly uncomfortable for the first time in the interview. "What does Mr. Fowler's death have to do with the Aurora?"

"I was hoping you could tell me," Candace shot back.

Leah laughed, or at least made the gesture of laughter. "I haven't the slightest idea what you're getting at."

"My understanding is that Mr. Fowler was involved in the embezzling from the Aurora," Candace said. "Isn't that your understanding as well?"

"I don't know anything about that," Leah said. "The man's dead, Candace. I hope you won't slander his name with unsupported rumors."

Candace decided to shift gears—she had no reason to think Leah knew anything about what Fowler had been up to. "Any comment on Jack Pellettieri's imminent indictment?"

"The only thing I know about that is what I read in your newspaper," Leah said. "I agreed to speak with you regarding our political donations, Candace, not the accident at the Aurora."

"Putting the accident to one side, then, how about Pellettieri's skimming from the project?"

"We've become aware of potential issues with some of the billing. Given that there's litigation, as well as the DA's investigation, I'm not going to comment further."

"Are you concerned that your brother is going to be implicated in Pellettieri's skimming?"

Leah's gaze turned cold. "Of course not," she said, the words quick and sharp.

"What I'm hearing is that your brother was actively involved in overbilling the construction costs, and that Sean Fowler was involved with it too. Of course, he's not going to talk, is he?"

"Print anything like that and we'll sue you," Leah said. "You've got absolutely no support for that claim—no witness, no documents, nothing."

Candace was puzzled by Leah's confidence in that regard. But the most interesting thing was that she was virtually certain that Leah had seen this coming. "I'm not just making this up," she said. "I do have sources. If you won't comment, perhaps your brother would?"

"I really don't think you do have sources. Tommy Nelson was pulling your chain. He's got a funny sense of humor."

Candace knew her composure had failed her. She remembered her call to the Aurora after the break-in, being told that Nelson was off the project. "I didn't say anything about who my sources are," she managed to say.

"And I didn't ask," Leah said. "I don't ask people to tell me things I already know."

·55·

"YOU WANTED to see me?" Duncan said.

Blake didn't look up from his computer monitor as Duncan came in and sat down in his office. Duncan had lost his comfort level with his boss: Blake had always been brusque—virtually all of the firm's partners were; it was an inevitable outgrowth of a life spent billing in six-minute increments—but before, Duncan had always been confident that he was on the man's good side. Lately that felt far from clear.

When Blake finally spoke, it was without shifting his gaze from the screen. "The murder case," he said. "We can't keep it."

Duncan thought he must have misunderstood. "What do you mean?"

Blake finally looked over, already seeming hostile. "A positional conflict has arisen with an existing client. We can't represent the guy on the murder anymore."

Duncan just sat there for a second, his mind scrambling, completely at a loss. "This is Roth pulling us off?" he finally said.

Blake frowned. "Are you under the impression I have to explain myself to you?"

Duncan shook his head but made no effort to hide his frustration. "It's not that simple, though. Rafael's indigent, for one thing, there's a trial date on the judge's calendar. We'll need the judge's permission to stop—"

"So we'll get the judge's permission," Blake interrupted. "I'll handle it."

"But the case is going really well," Duncan couldn't stop himself from saying, though he already realized that there was no point in arguing with Blake about it.

"So you'll pass on what you have to the kid's new lawyer, and he'll go from there. You're not irreplaceable, Duncan. We're off the case, and this is not a debate."

NOT KNOWING who else to talk to about it, Duncan went to Lily, going up to her office and closing her door behind him.

Lily looked up at him with a smile. "Again with the closed door?" she said. "Isn't it a little late in the day to get rumors started about us?"

"Blake's taking me off the Nazario case," Duncan said. "The firm is dropping it, saying we have a positional conflict. I don't even know what that fucking means."

"I think it just means that while there's not a conventional conflict, in the sense of two clients being on opposite sides of a case, the position we would take for one client conflicts with positions we're taking for another. Though how that connects to a murder . . ."

Duncan had a pretty good idea of how it might relate to the murder, but Lily didn't need to know that. "It's something to do with Roth, obviously. Blake won't even confirm that."

"I thought Roth signed off on your taking the case?"

Duncan hesitated, wondering how far in he wanted to bring Lily. "I think the plan was that we'd plead it out quickly."

Lily frowned at that. She started to say something but thought better of it. Duncan didn't blame her for stopping to think about whether she wanted to know the answer before she asked a question. "I'm not sure I'm following," was all she said.

"The point is, they wanted it to go away. When I started to break apart the DA's case, then all of a sudden there was a conflict. So what the hell do I do about it?"

Lily looked at him quizzically. "What can you possibly do about it?"

"I could resign," Duncan said, partly just to hear himself say it, see how it sounded.

Lily looked incredulous; then she smiled. "And do what, open up a solo criminal defense practice down on Pine Street? With your one non-paying client? Your protest is duly noted, but let's be serious."

Duncan shrugged, acknowledging the absurdity of it. Lily was right, of course: he wasn't going to resign. "Don't I have some kind of obligation here, though?"

"Duncan Riley trying to do the right thing," Lily mused. "How long have I slept?"

"This guy's my client, and I was getting it done for him. Am I really supposed to just turn that off on command?"

"If you've got another choice," Lily said, "I'm not seeing what it is."

Duncan went back to his office, if anything more frustrated. Out of nowhere the thought occurred to him that he was never going to speak to his mother again, that she was no longer alive. Not that he would've asked her for advice at a moment like this anyway, but if he could there was no doubt she would tell him that he had to do something.

"**WHAT'S SO** urgent?" Leah asked as she showed Duncan into her office.

Duncan understood the risk of coming here, knew he'd back out of doing so if he gave himself too much time to think. He owed this to Rafael; he owed this to his own sense of self.

"The Nazario case," Duncan said. "Suddenly Blake's telling me we're off it."

"And you're coming to me about this why?"

"You closed it down, didn't you?"

Leah smiled thinly, letting him see her ebbing patience. "If I'd felt the need to discuss this with you, don't you think I would have?"

She had sat down behind her desk while Duncan was still standing. He decided to sit across from her, hoping that would maybe cool the dynamics a little. "You guys knew I represented Rafael," he said, speaking slowly and softly. "I thought you wanted me to."

"What's that supposed to mean?" Leah said, her voice also going soft, though it only made her sound more threatening.

Duncan knew he was on a tightrope but tried to go forward. "I just mean it surprised me when I was allowed to keep Rafael's murder case at the start. I figured you guys wouldn't want us anywhere near it. And then the clear message I got from Blake was to plead it out right away. I assumed that message was actually coming from your family."

"I think we're having a misunderstanding of what's an appropriate way for you to interact with me," Leah said.

"I don't like being manipulated. Even by a client. Even by you."

Leah sighed and looked over at her computer, signaling her lack of interest in continuing the conversation. "Why are you so involved in this kid's case, anyway? If you'd wanted to be defending murderers, you wouldn't be working for Blake."

"I don't want to be defending murderers. But Rafael's my client. Look, it's easy to get lost doing this job. Fighting for my clients—no matter who they are, no matter what they've done—is what being a lawyer is. If I compromise that, then it's like it never really meant anything."

Leah considered Duncan carefully. "It's not your decision to make."

"I'm not starry-eyed. I'm not looking to draw some big line in the sand here. But no one will even explain to me what's really going on."

"What if it turns out you don't actually want to know what's really going on? You can't press 'undo' when it comes to finding things out."

"I understand that," Duncan said, wondering if he fully did.

"All I can say is that Fowler's murder had the potential to embarrass our business. We preferred that it be handled quietly. But that's not what you've been doing."

"You mean I've been doing too good a job," Duncan said. "But how does that embarrass your family?"

"I'm not going to draw you a map."

"He's innocent, Leah. I'm not trying to hurt your family or anyone else. I'm trying to get an innocent man out of jail."

Leah looked away, Duncan thinking maybe he was getting somewhere. "Did you know that back in the 1930s the rule of thumb on skyscraper construction was that one worker would die for each floor built?" Leah said after a moment. "Think of that the next time you walk past the Empire State Building."

"So you're saying what—Rafael's a broken egg needed for your omelet? I don't have a responsibility to help everyone, but I do have a responsibility to help him."

"Don't be naive, Duncan; it doesn't suit you. I'm saying any large building in New York has got some bloodstains hidden beneath its foundations. That's the reality of doing something on the scale we work on.

I'm not being cavalier about the cost; I'm just being realistic about it. You can be on our side, or you can be on Rafael's side, but you can't be on both. It's your choice, but I would imagine it to be a very easy one."

Duncan, feeling helpless, shook his head. "I don't want to be a part of this, Leah."

"You already are," Leah replied.

·PART·

THREE

·56·

DUNCAN HAD been waiting about twenty minutes when corrections officers finally brought Rafael in. A short time in jail had changed him: his thin features had turned a little puffy; bad food and lack of exercise had put some weight on him. But it wasn't the physical change that was the most noticeable: it was how Rafael's youthful enthusiasm had been burned away, leaving him sullen and withdrawn. Rafael hadn't been the same since his time in solitary, and Duncan knew his visit today was certainly not going to make things better.

"I'm afraid I'm here with some bad news," Duncan said once they were settled in. Rafael responded with a hard stare that made Duncan hesitate before continuing. "Something's come up with my firm, a conflict. As I told you before, we represent Roth Properties, the developer behind all the changes at Riis. Long story short, they've decided that our representing you conflicts with our representing them. I tried to talk them out of it, but . . ."

Rafael looked puzzled as Duncan trailed off. "What're you saying?"

Duncan hated to say it, but he forced himself to meet Rafael's eyes as he did. "My firm's going to have to withdraw from representing you. Meaning I won't be able to be your lawyer anymore."

Rafael shook his head, clearly struggling to process what he was hearing. "You're quitting on me? I don't have a lawyer no more?"

"You'll still have a lawyer—the court will supply you with one, a public defender probably. I'll turn over all my files to your new attorney. You'll end up with a far more experienced criminal lawyer than you had with me. Your defense shouldn't lose a step."

Rafael's response was a curled lip. "You told me I could trust you," he said bitterly.

"This ended up being out of my hands. But your case is in great shape. We're about to get the police statements from Dwayne Stevenson. Your new lawyer will hopefully be able to use him as a witness."

"You had me thinking you really believed I didn't do this shit."

"I do believe that," Duncan said. "That's not the issue at all."

"I should have known someone like you wasn't really going to be in my corner. Nobody ever been there for me; why you going to be any different?"

"If it was up to me—"

Rafael wasn't having it, his angry look unforgiving. "That's what people always say when they setting up to let you down," he said.

BY THE time Duncan made it back to his office his concentration was as shot as his morale. Not being fit for doing anything billable, Duncan turned to the mail his secretary had stacked in his in-box. Virtually nothing important came to him by mail; it was mostly law journals and pitch letters from legal service providers, so Duncan generally went through it only once a week or so.

At first the envelope didn't mean anything to him, the Bank of America return address not enough for his frazzled brain to make the connection. He opened it, only mildly curious what it was, then unfolded the half dozen sheets of paper. Bank records, he realized, for Sean Fowler. He'd subpoenaed them over a month ago, unsure whether the bank would really comply. But here they were.

"What the fuck," Duncan muttered to himself as he looked through the statement. Sean Fowler, an ex-cop who was working construction security, had well over two hundred thousand dollars in the bank at the time of his death.

·57·

CANDACE FINISHED writing her article on the Roth shell corporations' campaign contributions to Speaker Markowitz and sent it to her editor. It wasn't a breaking news story, and she had no reason to think any other reporter was sniffing around it, so Candace didn't expect it to run immediately. It was the kind of piece that would require careful review because of the potential political fallout, and especially because it touched on the highly litigious Roths. Because of the paper's recent history with the family, Candace expected that Nugent would loop their lawyers into the vetting, which meant it would take twice as long.

She e-mailed the story to Nugent around lunchtime, expecting to hear back in an hour or so. Instead most of the day crept by, and when Nugent finally did respond it was to ask her to come to Henry Tacy's office.

Candace had a bad feeling as she made her way to the editor in chief's lair. Tacy's office was in the far corner of the newsroom, the only proper corner office claimed by the paper's editorial side. It was spacious and open, one wall lined with grip-and-grin photos, Tacy alongside everyone from Bill Clinton to Bill Gates. Tacy was seated behind his desk, Nugent on the couch along the far wall.

"Am I being fired?" Candace asked as she sat down, only partially to break the tension.

"Nonsense," Tacy responded, a bit too brightly, Candace thought. Tacy was not really a man who did enthusiasm well. "I'd gotten some calls about your story, so I asked Bill to give me a heads-up when you had a draft."

"You've been getting calls about a story I hadn't even written yet?"

"Friends of Speaker Markowitz," Tacy said. "Apparently a lot of people think his future will be quite sunny."

"And they've been calling to tell you that?"

"People call to tell me all sorts of things," Tacy said. "It doesn't mean I listen. But here they've been calling Mr. Friedman too, and him I do listen to."

"So an up-and-coming politician has friends in high places," Nugent said. "Whoever would've thought?"

Candace smiled at Nugent as a way of thanking him for speaking up. Perhaps people put pressure on the paper's editor and its owner more often than she knew, but this was her first direct experience of it. She had no doubt the Roth family was playing a role.

"In any event," Tacy said, "I've had a chance to take a look at your article. It's all bloody good stuff, of course, but it seems to me you don't quite have the full story here. Now don't get me wrong; it stinks of quid pro quo, it looks unseemly at best, and clearly there's a loophole in the campaign finance laws that they're exploiting. But what we don't yet have is whether Roth and Markowitz are the only people doing this, either in terms of politicos receiving or big-ticket donors giving. Is the Roth family the only people using LLCs in this way, or is it a common practice among their kind? How many politicians are getting money?"

Candace wasn't sure she was seeing where this was leading. "I agree it'd be good to see how much of this is going on, but that's going to take a couple months of Freedom of Information requests and combing through public records to piece together. We can get the party started by printing what we know now."

"It doesn't make sense to rush part of the story out there when right now we have it to ourselves," Tacy said. "It's your get, and we'll free you up to pursue it."

Candace was trying to figure out whether Tacy actually believed he was doing her a favor, rather than shutting her down. "It's just that it's going to be a long project, and I'm in the middle of tracking down all the angles on the Aurora."

Tacy frowned slightly, then shot a quick look over to Nugent. "But this story doesn't have anything to do with the Aurora," he said.

"Not directly, but the trail from the Aurora is what led me to all of this."

She'd clearly lost Tacy. "This isn't a story about Simon Roth," he said. "And it's certainly not about the Aurora. It's about money and politics. Besides, it's going to be good for you to branch out a little."

"What's that supposed to mean?" Candace couldn't stop herself from asking.

Tacy shrugged but didn't meet her eye. "Just that I've seen it before, a reporter getting obsessed with their white whale."

"I don't have a white whale," Candace protested.

Tacy sighed, loudly. "Let's not make this something it's not. Everybody thinks you're doing slam-bang work. You've found a rich vein to mine here, something you can really dig into. So go do that, happily, and leave whatever else you were doing to the side for a while."

"And this is an order?"

Tacy's smile was not amused. "I wouldn't characterize it as a suggestion."

Candace realized she was being petulant and told herself to stop it. Tacy was right; it was going to be a big story. Who knew how broad the scope of it would prove to be?

Yet as they left Tacy's office Candace couldn't stop herself from confronting Nugent. "Did you sign off on this?"

"Henry didn't put it to a vote," Nugent replied. "I have bosses, same as you."

"My story isn't the LLC contributions; it's Roth buying off politicos so he can have the Riis project. Which in turn connects back to the Aurora, and buying people off there."

Nugent sighed. "Now let's stay within the reality-based community here. You're getting a lot of rope to dig deep into a story you've uncovered. You could close a major loophole in the state's campaign financing—and who knows what else you'll uncover along the way."

"So am I not supposed to notice that I'm being pulled off the Roth story?" Candace demanded. "This is how the Riis deal came into being. It has to be."

"It's also politics as usual."

"And then there's the dead security guard at Riis. I think his murder goes back to the Aurora. That's what I should be looking into."

"And you know this how?" Nugent said archly. "Women's intuition?"

Candace gave her editor a look. "I don't think people really say that anymore."

"Whatever kind of hunch you have, that's all it is. Simon Roth and Speaker Markowitz will still be part of the story. But let's see the whole picture before we decide what it shows."

·58·

I'VE SCARED you away, haven't I?" Leah asked. Duncan shifted slightly on her couch, trying to come up with a smile.

"I'm being pulled in some conflicting directions, is what I would say," he replied, taking a sip from the glass of white wine she had poured him.

He didn't want to be here, but when Leah had e-mailed saying she had something to discuss with him, Duncan hadn't felt he had any real choice. He suspected she wanted to talk about Jack Pellettieri's having gone on the run. Pellettieri had apparently gotten out of the country, was somewhere in the Caribbean.

Duncan wasn't quite sure what to make of it. It was likely the end of the criminal probe into the Aurora, which was good news for his clients. He wondered if the Roths had a role in Pellettieri's flight. Of course, Pellettieri might not have needed any encouragement to run: he was likely facing serious jail time. But the risk of his cutting a deal and testifying had clearly been on Leah's mind, and Duncan was fairly certain Pellettieri had something that could hurt the Roth family.

But he had no proof for his suspicions, and no reason to look for any. The smart thing was to just assume that Pellettieri had run on his own, and not ask any questions.

"I realize I've put you in a very difficult position," Leah said. "Both in terms of your professional obligations and in terms of dealing with me. No sooner did we start seeing each other socially than I became the diva client from hell."

"'Diva' isn't the word I would use."

"You don't have to be polite about it," Leah said.

"I wasn't," Duncan replied. "The word I would've used was much worse."

This got a smile from Leah, although most of the tension remained. "That's fair," she said. "I'm honestly sorry, Duncan, that I've made things difficult for you."

Duncan shrugged awkwardly. "Like you said, the Nazario thing wasn't my decision to make."

"If I made you betray a principle, I'm again sorry. But loyalty is rewarded."

"Meaning what?"

"Meaning do you really want to spend the rest of your life working at a law firm?"

Duncan was surprised by the question. "As compared to?"

"Surely you realize by now that even a lawyer like Steven Blake is little more than a captain in the army. The generals are people like me—the clients, the businesspeople. How many cases have you worked on that were heading to trial, you've spent two months working twenty hours a day getting ready; then it settles on the courthouse steps?"

"Happens at least once a year," Duncan replied.

"Because all that work you're doing, all that gearing up for battle, it's just a feint. A maneuver. You're just a foot soldier on one flank. You're only seeing a small part of what's happening."

"That's certainly all true," Duncan said, picking up his wineglass. "But it's probably a little late for me to drop out of law school."

"A law degree has plenty of uses outside a law firm. You've met Roger, haven't you, our GC?"

Duncan wondered if Leah was going where he thought she was. "We've met, but only to say hello," he said.

"Roger is pretty exclusively focused on the transactional side of things, not litigation. That's why I end up having a role in looking over your cases. But it's not really my skill set, and frankly it's also a distraction from my real work. I think a full-time in-house lawyer to oversee all of our litigation would be very useful."

"Is that so," Duncan said neutrally.

"The position would report to Roger, but it would carry a VP title. Our bonus payments to people at the VP level are quite generous."

Duncan felt equal parts bemused and confused. If this was intended as his payoff for dropping Rafael, it made him think that Leah didn't understand him very well. "You're offering me a job?" he said.

"Are you interested in accepting if I am?"

"So instead of just being my client, you'd be my boss too. Doesn't that just further complicate things?"

"I wouldn't be your boss, except maybe in a technical sense."

"The technical sense being that your family owns the company?" Duncan replied.

Leah smiled. "I guess maybe 'technical' wasn't quite the right word."

"I'm flattered, of course, that you would ask me, but I'm not seeing how it would bring clarity to our interactions."

"It would make it clear that we were allies. Look, Duncan: the grown-up phase of my life started some time ago. I'm not in the habit of sleeping with someone without trying to build something out of it."

Duncan could feel himself pulling away from Leah. His trust in her was broken, and he didn't think it was coming back. "I don't belong in your world, Leah," he said.

"You're a Harvard Law grad, for Christ's sake. It's not like you just got off the bus."

"But my background and yours are pretty close to opposites," Duncan said. He wasn't entirely sure where he was heading with this.

"I told you when we met: I'm a merit snob, not an Upper East Side snob. I don't give a shit whether somebody's family came over on the *Mayflower*, or how old their money is. Those people weren't letting my family into their clubs not that long ago. And we're getting ahead of ourselves, don't you think?"

Duncan nodded emphatically: he felt very uncomfortable having this conversation. He decided to shift back to the job. "And in terms of work, I've never really aspired to going in-house—the trenches are where I'm happy."

"You could be as hands-on as you wanted to be."

Duncan finished his wine, put the glass down on the coffee table. They were starting to talk in circles without really addressing the issue at hand. He thought it past time for a blunt question. "Why are you offering this now?"

Leah's look soured. "You think this is a bribe? For what? Your silence? I already have that, don't I?"

"Yes, you do, and no, I wasn't suggesting this was a bribe, as such."

"What's wrong with a simple recognition of your abilities?"

"Nothing whatsoever," Duncan said. "Only I don't quite think that's what this is."

"If you want to give it some thought, maybe set up a meeting with Roger, we can take it a step at a time."

"Sure," Duncan said, standing. "I'll sleep on it. I should get going, though—I've got a nine-o'clock conference call."

Leah looked up at him, her cool facade cracking a little. "You can stay if you'd like."

"I think it's better if we let the dust settle a little."

"Have I totally driven you away for good?" Leah asked.

"Not at all," Duncan said. He tried to put something in it, not because it was true, but because he was scared of what Leah might do if she realized it wasn't.

·59·

"WHAT'S GOING on with your favorite lawyer?" Costello asked Candace.

"I didn't know I had one," Candace replied, looking up from her computer screen. She'd spent the last two hours combing through campaign finance records for corporate donations, so a break was welcome. She'd hoped that Pellettieri's going on the lam would give her a renewed license on the Aurora, but it'd ended up being a one-day story. There was a money trail suggesting that Pellettieri had made his way to the Cayman Islands by way of Mexico. The authorities were searching for him, but so far it didn't seem like his capture was imminent. Candace had feelers out, hoping the story would grow legs, that it would extend into some clear connection with the other goings-on at the Aurora, but for now she wasn't pursuing it until something broke.

"I was referring to Duncan Riley."

"What's going on with him?"

"That's what I just asked you."

"Yeah, but you're the only one of us who knows what it is you're talking about."

"He's dropped the Nazario case."

Candace was taken aback: while she still wasn't sure if she fully trusted Duncan, she couldn't see him quitting a case, especially one where he was doing so well. Unless, she thought, his doing so well was the problem. "First I've heard of it. How'd you find out he'd quit?"

"There was a court appearance today, just a regular status conference. But lo and behold, Steven Blake himself shows up. Blake immediately asks to speak to the judge in chambers regarding some sealed motion. Off they go, and when they came back an hour later the judge announced that the case was being continued over until a new defense lawyer could be found."

"That does seem weird," Candace said, having no idea what to make of it. "You try to talk to Blake?"

"He gave me the dirt-off-the-shoulder treatment. Wasn't your whole thing before that Riley had taken the Nazario case to do Roth's bidding somehow?"

"Something like that, yeah, though I never put it all together," Candace said.

"You've spoken to Riley a lot more than I have. Think he'd talk to you now? I've called three times and can't get past his secretary."

"If he's not taking your calls, what makes you think he'll take mine?"

"Guys feel like they have to call a girl back," Costello said. "It's just one of those things."

"I'll reach out, let you know."

"Cool; thanks. And, hey, congrats on Serran's resignation. Big scalp."

Candace felt a little awkward accepting congratulations for Serran's resignation, part of a plea agreement with the AG's office to avoid jail time. Not that Candace thought Serran had been railroaded: it seemed clear that she'd laundered money through the ACCC into her campaign chest. But Candace suspected it was little more than the tip of the iceberg of the corruption connected to changes at Jacob Riis. "Thanks," she said. "Hey, while I've got you: ever hear anything linking Fowler to the accident at the Aurora?"

"Nada, why?" Costello said, looking surprised by the question. It wasn't the sort of thing Candace normally would have shared, but she figured since she was at a dead end with it there was nothing to lose.

"I've heard rumblings that he might have been involved in the embezzling that went on there."

"This is solid?" Costello asked.

"Can I get it in the paper? No. Do I believe it? Yes."

"Any reason to think it connects to his murder?"

"That's where I was hoping you might have heard something."

Costello shook his head. "I'm not really working the story, other than following the court proceedings a little. I figured it was pretty much dead."

Candace shrugged. Perhaps it was, she thought.

■   ■   ■

BUT AFTER Costello had left and Candace was facing the prospect of spending the rest of her day cross-checking campaign finance documents, she found her mind drawn back to Fowler and the Aurora. She'd obeyed orders and put it off to the side in order to focus on the political story, but now Candace brooded over her conversation with Leah Roth, how Leah had not only known what Nelson had told her but seemed confident he would retract it. Candace decided she needed to find out if Leah was right.

Finding Nelson's home number proved easy: she knew he lived near McGee's, and there was a listed number for a Thomas Nelson on West Fifty-second Street. Sure enough, Nelson picked up on the second ring.

"Tommy, hi, it's Candace Snow from the *Journal*. Listen, I heard you were off the Aurora for medical reasons, and I—"

"I can't talk to you," Nelson interrupted.

"I just had one quick—"

"I *can't* talk to you. They know we talked."

"The Roths?" Candace said, wanting to keep Nelson on the phone. She figured it was a good sign that he hadn't hung up on her.

"I told you before, my career's over if I cross someone like them," Nelson said. "I may be blackballed already."

"Completely off the record, Tommy. Just tell me what's going on."

Nelson sighed into the phone, Candace feeling her heart pound as she waited. "Couple of guys paid me a visit after we spoke. I pegged them for cops at first—before they beat the shit out of me."

"You go to the police?"

Nelson laughed harshly. "Right. That's not how things work."

"Why not?"

Nelson ignored the question. "They claimed to have seen the two of us at McGee's. I can't imagine they were watching me; any chance they were watching you?"

Candace hesitated before replying. "Actually I've been feeling a little weird out on the street lately. And my apartment was broken into recently."

Nelson offered a faint snort. "You start hearing alarm bells in your head, believe them," he suggested. "No offense, darling, but this is the last time we're going to speak."

"Are you going to be okay?"

"If they'd wanted to kill me, I'd already be dead. But I'm not going to give them any reason to think twice about it. Good-bye, Candace. Watch yourself."

Candace sat for a moment listening to the dial tone, her heart still racing, wondering what the hell she'd gotten herself into.

· 60 ·

NEVER HAVING been followed before, Candace didn't know how to go about losing a tail. She decided a good place to start was sneaking out of work: instead of leaving by the front entrance, she went to the rear of the building, where the delivery trucks loaded up from their basement printing press, and out onto a gritty stretch of Tenth Avenue. From there she walked over to Macy's, spent a few minutes zigzagging around the store, which was both enormous and quite crowded, exiting a block away from where she'd come in. She then jumped into the first free cab she saw. Comfortable that she'd done everything she could to escape detection, Candace made her way to Duncan Riley's apartment.

She'd gotten hold of Duncan at his office a couple of hours earlier, asking if they could talk after work. Candace had expected resistance, but instead Duncan had readily agreed. "Is there someplace private we can meet?" she'd asked. "It's a long story, but you don't want to be seen in public with me right now."

"That's truer than you know," Duncan had replied.

His apartment was in a high-rise in the West Fifties. The doorman called up for her, Duncan standing in his doorway when she got off the elevator. He'd obviously changed clothes since work: he was dressed in jeans and a black T-shirt, and his hair looked damp from a shower.

"Can I get you a beer or something?" Duncan asked, after showing her in.

"If you're having one," Candace replied. Duncan nodded and stepped into the kitchen.

Candace took the opportunity to scope out his apartment. It was new and stylish, with the accoutrements of a guy who had more money than he quite knew what to do with. There was a fifty-inch flat-screen hanging on a wall, home theater speakers arrayed around the room.

"Nice place," Candace said as Duncan returned, handing her a Bass ale.

"Thanks," Duncan said. "Here's hoping I make partner so I can actually afford it."

"How's that looking?"

"I try not to think about it," Duncan said with a shrug. He gestured Candace to the couch as he settled into the living room's lone chair. "The things I can't change, and all that."

"You must have a good shot, being a Blake protégé and all."

Duncan clearly didn't want to discuss it. "Things have been a little complicated on that front lately."

"Does that have to do with why you're off the Nazario case?"

"Is that what you wanted to talk to me about?" Duncan said. Having Candace in his apartment was making him uncomfortable; he wasn't quite sure how to settle in with her. There was inevitably something intimate about her drinking a beer on his couch, regardless of what they were talking about.

"You told me that there was nothing strange going on with you representing him. Can I assume that assurance is no longer operative?"

Duncan forced a smile. "I can't tell you anything other than that the firm had a conflict. Not even off the record."

"Does it have to do with Simon Roth?" Candace pressed.

"You're not expecting an answer, are you?"

"Hope springs eternal. Nobody would know it came from you."

Duncan found that good for a laugh. "I may not be the ideal target audience for your assurances of anonymity," he said, before taking a swig of beer.

"I've never burned a source, and the only time one has been outed is when you did it. Worried you'd have to go hunting for yourself?"

Duncan shrugged, looking away. "I don't even know the full story, anyway."

"I have to say, conflict or no conflict, I'm surprised you'd go along with dropping Nazario's case."

Duncan wondered if Candace was trying to butter him up. "You think I got a vote?"

"Was the conflict something you found in representing Nazario?"

"I can't answer that."

Candace tried not to show her frustration. She'd hoped Duncan would be more forthcoming. "I know you want to help Rafael. I saw that in you. Here's what I think happened: you uncovered the truth, or at least too much of it."

"What truth would that be?"

"You found something showing that Fowler's death went back to the shenanigans at the Aurora. You discovered proof that he was the bagman for divvying up the spoils of what Pellettieri took."

Duncan picked up his beer bottle, held it for a moment before taking a drink. Candace was wrong: he hadn't ever come close to linking Fowler's murder and the Aurora. "I'm afraid not," he said. "There is one thing I can tell you, but you can't say it came from me. I subpoenaed Fowler's bank records. He had way too much money at the time he died."

Candace leaned forward. "How much money?"

"Nearly a quarter million."

Candace showed surprise at the number. "That seems like a big cut for a bagman, I would think."

"I wouldn't know what the going rate is, but yes."

"I can try to look into it. You really have no leads on where it came from? If you still want to help Nazario, talking to me is your only way now."

Duncan chuckled in response. "You don't even trust me," he said.

"That's not true," Candace said. "I think you're basically honest, and that you're legitimately trying to help Rafael. I also think you're in over your head."

"And you're my way out," Duncan said skeptically. "Why on earth are you telling me your suspicions of the Roths in the first place?"

It was a good question, Candace had to admit. The answer was that she didn't have anyone else to talk to about it. Nobody at the paper wanted to hear it anymore. She didn't have the full story, and the only person she could think of who could potentially fill in the blanks was Duncan. But she didn't think she could say all that, and wasn't inclined to try.

"My apartment's been broken into," Candace said instead. "My laptop was stolen. One of my sources had the shit kicked out of him because he'd talked to me. I was mugged on the street a little while back. I'm being followed."

Duncan looked stricken. "Obviously I don't know anything about stuff like that—Jesus."

Candace believed him. "You still underestimate just how dirty they're playing," she said.

Duncan suspected she was right. He'd never thought of himself as naive, but when it came to the Roths he was beginning to think that was exactly what he'd been. "I thought about resigning," he said abruptly.

Candace looked over at him, surprised, before laughing quietly. "Me too. When they took me off the story."

"Why didn't you?"

"Nobody wins every battle, right? What good's it going to do—I've worked really hard to get where I am, and throwing it away won't change anything."

"I never felt bad about playing hardball, pushing up against the edge of the rules, because I was doing it on behalf of my clients. But a lawyer who doesn't stand up for his clients isn't a real lawyer anymore."

"So what are you going to do about it?"

Duncan leaned forward, giving way to an impulse. "What if you really broke the story open? Would your bosses keep you from publishing it?"

"If I handed it to them on a platter, said if they didn't run with it I was going to the *Times*, yeah, I think so. Why?"

"I want to get Rafael out of jail," Duncan said. "I want to blow this whole mess up."

"How're you gonna do that?"

"I haven't the faintest idea," Duncan replied. "Want to help?"

Candace gave Duncan a skeptical look. "Have a guilty conscience?" she asked.

"About what?"

Candace smiled. "Your career."

"Your father doesn't seem to have given you a good impression of the practice of law," Duncan replied. "Where's he a partner?"

"Cleary Gottlieb. And he doesn't complain about it, really. But I guess what always struck me was the disconnect between how all-consuming the job was and how little passion he felt for it."

"I know lawyers who are passionate about the job—Blake is. But it's the battle itself, you know? And I have that too, at least somewhat. But it can be a little . . . I mean, sure, it's nice to actually feel like you're on the side of the angels."

"A lawyer who wants to be on the side of the angels," she said. "Sounds like a recipe for disaster."

Duncan thought she might be right. "So you really think they broke into your apartment? And if so, who exactly are 'they'?"

Candace shrugged. "I have no idea who actually broke in. And I can't prove it was related to my reporting. But I think more likely than not it was someone acting on behalf of Simon Roth."

"Either way, it must be scary. You're still living there?"

"I stayed with a friend for a couple of days right after, changed the locks and all that. But if Roth's behind it, moving wouldn't solve the problem."

Duncan felt guilty: he was on Roth's team, after all, which implicated him in what they did. "And you're really being followed?"

"I can't prove it, but I'm pretty sure. I snuck over here, just in case."

"Are you scared?"

"Of course I'm fucking scared," Candace replied with a laugh. "I'm a reporter, not a CIA agent. These aren't things I signed up for, and they scare the shit out of me."

"But they haven't driven you off the story."

"I'm supposed to just let them run over me? First with the lawsuit, and then when that didn't work by breaking into my apartment? It's bad enough that Roth has managed to bully the paper. But I let him bully me, then I can't do my job."

Duncan found himself admiring Candace. He'd been skeptical of her at first, but he was increasingly impressed with her determination, especially in light of how she was being harassed. He restrained an impulse to say any of this, instead hoisting his beer and emptying the bottle. "You want another?" he asked, though as he said it he noticed that Candace's beer was still half-full.

Candace glanced over at her bottle as well, then hesitated. "I should probably let you get back to your evening," she said, standing up.

The thought of asking her to stay pushed into Duncan's mind, but things were too messy in his life right now as it was, and he also had no idea how she'd respond. Duncan stood, taking a step toward the door to show her out, and as he did so he found himself standing close to Candace, the two of them freezing for a second at the sudden proximity.

"Good night, Candace," Duncan said. "Be careful out there."

"Good night," Candace replied, turning toward the door. "And you'd better be careful too."

·61·

WANTING A chance to talk the case over with Rafael's new lawyer, Duncan arranged to personally deliver a copy of the file down to him. The file half-filled a banker's box, tiny as far as Duncan was concerned—most of his cases had hundreds of thousands, if not millions of pages of documents going back and forth.

Rafael's new lawyer, Robert Walker, had a solo practice out of an office on Thomas Street downtown. The building had an Art Deco charm, although it did not seem well kept: the slow and tiny elevator wheezed and clanked as it took Duncan up. Walker's office was small and derelict, the sort of office Duncan pictured a thirties private eye having. It was also a mess: papers everywhere, no sign of organization. Duncan's office looked the same way, but he had a support staff and a file room that kept track of originals.

"Thanks for the personal service," Walker said, gesturing for Duncan to put the box down on an empty patch of floor, the carpet discolored with age. He was a burly, bearded guy in his late forties who had clearly bought his suits twenty pounds ago. "But you could've just stuck it all in the mail."

"I thought it would be useful for us to talk," Duncan said.

"About?"

Duncan didn't quite know how to begin. "There're some unusual aspects about this case that may not be reflected in the file."

"I don't really know anything about it at this stage of the game," Walker said. "I can always give you a call if I have any questions after I've gotten up to speed."

"Sure," Duncan said, taking a card from his wallet.

Walker took Duncan's card. "Blake and Wolcott, huh?" he said, looking back up at Duncan. "This must have been what, pro bono for you?"

"It was, but—"

"I may not have a fancy office, but I've been practicing criminal law for over twenty years. I've handled literally thousands of felonies."

Duncan did not find the volume of cases reassuring; rather it just confirmed his impression of Walker as a low-end court-appointed lawyer who made his living by the sheer number of people he helped shuffle through the system. "It's not that I have any doubts about your ability or experience, Mr. Walker. I just wanted a chance to go over some things that you're simply not going to be able to pick up by reading the file."

"That all sounds very mysterious, Mr. Riley. I hope you're not taking everything your client says at face value, because in my experience most criminal cases are exactly what meets the eye."

"I have reason to suspect that the victim here was killed by completely different people for completely different reasons, and that Rafael was set up. Perhaps I need to back up."

Walker looked at his watch. "I have to be in court in twenty minutes," he said. "I'm sure your theory is a fascinating one, and if you want to write it up and send it to me I'll give it a read. But I've got a lot of cases, and I don't generally go looking for a conspiracy theory."

"If I could just have a couple of minutes—"

"As I just said, I don't have a couple of minutes, Mr. Riley. I'll turn to Mr. . . . . this case as soon as I can. Thanks for dropping off the files."

·62·

DARRYL LOOMIS was driving in a loose circle through the congested streets of Midtown, Leah Roth in the Town Car's backseat. It was early evening, the rush-hour traffic so dense pedestrians were moving faster than cars.

"So," Leah said. "We've finally gotten things under control."

Darryl glanced at her in the rearview mirror. "Not so sure," he replied.

"We've got the reporter boxed in; we've got the Nazario case out of Riley's hands. What's the problem?"

"I don't think we've really gotten either of them off our backs."

"Why do you say that?"

"Because she was over at his apartment the other night," Darryl said. He had laughed out loud upon hearing about the reporter's trying to lose her tail by sneaking out of her office and then dodging around Macy's before making her way to the lawyer's apartment. She'd succeeded in getting away from her physical tail, but it hadn't mattered. His men following Candace were mostly just meant to intimidate her.

After stealing Candace's purse, Darryl had downloaded a surveillance program onto her BlackBerry, then made sure it'd gotten back into her hands. Not only could he read her e-mails, but the device now worked as a GPS, allowing Darryl to pinpoint its whereabouts anytime it was on. Since the reporter carried it with her at virtually all times she was outside her apartment, Darryl could know her location even without any actual surveillance on her.

Leah felt personally jealous as well as professionally betrayed, her jaw clenching tight. "How long was she there?" she asked.

Darryl glanced back at her. It was clearly not a question he'd been expecting. "Maybe an hour."

"I just offered him a job at the company," Leah said. She tried to keep her expression composed, not wanting Darryl to glimpse the depth of betrayal she felt. "He was mad about being taken off the Fowler murder. I thought it would be a way to calm him down."

"How much does he know?" Darryl asked.

"He knows some, and I'm sure he suspects a good deal more," Leah said. "He's a long way from the full story," she added quickly, impulsively protecting Duncan.

"You're sure about that?"

Leah nodded briskly. "Besides, he's too much of a lawyer to have given the reporter anything that would directly hurt us."

"Maybe."

"His being too much of a lawyer is the whole problem. That's why he won't let the case go. Anything else on the reporter?"

"I've gone through her computer. She's trying to make a connection between Fowler and the Aurora, but it doesn't look like she has all the pieces. Mostly, though, she seems to be digging into Riis and the politicians. Could she take down Markowitz?"

"I doubt she can even try. Dad has an understanding with Friedman as part of dropping the libel suit, so Snow shouldn't have any room to operate at the paper."

"Let's say the reporter and Riley are pooling everything they know. They could piece most everything together, couldn't they?"

"Even if they could, it'd just be speculation, and what're they going to do with it? The *Journal*'s not going to print it without direct evidence. Riley isn't even Nazario's lawyer anymore. They can't hurt us."

"I'm not sure we're that protected," Darryl said, turning back onto the block where Leah's office was located.

"I'll deal with Duncan Riley and the paper. Everything went okay with Pellettieri?"

"He's off the map."

"I'm not going to ask for any details," Leah said as she opened the car door. "I don't want to know."

AS SHE made her way back to her office Leah wondered for the hundredth time how things had managed to come to this. When exactly had the line been crossed? It'd started with her insistence on knowing what

Darryl was going to do about Fowler. That'd led to their next conversation, when she'd become an active participant in planning a man's death.

After Darryl's reluctance to say much during their initial conversation as he drove her to work, Leah had insisted on their talking again the following evening. That'd been the same day that Duncan had taken her to lunch at Blue Fin, she recalled now. Darryl had parked the Town Car in front of her office around six o'clock, Leah going out and sitting in the back while he drove through Midtown.

Darryl clearly still hadn't wanted to tell her anything about what he was going to do. "I'm already in the middle of this, regardless of whether I want to be," Leah had said. "My biggest concern is how we eliminate the risk of someone connecting anything that might happen to Fowler to my brother."

"Like I said before, there are ways to contain the scope of a police investigation."

"By giving them someone to arrest?" Leah asked. "Is that what you mean?"

Darryl raised his eyebrows slightly, though his eyes stayed on the road. Leah had the sense she'd just impressed him. "That's a possibility, yes. Doesn't really matter what answers they come up with if they're asking the wrong questions."

"Because I had an idea with that," Leah said, speaking quickly, fully aware that she was an amateur giving advice to a pro. "A lawyer at our outside firm has a client who's being evicted from Riis because Fowler caught him smoking pot. A teenager. I was thinking, with the law firm, we could have some control over it. Make sure things didn't end up pointing in our direction." Leah couldn't read Darryl; she trailed off, unsure whether she was making a fool of herself.

Finally Darryl spoke. "That could work," he said. "We wouldn't want the lawyers in the loop, though. Too risky."

"The lawyers wouldn't even know," Leah said. "That's the beauty of it."

It'd been improvised, essentially, bringing in Duncan's client as the fall guy. Leah hadn't figured Duncan would find out. If he somehow did, she'd assumed his loyalties, like most people's, would be decided by pragmatic considerations. Choosing to be on the side of her family was an easy call, or at least Leah had expected it to be.

It'd been stupid to get involved with Duncan romantically in the midst of it. She'd seen it as a way to guarantee his loyalty; but instead it'd just put him on guard. Not that her own motives in seducing him had been limited to the strategic. She'd found him intriguing, especially as she waited to see when or if he would tell her the thing about himself that she already knew.

Darryl had run a background check on Duncan shortly after the murder, part of his due diligence. He'd presented Leah with a brief summary of what he'd found, including the unforeseen detail that Duncan's father was black. Once they'd started seeing each other she'd been waiting for Duncan to tell her himself, had been surprised when he hadn't. It hadn't mattered to her—if anything it'd made him more interesting. Leah had always felt slightly imprisoned by being born into a powerful family: she was attracted to those who were self-invented, and Duncan was his own invention more than just about anyone else she'd ever met.

Leah knew not everyone would feel the way she did about Duncan's background. Her father wouldn't approve of her getting involved with someone who wasn't white, as such, though he'd be smart enough not to say anything. She wondered if Duncan hadn't told her because he'd been worried she would have such feelings herself.

Leah remembered what she'd said to Duncan about playing her life like a chess game. Never had that been truer than the last couple of months. She'd seen a way she could use Duncan, and she'd done so, despite her interest in him.

But Duncan had made his own choices too. When the time had come for him to pick a side, he'd gone against her. His loyalty to a poor teenager from the projects apparently trumped his personal ambition. Duncan would have nobody but himself to blame for what was about to happen to him.

·63·

LIZ PIERCE was in ADA Castelluccio's office for an update on the case against her ex-husband's killer. Castelluccio's least favorite part of her job was dealing with victims' families. Some DAs took inspiration from it. The families were not their clients in a literal sense—that was the state—but they were obviously the people most invested in the case. And that was the problem: a grieving family reeling from the death of a loved one had little patience with the arcane procedures, evidentiary burdens, and loopholes of criminal law. No one could blame them for that, but that didn't make getting yelled at for the faults of the justice system any more pleasant.

Castelluccio had arranged for Detectives Jaworski and Gomez to be present at the meeting, as well as ADA Bream. Not that reinforcements would help if Liz Pierce got emotional: Castelluccio knew full well the three men would look to her to be the empathetic one.

"So before we get into recent developments," Castelluccio said, "I want to assure you at the outset that our case is still quite strong. We have had one significant setback—having to withdraw the GSR evidence—but the core of our case remains. The other thing that's come up recently is that a drug dealer who was sitting near Nazario's building at the time of the shooting denies seeing him run by. It doesn't mean anything, really—most likely this guy just doesn't want to get involved, be perceived by his crew as helping the police. And even if he's telling the truth, it's not really evidence of anything. But it's something the defense may try to use.

"Which brings me to the most recent development. The defendant's attorney resigned, and the judge is granting his new lawyer time to get up to speed. So it's going to take a little longer to bring the case to a close, probably."

"Something's wrong, isn't there?" Liz said after a moment.

Castelluccio shot a quick glance at Jaworski, whose attention stayed on Liz. "What do you mean?" she asked.

"This reporter came to see me yesterday. She'd somehow gotten hold of Sean's bank records. She knew that he had a lot more money in the bank than made sense."

Castelluccio had never looked into Fowler's finances, but ADA Sullivan from the Rackets Bureau had met with her and the detectives a couple of weeks back, raising questions about whether Fowler had been involved in an embezzlement scheme at a construction site. "I'm not sure I understand what you're telling us," Castelluccio said.

"I'm telling you that my ex-husband had put a quarter million dollars into his bank account a few months before he died. I have no idea where that money came from."

"Are you suggesting that this money was in some way connected to your ex-husband's death?"

"The reporter seemed to think so."

"Who was this reporter?"

"Her name was Candace. She was from the *Journal*."

Castelluccio turned back to the detectives. "She ever contact you?"

Jaworski shook his head. "Somebody from the *Journal* called me back when we made the collar, but it was a man."

Castelluccio turned back to Liz. "But you knew about this money, right? I mean, after he died."

"It went to our kids, so yeah. But I didn't know most of it had come in shortly before he died. I was surprised how much money Sean had, but I knew he was doing a lot of overtime and stuff, so . . ." Liz trailed off. Castelluccio got the picture: Liz had known for a while that her ex-husband had too much money, but hadn't wanted to say anything because she wanted her children to keep it.

"Why do you think this extra money has anything to do with your ex-husband's murder?"

Liz just looked back at Castelluccio, who wondered if she'd asked the question too aggressively. But Castelluccio didn't get why Liz was bringing this up. The more they talked about it, the more likely they'd have to reveal it to the defense as something exculpatory. Castelluccio saw no reason to think that the money had anything to do with Fowler's murder, but whatever Fowler had done, it likely wouldn't end up reflecting well on him. "I think Sean was in some kind of trouble before he died," Liz finally said.

"What makes you say that?" Jaworski asked. Castelluccio understood that the detective wanted to ask the questions if some new information relating to the murder was coming up. She leaned back in her chair a little, wanting to indicate that Jaworski had her blessing. This whole thing was looking like a disaster—what once had been a completely straightforward case finding yet another way to go sideways on her.

"I don't know; it was . . . There was the way Sean was talking that last month or so. I could tell he was drinking too much, and that something was nagging at him. I think it all had to do with that accident that happened at the building he was working at."

"The Aurora, yeah, we know he worked there. And you think Sean might have, what?" Jaworski said, clearly a little frustrated.

"I don't know," Liz said. "I think he knew about problems they were having down there."

"We can dig into it, I guess," Jaworski said. "But I'm not really seeing how that would relate to his being murdered off of Avenue D months later."

Liz looked over at Castelluccio, as though for support from the detective's skepticism. "I mean, if you're sure this Nazario did it over being evicted, then this is all probably just something else. But the people Sean worked for, they won't talk to me about what was going on with him. I asked Darryl Loomis about the money, and he just said it was from work, but wouldn't explain how. Chris Driscoll won't even return my calls. Why wouldn't he call me back?"

"Driscoll's an ex-cop," Jaworski said. "I can tell you, being on the scene, not being able to stop what happened, it probably haunts him. It may just be hard to talk to you."

"But you guys are sure Sean was killed by this Nazario?"

"It's a very solid case," Castelluccio said. "I haven't seen any reason to doubt that the defendant is who shot Mr. Fowler."

Castelluccio walked Liz out to the elevator, then returned to her office, where the detectives and Bream were waiting. She sat down and looked at each man in turn, deciding she wanted to let someone else speak first. For a long moment nobody did.

"Weird, huh?" Gomez finally said.

"Weird how?" Castelluccio said.

Gomez shrugged. "I don't remember ever having a victim's family doubt we got the right guy, this stage of the game. Even in cases where it's all circumstantial, the family wants to believe. It's hard enough for them without doubt."

"There's no right way to be the ex-wife of a murder victim," Castelluccio countered.

"Course not," Gomez said. "But that was still strange."

Castelluccio agreed, but didn't want to say so. "It syncs up with what Des Sullivan was telling us. Sounds like Fowler put some money in his own pocket a few months before he died. Did you guys ever look into this business with the construction accident?"

"Like we told Sullivan, we had this case down an hour after the shots were fired," Jaworski said. "We never looked at anything going on with Fowler."

"Should we now, maybe?" Gomez said, looking at Castelluccio.

"I've still got a winnable case here," Castelluccio said. "We've got an ex-detective as an eyeball wit on the scene. The ID is flawless; the doer had motive and opportunity. The GSR shows he shot a gun."

"It was thrown out," Gomez said.

"It was thrown out because CSU decided to play amateur hour," Castelluccio said. "But the fact is, Nazario did have GSR on his hands, even if we can't use it at trial."

"So should we look into Fowler?" Jaworski asked.

"To what end?" Castelluccio replied. "Create some *Brady* material for the defense? This case has become more of a headache than it should be. Anybody had any dealings with this new lawyer, Walker?"

"I had a murder trial two years or so ago where he was the lawyer," Jaworski said.

"What was he like?"

"Best lawyer you could ask for. For our side, I mean."

"That bad?"

"Put his client on the stand, guy had two priors, assault with a deadly. Asked me questions that allowed me to throw dirt on his guy's grave. Jury wasn't even out an hour."

"Hopefully he knows what a bad trial lawyer he is," Castelluccio said. "Because what I'm thinking here is that it's deal time."

·64·

DUNCAN HAD gotten home a little before ten—not an especially late work night by his standards. He was almost never home
much before nine: on those rare days he was able to get out of the office
by seven or so, he generally hit the gym for an hour.

Duncan ate dinner at his desk roughly three times a week, ordering
online through SeamlessWeb, charging it directly to a client's bill. But
lately he'd been feeling a little antsy in the office, more in a hurry to
get out of there. Six months ago he'd felt confident that he'd make
partner, spend the rest of his professional life at the firm. But that felt
blown off course now, even if he couldn't entirely put his finger on
why. He hadn't actually done anything to get on Blake's bad side, other
than not taking the hint about bringing the Nazario case to a quick
close.

He'd been home for only about ten minutes when the doorman
called up. Duncan, who got unexpected guests popping over approxi-
mately never, went to answer it. The doorman's thick Slavic accent made
understanding difficult, but it sounded to Duncan like he was announcing Leah Roth.

Not only had Leah never been to his apartment, but Duncan didn't
even know how she would have his address. Duncan had no idea what
would prompt Leah to stop by unannounced, but he was pretty sure
good news didn't make the list.

Duncan wasn't sure how to greet her, but did his best to force a
friendliness he did not feel. For her part, Leah's usual cool seemed
slightly manufactured; Duncan wondered if she was nervous.

"So," Duncan said, "how do you know where I live?"

"That's the least of what I know," Leah replied.

"Can I get you something? Water, beer, booze?"

"I won't be staying long. I told you, Duncan, to stay away from that reporter. Why couldn't you do that?"

Duncan felt a stab of something like fear, but tried to push it aside. "You mean the *Journal* reporter? She was interested in the Nazario case is all."

"Knowing when you're caught, Duncan, I would think is an important skill for a lawyer to have."

"What's that supposed to mean?"

"Candace Snow was in your apartment the other day. You'd already resigned from the Nazario case."

"How do you know who's been in my apartment?" Duncan asked, allowing himself to show anger. "What is this, Leah?"

Leah looked genuinely sad. "I offered you so much, Duncan. It was an extremely good offer, especially since all you had to do to get it was nothing."

Duncan noted the past tense, trying to figure out what he could do to make peace. "I haven't betrayed either you or your company," he said. "I don't know what's bothering you, exactly, but I haven't done anything wrong."

Leah had recovered her composure. "If you told that reporter one word that was privileged, I'll have your law license."

Duncan was tired of her threats. "I see we've moved from the carrot to the stick," he said with a half smile.

"Just remember, you made the choice here, not me," Leah said. "This is good-bye, Duncan. Life is about to get very challenging for you."

·65·

ONE LOOK at his new lawyer was enough to make Rafael miss Duncan Riley. Robert Walker was dressed in a cheap suit that no longer fit, a light dusting of dandruff on the shoulders. His tie was loose, the collar of his white shirt frayed. Everything about Walker seemed sloppy; he utterly lacked the sort of high-end professionalism that Duncan had always conveyed.

Walker stayed seated as Rafael was brought into the interview room and sat down across from him. The lawyer had some papers in his lap; he continued reading for a moment before finally extending his hand.

"I'm here with some good news," Walker said. "The DA's put an offer on the table, a good one."

Rafael hadn't thought about taking a plea, not since the one conversation he and Duncan had about it, back when he'd told his lawyer to go to war. But looking at Walker, Rafael wondered if going to war was really still an option. "What's the offer?"

"They're willing to go down to murder two, sentencing recommendation of eighteen years. That means with good behavior you'd get out in fifteen. You go to trial, you're looking at life without parole, meaning you'd go in knowing you never had any chance of coming back out. Given that the guy was an ex-cop, this is a hell of a deal."

Rafael was skeptical. "Fifteen years in jail is a hell of a deal?"

"When you could be looking at life without parole, then yeah, a hell of a deal is exactly what fifteen years is."

"But Mr. Riley thought he could get me off," Rafael protested, feeling again the betrayal of losing the lawyer he'd believed had enough juice to beat the system.

"I'll tell you, the last thing you want in your situation is some young-

Turk lawyer who's looking to make a name for himself while it's your life on the hook. Even the best criminal defense lawyers lose a lot more trials then they win; that's just a fact. I understand he was probably telling you what you wanted to hear, but counting on an acquittal isn't realistic. You're young; you take this deal, you can get out and still have a full life in front of you."

"So you saying I should take the fifteen."

"It's fifteen with good behavior, but yeah, I definitely think you should take it. You'd be making a big mistake not to."

Rafael wasn't sure what choice he really had here. Fighting made sense only if he had a chance of winning, and he was no longer sure he did, not with this guy in his corner. "You don't think you can win my case?" he asked.

Walker looked uncomfortable with the head-on question. "The witness against you is a former New York City cop. They've got a motive, they've got that you were right there when it happened."

"My old lawyer thought he could win," Rafael said again.

"Look, Ramón, I've met your former lawyer. He's young, full of himself, never even tried a criminal case before. I understand he probably seemed impressive, his credentials and whatnot, but believe me, what you need is a lawyer who actually knows his way around the city's criminal courts, who knows how things get done in the real world. That's how come I was able to get you a good deal like this right off the bat."

Rafael didn't want to plead guilty to a murder he didn't commit, could hardly believe he was even thinking about doing so. It hadn't been that long ago that Rafael had been sure he was going to beat the charges, walk away, maybe even get some kind of apology. But he certainly didn't like the idea of trusting this new lawyer who couldn't even get his name right to win his case in court.

Rafael needed to think; he needed to get advice from someone. His mother and grandmother clung to the fact of his innocence, as if that were enough. Rafael had thought so too, at first, but no more: he knew that innocence was not sufficient protection. He would've liked to talk it over with Duncan Riley, but that option was gone now. That left only one person.

■   ■   ■

IT TOOK Rafael a day to find Armando, spotting him at the cafeteria with a couple other Puerto Rican men, including Luis Gutierrez. Rafael had been avoiding Armando since hearing his pitch, still wanting to get through Rikers without joining up with anyone. But he forced himself to go over and ask if he could talk to Armando alone for a minute.

Armando looked surprised by the request, but after a moment he nodded. A quick look and the other men at the table dispersed, Rafael then sitting down.

"I got something with my case; I don't know who to talk to," Rafael said. "My lawyer, he wants me to take a plea. Says I could get out in fifteen."

Armando regarded him for a moment. "Fifteen on a murder, that's pretty good," he said. "You'd still have plenty of life left to live when you got out."

"But I didn't shoot nobody," Rafael said. "This whole thing's just a mistake."

Armando smiled at this. "It's not no mistake," he said. "You still thinking about it like what the system wants is to find the truth. What they looking to do is lock our people up. Don't matter what we did. What matters is what we are."

Rafael didn't want to believe that. He'd been actively fighting it off. But he could no longer pretend that his arrest was some misunderstanding that was going to be cleared up. He'd believed in Duncan Riley, but Riley was gone now. His new lawyer didn't have any interest in winning; he just wanted to get the case over with as quickly as possible. If Rafael went to trial it would be his word against Chris Driscoll's, and Driscoll was a white ex-cop. "So you think I should take the fifteen?" he asked Armando.

"It's a long time; I feel you. But you go to trial on murder in the first, get life without parole, that means you going to die in prison. That's the worst thing of all. And the fifteen don't have to be hard years. You come in with us, follow the seven steps and become a brother for life, you'll be taken care of. We got people everywhere."

Rafael wondered if he could really spend fifteen years in the system without the protection of a gang. It was one thing to survive on his own at Rikers; a long bid at a maximum-security prison would be a whole different beast.

Armando leaned forward, looking into Rafael's eyes. "I'm going to be taking a plea," he said. "Doing seven. Longest stretch I ever done. But ain't nobody going to fuck with me while I'm in. It's not just that; we get provided for too. You just tell me, *hermano*, you just say the word and I'll make you one of us."

·66·

CALLS FROM strangers who were skittish about giving their names but who claimed to have great secrets to share were part of Candace's stock in trade. But the call from the anonymous woman who said she had information regarding the Aurora Tower accident made Candace nervous. She'd had to fight off an initial impulse to refuse. That wasn't really an option: if she was too afraid to meet with a potential source, then it was time to hang it up. Candace had been rattled ever since the break-in at her apartment, but she was determined to push through it, not let it keep her from doing her job. She had, however, sent Nugent an e-mail about where she was going, something she wouldn't normally have done.

Candace agreed to meet her mystery source at a Starbucks just off Union Square. Maintaining her DIY attempts at evading surveillance, Candace again sneaked out the back of the building; then once she was on the subway she walked through the cars, keeping an eye out for anyone following her. When the N train got to Union Square, Candace waited until the last second to run out the closing doors, watching to see if anyone tried to follow. She felt foolish, like she was playing at secret agent, but at the same time it did seem necessary, especially on her way to meet someone who wanted to talk about the Aurora.

Candace had described herself over the phone, and after standing in the middle of the Starbucks for a few seconds she saw a hand being raised in her direction. Candace went over and introduced herself. The woman, who looked to be in her late twenties and who was extraordinarily pretty, hesitated slightly before shaking hands, clearly not something she was used to doing, at least with women.

"If we're going to talk, I need to know who you are," Candace said.

"You can be anonymous as far as any story, but I've got to know who I'm talking to."

For a moment the woman hesitated, but then she nodded. "My name's Alena Porter."

"So, Alena, what is it you wanted to talk to me about?"

"I read the article you did about the Aurora, so I figured you'd be interested in what I know about what was going on there."

Candace was skeptical this woman would have an inside track on a major commercial real estate project. "I'm guessing you're not a construction worker."

Alena looked confused for a moment, then smiled. "You mean how do I know? I dated Jeremy Roth."

Candace tried not to show her excitement as she wondered if she'd just caught her biggest break since getting William Stanton to talk last year. "And he told you about what was happening there?"

"He wasn't always exactly a model of clarity, but I picked up some things."

"Bad breakup?" Candace couldn't resist asking.

Alena's lips pursed slightly. "Excuse me?"

"Why are you willing to talk to me?"

"Bad breakup, yeah, I guess you could say that."

"It's just that, once you tell me things, you can't take them back; you understand?"

"I get that," Alena said defiantly.

"Okay," Candace said, not wanting to say anything more that might make her source bolt. "So what is it you want to tell me?"

Alena hesitated just long enough that Candace started to wonder if she was going to get cold feet. "Jeremy was involved in the stealing," Alena said, speaking quickly, the words pouring out. "He was working with that concrete guy, the one who took off, taking money out. And that's why they were allowed to get away with not doing what they should to keep the project safe."

This was basically old news to Candace, but given that her previous source for it had dried up, it was nevertheless valuable. It also told her that Alena was legit. "He told you this?"

Alena nodded. "Somebody who knew about it was blackmailing

Jeremy. He was really freaked out about it. But then he wasn't. He said the person deserved what they got."

It all came together for Candace. Fowler had known everything; Fowler had too much money in the bank when he died. Fowler wasn't killed because he knew too much; he was killed because he'd blackmailed Jeremy Roth over what he'd known. "Do you know who was blackmailing him?" she asked, hoping Alena would take her all the way across the finish line.

"It was somebody connected to the Aurora, and I'm pretty sure it was a guy. But that's all I know."

"Does the name Sean Fowler mean anything to you?" Candace asked. Alena shook her head. "Who's that?"

Candace tried to hide her disappointment. She was sure she had it pieced together, though she was nowhere near having it so solid that she could get it in the paper, not if Alena didn't know who the blackmailer was. "He worked at the Aurora, and was murdered a couple months ago. When did Jeremy indicate that the blackmailer was out of the picture?"

Alena blanched at hearing the word "murdered." For a moment she just looked at Candace. "I don't remember for sure," she finally said. "But it was a while ago."

"He ever say anything to you about Jack Pellettieri's disappearance?"

"No."

"You ever meet Pellettieri?"

"The only person I ever met in terms of business was one of the Arab guys Jeremy was trying to get money from."

Candace didn't know what Alena was talking about. "Trying to get money for what?"

"For the Aurora. I don't know the details, but his family needed a whole lot of money to keep that project going. They were looking for hundreds of millions of dollars."

"Did they get the money?"

"Not from the Arabs they didn't. Whether they got it from somebody I don't know."

"Do you have anything that backs up any of this? An e-mail, an answering-machine message?"

Alena shook her head. "Don't you believe me?"

"I completely believe you. But to actually get this in the paper my editors are going to want something more than your word. We'd need to figure out who was doing the blackmailing too—otherwise it's only part of a story."

"I've told you what I know," Alena said, looking frustrated. Candace had seen it before with sources who were leaking for personal reasons: they wanted what they said to simply be transcribed on the next day's front page. That wasn't going to happen, but Alena had filled in the last missing piece. Candace thought she had the whole story now. But she couldn't back it up, which meant she couldn't print it.

BACK AT the newsroom, Candace went to Nugent's office to fill him in on her new source, and what she thought it meant. Nugent listened carefully, and when she was finished he went over and closed his office door. Candace was surprised; she couldn't remember Nugent ever doing that before. "I thought you'd gotten the message on your own," he said.

"What message?"

"This conversation never happened, understood?"

"Now my own boss is going off the record on me?"

"That's right. Clear?"

"Fine, Bill, what?"

"It's not exactly a secret that we're losing money around here. The only thing falling faster than our circulation is our advertising revenue. The buyouts this summer didn't do nearly enough to stop the bleeding. We're looking at layoffs for as much as ten percent of the newsroom. Everybody's vulnerable. Hell, I'm vulnerable."

Candace didn't know where Nugent was going, but it was clearly someplace bad. "Are you telling me I'm about to be laid off?"

"No, though I can't promise you're not either. But that wasn't what I was getting at. The point is, we're losing money hand over fist here, and a certain amount of . . . caution is setting in. Defending against even a meritless libel case can run hundreds of thousands of dollars—and that would mean another half dozen people lose their jobs."

"So the paper is worried about Simon Roth suing us again?"

"The concern is that Roth sees you as having a vendetta against him. Rightly or wrongly, the thought is that anything you write about him is much more likely to lead to a lawsuit."

Candace couldn't quite believe what she was hearing. "Are you telling me this paper now has a policy of not reporting on Simon Roth?"

"Nobody's saying Roth gets a free pass from the paper," Nugent said. "He does, however, get a pass from you."

"But I've got sources developed. I'm the only person who's even close to having the whole story."

"You have something relating to the Fowler murder, pass it on to Alex Costello."

This was insult to injury. "Costello's not an investigative reporter. And besides, this is the biggest story I've ever had, a story that could break huge."

"This isn't something I got a vote in, Candace," Nugent said. "It came from Friedman himself. All I'm doing is conveying the word from on high. You weren't supposed to be working sources on Roth anyway."

"This source came to me; I wasn't looking for her. Which proves my point, by the way."

"She didn't give you anything we can print, regardless. Somebody was blackmailing Roth Junior, but she doesn't know who. You'd just be speculating that it was Sean Fowler. You printed that, it would be a libel suit we'd actually lose."

"She's a second source that Jeremy Roth was actively involved in the embezzlement. That's worth a story in itself."

"Potentially," Nugent said. "But you're not going to be the person to write it. Give what you have to Costello, and go back to the campaign finance story."

"This is bullshit."

"This is reality," Nugent said.

AFTER SHE'D left Nugent, Candace went looking for Brock Anders. His cubicle was in a small annex to the main newsroom—the gossip staff separated out from the news staff. Candace had never been clear whether this was to protect the reporters from the gossip columnists or the other way around.

Brock was in his cubicle writing an e-mail. He could tell at a glance that Candace was upset about something. Brock suggested she keep him company while he took a smoke break, and they went out to the loading docks in the back of the building, where the office smokers congregated.

"So what's wrong?" Brock asked after lighting up.

"I've got a big follow-up lead on my Aurora story, and the paper won't let me pursue it. They're apparently so scared of Roth suing again, even on a completely bulletproof story, that I've been shut down."

Brock shook his head. "We can't even afford to win a lawsuit these days, I guess. I heard another round of buyouts is coming. I'd take one, if I wasn't scared it'd mean I'd just never work again."

"I understand money's tight, and that we're a business. But still, when we let rich bullies dictate our news coverage, it may just be time to give up."

"But it's not like you're being told you can't do your job generally. I mean, I get that it sucks, but there're a lot of other dirty fish in this slimy sea of ours."

"All of whom now have a playbook for how to shut me down."

"See what happens when you take what you do for a living seriously?"

"I've almost got the whole thing," Candace said. "A huge scoop, just out of reach. It's killing me."

"Nobody gets every story, Candace," Brock said. "You know that."

"It'd be one thing if I just couldn't piece it together. That happens, sure. But this is my being sidelined by my own team."

"It just isn't a fight you can win right now," Brock said, taking a final drag off his cigarette. "Accepting that is really all you can do. Ready to head back up?"

"I'm going to make a call while I'm down here," Candace said, Brock raising his eyebrows but refraining from inquiring. After he left, Candace took out her cell phone and punched up the number of the one person she thought would actually care about what she'd discovered.

"What's up?" Duncan asked.

"I've figured out the real reason Sean Fowler was killed," Candace replied.

·67·

DUNCAN WAS antsy. He was spending his day supervising the production of the last batch of Roth documents to the DA's office—a tedious task made worse by the fact that his mind was elsewhere. He'd made plans to meet up with Candace at eight o'clock. She'd called that afternoon, saying she had a break regarding Fowler's murder, and now the day was dragging to a crawl as he waited to find out her news.

A little after five o'clock Blake called, telling Duncan to come up to his office right away. Duncan was a little surprised: he rarely met with Blake without knowing what it was about.

"Close the door," Blake said as Duncan walked in. Duncan did so, alarm bells ringing loudly in his head now. Blake glared at Duncan as he made his way to a seat.

"Did you go to bed with Leah Roth?"

Duncan had been expecting bad news, but he hadn't been expecting this. He was completely caught off guard and sure that it showed. "Excuse me?" he said after a moment, just to have said something.

"Answer the question."

"Since when is my personal life a concern of the firm's?"

"If you've slept with one of my clients, it's very much my concern."

Duncan was still scrambling for how to respond. The only way that Blake would know about this, he realized, was if Leah had told him. This was her move, her play to take him out. "Leah and I have spent some time together socially," Duncan said. "She was actually who initiated it."

"Last chance: if you're going to deny sleeping with her, do so now."

Duncan wasn't going to lie, but he wasn't going to confirm it either. "Jesus, Steven, why are you asking me about this?"

"Having sex with a firm client is a serious business," Blake said. "As I certainly would expect you to know without being told. Leah called to say she didn't want you working on any more of their cases. When I asked why, she said she wasn't comfortable with you because you'd had a brief personal relationship, and she'd come to have doubts about whether you were trustworthy."

"This has nothing to do with whatever relationship she and I had," Duncan said, trying to force a smile. "It actually concerns the Nazario case, and the so-called conflict we had there."

Blake held up a hand. "I don't want to hear it," he said.

"But I just want to explain my perspective—"

"I don't give a *shit* about your perspective. You understand? You broke the rules, and that's the only thing this is about."

"I'll talk to Leah. I'm sorry you had to get mixed into this, but I can straighten it out."

Blake shook his head. "You don't get it, Duncan. This is well past that. Leah Roth is the likely future CEO of one of this firm's anchor clients. You've jeopardized the firm's relationship with her and her family, and that cannot and will not be tolerated."

Duncan refused to believe this was going where he thought it was. "What're you saying, Steven?"

"I'm saying, yes, that you're fired."

"THEY *FIRED* you?" Candace said incredulously.

They were at Rudy's, a dive bar on Ninth Avenue, one of the last remnants of the old Hell's Kitchen. Duncan was already there when Candace arrived, and from the looks of things he'd been there for a while.

They were seated in one of the dark red booths along the wall. Duncan was a bit of a mess: his shirt untucked, his eyes a little glassy. She couldn't tell how much of it was alcohol and how much was shock.

"I'm fired, all right," Duncan said.

"What happened?"

"Long story short, I pissed off Leah Roth."

"How'd you manage that?"

"By talking to you. She knew that you'd been over to my apartment. She thought I was betraying her, I guess, by not standing down on Nazario."

"And just like that she was able to get you tossed from your firm?"

"Her family's got some pull," Duncan deadpanned.

Candace thought there had to be more to the story than that, but decided not to press it. "Her family has pretty much cut my balls off at the paper too," she said. "Though I realize that's not the same thing."

"No, it's not," Duncan said. "So what's your big news about Fowler, anyway?"

Candace felt bad talking business under the circumstances, but Duncan looked like he really wanted to know. "A source tells me that Jeremy Roth was being blackmailed by somebody relating to his embezzling from the Aurora. The source doesn't know who the blackmailer was, but it must've been Sean Fowler."

Candace could see Duncan's mind working as he added it up, his excitement growing as he did so. "That would explain the money."

Candace nodded. "Fowler gets too greedy, so Jeremy has him whacked. The eyewitness, Chris Driscoll, is in on it. Hell, maybe he's the murderer."

Duncan took a sip of whiskey, then chewed on an ice cube. "Can you print it?"

"Not even close," Candace said. "I don't even have enough to print the blackmail part, and if I did I wouldn't be able to connect it to Fowler."

"Even though we know he had the money?"

Candace shook her head. "Way too speculative. Especially about the Roths. I've been ordered to stand down on them."

"Why?"

"The paper's broke, and skittish about getting sued again. This would have to be completely rock solid before they'd let me print it, and it's not even close to that."

"I talked to Rafael's new lawyer the other week, but the guy's a putz. I can't imagine he's got what it takes to put this together."

Candace looked confused for a moment; then her eyes widened. "Shit, you don't know."

"Know what?"

"Nazario's pleading out."

Duncan cocked his head. "What are you talking about?"

"He's pleading on the murder. I figured you would know already. He's got a date to go before the judge."

Duncan looked ashen. "No fucking way. Rafael had no interest in taking a plea. He didn't do it, and he's a fighter. Why would he be taking a deal?"

"Beats me. I've never even met him."

Duncan finished his drink, rattling the ice in his glass. "Rafael can't take a plea. He's the last loose end we've got."

"There's that, plus that he didn't do it."

"Right," Duncan said, fuming. "I really didn't see a way for this day to get any worse, so thanks for that."

Candace reached out and touched Duncan's arm. He looked up at the contact, the look they exchanged catching him off guard.

"So what are you going to do?" Candace said, feeling self-conscious as she moved her hand. She wasn't going to go to bed with Duncan, she thought. Not tonight.

"Drink more whiskey. Hey, you have a job—you can buy a round."

Candace obediently went to the bar and got Duncan a drink. Her own beer was still half-full. "I was asking a little more long-term," she said upon returning.

"If Blake's really determined to burn me, no other first-rate firm's going to take me on. I'm fucked, basically."

"You're a Harvard Law grad. I'm sure somebody will hire you."

"I was a Blake baby, a few months away from making partner. You know what B and W's profits per partner are?"

"What's a Blake baby? Second thought, I don't want to know," Candace said. "They really fired you just for talking to me?"

"Not just that, but that I wasn't following orders. And Leah offered me a job, which I pretty clearly didn't want, and I think that confirmed that she couldn't trust me. I'm assuming now that she's had me fired the job offer is off the table."

"*Leah*," Candace said, and sure enough Duncan looked away. Her instincts told her that Duncan's involvement with Leah Roth had gotten a little personal.

"If Rafael takes a plea they're going to get away with it, aren't they?" Duncan said, his anger returning as he changed the subject. "All of it."

"They *have* gotten away with it, Duncan. I hate that as much as you do, but it's true."

"Not if I can get Rafael not to plead."

"How are you going to do that?"

"By becoming his lawyer again."

It took a while for Candace to realize that Duncan was serious. Of course, that he was serious now didn't mean he still would be in the cold light of morning. But it was also clear that Duncan had been thrown past the point of no return, and he didn't have anything else to focus his anger on.

"What about the so-called conflict you had?" Candace asked. "Could the Roths stop you from representing him?"

"I don't see how," Duncan replied. "They'd have to argue that I was using privileged material that I learned from representing them."

"Even if you do become Nazario's lawyer, are you sure you can win the case?"

Duncan laughed. "Hell, no," he said. "The first problem's Driscoll. He's got to be in on it, but proving that's another story. I don't think Driscoll's likely to break down on the stand and confess just because I ask him some tough questions. Right now I can't prove that Jeremy Roth and Chris Driscoll have ever been in the same room. It's entirely possible they haven't been."

Duncan took a gulp of whiskey. "Am I going to end up holding your ponytail tonight?" Candace said.

Duncan looked at her. "That sounds—well, I'm not exactly sure what that sounds like."

Candace ignored the innuendo. "You should at least eat something if you're going to pour that much booze down your throat," she said.

THEY ENDED up going for pizza at John's on Forty-fourth Street, Duncan insisting that he was only interested in eating something unhealthy. Candace figured he was at least entitled to that.

"So I realize nobody wants to get fired," Candace said after they'd ordered. "But is there really nothing in this that's a positive for you?"

"Meaning what? Now I have time to work on my poetry?"

"I thought everyone at the big law firms was dying to get out."

"So what you're really saying is, you think I should have sense enough to want to do something else?"

"Did you go to law school wanting to do what you've been doing?"

"I didn't have the slightest idea what I was getting myself into when I went to law school," Duncan said. "That's true of pretty much everybody there, or else the place would be empty."

"So why did you go?"

"You want an actual answer?" Duncan asked. Candace nodded, finding that she meant it. "In part it was that my parents both did stuff that's kind of similar to law—Dad's a union organizer, Mom was a social worker. But they were pretty working-class people, and I always had this understanding that I was supposed to go to the next step, you know, in the sense that I had the opportunity to get a different sort of education, and so on. Law seemed like the backstage pass to the world."

Candace was surprised to hear this—she'd assumed Duncan's background was similar to her own. "Small-town boy makes good, huh?" she said.

"I was born in Detroit, so not exactly."

Candace smiled. "Detroit as in what suburb?"

"Detroit as in Detroit," Duncan said. This was hardly the first time that someone had assumed that when he said Detroit what he really meant was Bloomfield Hills or Grosse Point.

Candace looked surprised. "I didn't know any white people still lived in Detroit."

"I'm not, actually," Duncan said without hesitation. "White, I mean. My dad's black."

Candace felt herself flush. "I'm so sorry if I—"

"No need to apologize," Duncan said, raising his hands. "I know what I look like."

Candace was impressed, though she wondered if there was something patronizing about this response. "I actually remember thinking you were, I don't know, *something*, first time I saw you. So you're biracial, working-class, and from Detroit, and yet you became Steven Blake's right-hand guy and consigliere to the Roths."

Duncan wagged a finger at her, apparently playfully. "Don't do that thing where that suddenly makes me interesting," he said.

"Okay, so I admit that I'd assumed you were some preppy shitbird from Connecticut."

"It's easy to say money doesn't matter when you come from it. I'm the first person in my family who really had a chance to get paid, and I took it. If my dad had been a New York corporate lawyer, I'd probably be doing something else."

Candace smiled. "I'm pretty sure you wouldn't be a reporter," she said.

"Are there even going to be newspapers in ten years?" Duncan replied.

"Maybe not, but there'll still be reporters. I'm not married to the actual print newspaper, personally, although a lot of people in the newsroom would view that as treason."

The waiter brought their pizza, pepperoni and black olives. Candace, who generally ate healthy, had to admit it looked really good. Duncan grabbed a slice, took a huge bite. "Grease meets alcohol," he said. "A match made in heaven."

AFTER THEY'D finished eating, the two of them stood outside the restaurant. "So," Candace said. "You going to be okay? Tonight, I mean."

"I'll get through," Duncan said. "What's the alternative, really?"

Before she fully knew she was going to do it, Candace stepped forward and hugged Duncan, who, caught off guard, took a moment to respond. "I need your help," she said, speaking softly into Duncan's ear. "Rafael needs your help. Stay in the game."

Candace leaned back, looked Duncan in the eye, their faces close, then quickly turned to go before he could say anything. Duncan stood, watching her walk away, his catastrophe of a day momentarily forgotten. He wished Candace was coming back to his apartment with him. But the day he'd been fired was not the day to start something, not if he wanted it to have a chance of working. So Duncan headed up Eighth Avenue toward his apartment, knowing he was in for a long and lonely night.

■   ■   ■

WAKING THE next morning was an extended exercise in disorienta-
tion. There was the hangover, for one thing, although under the circumstances the blurring it caused was almost welcome. At least he'd managed
to refrain from asking Candace to come home with him, although the
temptation had been strong. It was too soon, and his life was too much of
a mess, and their professional interaction was too important. But he
thought there was at least a chance she would've said yes.

Duncan got up and made coffee, starting his morning as he would any
other. But it wasn't, and the day stretched empty before him. He'd been at
the same job for seven years, working close to three thousand hours a year.
And then one five-minute conversation had taken it all away.

Duncan was far better off than most people who suddenly lost their
job; he knew that. He'd paid off most of his student loans; he had fifty
grand invested in mutual funds, over a hundred grand of equity in his
apartment. He'd listed his mother's house with a Realtor, and had also
inherited six figures from her life insurance. But his mortgage payments
were over three grand a month, and everything else cost so much more
in New York as well. He could easily go more than a year before he
would really start running out of money, but if Steven Blake was determined to burn him it might take longer than that for anyone to offer
Duncan a job.

Candace's question lingered: Did he really want to try to get back on
the corporate law treadmill? The fact was, representing Rafael Nazario
had excited Duncan in a way no other part of practicing law had in years.
He'd felt a sense of purpose, of actually helping somebody, that he
couldn't pretend his typical case gave him.

Duncan had been completely serious about the idea of representing
Rafael again, though the reality of the prospect was daunting. He didn't
have an office, a secretary, letterhead—let alone malpractice insurance.
All those things had been provided by the firm. The idea of renting
some office and setting out on his own seemed impossible.

But he also knew he couldn't let Leah Roth win. She'd tried to
destroy him, presumably believed that she had. Duncan's pride wouldn't
let him accept such a thorough defeat. He would expose the truth, bring
her down. It was just a matter of how.

Dressed in boxer shorts and a Knicks T-shirt, Duncan took his coffee to his desk. He sat down in front of his laptop and got to work.

·68·

JEREMY LET himself into the apartment where he'd let Alena stay. He'd come back here a handful of times in the increasingly unlikely hope that she would've returned. She still had a key, after all: it wasn't impossible that she would just come back. But as time passed this stopped being a real possibility, and Jeremy knew it.

The fifth of scotch in the kitchen was three-quarters empty; Jeremy poured most of it into a glass. He thought he would've forgotten about Alena by now, but instead her absence continued to gnaw at him. He missed her, he realized, marveling a little at the thought of it. Having her just vanish from his life had created a mystery that seemed only to grow with the passing of days.

All this drama over a stupid misunderstanding. Of course Jeremy hadn't meant to suggest that she should sleep with Mattar; could that really be what she thought? Have a drink with the guy, maybe flirt a little, sure, but nothing else. Just basic friendliness. It wasn't anything the least bit different from what she used to do around the clubs. Show Mattar a good time while he was in town, let him look at a pretty girl who was there to be seen. That was the only idea. He wanted to explain to her, make Alena understand that he hadn't been whoring her out, not at all. He wouldn't do that; they were dating, for Christ's sake. He had feelings for her, real feelings.

Jeremy walked over to the living room window, which faced the Hudson River, New Jersey vaguely visible in the distance. It was time to grow up, Jeremy told himself, as he often did. It was time to put away childish things, straighten himself out, stop drinking so much, getting high, focus his energies on the company. The Aurora was still a mess, but at least the full truth hadn't come out, not even to his father, and Jeremy didn't lose sleep anymore thinking he was going to jail. It'd been too close a call, though, and if that didn't tell him it was time to change things, then he didn't know what would.

Jeremy took a sip of scotch, the whiskey warming his chest. Fucking idiot: all these grand pronouncements about changing his life with a drink in his hand. And all this crap about how Alena had misunderstood him, when Jeremy himself had only the vaguest of understandings of what he'd been up to that stupid night. He hadn't trusted Alena, wanted to hurt her before she could hurt him, wanted to show her who had the power. He was no different from his sister or his father, the way they all wielded their money as a weapon, let its power isolate them.

If he was going to try to change his life, it needed to start with Alena. He needed a chance to explain, to give them both an opportunity to really try to be together, no bullshit this time. He pictured her on this couch, her robe undone, her body all soaring curves and sharp angles. He wanted to fuck her so bad right then and there that her absence made him feel like screaming.

He could track her down, Jeremy realized. Of course he could, with the resources at his disposal. Why not? Jeremy pulled out his cell and made a call.

"Darryl? What's up, it's Jeremy here. Listen, I've got a little situation I'm hoping you can help me out with."

"My man JR," Darryl Loomis replied. "Helping out with situations is what I do."

·69·

RIKERS STILL had Duncan listed as one of Rafael's lawyers, so he was able to schedule an attorney-client visit. He felt furtive as he was processed through, half expecting someone to stop him. But he made his way to an interview room without incident. About ten minutes later Rafael was brought in, stopping in surprise upon seeing Duncan.

"What're you doing here?" Rafael said as he sat down. "Thought you fired me."

Duncan smiled at this, though Rafael didn't. "I certainly didn't fire you, Rafael. It was never my decision to drop your case."

"But you did. So what you want now?"

"I heard you were going to take a plea," Duncan said.

"What do you care what I'm doing?"

"Of course I care. I know you didn't shoot Sean Fowler, Rafael."

Rafael shrugged, not making eye contact. "My new lawyer got me this deal. Says I'll have to do fifteen years, but if I go to trial I could get life, no chance to get out."

"But if you didn't do it—"

"Nobody gives a shit whether I done it or not," Rafael interrupted, his voice harsh with anger. "Took me a while to figure that out is all. You didn't give a shit neither, quitting on me."

Duncan shook his head, feeling defensive and embarrassed. "That's not what happened."

"Whatever. I don't feel like arguing with you about it."

"I understand you're angry with me, Rafael. But the reason I'm here is that I'd like to be your lawyer again."

This at least got Rafael's full attention. He cocked his head at Duncan, puzzled. "You just got done quitting on me."

"That was my firm, not me," Duncan said. He didn't know quite how to explain recent events. "Long story short, I don't work there any-more, so the conflict is gone. It may be a little complicated, but I'd like to help you keep fighting this. I've got a better idea now what actually happened."

"You going to promise me you can get me out?" Rafael challenged.

Duncan looked away, uncomfortable. "You know I can't promise anything, but I'll do everything in my power. You really want to spend years in prison for something you didn't do?"

"Course not. But I don't want to spend my whole life up in here nei-ther."

"I don't understand what's changed," Duncan said. "You wanted to go to war on this."

"That was back when I thought I could have a fair fight," Rafael said, his eyes dark and wrathful. "Look around you; see where you are. Fair got nothing to do with this place."

Duncan decided to offer a simple plea. "I'd like to help you, Rafael, if you'll let me. All that's left of the DA's case is the one eyewitness, and I have a good angle of attack on him. What do you say?"

Rafael was clearly unmoved. "Look, I liked you, Mr. R, and I don't want to get in a big thing with you now. But I trusted you and you dumped me, and now I don't trust you no more. You're part of the sys-tem, same as the rest of them. I know you say you're not, but you are."

"I can't even tell you how much I'm not," Duncan said, scrambling for a way around Rafael's defenses.

"I'm keeping my head down, doing the time. I can't take the chance of spending the rest of my life in here."

"Fifteen years in prison. A real prison upstate—Sing Sing or Green Haven. You realize what that'll be?"

Rafael waved his hand dismissively. "For a white boy like you, sure. But I got people in here. I'll be protected."

Duncan wondered if bringing up his racial background might cre-ate a bridge to Rafael, but this didn't feel like the time. "Your people in a maximum-security prison won't be people like you. This is every-thing you've managed to avoid becoming—don't give in to it now."

Duncan's words backfired; he could see the anger overtaking Rafael. "Man, *fuck you*. What do you know about me, what I've been through? You don't know *shit* about none of it, so quit talking like you do."

Rafael stood abruptly and turned to the bars. Duncan didn't know what he'd done to lose him, but he could see he had. "I really think I can take the case against you apart if you give me the chance," he said, offering one last try.

But Rafael didn't turn. "Guard," he called instead. "We done in here."

·70·

So how'd it go?" Candace asked.

Duncan smiled ruefully. "Rafael told me to fuck off," he said, handing a beer to her before sitting down in the chair across from her.

His apartment had somehow become their default meeting place. He wasn't quite sure what to make of that. Duncan rarely had people over unless he was sleeping with them; most New York socializing took place in restaurants and bars. But Candace didn't want to meet him in public, given that she was being followed, and in light of recent events Duncan certainly saw her point. But there was an intimacy to having her here, once again drinking beer on his couch.

It was a little after eight o'clock, Candace having come over after work. She was still dressed for the office, while Duncan was in jeans. He'd put on a suit to go see Rafael at Rikers, but otherwise hadn't bothered to look anything close to presentable since getting the ax.

"Nazario's still pissed that you quit on him?"

"I don't blame him for being pissed. But it's also that he seems resigned to taking the plea. I think he's so beaten down by the whole thing that he's made peace with the idea of spending years in jail for something he didn't do."

"I can't blame the guy for thinking a fair shake's not in the cards," Candace replied. "It can't just be a coincidence that they chose Rafael to be the fall guy. So which came first, you representing Rafael or his being set up?"

Duncan looked away, peeling off the beer label and then rolling it up in his hand. Candace, well versed in waiting people out, sat still. "We're off the record, right?"

"I told you before, I'm blacklisted from writing about any of this. We're just two guys talking."

Duncan fixed her with a look. "Is that what we are?" he said, Candace seeming a little caught off guard. When it became clear she wasn't going to say anything Duncan continued. "I obviously can't prove it," he said. "But I'm pretty much certain they picked him because I was already his lawyer."

Candace nodded. "Like I said before, I figured your guilty conscience had a role in all this."

"I don't feel guilty," Duncan protested.

"Really? Because my assumption that you did was part of why I was starting to like you."

Now it was Duncan's turn to be caught off guard. "I do feel responsible," he said. "There's a difference."

"To a lawyer, maybe," Candace said with a slight smile. "Anyway, so now what? If you can't represent Nazario, isn't that game-over?"

"Not necessarily," Duncan said. "I've got a potential angle to at least maybe get into the courtroom without actually representing Rafael. But that won't do me any good without a way to exonerate him once I get there."

"Which you don't have."

"I don't have that, no," Duncan said. "I need to talk to the person who came forward to you about Jeremy."

"You know I can't just hand over a source."

"Look, I play by the rules too. How's that working out for either of us?"

"I'll see if I can get her to agree to talk to you," Candace said. "I don't think she knows enough to help you, anyway. She doesn't have the slightest idea who Sean Fowler is."

Duncan took a long swig of his beer, trying to fight down the feeling that he'd already failed, and that all he was doing now was banging his head against an unmoving wall. "If you have a better idea," he said, "now wouldn't be a bad time to tell me."

"You either need somebody on the inside to give it up or you need some sort of physical evidence, right?"

"Actually it's a little worse than that. Evidence of Rafael's innocence isn't enough at this point, since I'm not his lawyer and there's not going to be a trial. I need to be able to show that he was framed, and by whom.

But I don't actually know who killed Fowler, and I don't have any evidence that the Roths gave the order."

Candace gave Duncan an appraising look. "So have you entertained the possibility that you've just lost here?" she said. "You don't have a client; you don't have evidence. Aren't those pretty essential things for a lawyer looking to win a case?"

She'd read his mind, but Duncan resisted conceding it. "What can I do but keep fighting?" he said. "This is the only thing I have left to do. If I don't try, it's game-over just the same as it is if I try and fail."

Candace offered Duncan a warm smile in response, Duncan finding himself smiling back, though it had nothing to do with what he'd just said. "Can I tell you something weird?" Candace said. "I got divorced today."

Duncan was a little thrown by the transition. Was this her way of telling him she was officially single? Of acknowledging the attraction in the smile they'd just exchanged? "I don't know whether to say congratulations or sorry."

Candace looked uncomfortable, like she might be regretting telling him. "Both. Neither. Shit, beats me."

"You were in court today?"

Candace shook her head. "We weren't contesting it, just a yearlong separation before I could claim abandonment. I got it in the mail. So anticlimactic, I suppose, in that sense."

"That must be strange. Though if you've been apart for a full year, I guess you've had time to get used to the idea."

"It's not like it's a surprise, except in the way that such things are when they actually happen," Candace said, looking like she was trying to fight off a sudden bout of sadness. "So how about you? How come you're not married?"

Duncan suspected Candace was feeling vulnerable and trying to turn the tables. "I've got nothing against the idea," he said. "It just hasn't happened. I've been working at least sixty hours a week for the past seven years, so that hasn't helped. And most of the people I meet are lawyers, and you know what they're like. Plus I don't come across a lot of great advertisements for the institution. How long were you even married?"

"About six years, not counting this past one, and we were together for about three before that. So as failed relationships go, we didn't do that terrible."

Duncan decided to probe further. "What ended it?"

"I guess I did. There wasn't a big scandal or anything. We got to the point where having a kid was the next thing, and suddenly the idea that I was in this for the next twenty years or whatever became something scary to me. Maybe we were a little too young—nobody in New York gets married in their twenties anymore. But really it was just that we had different approaches to life. Ben was such an academic—the world as it actually is just isn't that interesting to him. To me, it's the only thing."

Duncan finished his beer and put the bottle down on his coffee table before looking back over at Candace. "So why'd you just tell me?" he asked, no challenge in it, but no banter either.

"About the divorce?" Candace asked, looking taken aback. "No reason. I hadn't told anyone, and it seemed like something I shouldn't go the whole day without saying out loud."

"I think you just wanted me to know you were on the market," Duncan said, just playfully enough to leave himself some plausible deniability.

"Please," Candace said. "You don't even have a job. I do look for a certain amount of respectability."

·71·

DUNCAN HAD been waiting outside of the Roth Properties headquarters for over an hour before he spotted Leah Roth coming out. She was heading toward a small row of parked car-service Town Cars outside the building when Duncan intercepted her on the sidewalk.

Leah froze upon seeing him, frightened, like she thought he was about to attack her right out on the crowded street. Duncan held up his hands, palms up. "I just need to talk to you for a minute."

"We don't have anything to talk about," Leah said, struggling to regain her composure.

"We do. It'll take five minutes."

"You had plenty of chances to talk to me. You chose instead to betray your professional obligations, as well as any obligations you may have had to me personally."

"I'm not here to apologize or explain or grovel. I wouldn't be here if it wasn't important. So just hear me out for five minutes."

Leah hesitated, but then nodded. Duncan had been relying on her wanting to know what he was up to. "I'll listen to you for five minutes, but that's going to be it."

Duncan followed Leah to a Town Car, sliding in next to her in the backseat. It felt strange to be so physically close to her: he felt a sudden flare of violence, an impulse to physically hurt her for what she'd done to him. Leah must have felt it: she gave Duncan a sidelong look and put her back against the inside of the car door rather than the seat.

"In the course of my representation of you," Duncan began, "I became aware that you were a conspirator in ongoing criminal activity. That conspiracy included future criminal conduct."

"The hell do you think you're doing?" Leah interrupted, her gaze now shifted toward the car's driver. Duncan, who was seated directly behind the man, could see only the back of his head.

Duncan ignored the question. "Part of that future illegal conduct is an attempt to perpetuate a fraud upon a court, specifically in the prosecution of Rafael Nazario for the murder of Sean Fowler. I am therefore asking that you bring this fraud to the attention of the judge hearing that case. If you refuse to do so, I will have no choice but to do it myself."

The man in the driver's seat turned while Duncan was speaking, and to Duncan's shock he found himself looking into the eyes of Darryl Loomis. "I think you should assume our high-yellow friend here is recording this conversation," he said to Leah, his voice soft with controlled menace.

Ignoring Darryl, or at least seeming to, Leah permitted herself something like a laugh. Duncan found himself wondering if Darryl had already told her about his father, and whether she'd cared. "I have no involvement in a conspiracy of any kind," she said to Duncan. "Certainly not one involving Mr. Fowler's tragic murder by your former client. Any attempt by you to suggest otherwise would not only be slanderous, but would violate your ethical obligation as my former lawyer. It's bad enough you've lost your job from your inappropriate behavior toward me, Mr. Riley; do you really want to throw your law license onto the fire?"

Duncan was still trying to process what the hell Loomis was doing behind the wheel of the car. "I'm not recording this, or trying to get a confession out of you," he said. "I'm simply formally requesting that you notify the court of the truth about Fowler's murder."

"And what truth would that be?"

"That Fowler was murdered because he was blackmailing your brother over the Aurora. Driscoll was part of it; Mr. Loomis here probably was too. But you were behind it, all, weren't you, Leah?"

Other than a tightness in her face from clenching her jaw, Duncan didn't see much of a reaction from Leah. She was good. "I understand you're upset, Duncan," Leah said. "But really."

"I'm not letting you get away with it. If you hadn't made an innocent man the fall guy, that would be one thing, but I'm not standing by and watching Rafael go to jail for something he didn't do. If you won't find a way to get him out, then I'll go to the court and tell them everything I know."

Duncan spoke quietly, unable to fully keep a slight tremor out of his voice. Leah glanced up at Loomis, then back at Duncan. "Even if the judge agrees to listen to you, what proof are you going to show him? What evidence do you have?"

"I've shown you all the cards you're going to see. It was you who picked out Rafael as the fall guy; it had to be. You picked him because I was his lawyer—you had me implicated in this from the start."

Leah looked over at Loomis, trying not to react. "I couldn't have less idea what you're talking about," she said stiffly.

Duncan wasn't expecting a confession. "You've made me the most dangerous kind of person there is: a guy with nothing to lose."

"You've got plenty more you can lose, Counselor," Darryl growled.

Duncan opened the car door, got out, and slammed it behind him, walking quickly away. Leah made eye contact with Darryl in the rearview mirror. "What did you make of all that?" she asked.

"He was just fishing around for you to say something," Darryl replied. "He was wired, I'm sure."

"You think the cops wired him?"

"Nah," Darryl said. "I think he was just freelancing, hoping to pull out a rabbit. The question is, can he really go to the judge?"

"If he even tries I'll have his law license."

"Won't much matter to you if you're in jail," Darryl said. "It sounds like he knows what's been going on."

"Knowing and proving are entirely different things. He has no evidence. I shouldn't have gotten him fired, though: it meant I lost control of him. I overreacted."

"Even if he can't prove anything, there'd be some serious shit if he went public on this."

Leah shot Darryl a look by way of the rearview mirror. "I hope you're not suggesting anything. He's a lawyer, he's been talking to that reporter, he just got fired because of me—people would put it together, easy."

"There's no doubt he's a threat, though. This personal between you two?"

Leah was a little surprised that Darryl would ask, but then again, she figured the answer was probably obvious. "Not anymore," she said.

72

Rafael Nazario's guilty plea was scheduled to be heard at two p.m. Rafael hadn't been brought in yet when Duncan arrived at the courtroom at about a quarter to two. There were maybe ten people present, most of whom Duncan recognized: the ADAs; several reporters, including Costello from the *Journal*; and Rafael's grandmother. She was sitting next to a middle-aged Hispanic woman; Duncan wondered idly if it was Rafael's mother.

Bream spotted Duncan and muttered something to Castelluccio, who turned around, frowning. Duncan offered a nod, which she did not return. Duncan was sure Castelluccio would like him even less soon enough.

At five to two Robert Walker came hurrying in, walking past Duncan without appearing to notice him as he made his way to the defense's table up front. A couple of minutes later Lily Vaughan walked in. She sat down in the back, then looked around the room, her gaze quickly alighting on Duncan. Lily hesitated before coming over to him.

"What're you doing here, Dunk?" she asked by way of greeting.

"Don't call me Dunk. And I think the better question is, what're you doing here?"

"You probably have a better idea as to why I'm here than I do," Lily said.

"I assume you're here to see if I cause any trouble."

"That certainly could be," Lily said. "Why, will you?"

Duncan smiled. He wasn't going to take it personally that Lily was here to spy on him. "It's not like I have anything better to do."

Lily glanced around, then lowered her voice. "The fuck is going on? What'd you get up to that the Blake would fire you? What is this all about?"

"You don't actually want to know."

Lily shrugged, conceding the point. "Should I be worried? About the firm, I mean."

"I'm not going after Blake personally," Duncan said. "But if he turns out to be collateral damage, don't invite me to the pity party."

Lily looked away. "I guess I should tell you—I'm in."

It took Duncan a moment to understand. "You made partner?"

Lily nodded, pride fighting embarrassment. "It's not official yet, but Blake's given me his word. The competition got a little easier, I guess."

Duncan was surprised Blake would make a commitment like that, since partnership was never guaranteed, even to the star associates. He looked over at Lily, who still wasn't meeting his eyes. "You leveraged my getting fired, didn't you? That and Karen Cleary—you made a move, got Blake to commit."

Lily forced herself to look at him. "I'm sorry—I know it's not fair."

Duncan smiled at her, wanting her to see that he wasn't going to harbor it. "Since when did either of us expect things to be fair?"

"Are you okay?" Lily asked, looking at him with real concern.

"Are you kidding? I sleep till ten a.m., go to the gym every day. This is the life."

"Did you know it was going to get like this? That you'd end up out on the street over whatever was happening?"

Duncan shook his head. "Believe it or not, I wasn't trying to cause trouble. I was just doing my job. That's still all I'm doing."

"I'm sorry, Duncan. Is there something I can do that would help?"

"You don't owe me anything, Lily," Duncan said. "I think of you fondly and I wish you well. I'm sorry that nothing much came out of that, but let's part friends."

Lily looked at him sadly for a moment, then nodded. "So what's going to happen here now?"

"I'm kind of curious about that myself," Duncan replied, standing as Judge Lasky entered the courtroom and took the bench.

The court officers then brought Rafael in. The case manager read the docket number, formally beginning the proceeding.

As soon as he had done so, Duncan stood and made his way into the well of the court, his heart pounding. "Your Honor," he said, feeling every eye in the room on him. "Before you take this plea I need to bring some information to the court's attention."

Judge Lasky peered over his glasses at Duncan. "Mr. Riley, it is my understanding you are no longer Mr. Nazario's attorney."

"That's true, Your Honor. I'm speaking now not as a lawyer for Mr. Nazario, but rather as an officer of the court. I believe the rules governing attorney conduct obligate me to come forward."

"Mr. Riley has no standing to be addressing the court in this proceeding," Castelluccio said angrily.

"Chambers," Lasky said brusquely. "Lawyers only. That includes you, Mr. Riley."

AS SOON as they entered the chambers, Castelluccio continued her argument that the judge shouldn't even listen to Duncan. Bream and Walker followed her in, with Duncan bringing up the rear. "Why don't we hear from the one person in this room who actually knows what this is about," Lasky said to Castelluccio as he sat at the head of the table, gesturing for the rest of them to sit.

Duncan sat down next to Walker, who edged away from him, not wanting even the association of physical proximity. "Your Honor," Duncan began, "in the course of representing another client I became aware of an ongoing criminal conspiracy they were involved with. That conspiracy extended to perpetuating a fraud upon this court."

"You're in here planning to break attorney-client privilege?" Castelluccio demanded.

"I'll ask the questions," Lasky snapped at her, before turning back to Duncan. "But she does ask a good one. Are you proposing to describe privileged information you received from a client?"

"The relevant information was not disclosed to me as part of my representation of this other client, no. And even if there was concern about it being privileged, it would also fall within the crime fraud exception."

"Crime fraud is a narrow exception," the judge countered.

"There's also disciplinary rule 7–102(b)(1)," Duncan said. His big advantage as the only person prepared for this discussion was that it made him the only person who'd recently researched the issue. "That rule obligates a lawyer who finds out a client is perpetuating a fraud upon a court to call on the client to rectify it. I have unsuccessfully asked the client in question to do so. Since my client has refused, it is then my professional duty under that rule to notify the court."

"Does this relate to the positional conflict your firm had in this matter?" the judge asked.

"It does, yes," Duncan replied, though he was still fuzzy on what exactly Blake had claimed regarding that supposed conflict.

Lasky stared at Duncan for a long moment. "I don't know if you're right about disclosing whatever the specifics of this are, but I do know if you break privilege and I ultimately find that it was inappropriate for you to do so, I will report you to the bar. Good intentions will not be a defense."

Although this didn't come as a surprise to Duncan, actually hearing it said was not pleasant. But it was already way too late to retreat. "Understood, Your Honor."

Lasky looked at Duncan with something resembling pity. "I hope you know what you're getting yourself into, Mr. Riley. You're obviously a talented lawyer, but I worry you may be a little too fond of making the big splash. Let's hope you don't drown. Without naming the client in question, tell me in broad outline—and I mean broad—what you are alleging in terms of a fraud upon this court."

"I discovered that a former client of mine was engaged in illegal conduct, the details of which are not relevant to this case. However, I also came to discover that Sean Fowler was involved in the prior illegal conduct, and that Mr. Fowler had engaged in blackmail of my former client using what he knew about this illegal activity. In response to Mr. Fowler's blackmail, an ongoing conspiracy was formed to kill him and to frame Rafael Nazario for the murder. My representation of Mr. Nazario in effect made me an unwitting participant in the conspiracy, since I was pressured to plead his case out quickly."

The judge was silent after Duncan stopped speaking, but Castelluccio couldn't contain herself. "This is the most ridiculous thing I have ever heard in my life," she said. "We have an eyewitness that the defendant shot Fowler."

"Chris Driscoll is part of the conspiracy," Duncan replied.

Castelluccio laughed harshly. "Have you lost your mind? Seriously, have you? I suppose I'm part of this conspiracy too?"

"No," Duncan replied. "You're just bullheaded and bloodthirsty."

"Enough," Lasky said. The judge was still staring at Duncan, eyes narrowed. "If this is some kind of stunt, you are really going to regret it. I hope it goes without saying that if you can't back up this rather unbelievable story, your legal career may come to a very abrupt end."

"I believe ethics, and for that matter justice, require me to do what I'm doing," Duncan replied.

"Your Honor," Castelluccio said, struggling to contain her anger, "even accepting the truth of everything Mr. Riley just said, all that would mean is that he is a witness for the defense in this case, although one with some pretty major hearsay and privilege issues. The defense would be free to call him at trial, assuming they could provide a sufficient offer of proof. It would be his word against, among others, Mr. Driscoll's. I don't see any reason to treat him differently from any other witness."

"There isn't going to be any trial," Duncan said. "Rafael was supposed to plead today, and then this cover-up would be complete."

"What evidence do you have?" Castelluccio demanded. "We're supposed to just take your word? A defense lawyer who says his client's innocent—haven't heard that one before."

Lasky looked from one of them to the other, and then over at Walker, who was sitting with his arms crossed beside Duncan. "Do you know anything about any of this?" Lasky asked him.

"Nothing whatsoever, Judge," Walker replied.

Judge Lasky rubbed at his face, then sighed heavily. "A lawyer comes to me with a claim like this, however dubious, I can't just ignore it," the judge said finally. "So I suppose the question then becomes, how do you propose actually trying to establish this story of yours, Mr. Riley?"

Duncan wished he knew. "Hold a hearing," he said. "I will question witnesses. That way I'm not presenting information myself, and I won't be disclosing anything that's arguably privileged."

"You're willing to risk your entire legal career on convincing me at a hearing of an elaborate conspiracy to frame Mr. Nazario?"

"I guess I am," Duncan said. "If that's what I have to be."

They reconvened briefly in court, the judge offering a terse and inscrutable statement putting off the plea hearing. Rafael looked over at Duncan, completely in the dark, as the court officers took him out of the courtroom.

Costello was quickly over to Duncan, Lily lurking behind him. "No comment, sorry," Duncan said before the reporter could even ask him a question.

"Can you at least—"

"I can't," Duncan interrupted, moving past the reporter, who trailed after him, still asking questions.

"What the hell, Dunk?" Lily said.

Duncan smiled at her, then put his index finger to his lips.

"You're going to make me go back to the Blake empty-handed? Come on, give me a clue, at least."

"It's a little late in the day to worry about a fair fight," Duncan said, walking past her and out of the courtroom.

73

I DIDN'T think I'd be hearing from you," Candace said.

ADA Sullivan shrugged from across the table at Mustang Sally's, where the two of them had just ordered lunch. "I meant what I said before. I know your reporting is what got the Aurora referred to me in the first place. But what I'm telling you is way off the record—hell, it's past off the record. It'll be yours alone when you can print it, but that's only when you have my okay. Deal?"

"If I can't print it, why are you giving it to me now?"

"Because I'm hoping you'll tell me what you think it means."

Candace never turned down information, even if she couldn't print it, though normally she fought to get things on the record, at least on background. But she was clear that Sullivan was not about to negotiate. "Fire away," she said.

Sullivan watched as a man passed by their table on his way to the men's room, then leaned forward. "A body—well, most of one anyway—floated out of the Atlantic and onto the coast of New Jersey a couple of days ago. Badly decomposed, so we won't have a definite ID until the white-coat guys run some more tests. But preliminary indications are that the body formerly belonged to Jack Pellettieri."

Candace hadn't known what to expect, but Pellettieri's corpse washing up hadn't even crossed her mind. Her mind scrambled to figure out what it meant. "Murdered?"

"Can't say that for sure," Sullivan said. "We're missing the head, for one thing. But nobody's thinking fishing accident."

"I thought there was a paper trail showing Pellettieri in Mexico and the Caribbean?"

"Exactly," Sullivan said. "We haven't nailed down how long he's been in the water, but it was a while, which certainly suggests somebody was creating a fake trail for him after he was dead."

It took Candace a moment to catch up. "That sounds like a major investment. In resources and skill."

"Not exactly a drive-by, no."

"A lot of effort to spend on small-time Jack Pellettieri."

"Which, yes, is why I'm here. You told me before the Aurora didn't end with Pellettieri; now I'm pretty sure you're right."

"Pellettieri was killed because he knew too much about the Roths, and they couldn't risk his falling into your hands. But if you've come to me for proof of that, I don't have any."

Sullivan leaned back as the waitress brought their lunches. "I looked into that murder you told me about," he said, once she was gone. "The security guard, Fowler. I talked with the DA on the case."

"From what I've heard, she's a pit bull with her jaws locked."

"ADA Castelluccio is a talented prosecutor with a bright future in our office," Sullivan said. "And she didn't think there was any reason to think Fowler's murder had anything to do with a construction accident in SoHo."

"And so that was your attempt at investigating, and now you're coming to me?"

"One of the detectives, however, had a slightly different perspective," Sullivan said, ignoring Candace's dig. "He was agnostic on the charge against Nazario. I don't run into too many agnostic cops, not after a collar."

"But you don't have a link between Fowler's murder and Pellettieri's?"

"I don't have a link between Pellettieri's murder and anything. The trail's gone massively cold, obviously, plus we barely know where the trail is. We don't know where his body was dumped, or when. I can only keep it quiet until the ID is conclusive, so it's a short window before the killer gets a heads-up that we know about it."

"No wonder you're reduced to asking me for help," Candace said. She was uncomfortable with the idea of giving the DA's office a lead, even if she'd had one to give. But having Sullivan as a source could pay off huge if he did break the case. She decided to give him something.

"Fowler had a lot more money in the bank than he should have had. That's something you have better tools to dig into."

"How'd you get his bank records? Or shouldn't I ask?"

"Nazario's old lawyer, Duncan Riley. He's the other person who's pieced a lot of this together."

"Riley, from Blake and Wolcott? I've met him, on the Aurora wrongful death. I assume that's not a coincidence?"

"I wouldn't think the head of the Rackets Bureau believes in coincidences," Candace replied. "Riley's still trying to help Nazario, even though he doesn't officially represent him anymore. But time's running out."

"I can't help a defendant who my office is prosecuting," Sullivan said.

"You outrank Castelluccio, don't you?"

"She doesn't report to me, and I don't outrank her boss. The case isn't under my jurisdiction."

"It is if the Fowler murder opens the door to solving Pellettieri's murder, and goes back to the Aurora."

"Maybe then, yes," Sullivan said. "But I would need real evidence."

"I could do with some of that myself," Candace said.

·74·

LEAH COULDN'T recall seeing Steven Blake show surprise before. But Blake made no attempt to hide his incredulity as she told him that Duncan Riley had just subpoenaed her to testify at a hearing in the Fowler murder.

"I knew there was a lot I didn't know," Blake said after a moment. "But it sounds like I at least need to know some of it."

Leah nodded crisply. "Here's what I expect Duncan is going to claim, and then we can talk about possible responses. He's going to allege that my brother was involved in siphoning money out of the Aurora project, using Pellettieri to do so. That Sean Fowler was the middleman for that, and that after the investigation of the Aurora kicked up again, Fowler attempted to blackmail Jeremy about his involvement, and that Fowler was murdered out of that. To make sure Fowler's murder didn't lead to Jeremy, or back to the Aurora generally, Rafael Nazario was set up, with the idea your firm would reach a quick plea. And that because of the framing of Nazario, a fraud has been committed upon the court, which therefore frees Duncan up to disclose our involvement."

Blake's earlier surprise was nothing compared to the look on his face now. Despite herself, Leah felt a perverse sense of pride at knocking the veteran lawyer so far back on his heels. It was childish, she knew, and not an appropriate response to the situation. And really what it told her was just how completely off the rails she'd managed to go.

Blake started to say something, but then stopped himself before any words came out. He rubbed at his face, then glanced over at Leah, who forced herself to meet his gaze. Blake looked away first, his face ashen. A full minute had passed since Leah finished speaking.

"You've got me pretty far into this, haven't you?" Blake finally said. "You told me you wanted my firm to keep the murder case so that a defense lawyer didn't try to turn the whole thing into some kind of referendum on the redevelopment of Riis. 'Handle the case quickly and quietly so it doesn't become a distraction to the construction,' you said."

"I may not have been entirely truthful," Leah agreed. "It's probably best if you get past that quickly, under the circumstances."

Blake looked at her, his composure returning. "Does Duncan have any hard evidence to support any of these accusations?" he asked.

Leah shook her head. "As far as I know, he has pretty much nothing in the way of proof. This is just a theory he's put together."

"He's got to have some building blocks. I'll be able to counter him more effectively if I know what he's working with."

"How much do you want me to tell you?"

"I'm already going to look like an accessory, with the Nazario case, the positional conflict, firing him. I assume Duncan thinks I was part of this whole thing."

"You were," Leah said coldly. "You just chose to stay unaware of it."

"Is your father involved in all this?" Blake countered. "Does he even know anything about it?"

Leah tried not to show her reaction. "You don't have to concern yourself with my father."

"I've known Simon for twenty-five years," Blake replied. "He'll never forgive me if you get taken down on this on my watch."

"The easiest way to contain this, for all of us, is to keep Duncan from having this hearing at all. Does he really have a legal basis for it?"

"It's not a situation I've previously encountered," Blake deadpanned. "A lawyer does have an obligation to go to the court to prevent perjury, but this isn't that. Generally the only way he can break privilege is to prevent a future crime—that doesn't seem to quite fit either. But I've spent the last seven years teaching Duncan the fine art of fitting square pegs into round holes. . . . This would be easier to control if you hadn't had me fire him."

Leah immediately nodded; she'd been planning to bring this up. "It was an overreaction, and yes, obviously backfired. Perhaps we should bring him back into the fold?"

"We can try, though he can maybe use it against us if he says no."

"You think no is what he'll say?"

Blake thought about it. "He's an extremely ambitious guy who had a very bright future in front of him a month ago," he replied. "I would think he wants his old life back."

·75·

DUNCAN HAD agreed to meet Neil Levine at the Royalton for a drink. Neil had reached out, practically begging him to meet. Duncan figured he could try to pump Neil for information as to how the firm was preparing to respond to the upcoming hearing in the Nazario case. Although Duncan supposed that could be what Neil was planning to do to him.

Neil was already at a back table when Duncan arrived. He stood in greeting, extending a hand. Duncan thought he seemed nervous. "Don't worry," Duncan said. "I'm pretty sure getting fired isn't contagious."

Neil forced a smile, then clutched at his drink as he sat back down. "This is so fucked up," he said. "Nobody at the firm understands what happened."

"Does anyone actually want to know?"

"Of course. You were a rock star. It doesn't make any sense. What the hell happened?"

"It's really better if you don't know exactly what's going on."

"You're serious? Jesus, and I thought the problem with this job was how boring the work is."

"You haven't heard anything about what's going on in the Nazario case, the hearing that's coming up, nothing like that?"

"It's been complete radio silence. I went by your office one day; your nameplate was gone and the door was locked. I asked Lily and she claimed she didn't know shit. Did you see it coming?"

"I really didn't."

"I thought you were going to make the big time there."

The waitress came over, asked Duncan what he wanted to drink. He ordered a Knob Creek straight up with a water back, a little surprised that Neil didn't get another drink, although his glass looked empty.

"Tell you the truth," Neil continued after the waitress was gone. "I've been thinking pretty seriously about leaving. I know I've only been at the firm for a year, so it's probably a little quick to get out, but I already know I can't possibly spend my life doing this."

"I actually thought I could," Duncan said quietly. "I mean, I *was*. If I'd made partner—who ever walks away at that point? It already feels so distant."

Neil's attention had visibly faltered. "Listen," he said suddenly. "Don't be pissed, but I've got to tell you something."

"That sounds promising."

"Blake asked me to get hold of you. I don't know what it's about, but I felt like I couldn't say no. He said he needed to talk to you."

"Tell him to go fuck himself," Duncan said.

"You can tell him that to his face," Neil said, looking over Duncan's shoulder.

"Don't be pissed at Neil," a voice said from behind Duncan, who didn't need to turn to know who it was. "He was just following orders. Something law firm associates are expected to do, as you may vaguely recall from earlier in your career."

"I'm not pissed at Neil, much," Duncan replied as Blake came alongside the table. "More pissed at you for using him."

Neil stood up, Blake immediately taking his seat. "We need to talk," Blake said.

"Sorry, man," Neil said to Duncan. "I'll give you a call next week; maybe we can get dinner or something."

Duncan didn't bother to respond, debating whether he should get up and leave himself. But it would be useful to know why Blake was here.

The waitress brought Duncan his drink, pausing for a second as she realized that Blake was not the man who'd previously been sitting at the table, then asked if he wanted anything. Blake ordered a scotch, Duncan struggling to believe that the two of them were sitting here over cocktails. "How pissed at me can you really be, Duncan?" Blake said, after she was gone. "You think I wanted it to end up like this? You think I wanted to let you go? I'd been grooming you for years, for Christ's sake."

"I didn't sense a lot of hesitation."

Blake didn't bother looking contrite. "You ask me to choose between the Roth family and you, who the hell you think I'm going to pick? The firm's billed them probably twenty million the past decade; plus Simon and I go way back. What were you thinking, getting mixed up with Leah?"

"She came after me. And I was thinking what people usually are thinking when they go to bed with somebody, Steven. Plus, with her, there was that whole keys-to-the-castle thing; I'll admit that."

"Didn't it occur to you how it could end?"

"That she would have you fire me because she was worried I knew too much about why Sean Fowler was murdered?" Duncan said. "Honestly, no, I can't say that occurred to me."

"Now let's stick to the facts," Blake said. "Leah is . . . She's used to getting what she wants. I don't know exactly what's been going on, but I want to assure you I knew nothing about it at the time."

"You knew that she'd given you orders to reach a quick plea for Nazario," Duncan shot back.

"That's not true," Blake said immediately, Duncan rolling his eyes in response.

"For Christ's sake, Steven, I'm not wired. I thought I was meeting Neil for a drink, remember?"

"I don't think you're wired, Duncan, but I do think you seem to be out for revenge. I understand that you're mad at me. I thought Nazario was guilty, and that the best thing we could do for him was get him a good deal. The only thing Leah told me was she didn't want some lawyer using the shooting at Riis as a way of rabble-rousing about the development."

Duncan didn't buy it. But he did imagine that Blake hadn't been fully in the loop about what was really going on. Blake must have known something was off, but knew better than to ask questions he didn't want answered.

"Okay," Duncan said. "So she told you that then, and you chose to believe it. What about now?"

"This isn't what you think. There's never any big conspiracy. People are way too greedy and disorganized for that. Everybody's playing their own separate angle, and you end up with something that maybe looks like it has a pattern."

Duncan figured Blake hadn't brought him here to debate, and decided it was time to make the man get to the point. "What do you actually want, Steven?" he asked.

"I want to try to make this right for you. Under the circumstances, I realize that I can't just ask you to go back to the way things were. But I don't want you to be left out in the cold like you have been. So here's what I'm thinking: I'll put you back on salary, give you a year to look for a new job. During that time you will keep your office at the firm, but we won't expect you to work for us. I'll not only give you the best reference I can, but I'll personally, along with the rest of the partners, beat the bushes on your behalf."

"Let me guess," Duncan said. "All I have to do in exchange for all this is cancel the Nazario hearing."

"I already assumed you weren't actually going through with that," Blake replied with no hesitation. "You don't have any proof to present to the court, and if you violate attorney-client privilege you'll lose your law license. And for what? It won't change anything for this kid."

"It's interesting to find out what people think you can be bought for," Duncan said. "So you think my price is a quarter million, plus references."

"Don't be silly. It's about getting back everything you've worked so hard to achieve."

Duncan knew there was a pretty good chance that Blake was right: he could go to the wall fighting this, and not accomplish anything other than his own disbarment. Blake was offering a lot more than money: Duncan's whole career would be put back on track. It would be nice to have.

Duncan pushed the thought away and smiled at Blake. "And if I say yes, what am I then? I take your money, look the other way, turn my back on Rafael—what am I, Steven? At best, I'm you. And you know what? I don't want to be you, not anymore."

"You really think you can pull this off?" Blake said. "You really think you can pull this off against me?"

Duncan took a sip of his bourbon, then stood, so that he was looking down at Blake. "I'm sure as hell going to have fun trying," he said.

·76·

ALENA WAS staying at her friend Ivy's apartment—Ivy was gone for three weeks on a job in Milan. She was looking for a place of her own, though money was a little tight to get together a deposit. Alena hadn't worked in well over a month—long enough that she couldn't quite remember how long it had been—hadn't much tried to, but it was getting to be where that was a problem.

Walking through the East Village on her way back from meeting with the lawyer, Riley, Alena felt acutely aware of just how hard it was to live in New York City. She'd come here at seventeen from Decatur, Illinois. A little over a decade later and here she was, riding out the last flickering vestige of her glamour years. And there had been real glamour, early: when she'd first been signed by Elite, the seasons spent jetting from Paris to Tokyo. At first it had seemed like all of her childhood dreams were coming true. After a couple of years, though, her success had crested, settled into the midtier. She'd realized she was never going to be a name-brand star, just a working model who had a pretty good run but whose shelf life was already running out. Even then, though, she'd never really given any thought to what happened next.

By the time she'd turned twenty-seven her career was officially stalling out. And not just that; her life too had thinned, as most of the people she'd known in her first years in New York had vanished. Often nobody even seemed to really notice their departure: they were just gone, off the scene, out of the mix. Some got married, some moved back to where they came from, but usually Alena didn't know what had happened to them. A new crop of girls appeared as steadily as the seasons, but after you'd been around for a while the last thing you wanted to do was make the acquaintance of some bright-eyed kid just into town. You knew the mistakes they were going to make and the lessons they were going to have to learn the hard way. It was like watching a rerun of a show you'd already seen a half dozen times, the same story playing out with all the surprise and drama completely leached away by the familiarity. So mostly she hung out with people she'd known since she'd first moved to New York. She sometimes wondered if they were just the foolish ones, the people who stayed at the party that had long ago wound down, clinging to the desperate hope that something would still happen before the night was over.

And then Jeremy Roth had appeared in her life. Alena had been in the market for her ticket out, she wasn't ashamed to admit it, and Jeremy had seemed like maybe that was what he was. He hadn't been the first rich man she'd ever been with. He hadn't even been the first rich man to put her in an apartment—a married hedge-fund manager from Greenwich had been. But with the hedge funder there'd never been any suggestion he was going to leave his wife, or otherwise disrupt his existence for her. Their affair had lasted a year, almost exactly, Alena suspecting he'd had a clock running in his head the whole time.

With Jeremy, however, she'd actually allowed herself to imagine the possibility of a future. From the start she'd been able to see the scared boy lurking under his expensive men's suits. Jeremy's mother had died when he was a teenager, and Alena couldn't imagine that a man like Simon Roth had been particularly up for the task of finishing the raising of two children on his own. Alena gathered that it was Jeremy's sister who was closest to him.

Alena hadn't loved Jeremy, hadn't really come close, but all her life her relationships with men and been calculated and she hadn't necessarily seen the absence of love as a deal breaker. It bothered her sometimes, sure, but she knew how to live with it. And who knew where her feelings would've gone eventually? She'd thought that Jeremy just needed a woman to help him finish the task of growing up, that most of what was wrong with him could be fixed by his becoming a fully fledged adult. Though that was easier said than done when he was usually drunk and high. She'd also underestimated the full depths of his selfishness.

She supposed that was the biggest downside to growing up as rich as Jeremy had: it took away any incentive to correct your flaws, because the world you inhabited would always work around them. Jeremy expected the world to conform to him, not the other way around. Perhaps it wasn't an unreasonable expectation; perhaps that was the ultimate luxury that money could buy.

Looking back, Alena couldn't believe she'd ever let the idea that they could build a real and lasting relationship cross her mind, let alone taken it seriously. He'd kept her in a separate apartment, for Christ's sake, never introduced her to family or friends, never actually intermingled her into his life. She'd simply fooled herself, gotten greedy. She'd wanted to believe, because of all the money. If he hadn't stood to inherit a multibillion-dollar real estate empire, she would've seen right through him.

And all that time he'd just been thinking of her as a whore. There'd been signs all along, things she'd forced herself to ignore. But there'd been no ignoring his leaving her with Mattar Al-Falasi, especially since Mattar had been overtly hitting on her from the second they'd met. In fact, he'd been so overt about it that Alena had suspected from early on that it wasn't about her at all, that it was a power move between the two men.

She'd just let Jeremy leave the bar that night. What choice did she have, really? It wasn't her way to make a big scene there in the bar; she wasn't a tears-and-screaming kind of girl, and besides, she'd just been too blindsided. Was it really possible that was how little Jeremy valued her, that he really saw her as someone he could just hand over as a gift? Or was it simply meant as a brutally efficient way of saying he was tired of her, that it was over?

Mattar had smiled at her after Jeremy had left, a gentle smile, not predatory. Alena huddled in on herself, as if for warmth, though the night was pleasant. "I must admit," Mattar finally said, "if it was me you were with, I would not leave you alone with another man."

Alena offered him her coldest smile. "Wouldn't want your property stolen?"

Mattar registered the slight. "I can only assure you that I'm far less crude than you think I am," he said. "Tell me, what do you understand of the business between Jeremy's family and mine?"

"I understand that they want your money."

Mattar smiled again, seeming more genuine now that they were alone. "They *need* our money. I have gone over the paper for the Aurora myself. All of their construction loans are coming due, and they do not have anywhere near the sales to cover them. The banks are nervous now, especially after that unfortunate business with Lehman Brothers the other week, and they will not get more money from them. So without us, we will have to see if the Roth family actually has hundreds of millions of dollars they can pull together. This is no easy thing, even for those who may have so much in assets. It is not a good time to be seeking to turn your property into actual money."

"I understand," Alena said.

"I see that you do," Matter said, looking at her appraisingly. "I for one have never seen the charm in those who do not understand about money. They lack the ability to truly see what is taking place around them. This evening, for example. The fact that you and I are now sitting here, alone. What does that tell me about these people who my family is contemplating doing business with?"

Alena normally hated being quizzed, but found herself enjoying this question. "It tells you they're desperate," she said.

"That, absolutely, but that I already knew. It tells me something else, something very important. Their loyalty to others may not be so strong, yes? Why would I do business with such people?"

"So, a test? That's what this was tonight?"

Mattar waved his hand, whether in acknowledgment or dismissal Alena wasn't quite sure. "You are a most beautiful and interesting woman, and I am very happy to be sitting here with you. But I also learned things here tonight that relate to business."

"So how much of all of this has been an act?"

Mattar permitted himself a small smile. "You have never been to Dubai?" he asked. Alena shook her head. "We are trying to become a city of the world, such as New York. We are not yet the equal of this city, of course, but we are not so far apart either. The life I lead there, it is not so different, really, than the life I lead here."

"I thought maybe you were playing the ingenue," Alena said.

"Did Jeremy tell you much about my family?"

"Just that you were rich and from Dubai."

"He does not know what he has in you, does he? He sees only your beauty, which is abundant, but it is not everything."

Alena did not think a response was required, instead picking up her wineglass and taking a sip, then gently swirling the remaining liquid. Mattar's gaze was frankly appraising.

"I am in New York often," Mattar continued, studying her. "My family owns several apartments here. Nice apartments, I must say, though often they are unoccupied."

The brutal truth was that Alena had allowed herself to be bought before, and more than once, but never quite as nakedly as this. Mattar's indirection was really just a form of aggression, and she felt a sense of disgust rise up in her. She finished her wine, then put the wineglass down on the table, too hard, so that it rang out. "Would you like me to get you another?" Mattar asked.

"Sure," Alena said. "I'm just going to run to the ladies' while you do that."

Alena stood before Mattar had a chance to respond, and hadn't looked back as she made her way out of sight, going past the bathroom and down the stairs leading out to the street. She wondered how long it'd taken Mattar to figure out she wasn't coming back, or if he'd sensed it the instant she'd stood up.

It'd been as much disappointment with herself for believing that she might have a future with Jeremy as anger at him for handing her out like a party favor that had prompted Alena to look up the reporter. People in fashion leaked dirt to the gossip press all the time, avenging slights real or imagined. Perhaps it had been petty, but she'd wanted to show Jeremy that he couldn't just treat her like something cheap and disposable and get away with it, that she had ways of striking back.

It turned out to be a lot easier to plant a piece of gossip in the paper than it was an actual news story. Of course, she'd had no idea the reporter would think her tip was tied into a murder case. Alena still found it pretty much impossible to picture: Jeremy was simply too weak. But then again, how strong did you have to be to give the order, let someone else carry out the deed?

Plus, three construction guys had died in the accident. It hadn't been deliberate murder, but how much of a difference did that really make? If greed allowed you to risk people's lives to increase your own profits, wasn't that basically murder? How big a leap was it from there to deliberately killing someone who posed a threat to you? Didn't anyone with as much wealth as Jeremy Roth have to be at least somewhat indifferent to others in order to live such a lavish life?

The reporter, Candace, had called her yesterday, asked if she was willing to meet with the lawyer who was representing the guy accused of killing Fowler. Alena had said she didn't know anything that would help, but had found herself agreeing to meet with Duncan Riley anyway. Alena had rarely dealt with lawyers, who made her nervous, but Duncan had been young and casual, not her mental image of an attorney. He had asked her similar questions to what the reporter had; Alena had the sense that her answers had disappointed him.

It was weird, Alena thought, talking to people like Candace and Duncan. They seemed similar: two intense workaholics who were professionally obsessed with bringing out the truth. While it was clear that they both firmly believed the Roth family was behind the murder, it also seemed clear that they didn't have enough to actually pin it on them. But Alena wouldn't want to be on either of their bad sides.

Lost in thought, she was unlocking the door to Ivy's building without noticing the man getting out of a parked car and rushing across the street toward her until he was practically right behind her. She turned quickly, alarmed, and found herself facing a well-dressed African-American in his late forties. "Excuse me," he said. "Ms. Alena Porter?"

"Do I know you?" Though his suit was new and well tailored, something about the man made Alena doubt he was a lawyer or banker—there was something too rough about him despite his clothes.

"You and me, we have a mutual friend," Darryl Loomis replied. "A man who's just dying to see you."

·77·

"WHAT'S SO urgent?" Leah asked, eyeing her brother warily. It was just after nine a.m., and given that Jeremy rarely showed up to work before ten, his mere presence in her office was cause for concern. Then there was how terrible he looked: bloodshot eyes, haggard face, like he'd come straight from a bar. Once they'd gotten through this mess, perhaps the next thing would be an intervention.

"The reporter, Snow," Jeremy said. "She's got the story on the Aurora, all of it."

Leah blanched. She tried to stem panic by telling herself that she couldn't take her brother's word for such things. "What makes you say that?"

"She's been talking to people from my personal life, asking them about it. She knows about the money, knows about Fowler's role and why he was killed."

"If she really had the whole story you wouldn't be hearing rumors about it; you'd be seeing it on the front page of the paper."

Jeremy was looking carefully at his sister, a queasy expression on his face. "What really happened to Jack Pellettieri?" he asked after a moment.

Leah was puzzled by the question. "What're you talking about?"

"The reporter's telling people his body washed up in New Jersey. Did you have Darryl kill him?"

"Of course not," Leah said, relaxing a little at this. "That proves it; she's running a bluff is all. She's trying to get us to panic by throwing a bunch of shit at the wall."

Jeremy didn't look reassured. "You promise that Darryl didn't take out Pellettieri?"

Leah found herself hesitating. She wasn't entirely sure whether Darryl might have made an executive decision to kill Pellettieri and not told her. "As far as I know, Pellettieri is quite alive, on a beach in the Caribbean somewhere. What is the reporter claiming?"

"That Jack's body washed up, and that the police are looking at us for it. That Darryl's guys did it, on our orders."

Leah was getting a bad feeling about this. Would the reporter really just make up a phantom dead body? She needed to confront Darryl, see if there was something she didn't know. And if Pellettieri's body really had just washed up in New Jersey, and the cops were looking at them? It was ridiculous, of course: she hadn't arranged for Pellettieri's murder; she hadn't even known about it. Could her family be brought down by it regardless? It was an irony too terrible to contemplate.

"I'll talk to Darryl," Leah said.

"Call him now."

"Darryl isn't much of one for phones," Leah said dryly.

"This reporter's going to run a story saying we had Fowler and Pellettieri killed. It's going to ruin us, even if we don't end up getting arrested."

"Just because she's sniffing around on this doesn't mean she has anything," Candace replied. She was trying to figure out whether there was any way the reporter could have enough to actually publish a story. She didn't see how she could, but then, she didn't know what the reporter knew. The story on the Aurora had caught them off guard, after all. "And besides, Dad has pretty much shut her down over there anyway—unless she can back up every single word there's no way they're running any story."

"I think we need to tell Dad," Jeremy said.

"Tell Dad what?"

"All of it."

Leah never would have thought she'd hear Jeremy suggest taking a problem to their father, let alone the particular set of problems they were facing now. "Are you crazy?" she replied. "First of all, he'll kill us. And what is it you think he can do that we can't do ourselves?"

"He's been at this a lot longer than we have. He knows all the tricks."

"I can't believe you're serious about bringing Dad into this. You made me promise I wouldn't tell him about any of it."

"'Cause I thought we could handle it. If I'd known then . . ."

Leah's eyes narrowed, her whole face going tight. "What's that supposed to mean?"

"Just that this never seems to end. People get killed, and it just gets worse."

"Don't you dare blame me for the mess we're in," Leah said angrily.

Jeremy did blame her. He knew it was his mistakes that had started it, but it was her decisions that had escalated it to where it was now. But he knew better than to say that.

"We need to find out exactly what it is the reporter knows," Leah continued. "Who's she been talking to?"

Jeremy didn't want to bring Alena into this, didn't want his sister dragging her in for some kind of interrogation. "I told you," he said. "It's people I know socially. I have no idea why the reporter would think they'd know anything."

Knowing her brother, Leah was sure a woman was involved. "Does she?"

Jeremy pretended not to understand. "Does who?"

"Whoever this woman is that Snow's talking to. Does she know anything about the Aurora?"

"You don't have to worry about that," Jeremy said. "The question is, does the reporter have enough to run a story, and if she does, how can we stop it?"

"I'll talk to Darryl today," Leah said. "You just lie low."

DARRYL ADMITTED it at once. "I went there to get him to run, like we'd talked about," he said, his eyes meeting Leah's via his Lincoln's rearview mirror. "He wasn't interested. We couldn't trust him, so I did what had to be done."

This wasn't close to good enough. "And you never told me?"

"You said you weren't going to ask about Jack because you didn't want to know," Darryl countered.

Leah wasn't buying it. "I meant ask where he was, not whether you'd decided to kill him, for Christ's sake. You can't do something like that without our okay. Who else are they going to look at for killing Pellettieri than us?"

Darryl didn't look particularly defensive. "Why would they look at you?" he said. "You never even met Jack Pellettieri."

"You know that's not the point."

"Sure it is. You didn't know Pellettieri was dead, let alone tell anyone to smoke him."

Leah wasn't persuaded her lack of knowledge really meant she was out of harm's way. "Why would the police be keeping his death a secret? Can they do that?"

"Not for long," Darryl said. "And not for a damn good reason. The strangest thing is that someone would leak it while the lid was on."

"Doesn't that suggest the police are up to something? Planting a trap?"

Darryl shrugged. "I can find out what the reporter's got," he said.

"How would you do that?"

"It may take some pressure."

Leah didn't like the sound of that. "What are you suggesting exactly?"

"Accidents do happen," Darryl said. "Even to reporters."

Leah shook her head sharply. Jeremy was right: violence had only made things worse for them, and going after a reporter who was known to be working a big story about their family was not something they could get away with. "No way," she said. "All that does is get us deeper into shit. You stay away from the reporter. Are we clear?"

Darryl looked at her, his gaze blank. "Yes, ma'am," he said.

SIMON ROTH made no attempt to hide his displeasure at his son's abrupt appearance in his office. "Can't it wait?" he demanded, then stopped short when he saw the look in Jeremy's eyes.

"I'm in big trouble, Dad," Jeremy said.

·78·

JUDGE LASKY was holding the hearing under seal, closing the courtroom. Duncan would've preferred to be in open court, so that no matter what happened there would be a public record out there, but he'd already used up too much of the judge's patience to put up a fight about it.

Duncan arrived a few minutes before ten. The judge's deputy was chatting with the court reporter; two court officers stood near the door through which they would bring Rafael up from the holding cell. Duncan hadn't made any attempt to see Rafael; he assumed the guards wouldn't let him. If they did, he didn't know what Rafael's reaction would be: his former client had told Duncan in no uncertain terms to get lost, and he was sure Rafael had no idea what was going on. Duncan figured he'd have plenty of time to explain if he pulled this off, and if he failed, then it wouldn't really matter.

He walked through the empty rows of seats, then past Steven Blake and Leah Roth. Blake nodded to Duncan, one old pro to another, while Leah ignored him completely. Duncan sat down in the front row, directly behind the defense table.

This was the worst time of all, the couple of minutes where nothing was happening, just before the battle was joined. Duncan had been thrown out of sleep at six a.m. sharp, well before his alarm was to go off, instantly completely awake. His nerves were thrumming, his hands clammy. He took a bottle of water out of his bag and had a large sip, though the dryness in the back of his throat returned seconds later.

Robert Walker came in, sat down at the defense table in front of Duncan without acknowledging his presence. Duncan smiled at the thought that he'd managed to have every possible side in the case—judge, defense, prosecution, and witness—all pissed at him at once. It was an accomplishment of sorts. Here he was, an unemployed, clientless lawyer, with nobody in his corner. There was no safety net, no next time if he failed.

Finally Judge Lasky entered from the back of the courtroom, everybody obediently standing as he made his way to the bench. The judge peered out at each of them in turn, like he was silently taking attendance. "Let's bring the defendant in," Lasky said to the court officers, and a few moments later Rafael was brought to the defense table.

To Duncan's surprise, the judge then turned not to him, but to Steven Blake. "Mr. Blake, I assume you would like to be heard on your motion before we begin?"

Blake readily agreed, making his way into the well of the courtroom, buttoning his suit jacket as he did so. Duncan also stood, not understanding what was going on. "Your Honor," he said, "I'm not aware of any motion filed by Mr. Blake."

"Did you not serve a copy of your motion on Mr. Riley?" Lasky asked Blake.

"I didn't know that Mr. Riley had opened his own law practice, Your Honor," Blake said. "We served the defense counsel of record."

"Mr. Blake certainly knows how to find me, Your Honor," Duncan replied. "We worked closely together for a number of years, and he's contacted me at home on numerous occasions."

"Seeing as this morning is all about indulging you, Mr. Riley, I'm inclined to indulge Mr. Blake, though he certainly should have served you with papers. I don't want to postpone this hearing, so, Mr. Blake, why don't you summarize your argument?"

"Certainly, Your Honor. We think there are several reasons to quash the subpoena of Leah Roth. As a procedural matter, we think it was entirely inappropriate for Mr. Riley to file a subpoena when he is not representing any party in the case and he is not maintaining an actual legal practice. More substantively, Ms. Roth simply has no relevant information to impart regarding this case. And if we assume for the sake of argument that she did have relevant information, the only way that Mr. Riley would know about it is through privileged communications, and his questioning her based on what he learned in those conversations would violate not only the attorney-client privilege but also my firm's work-product privilege. Lastly, we believe that Mr. Riley has served this subpoena out of, frankly, personal animus, and that the court should not allow him to use the judicial process to work out his own private agenda."

Duncan was alarmed to see that the judge was paying close attention to Blake's argument. "So in your view," the judge said, "Mr. Riley could be breaking privilege simply by asking a question where he was drawing on his knowledge of privileged matters?"

"Absolutely," Blake said. "If he knows the information through privileged communications, it hardly matters whether he is relaying it himself or doing it through the questioning of a witness, especially when the witness in question is a former client. Clients have the right to expect that their lawyers won't turn around and use their confidences against them."

"But the attorney-client privilege is not absolute," Lasky said. "And it does not extend to future criminal conduct, which I believe is what Mr. Riley is alleging, at least in part. I couldn't help but notice, Mr. Blake, that your motion was silent regarding your firm's positional conflict in this matter. It seemed a curious omission."

Blake appeared confused by the question, though Duncan wasn't buying it. "In what sense, Your Honor?" Blake said.

"Your argument then suggested the Roths had some interest in the outcome of this case. The conflict was because the victim of the shooting was in effect an employee of Roth Properties, and that your firm was therefore constrained from investigating the recent allegations in the press that Fowler was involved in improper evictions at Riis as part of Mr. Nazario's defense. That does at least lend some credence to Mr. Riley's claim that there is a connection between Roth Properties and this case."

Duncan was trying to catch up. This was the first he knew about how Blake had gotten the firm out of representing Nazario. "Here's the way I see it," Lasky continued. "I don't know right now whether this proceeding is going to prove a waste of time. We will all know soon enough. Once that has become clear, I will take appropriate action. If it turns out that Ms. Roth's time has been wasted here today, well, I'm sorry for that, but I can assure her that Mr. Riley will face steep consequences for having wasted it.

"That still leaves privilege issues. You, Mr. Blake, will be free to object to questions that you think implicate attorney-client privilege, and to counsel your client, within limits, if you think privilege is implicated by her answer or potential answers. If I ever contemplate unsealing the transcript of today's proceedings, I will first allow you to note any privileged material that you would like redacted. If I find that this hearing has been meritless, I will strike the proceeding from the record in its entirety and no transcript will exist. Fair enough, Mr. Blake?"

Blake looked unhappy but resigned. "I appreciate Your Honor's efforts to protect my client's interests, but the easiest way to do so is simply to quash this subpoena. There're also the procedural issues—particularly that Mr. Riley does not actually represent a party in this case."

"Mr. Riley appeared before me as an officer of the court alleging a fraud. I think he is entitled, and I am obligated, to find out whether there is merit to that claim. If there's not, I assure you it will be dealt with. Mr. Riley, call your witness."

LEAH ROTH was dressed in a black suit, the jacket buttoned, a steel gray shirt underneath. Her hair was pulled back, adding to the austerity of her appearance. Her thin face appeared almost gaunt, her paleness turned to pallor. She looked her wealth, Duncan thought, but she did not look well.

After she'd been sworn in, Duncan stood and made his way to the podium. He started with some basic background questions, necessary to establish who she was, where she worked, and what she did there, as well as the roles in the company occupied by her brother and father. Leah answered quickly and crisply, doing a fairly convincing show of boredom.

"Roth Properties was the developer of a building project called the Aurora Tower, correct?" Duncan asked.

"That's right."

"Can you describe the Aurora Tower?"

"It's a thirty-six-story high-end condominium development."

"Have there been problems during its construction?"

Leah shifted in her seat. "There was an accident, yes, if that's what you're referring to. Three workers were killed, and others injured, due to a partial collapse."

"Were you the Roth Properties executive supervising the Aurora's construction?"

"My brother was in charge of the project, though as the developer we do not supervise the actual construction. That's the general contractor's job."

"Do you have an understanding as to what caused the accident?"

"I'm not an engineer."

"Understood. But please answer the question."

Leah's mouth tightened slightly. "My understanding is that the subcontractor who was responsible for pouring the concrete did not undertake standard safety measures. As a result the concrete wasn't properly supported, allowing for the collapse."

"Who was that subcontractor?"

"Pellettieri Concrete."

"Who was in charge of the company?"

"Jack Pellettieri," Leah said, spitting out the name.

"Mr. Pellettieri has disappeared, correct?"

"Apparently so," Leah said, shifting in her seat. Duncan guessed she was braced for him to bring up Pellettieri's death. He wasn't going to do so, however: he couldn't prove that Pellettieri was in fact dead, and raising it without proof risked making him look crazy. There was enough danger of that as it was.

"Is it your understanding that Mr. Pellettieri was skimming money from the Aurora construction?"

"Unfortunately, yes."

"How was he able to do so?"

"He did a few things. Billing for work that wasn't performed, no-show jobs."

"In essence, he was stealing money from your company, correct?"

"Yes."

"Was anyone else involved in this skimming?"

Leah hesitated for a moment, Duncan thinking she was worried about a trap. "I don't know," she said. Okay, Duncan thought, so you are going to lie under oath. He'd assumed she would, but hadn't been sure. Now the question was whether he'd be able to expose it.

"At the time of his disappearance, Mr. Pellettieri was under investigation by a grand jury, correct?"

Leah glanced over at Blake, apparently expecting an objection. "I have heard rumors to that effect," she said. "But I obviously don't know whether or not they are true."

"Your Honor," Blake protested, "what does this line of questioning about the Aurora possibly have to do with the murder of Sean Fowler?"

"It's a fair question, Mr. Riley," Judge Lasky said, peering down at Duncan. "Tie it together or move on, counsel."

"Certainly," Duncan said to the judge, before turning back to Leah. "Do you know who Sean Fowler, the victim in this case, was?"

"I never met him, but I know he did security work for our company."

"When do you first recall hearing of Sean Fowler?"

"I believe it was the day after he was killed. It happened on our site, and he was working for us at the time, so obviously we heard about it, were concerned."

"Your brother had never mentioned Mr. Fowler to you?"

Leah hesitated slightly, Duncan not sure if it was sincere or a pose. "I don't believe so," she said.

"Were you aware that Mr. Fowler worked at the Aurora?"

"It doesn't surprise me. His employer does virtually all of our security work."

"Mr. Fowler was involved in Mr. Pellettieri's skimming from the Aurora, correct?"

For the first time Duncan saw a little fear in Leah. "I don't know the details of Mr. Pellettieri's skimming," she said after a moment. "As I said, I believe it was being investigated at the time of his disappearance, but I don't know what conclusions were reached. You'd have to ask the district attorney's office."

"You are aware, are you not, that your brother knew about Mr. Pellettieri's embezzling?"

"I don't know anything of the kind," Leah said coldly.

"As you sit here today, Ms. Roth, you know that your brother was actually involved in the skimming, correct?"

Leah's anger appeared genuine enough. "That's an outrageous accusation."

"Are you denying it?"

"I am absolutely denying it," Leah said. Duncan thought she probably seemed convincing to someone who didn't know she was lying.

"Did there come a time when you learned that your brother was being blackmailed?"

"No."

Duncan tilted his head skeptically. "It's your sworn testimony that you had no knowledge your brother was being blackmailed?"

Leah look was filled with contempt. "I understood I was under oath the first time I answered the question."

"Isn't it true, Ms. Roth, that Sean Fowler was killed because he was blackmailing your brother?"

"That's an absurd question."

"Please answer it, rather than giving your opinion on its merits."

"I thought I had answered it by calling it absurd. No, it's not true."

Duncan wasn't going to get anywhere by pressing the point. She'd made her denials, and that was what he was going to have to work with. It was time to shift tacks. "How did you first hear of Rafael Nazario?" he asked.

"I guess when I read in the paper about his getting arrested for murdering Mr. Fowler."

"Didn't you and I have a conversation about Rafael Nazario prior to the murder?"

Leah's confusion looked real enough, Duncan thought. "Why would we have talked of Mr. Nazario?"

"I was handling his eviction case. You and I discussed it briefly the first time we spoke, and then at length the second time we spoke."

Blake stood. "Your Honor, clearly the conversations in question were privileged."

"I'm not disclosing anything relating to my representation of Ms. Roth or her company," Duncan protested. "Just that she and I discussed, in broad strokes, my representation of Mr. Nazario."

"I'll allow it," Judge Lasky said.

"I vaguely recall your mentioning something about a pro bono case," Leah said. "All I remember about it was that you seemed to feel it was too small-time for you."

All right, Duncan thought, left myself open for that one. He smiled slightly at Leah, acknowledging the blow. "Once Mr. Nazario had been accused of this crime, my then firm sought permission from you as to whether or not we could keep his case, correct?"

"That clearly gets into work product," Blake objected.

"I'm going to allow it, at least in general terms," Lasky said. "Especially in light of the conflict issue that arose, I think any work-product privilege has been vitiated."

"Yes, I had a conversation with Mr. Blake about it."

"And you originally gave Mr. Blake permission for his firm to take the case?"

"Yes, I did."

"You instructed my firm to try to reach a quick plea bargain for Mr. Nazario, correct?"

Leah glanced over at Blake. "My only concern was that I didn't want a lot of extraneous bad publicity to hobble the work we were doing at Jacob Riis. But I certainly didn't offer any instruction as to legal strategy. Nor did I suggest that the firm do anything that wasn't in your client's best interest."

"Did there come a time when you told Mr. Blake that you no longer wanted his firm to represent Mr. Nazario?"

Leah was growing increasingly uncomfortable, the pauses longer between each answer. "Yes," she finally said.

"Why?"

"As Mr. Blake alluded to earlier, there were allegations regarding the security staff who were working at Jacob Riis relating to evictions that were taking place. Mr. Blake expressed concern about whether his firm could investigate that aspect of the case without the risk of creating a conflict with our company. If evidence emerged showing that Mr. Nazario's eviction had been set up by security guards in our employ, he could potentially have had a lawsuit against us, for example."

Bulllshit, of course, but not bullshit Duncan could disprove. "Do you have an understanding of the motive that has been alleged for why Mr. Nazario would want to kill Mr. Fowler?"

"I understand that it concerns the eviction."

"Specifically, that Mr. Fowler had claimed to catch Mr. Nazario smoking marijuana, which led to the Nazario family facing eviction?"

"I don't recall the details, but that sounds right."

Duncan entered Candace Snow's article about the Riis evictions into evidence, then presented a copy to Leah. "Did you read this article when it was published?"

"Yes," Leah said. Duncan thought it was the first truthful answer she'd given in some time.

"Were the private security guards at Jacob Riis planting drugs on people?"

"Not to my knowledge."

"The fewer existing residents your company had to move back into the project, the more room there'd be for market-rate tenants, true?"

"It's a good deal more complicated than that," Leah said, shifting slightly in her seat. While Duncan knew this issue wasn't directly relevant to Fowler's murder, it was one where Leah had little plausible deniability.

"Did your company, Roth Properties, know that security guards were looking to cause people to be evicted from Jacob Riis?"

"I certainly did not. I can't speak for my entire company. And I have no personal knowledge that our security guards did anything inappropriate. Just because something is printed in the newspaper doesn't make it true."

"After this article appeared, did you investigate the allegations in it?"

"I did not, no."

"Did your company?"

"Not that I know of."

"You didn't think it was worth checking out?"

"We've had previous dealings with this particular reporter," Leah said. "We know her to be unreliable and inaccurate."

"The newspaper article quotes Riis residents accusing Mr. Fowler of being one of the security guards who planted drugs on people in order to secure their evictions?"

"I think that's right."

"Would you like a chance to review the article?"

Leah glanced over at the judge before looking back at Duncan. "There are accusations regarding Mr. Fowler, yes," she said with a slight shrug.

"The city announced it was investigating the evictions in which the security guards were involved, correct?"

"I believe they did, though there haven't been any charges or anything out of it."

"In fact the city has suspended the pending evictions where the security guards had a role?"

"While they were looking into it, yes. I don't think any final decision has been made."

"Have you ever met Chris Driscoll?"

"Not that I recall."

Duncan wondered if that could be true. He supposed it was possible: there was no reason to think Leah had actually sat down with Driscoll and hatched out a plan. "You do know that Chris Driscoll worked at the Aurora as a security guard, right?"

"Yes."

"You're aware he is the state's sole witness against Mr. Nazario?"

"I'm aware he saw the shooting," Leah said. "I don't know whether your characterization is correct."

"Did you ever discuss Sean Fowler with Mr. Driscoll?"

"Like I said, to the best of my knowledge I've never had a conversation with Mr. Driscoll about anything."

"But you do know, as you sit here today, that Chris Driscoll is not telling the truth when he claims to have seen Rafael Nazario shoot Sean Fowler?"

"I do not," Leah said without hesitation. It wasn't obvious by looking at her that she was lying, and Duncan assumed the judge didn't think he was getting anywhere.

"Do you know a man named Darryl Loomis?"

"He's the head of a private security company that does a lot of work for us. Sean Fowler was one of his employees."

"Did you ever discuss my representation of Mr. Nazario with Mr. Loomis?"

"Yes. Your firm asked whether we objected to your representing Mr. Nazario on the murder charges and I in turn raised the issue with Mr. Loomis, given that Mr. Fowler was his employee."

"You and Darryl Loomis ever discuss the fact that Sean Fowler was blackmailing your brother?"

Leah leaned her head back, as if repulsed by the question. "Of course not."

"Isn't it true that you and Mr. Loomis came up with a plan to kill Mr. Fowler and frame Mr. Nazario for the crime?"

"Absolutely not," Leah said immediately, maintaining eye contact with Duncan.

"Are you aware that Darryl Loomis arranged to have Sean Fowler killed?"

"No. I don't believe that he did."

Blake stood. "Your Honor, what is the point of all this? The witness has repeatedly and emphatically denied every accusation that she has any knowledge relevant to the criminal case here. Mr. Riley has not presented any documentary evidence that contradicts her denials."

Judge Lasky nodded, turning to Duncan. "I must agree, Mr. Riley. If your only goal here is to ask accusatory questions while getting blanket denials in response, then your mission is accomplished and the court's patience is at an end. Do you have any evidence to present to this witness that will actually establish that she has taken part in a fraud upon this court?"

"I believe I have already laid the groundwork for establishing that, Your Honor," Duncan said. "Ms. Roth's answers have been untruthful in the extreme."

"She has denied your accusations in no uncertain terms," Lasky replied. "Unless you have some evidence that establishes she is not being truthful, Ms. Roth is excused."

"I do have evidence, Your Honor," Duncan said. "I have one more witness to call."

·79·

THERE WAS nothing Candace hated more than sitting on big news. She'd promised to keep quiet about the Nazario hearing until Duncan called her after it was over. Candace was braced for a dull day of waiting around, but that was before she received an e-mail from Tommy Nelson. Candace's surprise grew as she read it: Nelson said he had something to show her. He asked her to meet him in Tompkins Square Park in one hour, and instructed her not to call him.

This felt wrong. Candace remembered what Nelson had said to her the last time they'd spoken, how she should believe her own alarm bells. After a moment she picked up her office phone and called ADA Sullivan. "I think someone's about to try to kill me," she said.

A HALF hour later she found herself in a conference room off the newsroom with Sullivan and a Detective Gomez. Gomez had given her a small wireless transmitter, instructed her on attaching it to the clasp of her bra.

"We're going to have a dozen plainclothes all over the park," Sullivan said. "We'll have sharpshooters on a roof. We'll be able to hear every word, will come in once we've heard enough or if you seem to be in any danger. If you want us to break it up just say, 'Enough is enough.'"

"What do you think their play is here?" Candace asked.

Sullivan shrugged. "I assume they really want to talk to you, find out what you know. They could just try to do that through subterfuge, or they could try something worse than that. As long as you're in a public place with us all over it, you should be okay."

"Should be?" Candace said. She was scared, and didn't mind if Sullivan knew it.

"If they just wanted to shoot you, there's no reason to set up a meeting, but obviously this isn't risk-free. You don't really need me to tell you that."

CANDACE TOOK the N train down to the East Village, then walked down Saint Marks Place to the park. While even Saint Marks wasn't immune from gentrification, the mohawked street kids and punk rock T-shirt stores were still the same as when Candace was a teenager, though now they were interspersed with Japanese restaurants and tourists.

Tompkins Square bore virtually no resemblance to the place Candace remembered from twenty years ago. Back in the late eighties the park had been full of a volatile mix of anarchists and hard-core addicts, largely surrounded by dilapidated squats. Now the park was surrounded by condos, and the people gathered in it looked little different from those in Central Park.

Candace walked over to the benches near the chess tables. All of her senses were on high alert, and fear had knotted her stomach into a tangled ball. Candace noticed every passing face, the wind through the trees, the angry sounds of city traffic. She'd been sitting there for about five minutes, scanning the crowd, when a well-dressed middle-aged black man came and sat down beside her. Candace glanced over at the man, who looked back, smiling.

"Excuse me," he said. "Are you Candace Snow?"

Candace gave the man a long look. She couldn't swear to it, but she was pretty sure he was Darryl Loomis. They'd never met, but Candace had looked up a photo of him while writing the eviction story. If she was right, Candace was surprised Darryl would show up himself—it seemed like an unnecessary risk. "Do I know you?" she asked.

"I'm a friend of Tommy's. He sent me to come get you."

"Come get me?" she said, stalling. The plan was for whatever was to happen to take place in the park. It was risky enough to be here, even with police surveillance in place and a mic under her shirt; it was something else entirely to leave with this man.

"To take you to Tommy, and what he's got to show you."

"Tommy didn't say anything about any friend," Candace said, still thinking it through. It would be dangerous to go, obviously. But Candace thought it didn't make sense for Darryl to go about it this way if all he wanted was to kill her.

"He's worried that you're still being followed," Darryl said. "The last time he talked to you, he ended up with his ankle broke. Besides, what he has to show you, it's not portable. You got to go to the source."

"Where's the source?"

"The building he used to work at, down in SoHo."

This came as a surprise to Candace. "The Aurora?" she asked.

"That's it, yeah."

Candace wanted to get Darryl talking here at the park, but she wasn't sure how. "This seems awfully cloak-and-dagger," she said. "I mean, no offense, but I don't have any idea who you are."

"The name's Reggie Watson," Darryl said, putting out his hand. Candace looked at it for a moment, then shook.

"Can I call Tommy and find out what the deal is?"

Darryl shook his head. "No phones. Whoever these people are you're looking into, they've got Tommy more spooked than I've ever seen him."

"So what's the idea, exactly?"

"My car's parked over on C. We drive a little, make sure nobody's following; then I take you to the Aurora, Tommy shows you what he's got to show you."

"Which is?"

Darryl shrugged. "Just the messenger."

Candace made no attempt to hide her discomfort. Darryl smiled at her. It was clear he wasn't going to say anything while they were here. If she was going to get him to incriminate himself, she was going to have to go along with whatever he was up to. After a moment Candace stood. "All right," she said. "Let's go."

·80·

"WHO THE hell is Alena Porter?" Blake whispered urgently to Leah.

"I have no idea," Leah replied. She turned and watched as a beautiful woman she'd never seen before made her way through the courtroom to the witness stand.

Blake stood. "Your Honor, I object to the calling of this witness. My client tells me that she has never met Ms. Porter. If the purpose of this hearing is to establish whether there has been a fraud upon the court perpetuated by my client, then surely the witnesses should be limited to people who have direct knowledge of my client's actions."

"This witness has very direct knowledge, Your Honor," Duncan replied. "As will quickly become clear."

"I'll see what the witness has to say," Judge Lasky said. "But, Mr. Riley, let's not have any song and dance here, understood?"

Leah studied this woman Alena. She looked to be in her late twenties, dressed well, surprisingly composed under the circumstances. Then again, with her looks she was probably used to being the center of attention, Leah thought. Then it came to her: this woman must know her brother. Was she the woman who had told her brother about the reporter? If so, what was she doing here in court?

Once Alena was sworn in on the witness stand, Duncan led her through just a few background questions before getting to the point. "Ms. Porter, do you know Jeremy Roth?"

"Yes, I do."

"How do you know him?"

"We dated."

"Did you and Jeremy Roth ever discuss the Aurora Tower?"

"Yes."

"On how many occasions did you discuss it?"

"Three that I can think of."

"Did you discuss the accident at the Aurora?"

"Some."

But Duncan wasn't quite ready to get into the heart of Alena's testimony. "Did Jeremy Roth ever say anything regarding Pellettieri Concrete's work at the Aurora?"

"Objection," Blake said quickly. "Hearsay, Your Honor."

"It's a party admission," Duncan said to the judge, invoking one of the exceptions to the rule against hearsay testimony.

"Jeremy Roth isn't a party to this matter," Blake rejoined. "So nothing he said could be a party admission."

"Obviously the nature of the present hearing complicates who the parties are," Duncan said. He'd been expecting Blake to raise hearsay issues, knew that he was on thin ice in that regard, but hoped the unusual circumstances would get him some leeway. "If the court isn't willing to treat Mr. Roth's statements as party admissions, they are statements in furtherance of a conspiracy and against penal interest, and therefore exceptions to hearsay."

Lasky looked at Duncan for a long moment before turning back to Blake. "The hearsay issues here are complicated, especially given the unusual procedural posture of this hearing. Since there's no jury, and I'm still unclear as to the nature of the evidence Mr. Riley intends to introduce, I'm inclined not to rule on the hearsay issues until I know where this is going. You'll have a standing objection, Mr. Blake. Mr. Riley, you shouldn't assume that any arguably hearsay evidence you present will ultimately be considered by me. I may well strike all of it. Clear?"

Duncan nodded, figuring this was as good as he could hope for. He turned back to Alena. "The question, Ms. Porter, was whether Jeremy Roth ever told you anything regarding Pellettieri Concrete and the Aurora?"

"He told me he knew they were skimming money."

"If he knew about that, why didn't he put a stop to it?"

"Most of the money was going to Jeremy. He was basically pocketing company money out of the project through the concrete company."

Duncan paused, wanting to let this sink in to the judge. Blake stood once again. "Your Honor, even if these accusations were true, of what possible relevance are they to the murder case before this court?"

"That will be clear quite soon, Your Honor," Duncan said quickly. Judge Lasky gestured for him to continue.

"Did you ever have a conversation with Jeremy Roth regarding the accident at the Aurora?"

"Yeah. He felt guilty about it, because he knew how the concrete guys were cutting corners."

"What, if anything else, did he tell you about the accident?"

"He told me he was being blackmailed because of it."

"Did he say anything regarding who was blackmailing him?"

Alena glanced over at Leah before answering. For a moment the two women just stared at each other, as though they were the only people in the room. Then Alena turned back to Duncan, her composure showing a crack for the first time since she'd taken the stand. "It was Sean Fowler," she said.

"When did Jeremy Roth tell you that Sean Fowler had been blackmailing him?"

"Two days ago."

Leah couldn't believe what she was hearing. If this woman was telling the truth, Jeremy had not only told her his darkest secrets, but had done so on the eve of this hearing. Did he want to get caught? She knew her brother was self-destructive, but this was something else entirely.

"Did you and Jeremy Roth ever discuss the murder of Sean Fowler?"

Blake again stood. "Your Honor, I must object. This is rank hearsay. If Mr. Riley wanted Jeremy Roth's testimony, he could've called him as a witness. If Ms. Porter has no direct knowledge, she shouldn't be testifying."

"As I said, Mr. Blake, I'm going to reserve ruling until I know where this is going," Judge Lasky said. "You may proceed, Mr. Riley."

Duncan nodded, turning back to Alena, who had remained impassive throughout the back-and-forth. "You can answer, Ms. Porter."

"We did discuss the murder, yes."

"Did Jeremy Roth explain to you how Sean Fowler came to be in a position to blackmail him?"

"He told me Fowler was involved with the skimming at the Aurora, as a go-between, I guess."

"Did Mr. Roth tell you anything else about his interaction with Sean Fowler?"

"Jeremy told me that he paid Fowler off, but that he came back for more. That's why he was killed."

"What if anything else did Jeremy Roth tell you about Fowler's death?"

"He said he didn't have anything directly to do with it. That his sister made the arrangements, working with these security guards they used."

Blake had again stood. "This has become utterly outrageous, Your Honor. It's all unsupported. Leah Roth tells me she's never even heard of this woman who is making these outlandish accusations. I have no idea whether Jeremy Roth has actually ever met her."

"I have no objection if Mr. Blake would like an opportunity right now to probe the basis for Ms. Porter's testimony," Duncan said calmly.

Blake glanced over at Duncan, his suspicion of the offer doing battle with his need to derail Alena's testimony.

"I would like to question this witness, yes," Blake said after a moment. "But I'd also like at least a few minutes to consult with my client first."

"All right, then," Judge Lasky said. "We'll take a ten-minute recess to catch our breath, finish with this witness, then see where we are."

81

JEREMY WAS unable to sit still. He was pacing around his office, feeling trapped as he waited for word from his sister about what was happening in court. Jeremy had wanted to go down and see for himself, but Blake had strictly forbidden it. So he'd come to work, despite knowing he wasn't going to even attempt to be productive.

His sister hadn't seemed especially worried about the court proceeding, or at least she'd put on a brave front. Leah continued to insist that nobody had any actual evidence linking the family to any murders, and that all she had to do was deny the lawyer's accusations. Even if true, that still left the prospect of the reporter running a story.

All of this because he'd taken some of his own money. That was all he'd done, really, taken a loan from his future self. Why should anyone even care? Yet out of that, five people had died.

And now his father was in the mix too, although he was being characteristically tight-lipped about what he was doing. In fact, they hadn't spoken at all since Jeremy had come clean to him. Jeremy had expected it to be an ugly conversation, but Simon's response had been even worse than he'd been braced for. He honestly wasn't sure if his father would ever speak to him again, but he did know that Simon was trying to prevent the story from coming out.

Jeremy's office phone rang. He checked the caller ID, saw that it was his sister, and grabbed it. "Is the court thing over?"

"What does Alena Porter know?" Leah said.

Jeremy's mind reeled as he tried to imagine why Leah was asking him that. "Alena? Is she there?"

"What does she fucking know, Jeremy?"

He heard a tinny echo in her voice. "Am I on speaker?" he asked, stalling.

"Hello, Jeremy," Blake said. "It's important that this call be privileged."

"Having a lawyer on the phone with you is the sort of thing you're supposed to tell a person," Jeremy said to his sister.

"Now's not the time for your shit, Jeremy," Leah said. "Alena Porter."

"What's happening there?" Jeremy replied. "What does Alena have to do with anything?"

"We don't have much time," Blake said. "Do you know this woman?"

"Fuck. Fine. Yes. So?"

"She's testifying against us," Leah said. "She's claiming you basically admitted everything to her."

Jeremy couldn't understand how that was possible. Alena was the one who'd warned him about the reporter. They'd left things in a good place two nights ago, even if not completely resolved. Alena had said she wasn't ready to move back to the apartment, had refused to go there with Jeremy the night they'd met for a drink, saying she needed some time to process everything. Jeremy hadn't pressed it, especially in light of the conversation they'd just had, but he'd kissed her good-bye, a real kiss, with clearly implied promises of things to come. She'd make him work a little more, but he was sure that was all it was, just wanting him to pay some more dues before she came back to him. And now she was somehow in court, testifying against him? Was she telling them all the things he'd told her the other night? Could she be doing that?

"This Alena Porter is claiming to have dated you," Blake said. "She's testified that you told her that you were taking money out of the Aurora, using Fowler as a middleman, and that he blackmailed you about it after the accident. She alleges that your sister then engineered Fowler's death. Did you actually tell her these things?"

"Jesus Christ," Jeremy muttered. For a long moment it was the only thing anyone said.

"I need to know every speck of dirt you have on this girl," Blake finally said. "Anything I can use to hurt her, I need right now."

82

WHAT DO you do for a living, Ms. Porter?" Steven Blake asked once court had resumed. They'd ended up breaking for fifteen minutes, everyone dispersing to their separate corners to confer. Duncan had left with Alena, spent the time huddled with her on a bench in the hall. He'd exchanged a glance with Rafael, but hadn't talked to him. Duncan hadn't been able to get a read on what his former client was making of all this.

"I'm a model," Alena replied, regarding Blake warily. Duncan had done his best to prep her for being crossed in the little time they'd had, but he knew she wasn't close to fully prepared for it.

"When was the last time you worked?"

Alena's hesitation was noticeable. "I'm not sure," she said after a moment. "It's been almost two months, maybe."

"Where do you live, Ms. Porter?"

"Right now I'm staying at a friend's who's out of town. I'm looking for my own place."

"And where were you living before that?"

Alena again hesitated. "In an apartment on the West Side."

"Were you paying rent on this apartment?"

"Jeremy Roth owned it. He let me stay there."

"You lived in this apartment by yourself?" Blake said, picking up his pace in a way Duncan recognized, trying to establish a rhythm.

"Jeremy stayed there sometimes, but he didn't live there."

"And Mr. Roth let you stay in this apartment for free?"

"Yes."

"And this was while you were romantically involved with Mr. Roth?"

"Yes."

"You are no longer involved with Mr. Roth?"

"That's right."

"Where did you and Mr. Roth meet?"

"At a nightclub."

"A nightclub," Blake repeated, the insinuation clear. "Did someone introduce the two of you?"

"One of the owners did, yes."

"Was the owner a friend of yours?"

"We've known each other for a while," Alena said.

"Is he in the habit of introducing you to rich men?"

Duncan was quickly to his feet, not having to feign his anger. "Objection," he said. "This is badgering, and it's irrelevant."

"I'm simply exploring the motivation that brought this witness to court today, Your Honor."

Lasky gave Blake a long look. "Move forward, Mr. Blake," he said.

"Was there a specific incident that caused you to move out of the free apartment that Mr. Roth had supplied you with?"

"I don't think it was that simple."

"Were you out with Mr. Roth and another man the night before you moved out?"

Duncan didn't know anything about this. There was only so much you could do to prepare a witness who didn't tell you everything. If Alena was about to get embarrassed, she was just going to have to take the hit. "Yes."

"A business acquaintance of Mr. Roth's?"

"I guess."

"And at some point in the evening, Mr. Roth went home, and you stayed out with this other man."

Alena looked at Blake, her sharp cheekbones heightened by her clenched jaw. "I'm not a whore," she said, her voice quiet but with a faint tremor.

Blake feigned confusion. "Excuse me?"

"You heard me," Alena said.

"I don't believe I suggested that you were a prostitute, Ms. Porter," Blake said with a slight smile. "But you are an unemployed model who lives off of rich men who you are introduced to at nightclubs; we have agreed on that, yes?"

"Your Honor," Duncan protested.

Lasky shook his head at Blake. "There's no jury here for you to inflame, Mr. Blake," he said. "Get to the point."

Blake nodded, not looking away from Alena. "You were angry at Mr. Roth for leaving you with this other man, weren't you?"

"Actually, Mattar and I ended up having quite an interesting conversation that night," Alena replied.

Blake resisted any impulse to inquire, following the rule of thumb that a lawyer on cross-examination shouldn't ask questions he didn't already know the answer to. "But you were angry at Mr. Roth for how he treated you that night, were you not?"

"I was disappointed with Jeremy, I suppose, yes."

"You thought that you were in a serious relationship with Mr. Roth, and were surprised to learn that his view was quite different, correct?"

"I wouldn't agree with that at all, actually."

Blake wasn't really trying to get concessions from her anymore, Duncan knew. At this point Blake's focus was on the questions themselves, endeavoring to establish a scenario in the judge's mind regardless of what answers Alena gave. Duncan felt bad for her, but he figured it was soon coming to an end. "Isn't it a fact, Ms. Porter, that you are angry at Mr. Roth, that you are looking to get revenge on him, and that you fabricated your testimony here today in order to do so?"

Alena didn't react to the heightened bluster. "That's not true."

"You are clearly the very definition of a woman scorned. Why should this court put any stock in this story you've put forward?"

Alena looked to Duncan, who was doing his best to keep his poker face as he offered her a slight nod. "Because I have it on tape," she said.

·83·

SIMON ROTH prided himself on his ability to get a good night's sleep. No matter how much pressure he was facing, no matter how many hundreds of millions of dollars were hanging in the balance, Simon had always been able to unplug from it all and sleep through the night. He considered it proof of his strength of will.

But last night he'd barely managed an hour's sleep, and today he was so distracted that he couldn't even escape into his work. He'd come to the office, tried to go about a normal day, but he wasn't hearing anything that anybody said to him.

Never in his life had he had more at stake in a single day. His daughter was being dragged into court by a lawyer who was intent on accusing his family of murder and corruption. A reporter was putting together a story making the same accusations. He was less concerned with the lawyer, who would need hard evidence, while the reporter could use rumor and innuendo. Simon had his counterattacks in place, and now there was nothing for him to do but wait to see if they worked.

He should have seen it coming. If it hadn't been his own children, he would've caught it. But he'd made a point of giving Jeremy and Leah room to operate, however against his nature it went. While Simon was in no hurry to retire, the reality was that he needed to start handing over the reins if he wanted his children to be ready to take over the company. So he'd given Jeremy control over the Aurora, stayed out of the way. Even after the three workers were killed, he hadn't really gotten involved: accidents happened in construction, and Simon had seen no reason to think it had anything to do with his company.

Then Jeremy had come to him yesterday, confessed a story whose sheer awfulness Simon was still unable to fully bring himself to contemplate. Simon was good at dealing with crises: although he had a famous temper, it was mostly under his control, something he utilized strategically. In the face of disaster he could be the calmest person in the room. So he'd set aside his vast disappointment and focused on finding out what exactly their exposure was.

"The reporter's telling people she has the whole story?" Simon had asked his son after hearing his confession. "That she's going to print it?"

Jeremy nodded. "Leah thinks she might be bluffing."

Simon thought that possibility was a luxury they couldn't afford to believe in. "She's a reporter who's out to get us, and now here's your head on a plate. She can do what the media always do when they can't actually prove anything, say that questions have been raised, *suspicions*, that kind of bullshit. And once it sees print, even as a rumor, we're never going to outrun it."

"What about your deal with Sam Friedman?" Jeremy asked. "I thought he was keeping the reporter away from us."

"If she's really got enough to take us down, Sam will sharpen the knife for her personally. Our understanding will last only as long as it benefits both of us."

"So there's nothing you can do?" Jeremy asked, pleading, just like when he'd gotten into trouble as a teenager and it had fallen on Simon to fix it.

Simon looked at him sharply. "There are always things that can be done," he said. "You just stay out of the way."

"Listen, Dad," Jeremy said, "I know I fucked up on this, big-time. I'm sorry, okay?"

Simon studied his son, his gaze more calculating than anything else. "Once this is over," Simon said, his voice calm, "once you're safe, I'll expect your resignation."

Jeremy leaned back in his chair, caught off guard. Simon was stone-faced, outwardly calm except for a small vein throbbing on the side of his forehead. "I said I was sorry—"

"And I don't give a *fuck* about any apology from you," Simon interrupted. "Getting you out of this is the last thing I'm ever going to do for you, understand? You're on your own."

Jeremy had a queasy smile on his face. "I get that you're angry—"

"I'm not angry," Simon said, again interrupting. "I'm past anger, past disappointment. I'm giving up on you, Jeremy. I've given you everything I can imagine a person having, every advantage, and you've turned it all to shit."

Jeremy started to say something, then abruptly stood up and walked out. After he was gone, Simon had sat perfectly still for several minutes. He wondered if this was all his fault somehow. On some level he was sure it was—that he'd let things be too easy for Jeremy, made him spoiled and soft. Although if anyone was to blame for spoiling his son it was his late wife. Simon pushed that thought aside: he wasn't going to blame Rachel for the sins of her son.

Perhaps it was simply that wealth always corrupted. Simon himself had been raised quite comfortably, but with nothing like the money he now possessed: his father, Isaac, had started the business, eventually owning a string of apartment buildings in Harlem and Brooklyn. Isaac Roth had come to this country as a boy, grown up on the Lower East Side with nothing to speak of. He had started Roth Properties with a single four-story building and ended up with over a dozen, accomplishing it all on a City College education and an appetite for risk.

Isaac Roth had been, technically, a slumlord, though Simon considered the label unfair—there'd been no horror stories of rat-infested apartments or holes in the roofs of his father's buildings. But they'd been tenements, their occupants poor and mostly nonwhite. Isaac's business model had been simple: he spent as little as possible on buildings that had fallen into disrepair, often those with numerous citations from the city, fixed them up, and then doubled the rent. Many existing residents hadn't been able to afford the new prices, and a certain amount of displacement had followed.

His father had been criticized for this, of course. But the reality was that he had often taken over buildings that were barely inhabitable and made them into someplace livable. Entire neighborhoods would've fallen apart completely if it weren't for people like his father. You were damned either way: you left the buildings in their squalor and you were exploiting the poor; you fixed things up and charged rent accordingly and you were disrupting their neighborhood.

Not that his father had been a saint. Sometimes, yes, it was necessary to remove tenants who didn't want to leave, and the best way to accomplish that was by making staying too unpleasant. Isaac had employed people—off the books—who specialized in such things. Lack of heat was one way; breaking the front lock of the building to allow vagrants to sleep in the lobby was another. Actual violence was rarely necessary, but Simon had no doubt that his father had done things he wasn't proud of, and which his son had never known about.

While his father had never tried to hide his humble origins, Simon had joined the company after obtaining a Columbia MBA. The education hadn't just taught him different ways of conducting business; it had taught him how to interact with the city's blue bloods in a way his father had never even considered attempting. Simon had understood from his first day that the company needed to go more upscale, that no matter how much money came from renting out tenements in the city's minority neighborhoods it would never buy them real power. His father hadn't concerned himself with such things: the idea of joining New York society had never crossed his mind as a possibility. But things had changed, and New York's WASP elite could no longer afford their snobbery: people like Simon had simply taken over too much of the city from them.

From the start, Simon's focus had been on commercial real estate, betting big on Midtown office space just as many of the large Wall Street players had started migrating uptown. The money had grown exponentially, until the family was one of the top five developers in the city.

Simon had thought of the Riis development as taking the family business full circle. His father had owned tenements; now Simon was playing a central role in transforming the city's housing for the poor. He wanted to turn a profit on it, sure, had authorized Loomis's people to be on the lookout for evictions—a mistake, he now realized, although it'd seemed harmless at the time. But Jacob Riis was also a once-in-a-lifetime opportunity to put his stamp on the city, his Robert Moses moment. Simon thought it would end up being his most enduring legacy, assuming they weren't engulfed by scandal.

Twenty years ago he'd expected Jeremy to one day grow the family's empire, though certainly not as dramatically as he himself had. He'd even imagined his only son going into politics, expanding the family's position that way. Of course, that particular dream had been dashed by the time Jeremy was a teenager, when he'd nearly been thrown out of Horace Mann after getting caught with ecstasy.

Perhaps Simon's big mistake had been not cutting his losses with Jeremy early, doubling down on Leah instead. She'd always been the more talented of the two; there was no doubt about that. Simon had been old-fashioned about it, unable to imagine that his daughter would one day run a major development company. When Leah was born, there were no women in the upper reaches of New York real estate. But that too had changed, and once he'd realized it Simon had welcomed Leah into the business. Still, he hadn't encouraged her to think that way when she was growing up, and she'd never quite forgiven him for initially favoring Jeremy as the heir apparent.

And now here Leah was, maybe even more exposed than Jeremy, even though she'd just been trying to protect her brother. Simon was pissed that she'd tried to handle it on her own, that she'd dug them in deeper rather than gotten them out. Leah had always been protective of her brother; even as a child she'd had that. She'd taken that loyalty too far, but as faults went it was better than most. And no doubt she'd worried that if she'd brought it to him, he would respond by cutting Jeremy off. She hadn't been wrong about that.

It was too late for Simon to undo any of it now; all that was left was trying to keep it from destroying his family completely. So that was what he would do. He would finish it. He would stop the reporter the only way that was left. If suspicions fell on him, he'd just have to ride it out.

So yesterday Simon had picked up his office phone and called Darryl Loomis.

It was the first time Simon had even contemplated having someone killed, and he still couldn't quite believe it. Simon had hired Darryl a couple of years ago, and he'd quickly proved indispensible. Roth Properties had always had private security guards on retainer, used them on-site. They were the people on the front lines, doing battle with the assorted unions that controlled the city's construction industries. Although the situation was much better than it used to be, the unions were still occasionally entangled with organized crime, and even the ones that weren't tended to corruption of one sort or another. Bargaining took you only so far; you needed to be able to back it up. Simon had hired Darryl because he was tougher than the rest, and Darryl's ability to intimidate had quickly paid dividends.

Darryl had certainly gone right up to the line for him before, if not past it—wiretaps, surveillance, snatching up the trash of competitors and scouring it for information. But Simon had never known just how far Darryl would go, had never wanted to know. It appalled him that Leah had authorized Darryl to kill someone, no matter how big a jam Jeremy was in. But he couldn't undo what had already been done.

They were already all in: both his children at risk of going to prison for the rest of their lives. Simon was used to thinking big-picture; it was part of his job description. There were all sorts of cost-benefit trade-offs to any big real estate project, people whose lives were hurt by it in one way or another. Murder was different, of course, but how different was it, really? Construction workers died, as they had at the Aurora, and no one called for the abolition of skyscrapers.

He was a builder; that was his function, and society needed its builders to be capable of ruthlessness. So the only question for Simon was whether they could pull it off. There was nothing for him to do now but wait, and there was nothing Simon hated more than waiting. He felt powerless, but he also knew that he had his best soldiers on it, that both Blake and Loomis would go to the wall, and would keep their mouths shut if things broke badly.

He wasn't letting himself think about what came next. Simon hadn't talked to Leah since Jeremy had told him the truth. He would forgive her eventually, but wasn't quite ready to do so yet. As for Jeremy, Simon had meant what he said: his son was not getting another chance from him.

He'd have someone's blood on his hands, have to see what living with that was like. But what Simon could not live with was the destruction of everything he'd built.

·84·

DUNCAN STUDIED Leah as Alena announced that she'd made a recording. Even from across the room he could see the muscles in her jawline clenching. He wondered if there was any part of her that felt relief, or if she'd been willing to just keep fighting, no matter how many more crimes it meant committing and how many more people it hurt.

Duncan turned his attention to Blake, who was uncharacteristically hesitating. Blake was clearly aware that he'd fallen into a lawyer's worst nightmare on cross. On the one hand, asking further questions was risking more unpleasant surprises, but on the other, there was no way to shove the genie back into the bottle. If Blake sat down now it would just allow Duncan to apply the coup de grâce.

It was the judge who spoke first. "You recorded conversations between yourself and Jeremy Roth?" he asked Alena.

"Just one conversation."

"And you have that tape here with you?"

"I do."

Blake turned to the judge. "Your Honor, obviously there are issues of authenticity, of chain of custody, not to mention the legality of any purported recording."

"New York is a one-party-consent state to recording conversations, Your Honor," Duncan said, his mind flashing briefly to Candace and the digital recorder she kept in her pocket—the very same recorder that Alena had used. "Ms. Porter did not make this recording at the direction of law enforcement, so there's no issue of entrapment or the like."

"I'll hear the recording," Lasky said. "I'm reserving judgment on its admissibility. Let's get all the cards on the table, then go from there."

Alena stayed in the witness box while Duncan produced a CD containing the recording of her conversation with Jeremy Roth. There was some wrangling among the lawyers and the judge over the disc's origins, but Alena didn't pay attention. Those years on the runway had made her an expert at separating her mind from her body. So while she sat poised attentively in the courtroom, her thoughts went back to the events that had brought her here.

She never would have imagined that calling the reporter would ultimately bring her to the witness stand at a murder trial. She hadn't even heard of Sean Fowler or Rafael Nazario when she'd first met with Candace Snow. If she'd had the slightest idea where it would all lead, she was pretty much certain she would've kept her mouth shut.

But it hadn't been the reporter who'd made it go this far; it'd been the sudden appearance two days ago of the man who'd been waiting for her outside Ivy's apartment. They'd talked out on the street for a few minutes, Darryl trying to get her to come with him right then to go see Jeremy. Alena hadn't even considered doing so; she'd claimed to have an appointment for later that afternoon. Darryl clearly hadn't wanted to take no for an answer, but was trying to seem nice about it too. She'd finally agreed to meet Jeremy for a drink that night.

Alena had felt something like terror at the thought. She'd been frightened of Darryl the whole time they were talking, even though it was on a busy street in broad daylight. She hadn't been able to shake the thought that Jeremy must've found out she'd talked to the reporter. She knew too much about the Roths, and now she also knew the danger that could bring.

She was scared of Jeremy now. People who'd stood in his way ended up dead; she believed that. She recognized that there was no limit to his selfishness, nothing that restrained him from hurting other people—or causing them to be hurt—to get what he wanted. The way he had treated her before, how he had used her, was just a symptom of his larger disease.

So she'd called the reporter, told her about the man who'd been waiting for her outside Ivy's apartment. "The first thing you should know is that you may be being followed," Candace said. "They can probably get inside your apartment too, so don't leave anything around you wouldn't want them to see."

"You're not helping," Alena said after a moment.

"We don't have time for sugarcoating. How did you leave things with Darryl?"

"I said I had an appointment with someone from my agency this afternoon, but that I'd meet Jeremy tonight for a drink."

"Then you should go meet somebody, in case they're watching you. Listen, Alena, you can get an innocent man out of jail, help solve two murders. Are you willing to do that?"

"Jesus Christ," Alena said. "I'm an unemployed model who doesn't even have an apartment. I'm not a lawyer or a reporter or anything like that."

"Which is exactly why you can do things here that we can't."

Alena had closed her eyes, trying to figure out how she'd gotten herself in the middle of this. The reporter couldn't stop Jeremy; neither could the lawyer. Both had admitted they didn't have the ammunition. And neither could even begin to penetrate the layers that insulated him from the actual violence. There was only one person who could slip through, Alena realized. There was only her.

She was scared, but also angry, and she had never really had a chance to help someone like this. "What is it you want me to do?" she'd heard herself say.

As arranged, Alena had waited an hour and then walked up to a coffee shop called Mud, a few blocks from Ivy's apartment. A few minutes later a man she'd never seen before had come in, looked around, and then hesitatingly come over to her. He'd introduced himself as Alex Costello, said he was a reporter at the *Journal*. He'd made a call on his cell phone, and then handed it over to Alena. The lawyer, Duncan Riley, had been on with Candace, and they'd walked her through the plan they'd scrambled together. Costello had given her a small padded envelope containing a digital recorder, telling her not to open it until she was home.

At nine o'clock she'd met Jeremy at the Flatiron Lounge, a deliberately retro bar in Chelsea that Jeremy had always been partial to—Alena suspected it was because the drinks were so strong. Jeremy was already there, seated at a far back table, nobody else near him. He'd stood in greeting upon seeing her, kissing her awkwardly on the cheek. Jeremy was dressed in a suit without a tie, and seemed as eager as a teenager on a first date as he got her a drink.

"I've been trying to get hold of you for a while," he said. "I'm glad you agreed to meet. I'm sorry for whatever misunderstanding we had before."

She wasn't here to fight with him, Alena reminded herself. She wasn't going to get what she'd come for if she reacted honestly. "Okay," she said, unable to come up with something more that would seem even remotely plausible.

"That's what you were mad at me about, leaving the bar that night? I was just tired, is all, and Mattar wanted to stay out and I needed to be on his good side. He was harmless, though, right?"

"I'm not sure 'harmless' is a good word to describe Mattar," Alena said. "He didn't end up doing business with you, did he?"

"But I mean nothing weird happened? I tried calling you a few times later on that night, but you never picked up."

Christ, Alena thought, Jeremy was actually jealous of Mattar after leaving her alone with him. She didn't know how to respond, especially given her awareness that every word was being recorded and might end up on the front page of a newspaper. "Mattar was just fucking with you, you know," she said. "It was a power play is all. They'd already decided not to buy in."

"It's not like I liked him either," Jeremy said, Alena surprised by his lack of reaction. "I just had to hang out with him. It was always business. Did he make a move on you that night?"

"I left a few minutes after you did," Alena said, wondering if the whole reason Jeremy had been so desperate to see her was simply because he needed to know whether she'd slept with Mattar. She doubted that Jeremy was self-aware enough to know it, if that was the case. "But listen, before we talk more about anything else, there's something I've got to tell you about. A reporter tracked me down yesterday. She said some pretty wild things."

Jeremy's reaction was immediate: he leaned forward, his eyes narrowed. "Was it the woman from the *Journal*?"

"Yeah, it was the reporter you guys sued. She's still going after you, I guess."

"Why the hell was she coming to you?" Jeremy said. "How did she even know who you were?"

"Beats me," Alena said. "She wouldn't explain any of that—just showed up at my door. Apparently I'm not that hard to find," she added, but Jeremy was too worried to catch the reference.

"So what did she want to talk to you about?"

"She's digging into you, Jeremy. She said you were taking money out of the Aurora, and that somebody who was part of it—a guy named Fowler, she said—was blackmailing you." Alena paused, looking Jeremy in the eye. It wasn't just about getting something on tape: she wanted to know if Jeremy really had a man killed, if he was capable of that. "She said the guy who was blackmailing you was murdered."

Jeremy picked up his drink, then immediately put it down. Even in the dimly lighted room Alena could see sweat at his temples. "What did you tell her?" Jeremy asked, his voice tight. He was afraid, Alena realized.

"I didn't tell her anything. I mean, I told her I had no idea what she was talking about. It's not like I know anything about stuff like that. Jesus, Jeremy, is it true?"

Jeremy used both hands to lift his drink this time, taking a long sip. It *was* true; Alena could tell just by looking at him. She'd come here believing it, but that still hadn't quite prepared her for this moment. "You don't want to get mixed up in this shit," Jeremy said.

"That's all you have to say? How am I supposed to even be here if you've done something like this?"

"I didn't kill anyone, obviously, if that's what you're asking."

"The reporter wasn't saying you shot the guy yourself, just that you were behind it."

Jeremy had recovered at least a little of his composure. "We're not going to talk about this," he said.

Alena had expected Jeremy to want to confess. But he wasn't just looking to tell her. She was going to have to dig it out of him.

"That's basically the same as admitting it," she said, studying Jeremy as she spoke. "You're not that sort of person. Are you?"

"There're some things that happened at the Aurora. Yeah, I took some money out—but it was my goddamn money anyway. If my father wasn't such a hard-ass I never would've needed to use Pellettieri to take it."

"So you knew he was skimming?"

"It happens all the time on construction," Jeremy said. "The only difference here was that I was getting my fair share. It's not like I can really rob myself, can I? And no, I didn't kill anyone, or order somebody to kill them, or anything like that."

"Then why is the reporter writing a story that says you did?"

"Because she doesn't know what she's talking about," Jeremy said. He seemed angry now, although at what exactly Alena couldn't say.

"But she's not just making the whole thing up," she protested. "You'd told me you were being blackmailed before, and then you told me it was over with, the guy deserved what he got. Was he killed?"

For a moment Jeremy just looked at her, a violence in his eyes. "None of it was fucking *me*, okay? None of it. I mean, yeah, I fucked up a little bit at the Aurora; that's on me, but I didn't have shit to do with the rest of it."

"The reporter told me that somebody's on trial for the murder. She said he's got nothing to do with it, that he's been set up."

"Just don't talk to her, okay? If she comes back, I mean. Did you tell her *anything*?"

"I admitted that I knew you, before I had any idea what she wanted to talk about. I didn't say anything once she got going. She just kept throwing new stuff out there—kept piling on. She seemed sure I already knew about it."

Jeremy looked ashen. "Was there anything else she said about the murder?" he asked.

"She said your security guards did it. That was the other thing. Do you have people who do these things for you, really?"

Jeremy didn't answer, cradling his drink in his hands. The idea that the reporter had this much clearly had him scared. Alena decided it was time to play her final card. "That wasn't even the end of it. The contractor you were working with, the police were about to arrest him and he disappeared?"

"Jack Pellettieri? He went on the run, yeah, so what?"

"She said his body just washed up in New Jersey."

Jeremy seemed equal parts puzzled and afraid. "Pellettieri's dead? I don't know anything about that."

"You said you wanted to see me again, Jeremy. That you wanted to fix things. I can't have someone make these accusations about you and then just pretend that I haven't heard them."

"It wasn't me," Jeremy said again, his voice fraying.

"But it did happen, didn't it?" Alena said, not having to act to show her own fear. "God, Jeremy, you *know*, don't you?"

"I can't talk to you about this."

"Meaning you don't trust me?" Alena said, aware of the absurdity of asking for the trust of a man she was secretly recording.

Jeremy looked at her, and Alena could see in his face the burden he'd been carrying. Then something broke in him; she watched it break. Jeremy was not somebody built for carrying around a terrible secret; his nature wasn't self-contained enough for it. He needed to confess.

"It was my sister," Jeremy said, his voice trembling. "Fowler was involved in skimming money, and then after the accident he came to me with his hand out. I paid him off, but the fucker came back. So I told my sister what was happening with Fowler, and she said she'd take care of it. Then she went to our security guy, Darryl, told him what Fowler was up to. I didn't know what they were going to do; I didn't know what was happening. You can't ever talk to the reporter again, not one word. You understand? I won't be able to protect you if you do."

Alena felt a chill. "Are you threatening me?"

"Of course not. But once you know about something like this, you've got to keep it to yourself."

"I'm glad it wasn't you, Jeremy," Alena said. "I'm glad the reporter's got it wrong. I mean, it's still pretty fucked up that you let it happen, but it's good you weren't directly involved. But is it true that some innocent guy is being charged with killing Fowler?"

"I didn't have anything to do with that. Darryl ran the show. Leaving it unsolved was too risky, I guess, but nobody asked me my opinion. I mean, you do something like this, the idea is to get away with it."

"But you're letting it happen. You could stop it if you chose to."

"It's too late. Things take on a momentum of their own. I can't change any of it now."

LOST IN thought, Alena barely noticed that Duncan had stopped the tape, the courtroom falling silent. As the room came back into focus the first thing Alena noticed was the cool hatred in the gaze of Leah Roth. Steven Blake stood, though more slowly this time. Alena thought the lawyer had to know the game was lost, that he wasn't going to spin his clients out of this.

"There are multiple issues with this recording, Your Honor," Blake said. "We don't know for a fact that the voice on the tape is Jeremy Roth. We don't know if this recording has been spliced or altered in some way. It is also clear that Ms. Porter is being deceptive, at best, in the recorded conversation. And even if the tape is what it purports to be, it's still hearsay. There is no supporting evidence to the claims made on the recording."

Judge Lasky looked exasperated by Blake's arguments. "Are you suggesting that Mr. Roth was lying on that tape? And as to whether it's his voice, you know him personally, do you not?"

Blake hesitated. "He's my client, yes."

"Standing before me as an officer of the court, did you think it was him?"

Blake clearly didn't want to respond. "It sounded generally like him, but I am by no means an expert in such matters."

Lasky offered Blake a withering look before turning to the DA's table. "Would the People like to be heard?"

Castelluccio stood, looking shell-shocked. "Your Honor, I have no way of knowing whether that tape is what it purports to be. At a minimum, I would like to have our technical experts review it. Obviously too we can simply ask Jeremy Roth whether he disputes it."

"Where does that leave Mr. Nazario in the meantime?" the judge asked.

Castelluccio hesitated. "It would be premature for my office to make a decision as to what, if any, effect today's hearing has on the case against Mr. Nazario. This tape by itself does not exonerate him, though it certainly raises questions."

Duncan had told himself to be quiet for as long as he could, see how things were shaking out. Now he stood and faced the judge. "This tape does not raise questions, Your Honor. It establishes that the defendant was framed, by whom, and why."

"It does no such thing," Castelluccio said. "I would remind the court that Mr. Nazario was prepared to plead guilty to this crime. It remains to be seen whether this new information will actually exonerate him."

Judge Lasky looked at Castelluccio, then over at Rafael for the first time. After a moment he turned back to the ADA. "Even on its own, this tape is pretty much fatal to your case against Nazario," he said. "Reasonable doubt is certainly established by it. You don't have a case here anymore, counsel."

"It would be premature to dismiss this case entirely," Castelluccio said quickly.

"Jeopardy hasn't attached, Your Honor," Duncan said. "You can dismiss without prejudice, and the DA will be free to refile if they come up with anything."

"There would be a risk of flight," Castelluccio said.

"My client has no resources to speak of," Duncan said, realizing that he'd mistakenly called Rafael his client but not feeling any need to correct it. "He doesn't even have a passport. And why on earth would he run, under the circumstances?"

Judge Lasky looked over at Rafael. "The defendant shouldn't have to be in jail while the police try to build this case all over from scratch," he said at last. "And the goal should be trying to figure out what actually happened here, not keeping this prosecution alive. *People v. Nazario* is hereby dismissed without prejudice. Mr. Nazario, you are free to go."

Duncan walked over to Rafael, ignoring Walker, and put his hand on Rafael's shoulder. "Let's get you home," he said.

·85·

DARRYL LOOMIS parked on Sullivan Street, about a block away from the Aurora Tower. "We're actually meeting Tommy inside the Aurora?" Candace asked as she got out of the car, an aging Ford Taurus. She was assuming that the police were hearing every word she said, and she was trying to give them a play-by-play without being too obvious about it. She hadn't been able to see any sign that the cops were following them, but was taking it on faith that they were. "How are we getting in?"

"Tommy arranged it," Darryl said.

"Aren't they still doing construction?"

"They're doing the interiors now. We're going around to the back."

They walked past the front of the Aurora and turned the corner. From the outside it no longer looked like a construction site. The building was stylish, she had to admit: it appeared to undulate like a gentle wave. It was by far the tallest building on the block, a showpiece. Candace supposed it should be, for half a billion dollars.

Darryl stepped into an alley in the middle of the block, Candace hesitating a little. Darryl noticed, stopped, and turned back. "It's just down here. The freight entrance has been left open. Come on."

"You say so, Reggie," Candace said, forcing herself to go forward. The alley was actually well kept—this was SoHo, after all—and they walked about twenty feet to the back of the Aurora. The freight entrance was unlocked.

Candace followed Darryl inside, finding herself in a grimly functional, fluorescent-lit hallway, a part of the building that the wealthy residents would presumably never see. Darryl led the way to the freight elevator, Candace following him in. The elevator was large and had clearly recently seen heavy use: it was scuffed, with dirt and sawdust on the floor.

They took it up to the twenty-seventh floor. Once in the hallway Candace could see that she was in an unfinished building. There was plywood on the floor and the overhead lights weren't on, plunging them into an evening gloom.

"What's on the twenty-seventh floor?" Candace asked, wanting to make sure the police knew exactly where she was. Assuming they still had a clear signal from her. Candace was beginning to think she'd made a very bad mistake, and she wondered if the smart thing was to just get back in the elevator and get the hell out of there.

Darryl gave her a look. "This is where Tommy said he'd be," he said.

"It's weird up here, Reggie," Candace said.

"You get used to it," Darryl replied. "If you're in construction, I mean."

"You're in construction too?"

"Yeah, I work with Tommy," he said.

"You must be management," Candace said.

Darryl looked puzzled. "Why you say that?"

"Your suit," Candace said. "I'm betting it's hand-tailored."

Darryl looked at her for a second but didn't respond. He walked halfway down the hall, then stopped at an apartment door. The slots for a lock and a doorknob were both empty. "In here," he said, pushing the door open.

Candace followed Darryl inside. She found herself in a large unfurnished apartment. As she passed the island kitchen Candace noticed that the refrigerator was in the middle of the room and the marble countertop was lying beside it, covered in bubble wrap. The living room was empty, except for a man who was not Tommy Nelson.

"Chris Driscoll?" Candace said after a moment, recognizing Driscoll from the time she'd spotted him talking to Duncan. "The hell are you doing here?"

"I work here now, the Aurora," Driscoll said. "Got transferred off of Riis after your little article came out."

Driscoll was leaning against the far wall of the living room, Candace in the middle of the room facing him with Darryl behind her. The wall in front of her was glass, looking south onto Lower Manhattan. Candace took a couple steps backward so that she could have both of them in her sight.

"It was nothing personal," Candace said reflexively—what she always said to somebody who was pissed off about something she'd written.

"Just my name in the paper, being called a liar, right?" Driscoll said. "My father saw that, my wife."

Candace was through playing nice. "What's the idea of bringing me here?" she said instead. "Look, I'm sorry if I pissed you off, Chris, but this isn't the way to get a meeting with me."

"It's not that simple," Darryl said. "Chris's not the only man I know who feels you've been talking too much."

Candace turned to face him. She decided there was nothing to be gained at this point by pretending she didn't know who he was. "You're Darryl Loomis, aren't you?" she said.

Darryl was caught off guard, knew he'd shown it, then smiled. "Very good," he said. "So then I'm guessing you can figure out why you're here."

"You realize my editor knows where I am, right?"

"With Tommy Nelson in Tompkins Square?" Darryl rejoined.

"What is it you want?" Candace said.

"First, I want to know if it's true about Pellettieri."

"That he washed up in Jersey? Yes, it is."

"And you're writing a story about it?"

"You can buy a paper same as anyone else," Candace said. "Or you can go to our Web site—it's free, you know."

Darryl shook his head as though disappointed. "You need to take a look around, figure out the situation you find yourself in. You're alone with two men who you think are killers. There is nobody else within a hundred feet of you. I ask you a question, answering is a real good idea."

Candace was trying to understand what Darryl's actual plan was. If she told him everything she knew, what was he going to do then? If he let her leave, he'd have to assume that Candace would go straight to the police and file charges against him. Maybe not serious charges, not if he didn't hurt her, but still, he'd have a lot of explaining to do. "Are you planning on killing me?" she asked. "Because otherwise I don't really see your move here."

"I'm just looking for information," Darryl said. "Have you written a story regarding Pellettieri's death?"

"I've drafted something, yeah," Candace said, lying. "It's on the network at work."

"What is it you think you know?"

"About Pellettieri?"

"About all of it."

"Let's see. I know that Driscoll here lied about seeing Nazario kill Fowler. I know that the real reason Fowler was killed was because he tried to blackmail Jeremy Roth about what happened at this building. I don't know who actually killed Fowler, though you'd certainly make my short list. Whoever it was, they were following orders from the Roth family."

"And have you written this?"

"Yes, though it's not finished," Candace said. "I guess my asking around got back to Jeremy?"

Darryl ignored the question, studying her with a slight smile. "I'm calling bullshit," he said. "I don't think you've written a goddamn thing. What proof of any of this do you have?"

"The DA is building a case against you for Pellettieri right now," Candace said. "How do you think I know he's dead and yet it hasn't been reported anywhere? And once they do that, they'll look at you for Fowler too. You killed your own guy, for Christ's sake."

Darryl's face went cold. "Fowler wasn't my guy, not after what he did. He was a dead man the second he put his hand out to a client. I'm in a business that requires absolute trust. People come to me with their worst problems. The secrets I keep are beyond your ability to imagine. You think your little paper conveys the truth about how this city really works? You barely have a clue."

"Now's the time to protect yourself," Candace said. "The Roths won't hesitate to throw you over, the shit hits the fan. Tell me the story, make a deal with the DA, cash out while you have the chance."

Darryl offered a tight smile. "I don't think so," he said. "I don't think you're going to be writing any more stories. I think you broke into this building, snooping around for some shit, and had yourself an accident."

Candace braced herself. "Enough is enough," she said, then took two quick steps back toward the wall.

Nothing happened. Darryl looked at her, puzzled. Candace, in a panic, thought something must have gone wrong, and that the police where nowhere near her. She considered trying a sprint toward the apartment's front door, but didn't think she'd make it past Darryl.

Then there was the sound of quick movement over by the door, followed by a loud voice from behind Darryl yelling something about showing hands.

Things happened in a jumble after that. Darryl spun quickly to the door, his hand going inside his suit jacket as he did so, emerging with a pistol. The sound of gunfire was deafening in the empty room, Darryl falling in a heap. Driscoll stood frozen in place, then slowly lifted his hands. Detective Gomez was at Candace's side, asking if she was all right, while several other cops, guns drawn, clustered around Darryl's body.

"Is he dead?" Candace asked, barely able to hear herself over the ringing in her ears.

Gomez glanced disdainfully over at Darryl's body. The only movement was the blood slowly pooling around it. "Don't look good. It might've been useful to have him alive, but fuck him anyway. He disgraced the job."

"He went for his gun," Candace said, still dazed. "Why would he do that?"

Gomez shrugged. "Let's get you out of here," he said. He placed a hand on Candace's shoulder and gently pushed her out of the room.

Gomez led her to the elevator, down to the ground floor, and then out of the Aurora. Sullivan was waiting for her just outside the door, an earpiece dangling around his neck.

"Is he dead?" Sullivan said to Gomez.

"I think so."

"Suicide by cop?"

Gomez shrugged. "Happened fast."

"Driscoll?"

"He's cuffed. Didn't resist."

Sullivan nodded, then turned to Candace. She could tell by the way his face changed that she did not look good. She felt herself going fuzzy. All the fear of the past hour had come out now, her entire body buzzing with it.

"You okay?" Sullivan asked. "You're shaking."

"Am I?" Candace said, then looked down at her hands, which were fluttering like butterflies. "I guess I am. I think I might not see okay for a while."

Sullivan nodded. "Let's get you to the station, get a quick statement; then we'll let you go home. You can have a glass of wine and a long bath."

Candace looked at Sullivan like he was nuts. "You kidding me? In case you missed it, I'm sitting on a huge fucking story."

·86·

DUNCAN AND Rafael ended up walking from the courthouse to Jacob Riis. Duncan had suggested a cab, but Rafael, relishing his freedom, said he wanted to walk. As they emerged on the street Duncan offered Rafael his cell phone to call his family, who had no idea what'd happened. Rafael refused, saying he wanted to be able to see their faces when they learned he was free.

"You did it, Mr. R," Rafael said, as they crossed through the crowds of Canal Street, the smell of dead fish from the Chinese markets in the air. "I'm sorry I didn't think you were for real before."

"You got screwed over by pretty much everyone, Rafael," Duncan replied. "Why should you have thought I was any different?"

"But you came through for me."

"In some way I bet it's my fault that you got mixed up in all this to begin with," Duncan said. "They probably picked you as their fall guy because I was your lawyer."

Rafael looked over at Duncan. "You didn't know nothing about that when it happened, though, right?"

"Not at all. But that's part of why I wouldn't let it go."

"You kept fighting for me even when I dissed you, told you to stop."

Duncan didn't feel comfortable accepting Rafael's gratitude. "That's what it is to be somebody's lawyer. It might sound silly, but I believe that."

"So who shot Fowler?"

Duncan laughed. "I don't actually know," he said.

"Don't you want to know who did it?"

"Sure, but whoever pulled the trigger wasn't really behind it. Leah Roth is the person responsible."

"They going to arrest her?"

"They're not going to be in a hurry to do so. Somebody with her amount of juice, you're going to need everything just so before you make a move. We'll see."

"It was because of her that you had to drop me before?"

"Basically she was worried that I was doing too good a job—she didn't want the case against you to completely fall apart."

"I want to see her go to jail, man. I want to know she's trying to survive the same shit I just had to get through."

Duncan certainly didn't blame Rafael for feeling that way, but he didn't want to talk about Leah. "I talked with your old boss, Marco, a while back," he said. "I'm betting he's kept a spot for you at the restaurant. And also, in terms of money, the other thing is, you're in a position to sue some very wealthy people."

Rafael's eyes went wide. "You serious?"

"Hell, yeah, I'm serious," Duncan replied with a grin. "And if you need a good lawyer to take your case, it just so happens that I have a lot of free time at the moment."

They turned east on Ninth Street, crossing into the alphabets, the Jacob Riis project coming into view. Construction and demolition were both still under way, the project's transformation continuing. Even if Roth Properties collapsed in scandal, Duncan assumed some other developer would come in to take their place. Change was the one constant in New York; every morning you woke to a slightly different city. That was the source of its greatness and its grinding cost.

Rafael stopped walking, his gaze drawn to the towering buildings that he'd called home. "But there's plenty of time to talk about all that," Duncan continued. "Now you need to go surprise the hell out of your family."

"SO," DUNCAN said to Candace. "Ready for your exclusive?"

He'd called her as soon as he'd left Rafael outside the Riis project, arranged to meet her back at the Life Café. Duncan walked her through the events of the day. It might get him in some trouble with Judge Lasky, but it was part of the deal he'd made with Candace, and under the circumstances he expected the judge would let it go.

"What about Rafael?" Candace said when Duncan had finished. "Can I talk to him?"

Duncan hadn't really considered the fact that Rafael would likely be in the spotlight. "He's gone home to be with his family, so I'd like to give them some time. I'll call him in a couple of hours, see if he's willing."

"I promise to be gentle. He's the real victim here, and his story deserves to be told."

She had a point, Duncan thought. "I'll tell him if he's going to talk to anybody, it's you," he said. "But it's up to him. Meanwhile, Alena Porter's waiting for your call."

"I've had a bit of an exciting day myself," Candace said. "Darryl Loomis is dead."

Duncan looked equal parts shocked and confused, and Candace filled him in on what'd happened.

"Jesus," he said when she was finished. He'd encouraged Candace to reach out to Sullivan for protection when they'd cobbled together their plan, worried that it might put her in danger. But he'd never envisioned her conducting the sort of sting she had today. "And you just come in here like nothing's happened? You could've been killed."

"I didn't think they'd really kill a reporter," Candace said. "But actually yeah, I'm pretty sure they were going to."

"You risked your life for a story?" Duncan said incredulously.

"It's not like I'm embedded in Iraq or something," Candace said. "There're reporters who take bigger risks than what I did all the time."

"Still," Duncan said, "I wouldn't have wanted you to float up on a beach in Jersey."

Candace grinned at him. "That's sweet," she said.

Duncan smiled back, feeling genuinely amazed at what Candace had put herself through. "So," he said, "I guess we actually did it."

"It looks like we did. Listen, I'd love to stay and ponder how awesome we are, but it's going to be a long night at the office for me," Candace said, her eyes bright as she said it. Duncan could practically see the adrenaline pouring through her, the excitement of breaking a big story. "But yeah, congratulations. You should celebrate. I'd buy you a drink later, but I'm guessing I'll be in the newsroom until midnight."

"I don't exactly have to get up for work tomorrow morning," Duncan said.

Candace looked at him, her smile fading into something more serious. "If I buy you a drink at midnight, is that going to give you the wrong idea as to the kind of girl I am?" she said, though her voice failed to convey the playfulness she was aiming for.

"I think I already have a pretty good idea as to the kind of girl you are," Duncan said quietly.

Candace considered him, a slight smile playing around the edges of her lips. "You know how many times I've promised myself I'd never get involved with a lawyer?" she said.

"It's not entirely clear that I actually still am a lawyer," Duncan said.

"There's that," Candace agreed. A moment passed where the two of them just sat there, looking at each other. "I've got to go," Candace said, making no move to get up.

"Go already."

"I'm calling you later."

"I'm answering the phone."

Candace stood, then impulsively leaned down and kissed Duncan. "You're going to have a lot of explaining to do about Leah Roth," she whispered in his ear, before turning on her heels and walking quickly away.

Duncan gave her a minute, then also headed out. He didn't have the faintest idea what to do with himself. He began walking in the general direction of his apartment.

The weight of what he had just lost came crashing down on Duncan: his perfect upward trajectory had been completely wrenched off course. He didn't think he'd want it back, even if he could have it. He was free, Duncan realized with wonder, free to invent a new life for himself. But what would that life consist of?

There'd be a media feeding frenzy to start with. Duncan would get a certain amount of attention focused on him, which might bring forward some job offers, or at least put him in a position where opening his own practice didn't seem completely absurd. Something would happen. Something always happened: the next wave came, and you rode it as long and as well as you could. Duncan thought of F. Scott Fitzgerald's line about how there were no second acts in American lives. It had always struck him as categorically wrong, but never more so than today. The story of America was the story of second acts.

His was about to begin.

ACKNOWLEDGMENTS

Thanks to my wife, Melissa Goodman, without whom none of this would ever have happened.

Thanks to my agent, Betsy Lerner, and my editor, Gerry Howard, both of whom provided indispensable guidance and encouragement throughout the writing of this book.

Thanks to Anna Roberts, for her eagle eye and her insights into the New York City criminal justice system.

Thanks also to Brendan Deneen, Rachel Lapal, Loren Noveck, Sally Wilcox, and Tiffany Ward.

Numerous works of nonfiction were extremely helpful in the writing of this novel. For insights into Rikers Island, the documentary *Lock-Up: The Prisoners of Rikers Island* by Jon Alpert (DCTV, 1995) and the book *Inside Rikers* by Jennifer Wynn (St. Martin's, 2001) both offer a compelling view into daily life at the jail. For insights into commercial real estate, skyscraper construction, urban policy, and city politics, thanks goes to *The Death and Life of Great American Cities* by Jane Jacobs (Random House, 1961), *The Power Broker* by Robert A. Caro (Knopf, 1974), *Skyscraper* by Karl Sabbagh (Viking, 1990), *From the Ground Up* by Douglas Frantz (University of California Press, 1993), and *Skyscraper Dreams* by Tom Shachtman (Little Brown, 1991), as well as the reporting of Michael Idov of *New York* magazine, Danny Hakim and Ray Rivera of the *New York Times*, and Christian Berthelsen and Lance Williams of the *San Francisco Chronicle*. Lastly, I wish to acknowledge the reporting of Julie Bykowicz and Stephanie Hanes of the *Baltimore Sun* on problems with gunshot residue evidence, in particular that paper's coverage of the case of Tyrone Jones, who was convicted of murder as a result of shoddy forensics and is still in prison for a crime he almost certainly didn't commit.